CW00695225

A CHRONICLE OF LOST CAUSES BOOK
NO MAN'S LAND
STORY AND ART BY A. R. BLACK

ISBN: 979-8-9853091-3-3

Chapter Zero

(FELL'S POINT, 2 MONTHS PRIOR)

"Show me a hero, and I'll write you a tragedy."

— F. Scott Fitzgerald

"Don't be shy now—you didn't buy that sidearm for it to be a paperweight, Doctor," I say, as I lean on the Compression Ax I just used to decimate the door into the shabby animal testing lab.

"W-What the... No no no no—You don't have to do this, *please*!"

"That depends on what you mean by 'this', Doctor. I *do* have a job to do here, but you don't have to be present for it—I was paid to sanitize the place and collect your research—not for an execution. So, it's your choice—fight or flight?" I reply.

I'm more than slightly annoyed that Prosper Electronica's intel has failed me—the good doctor wasn't supposed to be working late tonight, according to the Pattern of Life they provided.

The doctor grabs the firearm and takes aim.

The man's face is, of course, hidden behind his mirrored medical face shield, but I can read the terror in the unsteadiness of his hand, now that it has a pistol in it—aimed at my center of mass.

"Fair warning—if you're going to do it, it'll need to be a bullseye right here," I tap a finger on my metal mask—right between the eyes. "Nothing else will cut it with a single shot—and I won't wait for a second one to respond."

"B-Body armor...? No matter—I can manage that from this distance—DON'T TAKE ANOTHER STEP!" he shouts, as I'm in the middle of doing just that.

I finish taking my step.

"No, I don't think you can. Feel free to prove me wrong, but... if you try and fail, I'll be forced to kill you—just as a matter of principle."

The lab positively drowns in the silence.

Even the test animals seem to sense the tension and are polite enough to recognize that their usual squeaking and chattering might be enough to push the doctor over his limit. Only the steady drip of water from some long-neglected pipe—and the doctor's labored breathing—proves to me that my hearing has not suddenly failed me.

Unsteady hands—which I'm sure were normally perfectly deft with a scalpel and precise in the taking of measurements—awkwardly search for a comfortable grip on the 45 he's clearly been too busy mad-sciencing to train with.

"Not to be rude, but ah... I think you have the safety on, Doc."

Flustered, the man switches off the safety before leveling the barrel at me once again.

I take yet another step.

Only six paces away now—far enough away for him to *feel* safe, but... he's anything but.

Then the doctor surprises me anew with his stupidity... by turning the weapon on himself.

"Whatcha doing there, Doctor?" I ask conversationally.

"Isn't it obvious?"

"Fair enough. *Why* are you doing it?" I correct, bemused.

"Because it's o-over for me. Even if I killed you, more would come. You say I can leave, but what would be the point if my life's research is stolen from me?"

I think it over for a moment.

"True, more Freelancers would be sent. It probably is pointless. But... you should try to kill me, regardless."

The doctor's head tilts to the side slightly—clearly taken aback.

"Why?"

"The principle of it. You have a right to defend what's yours—a right to strive for the future you want. More than that—you have a moral obligation to fight back—otherwise, you'll just encourage people like me to take from people like you."

...

"But you also have a right to make a living... You have people who love you, people who depend on—" begins the doctor.

"Nope. I don't. Not a single one. Don't package your cowardice as a virtue—nothing wrong with fear, but there *is* something wrong with pretending giving into fear is a virtuous act. Now, take a deep breath, line up your iron sights with my skull, and take a single, steady squeeze of the trigger—if you can."

...

"Are you insane?" he asks.

"Insane or bored—I've lost track of which it is today."

"No... This is how I'll fight back—I won't let you kill me in self-defense, I won't let you leave here feeling like you gave me a fair chance—but bested me irregardless, as you so obviously want. Whatever code of honor, or suicidal impulse, or insane thrill-seeking this is, I won't play along. I will die on my own terms. And you will have to live with the memory of it—of driving a man you have no personal grievance with to suicide. Or... you can leave—tell your boss that I was already gone when you got here—along with my research and animals," rages the doctor.

A burst of indignation flares up inside my chest.

"Are you seriously trying to hold yourself hostage to *my* conscience? You're making a fool of yourself—not least because you can't kill yourself with any gun made in Prospera the last 20 years—they are all made with a suicide prevention lock feature—even if you're wearing the trigger unlock ring.

"Y-You're ly—"

"Do it then," I interject.

After a moment's hesitation, he does.

A whole lot of nothing happens.

"Told you so," I say.

The doctor lowers the gun, and to my horror, breaks down sobbing.

I sigh, disappointed.

...

I walk around the dingy makeshift lab and place incendiaries at even intervals while keeping one eye on the doctor to make sure he does not try to grab any of his research before making a break for it.

A familiar cacophony of animal screams fills my ears as I work—mice, dogs, and a few birds are the primary audience of my work. The Compression Ax I used to take down the door is now magnetically holstered to free up both hands.

I set the last incendiary device next to a surprisingly calm horse, which sits in a homemade stable the doctor obviously constructed himself—the guy is clearly no great handyman. I know this creature is the main reason I'm here—the doctor had a breakthrough in his gene editing work that would probably make this horse officially the fastest that ever lived—if it is ever allowed to race. If so, the doctor would then stand to become lavishly rich off trademarking and selling the gene edits he invented... and would humiliate the two titans of genetic engineering in the process—Prosper Electronica and Restless Industries. Hence why a Freelancer like me was sent.

As I finish up, I notice a dusty bottle of whiskey, two glasses, and some stainless steel straws sitting on a shelf.

I grab them.

"Are you offering me my own whiskey?" asks the doctor—who I'm glad to see has managed to stop his sobbing.

I shrug.

"Either drink it, or it goes up in flames along with everything else. You can call me 'Roach' if you like—not that you asked."

We both drink in silence, using metal straws that let us keep our faces covered while we do—as is considered the decent, respectable way in this city.

The doctor's gun rests on the improvised table next to his glass.

"Would you do it, if our roles were reversed? Would you shoot?"

I nod.

"Do you think I'm weak for not being able to?"

I nod again.

"You are lucky that Prosper Electronica is the one who came after you first—Restless Industries would immediately escalate to having you killed. Prospera is not the place for a person like you," I say.

"A weak person?" he asks.

"Weak, decent, indecisive, idealistic—whatever framing we want to use—Prospera is not the place for people like you, Doc," I repeat.

"But Prospera is the most idealistic city in the world... it's the freest city left standing—science without the limits, art without the censor, a legal system intuitive and short enough to become an expert in with a single day's study... Prospera is the only place where people still celebrate human greatness—where great men have a chance at rising up..."

I take another drink while I think on his words.

"If you think we have science without limits, try to research Artificial General Intelligence and see how long you're left breathing here. You can make any art you like, but you'll never make a cent as an artist unless you lick a blueblood's boots. The legal system is short and sweet in theory, sure—but might makes right here—laws are only *simply* and *intuitively* enforced on the losers in this king of the mountain game we have. It is indeed the freest place in the world—so free that most people here are in freefall straight to the bottom—and ironically, we are the only place where people are free to sell themselves into literal slavery. You tell me if that seems better or worse than the insanity of the crowds that rule Kallipolis, or the supposedly benevolent

AI nanny state of Neo Kyoto. I've never been to either—I wouldn't claim to know."

...

"Would you mind... I don't... I don't want her to burn to death. She shouldn't have to suffer," says the doctor as he glances towards the racehorse that he had been betting his future on.

"I could. But it would be better if it was you—all I have here is my ax, and she will probably sense my intentions. She trusts you. And I'm sure you have some syringe here that would make it relatively painless—my employer first got wind you were up to something because of all the dead animals you disposed of while experimenting, you know."

...

"I don't deserve this! I'm cleverer than them—more industrious than them... How dare those reprobates look down on me because my genes are not enhanced like theirs!" fumes the doctor, taking me aback for a moment with the sudden change of mood.

I shake my head.

"You're not. If you were smarter than them, Doc, then you would have taken proper precautions—you wouldn't—let's say, have bragged to the pretty women in bars about what you were working on. You wouldn't have let that meal ticket of yours do a test run out in the open where others would notice its freakish speed. And most importantly, you wouldn't have tried to take on the city's most powerful corporate empires and families by yourself—as a nobody. You wanted to be noticed for your scientific genius, well... You got your wish."

The doctor stands up without a word and begins to walk towards what I presume to be a large animal crate or storage bin draped with a thick, filthy blanket.

"Doc... what do you think you're doing, exactly?"

The rattling of metal bars and the slight movement of fabric confirms that the mystery box is indeed an animal cage.

I've been around enough desperate men to recognize the kind of resigned determination that comes over a man when he's given up on a happy ending—the same instincts that told me this guy was not a serious threat a few moments ago when he pointed a gun at me, now scream at me to prepare for a fight.

I rise.

I did very literally ask for this—I told the man he was a coward, told him he had a moral duty to resist—I shouldn't be that surprised that a few rounds of whiskey and time for the initial panic to subside would be enough for him to decide to do just that.

I ready my ax.

The doctor pulls the filthy blanket away.

"You have some very exotic pets, Doc," I say, taking in the sight of a freakish reptile/insect hybrid—pitch-black scales armoring a many-limbed body vaguely resembling a scorpion. Behind its back arches not a stinger, but instead, a long, blade-like appendage that suggests a slashing function instead of a piercing one. A forked tongue darts in and out—tasting the air—as large, snake-like eyes study me with surprising intelligence.

"A poacher brought her back from No Man's Land as a hatchling—cost me every cent I had at the time. But one must spend money to make money; as the saying goes,"

"*How lovely*," I reply.

The doctor raises open the barred cage door—I tense, watching the motor-cycle-sized chimera who seems only to have eyes for me—even as its chance for escape presents itself.

The insect's black scales glint like polished metal under the dim light, while more limbs than I personally consider morally acceptable move with an eerie kind of grace—oozing lethality.

"Does she bite?" I ask pleasantly.

"Not the hand that feeds her, but as for you..."

I blink, and when my eyes reopen... the cage is suddenly empty.

My eyes scan the room, searching between stacked cages and in shadowy corners for the glow of yellow eyes or the flicker of a reptilian tongue.

"You didn't invent the gene modifications, did you? You just spliced some genetic code out of your ugly friend and pasted it into a horse embryo.

Did you just trial and error your way until you landed on a few genes that contributed to fast-twitch muscle fibers or something?" I ask, legitimately curious for his answer.

The racehorse whines, showing anxiety now for the first time since I arrived.

A flash of motion to my left alerts me—I strike down with my Compression Ax, sending chips of the concrete floor exploding into the air.

At the last possible instant, the beast diverts course—once again, nowhere to be seen.

My heart beats fast from the sweet flood of adrenaline, making me smile under my mask.

"Heeere, kitty kitty kittyyy..."

"Y-You really do have a Deathwish, you suicidal maniac," says the doctor, sounding astonished.

"Na, I don't wanna die per se—I just... enjoy the view of life from its edge," I answer.

.

..

...

No sign of movement—other than the various small test animals in their neglected cages.

"If you don't want to die, get behind me right now!" I order.

"Wh—"

The doctor disappears behind a blur of blackness as his pet decapitates him with a single slash of its bladed tail.

Slowly, I retreat to the door without ever showing the feasting bug my back.

I don't know much anything about animals—least of all the freaks of evolution that prowl No Man's Land—but I know the human animal well enough. Humans who have lived a life rough enough develop a sharp instinct for sizing up how dangerous potential opponents are. I doubt it's any different for the non-human animals of the world.

I clear the threshold and step out into the dingy alleyway.

I was not easy, low-risk prey—the doctor was—and it didn't take long for the monster to figure that out.

The sounds of ripping and tearing are fading now to a faint unpleasantness.

I finger the detonator for the incendiaries in my jacket pocket.

I hesitate for a moment, conflicted by practicality and my professional pride—I was tasked to burn the lab and its animals to the ground—but secondarily, I was supposed to gather as much of the doctor's research as possible. Pulling the trigger now will forfeit any chance at that.

I'm about to march back inside to cut the insect-lizard's meal short when the sounds of weapon safeties being flicked off causes me to turn.

"It looks like the Doctor was double-booked this evening—I *told* you we should have left the house earlier, Wheeler," a tall man in a wolf's mask says, his hand resting casually on the hilt of a Burner Blade. Next to him, a stocky man with salt and pepper hair and a mask made to resemble the face of a stone statue stands, his gloved hands holding a sawed-off shotgun at the ready. Behind them both, a fire team's worth of Restless soldiers stare down the sights of silenced sub-machine guns.

The Freelancer in the wolf's mask, I recognize as being something of a famous player who goes by the name "Okabe". More interesting to me are the Restless soldiers—they each wear identical jet-black light armor and the weeping full-face helmets of Restless Erasers.

These are not your standard House Guards—these men exist not to protect but only to make people disappear without a trace. Each of them have white teardrops on their masks to mark how many confirmed kills they have to their names.

"Did they send all this—just for the likes of me? I'm flattered, truly," I say.

"Not you. Not today. Have you done our work for us, traitor? Is the horse breeder with delusions of grandeur already lights out?" asks one of the soldiers, the insignia on his breastplate marking him as an NCO.

I nod as I study the pack of killers—not understanding why such a muscular crew was sent to deal with one nobody scientist—one competent Freelancer like myself should be plenty.

"Hold on—what does that mean for our compensation?" demands the Lancer in the faux-stone mask, looking back at the line of Restless Erasers.

"Nothing good. You'll get paid for the services you provide—no one left to kill means no payment for the killing, *Freelancer*," sneers the same NCO, his tone making his opinion of our ignoble profession abundantly clear.

Doing some quick mental arithmetic, I decide Prosper Electronica would probably rather no one get the fruits of the Doctor's labor than for it to end up in the hands of their main competition.

"Then let's put him down and get to collecting the data," says the Lancer in the stone mask—his weapon rising.

"Hold it! That man is off limits—he's on our No Strike list—so long as he stays off of Restless grounds, he is NOT a cleared target. Our work is done—time to go home," says an officer from the back of the group.

"He probably has the Doctor's data on him! If you don't want to kill the son of a bitch, fine—but your boss wants the info and we want our pay," says the stone mask Lancer.

"True enough..." allows the officer.

I shake my head.

"That's not gonna work—I have nothing to give you, but I'm also not going to submit to a strip search to prove it, I'm afraid."

By all good sense, I probably should just let them—I truly have nothing on me for them to find. But I can't bring myself to care at the moment.

There is silence, and I know the soldiers are talking on their helmet's internal comms—orders are being passed on how they are to take me with minimum risk of caving my skull in.

I pull the trigger on the incendiaries.

Flames roar to life in the building, and a cacophony of animal cries fills the night in reply.

"You piece of fifth—he's burning the research!" snarls Okabe as he pulls his Burner from its sheath.

"Don't matter—he wouldn't be leaving if he didn't already have it on him!" says the other Lancer.

I sense movement behind me and dive to the side—just as a flaming nightmare leaps out of the only exit from the burning building.

The soldiers open fire—and with an alien shriek unlike anything I've ever heard, the monstrosity dies.

I make a break for it down the side street, my feet carrying me on the blissful wings of adrenaline. I glance over my shoulder in time to see the Lancer with the shotgun take aim at my retreating back and roll to the side just as a hail of lead explodes from the barrel.

Scrambling, I get back to my feet and continue to run—determined to put enough distance between myself and the shotgun to be out of range, but I know I won't succeed—the killers were not distracted by the giant bug for as long as I'd hoped.

There is a second gunshot—this one comes not from a shotgun—but from a silenced sub-machine gun, and I hear a body fall to the floor.

"Was that really entirely necessary?" asks Okabe in a voice of mild indignation as soldiers' boots rush forward, and I hear the sounds of something metal skidding across the ground—presumably the shotgun.

I'm rather surprised that the Erasers are taking the No Strike order so seriously—to not kill me themselves is one thing—but to kill a Lancer in their employ, in my defense, is to go above and beyond the letter of the order.

I laugh as I run—loving how awfully alive it makes me feel to prove the old cliché of "fortune favors the bold" true—yet again.

...

My contact at Prosper Electronica answers my call on the third ring, her slightly flirtatious greeting full of expectation.

"There's been a fire in Fell's Point. The old man was in the building after hours. The Fire Company didn't arrive in time to stop it. Nothing to hand off—some vultures got in the way—tried to loot the place for themselves," I say.

"Oh no, how *ghastly...*" replies the woman delightedly.

In the internal display of my mask, I receive a notification of a substantial deposit into my account having been made—I'd expected Prosper Electronica to hit me with a pay deduction for failing to retrieve any of the Doctor's data, but instead, I'm rewarded with a healthy bonus. I was right to think they would rather see the research data burn, considering the alternative in this case.

I hang up on her.

1

Too Good to Refuse

No Man's Land *noun*

A vast and ever-expanding wilderness inhospitable to human beings. Human efforts to contain or counteract its spread have all been largely unsuccessful. All species native to No Man's Land evolve at a dramatically accelerated rate, to include even viruses and microbial life. The mechanisms responsible for this phenomenon are still unknown.

My alarm screams a song at me that I vaguely recall liking at some point.

I take a mental inventory of the things I need to do today—no jobs booked and nothing left to clean. Two hours I owe to the weights, another hour I will invest in staring at a blank canvas before I give up and go through the motions by following another Step-by-Step tutorial on perspectives—which will consume another hour, give or take.

Wait—I gave the damned HoloStreamer away a month ago. That evil thing was far too good at hypnotizing me into being a lazy waste of space. I could watch the tutorial in 2D with my mask's internal display, but... I know I won't. That frees up another hour... Three showers will take 1.5 hours, and three instant meals will cost me another hour.

Five and a half hours total, then—out of 16 waking hours.

I pull a cigarette and lighter out of my jacket pocket—I'm still fully clothed because I was too drained last night to bother with undressing.

The headrush hits me as I stare transfixed at the burning tip. Vivian would rip me a new one if she could see this now—she'd say I was an imbecile for literally burning years of my life away—I'd counter that I won't live long enough for it to matter—and she'd win the argument by reminding me that I need to maintain my lunge capacity if I was going to keep up with her.

But she's not here, so... *burn baby burn.*

I swore to myself today would be caffeine-free—I spent two hours yesterday laying in bed with my heart aching like an old war wound—the only suspect I have lined up so far is my daily 1,000mg of liquid motivation.

Baby steps... I don't want to trade chest pain for headaches—I'll cut it in half and keep it at 500mg today. Half is still a major improvement, surely.

My gaze drifts down to the authentic wooden floorboards where I have a stash of faded old photos, worthless childhood trinkets, and pain meds hidden away.

Those wooden floors were my pride and joy when I first bought this place—the one luxury I splurged on in an otherwise entirely practical purchase—yet now I mostly forget they exist... That is, other than when I get annoyed at the way they already creak in protest when I step in certain spots. There is a lesson there somewhere on the futility of buying shit you don't need for a temporary dopamine hit—a lesson I'm sure I will need to suffer through a time or two more before it will totally sink in.

I drift off into unconsciousness with the cig still burning between my lips.

.

..

...

I'm woken up by pounding at the front door. I put my mask on and grab the ax from its resting place near my bed.

Three unlocked deadbolts later, and I'm looking into a pair of glittering gold eyes that belong to Britannica—a recruiter and contract manager for Prosper Electronica—one of the biggest biotechnology and genetic engineering companies in the world.

"You... should *not* be here," I say, looking at a woman so beautiful that I'm tempted to slam the door in her face for that crime alone. The mask she wears is a metallic baby blue and is intended for sex appeal—leaving her eyes, full lips, and the gentle curve of her feminine jaw exposed while still concealing her nose, eyebrows, and cheekbones... This is barely enough to make her fit for public eyes—if she passed any children on her way here, I'm sure the outraged parents covered their innocent little eyes as soon as they noticed her.

More to the point—her presence here is not just unwelcome... it carries an implied threat—and I am sure that is just as intentional as all the skin she shows on her face.

Britannica gives a very slight bow of apology.

"Both my employer and I apologize, Roach. But we have a sensitive issue that we would like to hire you to address—sensitive both in time and in its legality. Sending an intermediary to speak to you about it in person made the most sense. May I come in?"

This justification is flimsy, and the laziness of it further irritates me—she does not respect me enough to even put effort into the lie.

Yes, the usual way of putting out a request for FreeLancer work isn't great for time-sensitive tasks—particularly if you want someone specific... but this will hardly be the first time someone has been in such a situation. There *are* other ways to try and reach someone to arrange for a conversation—ways short of hunting down where a man lives and knocking on the front door.

The real reason she is here is to demonstrate that the people she works for have figured out where I live—they want me to know that they know.

"If you're going to threaten me, please don't be passive-aggressive about it next time. I would request that all future threats be just plain old, *aggressive* aggressive. I'm a simple guy—shades of gray give me a headache."

Britannica chuckles.

"Threaten you? You're the one with the ax... How about we compromise, and I just promise to bring some ibuprofen with me next time?"

I stiffen for an instant—my mind racing with unspoken questions—before resigning myself and stepping aside.

"You can come in, but... don't hold it against me if I leave my mask on. We might be so close that we're dropping by for house calls now, but that doesn't mean we are dear old friends," I say as I wave her in with mock grandeur.

"Hmmm, now that won't do at all—business partners should trust one another, and if you won't even share your face with me, how can we claim any trust between us? Trust is optional in romance, but it is certainly not in business—you should know that by now," quips Britannica as she walks past me.

"Interesting relationship advice—how's that worked out for you so far? Doesn't sound healthy... No offense," I reply.

"None taken. But I'd dare say it's gone somewhat better for *me* than it has for *you*... Forgoing relationships altogether can hardly be considered healthy either, can it? And the one relationship you did have, well... that was so unhealthy it's literally considered a crime in some of the more... *sensitive* parts of the world... You poor thing," she purrs.

I can think of nothing to say to that.

In a couple of well-crafted sentences, Britannica both flexed her extensive knowledge of my life—which she by all rights should *not* have—and trampled over my dignity.

Britannica says all this in a perfectly sultry, silky-smooth voice designed to wrap the more smooth-brained of men around her finger.

I wonder, not for the first time, what this siren's true voice sounds like—because I have to presume I've never actually heard it. In a world where black-market Deep Fake technology from Neo Kyoto makes revealing your true face or voice an invitation for identity theft, blackmail, and framing, such things are kept closely held secrets by necessity—at least in Prospera, where the cutting-edge tech required for identifying the fakes does not exist.

Neo Kyoto is the birthplace of both this high-tech poison and its equally high-tech cure—yet they are somehow incapable of preventing the Deep Fake tech from escaping—while managing to maintain a perfect track record for hoarding the tools they use for combating it—one of the many reasons for piss-poor relations between the two city-states.

"Oh! So clean—downright spartan, actually; if I didn't know better, I'd think you served a tour or two in the FireJacks... Abysmally depressing. You're admittedly *cleaner* than most men... but you still have no appreciation for interior décor. Do you really not make enough money to afford decent furniture?" chimes Britannica, as if we are just a pair of old pals exchanging some good-natured jests.

"Maybe I've just decided to prioritize the ability to leave in a hurry over aesthetic charm..." I reply.

"Oh, we do love us a pragmatic man, but... the world is a much smaller place than it used to be, isn't it? You can stay in Prospera, go be a slave to the algorithm in Neo Kyoto, or drown under the constant failures of idiot politicians in Kallipolis... The world is too small a place to simply walk away from your problems anymore. So, let's hope the need never arises," Britannica says, her metallic light blue mask glinting in the pale green light of the mercury vapor bulbs overhead.

"Yeah, you're right. I'm sure I could be found... If someone with the resources really cared to put in the effort. Knowing that, I might make finding me almost as unpleasant for the finder as it is for the one being found."

I'm getting tired of beating around the bush.

Britannica laughs her perfect little laugh.

I don't know that I'd say she exactly has a nice laugh, but she certainly has an effective one. It's the kind of laugh that lets everyone know she's clever enough to always be in on the joke... and if you don't see what's so funny, it's probably because the joke is about *you*... and you have simply yet to catch on.

"Exactly right! That's why we want to *hire* you, once again, and I'm sorry if I've come off rather insistent, but... We want to *pay* you, not *threaten* you. We paid you last time, and that went swimmingly, so... why change tact now?" says Britannica airily.

"Or maybe a little bit of both, right? No need for a carrot to be mutually exclusive from the stick. But why not—let's hear it," I reply, while internally, my mind races with speculation on how this woman has found out so much about a personal history I've tried so hard to erase.

"As a general rule, I'd say that's right, but... once you hear what we have to offer you, you will be *begging* to take this job. We've gathered a lot of intelligence on you, as you're smart enough to have already surmised. We think we have an offer for you that's too good to refuse."

I raise an eyebrow—though it's under my mask and thus invisible to Britannica.

Now, I'm certainly curious—I'll grant her that much.

"So... it isn't money, I presume. You noticed my minimalist lifestyle. No amount of money could make me do something I really don't want to do... And what is it that you want me to do, exactly?" I ask.

...

"We need people for a search and rescue. Someone very important is deep inside No Man's Land after a flight they were on went down about... 36 hours ago, now. Very sophisticated life preservation systems on board—we don't think the crash itself will have been enough to kill them all. Prosper Electronica is willing to pay extravagantly to get a particular person back... Preferably, *before* something else manages to do what the crash could not."

...

It is my turn to laugh.

"You might as well stop there. There is nothing you could offer me that would do me any good if I'm dead. So, what's the point?

"Oh, come now, you have such a fine reputation for daring—don't tell me you're suddenly averse to a little risk? More importantly, you haven't heard what we have to offer in return."

"I do, but I also rather enjoy having a reputation for being, you know... *alive.* Out with it—what can you possibly offer me in exchange for dying, Britannica?"

She takes a deep breath as if preparing herself to say something very difficult.

...

"It's Vivian Restless... She's sick. Very... *seriously,* sick."

...

What a crap lie—again, I am insulted that she would put so little effort into her attempt to manipulate me.

"She's an Amelior; she doesn't *get* sick—premium, luxury genetics like hers... and the few things that could affect her, well... her family can afford any medical treatment money can buy," I reply, waving a hand dismissively.

"Very true. Only.... she *is* sick, and money *can't* buy the medicine she needs. Only you going into No Man's Land can do that, Roach."

I scoff.

"Oh really? I think the suspense has been successfully built up by this point, so how about you just tell me what she allegedly has?"

...

"She has The Fade."

...

"Prosper Electronica has developed the world's first treatment; it's very promising but still years away from seeing the light of day... Unfortunately, it will hit the market too late for it to be of any help to the youngest Restless daughter. But we are willing to give her early access... *if* we get what we want."

...

"But... she's *only* 20! How... How can you know that, anyway? It's not like the family would announce it..." My tone starts off accusatory but trails off into something far less threatening.

"The answer to that is simple; we were the ones who did the tests to confirm. Obviously, we're not supposed to share a paying customer's medical information, but... we decided to make a special exception for her old knight in shining armor. Her being so young is a tragedy, but... it's not totally unheard of. Here." Britannica hands a folder of papers over to me.

I open it.

Inside are medical charts, all with Vivian's name in the top left corner.

I skim through them.

The last page of the document stands out the most to me; it is titled "Time Estimates for Onset of Memory Degradation".

On it is a list of times and percentages.

...

Within the next 180 days: 99.7%

Within the next 90 days: 90.1%

Within the next 45 days: 78.3%

Within the next 30 days: 64.4%

Within the next 15 days: 49.2%

Within the next 7 days: 23.8%

...

I stare at those percentiles until they are burned into my retinas, the afterimage of them remaining even after I try to blink them away.

On the one hand, this would suggest The Fade hasn't started to affect her yet, but...

Desperately, I rack my brain for the early symptoms of The Fade, struggling to remember a childhood I've spent so long trying to forget—my mother's case is the only personal experience I have ever had with The Fade, and she was as good as gone before I was even seven.

The only symptom I come back with is the way her hands used to shake; the neurogenic tremors start before the memory loss does, right...?

I'm absolutely positive I would have noticed if Vivian had been presenting with neurogenic tremors back when I was with her.

I refocus my attention on the list of percentages.

The difference between a week and half a year... is all the difference in the world.

Yet even that comparatively small 23.8% is far too large. There is nearly a one in four chance that it starts, well... Right now—for all intents and purposes.

Even if I *accept* the job, leave *this instant,* and it turns out to be a *total success...* I can't imagine it taking less than a week—from its onset to giving Vivian the medicine.

"What... What happens if the memory loss starts *before* the treatment is administered? Would she... get back the things she'd forgotten?" I ask numbly.

"No... No, I'm very sorry, but... The treatment seems effective at halting the deletion of memories, and it also restores the capability for long-term memory formation to the individual, but... Whatever they forgot... that's gone for good," says Britannica.

The worst part about what she just said... is the tone of voice she used to say it.

There is pity there—real, heartfelt empathy.

That scares me.

...

"*Get out*, Britannica. Forget my address—since you shouldn't have known it to begin with. First, you threaten me, and now you bring me... *this*? This is trash—it would be *so* damn simple for you to fake some paperwork. It proves absolutely nothing. And your information can't be all that good because if it were, you'd know that I haven't spoken a *single* word to Vivian Restless for over half a year. But you still think I'll go die for her? And when this job inevitably ends in failure, you wouldn't plan on giving her a damn thing, anyway..."

I suddenly want to smash something expensive and irreplaceable—what a pity that I have nothing worth destroying.

"...So, would you kindly get the hell out of my bloodydamn house?" I finish.

...

"I thought you'd say something like that... Oh well, *here*... for when you change your mind..." Britannica holds out a slip of paper.

I make no move to take it.

"It's the address for a SpeakEasy named The Night Library—It's in one of the underground districts. There will be a meeting tonight—the others we've hired will be there. I'll be going over the fine details, like who exactly you're looking for and what the last known location is."

Resentfully, I accept the slip.

"Taking this doesn't mean I've agreed to anything, Britannica."

She smiles at me; she's only wearing a half-mask, so it's a smile I can actually see.

"Whatever you say, Roach. But... If you do come, you need to be all in. There can be no backing out once we've given you all the dirty details."

2

The Subways are Privately Owned

Amelior *adjective*

A genetically enhanced person, typically exhibiting distinctive physical features such as hair and eye colors that do not occur naturally in Homo sapiens. Derived from the word "ameliorate", which means to improve upon something previously deemed unsatisfactory.

There is not a lot of time left to make up my mind—the meeting at the Night Library is only a few hours away.

But that's okay. I do all my best thinking while walking.

So, I head in the general direction of the SpeakEasy while debating my willingness to give up my life for a girl I've known for more than half my life.

If this had happened six months ago, my answer would be an instantaneous, unambiguous "yes".

But now...?

My relationship with her is a complicated one, but I spent over a decade as some combination of her servant, bodyguard, and best friend.

A few years ago, my relationship with her got more complicated when she told me she wanted to be more than servant and master—I knew it was a mistake—knew it was destined to end in tears, but... rejecting her was never a possibility—I'd have more luck commanding my heart to stop its beating.

All that complexity was then painfully simplified half a year ago when she told me to get the hell away from her—without any prior warning or decent explanation as to what I had done wrong.

I have not, thus far, enjoyed my newfound freedom very much.

I turn up my jacket collar to help keep out the rain.

Well... it's not *technically* rain, not here in the Underground Districts of the city, but...

It's close enough that, in practice, it might as well be raining.

A weapon called a "Compression Ax" hangs from my belt; the heft of it is something reassuring.

It so happens to have been a 16th birthday gift from none other than Vivian Restless herself, and it is my second most prized possession in the world.

Walking around Prospera openly armed does little to attract attention, as most people are armed in Prospera, most of the time—the anonymity of our culture's masks and Voice Modifiers making self-defense all the more necessary.

Other people just usually opt for something a little less cumbersome—a Compression Ax is a tool favored by the FireJacks in order to help fell the titanic Earth Breaker and Strangle Root trees.

But I make sure to keep myself at least moderately encumbered at all times as something like a moral imperative—to do otherwise feels akin to slothfulness.

It's a nice night to go for a walk, not despite the rain, but at least partially because of it.

The green glow of mercury vapor bulbs mixes with the neon lights from storefronts and refracts the rainwater like diamonds.

Prospera is at its best at night, even if it's a little more dangerous.

And it's *always* nighttime when you're underground.

Once again, not technically, but practically speaking.

In the same way some people look their best when the lights are dim, Prospera is a city that benefits from a little low-light imposed mystery to draw attention away from its faults and shift it firmly onto its much more appealing, shinier features.

I try to enjoy it, but it is impossible to avoid dwelling on Britannica's words.

I take a deep breath, then try to call Vivian using my mask's internal display.

Again.

...

No answer.

No surprise there.

I can't entirely blame her. I spent weeks after she sent me away trying to contact her incessantly, but all the same...

I'm supposed to give up everything for a girl who won't even answer my calls?

Suddenly, anger flares up inside my chest.

Screw that.

I spent years absolutely devoted to her, and *this* is what I get in return?

If she wants my help, she can ask for it herself, not Britannica.

But regardless of my indignation, I still get on a subway car headed in the direction of the SpeakEasy.

I've only made it one station before my peaceful agonizing and obsessing over an uncertain future is interrupted by the uncomfortable sounds of a public argument.

"Miss... I'm sorry, but you need to have some form of payment to ride the trains... You're going to have to leave now."

"Payment? Please... I-I'm so confused. I don't know where I am—I don't recognize anything besides the names of some of the stations... I took the train only a few days ago—it was free... a public service... it's *always* been free..."

My hand freezes on the side of my mask—a second before I would have turned on the noise canceling.

"It's no longer free. Hasn't been free for... It *was* free, but not anymore... not since... the last time you used it. New policy. The subways are privately owned now. Now please... we need you to leave the station."

A few other people file past the woman, annoyed by the disturbance blocking the entrance.

"Oh... privately owned... I see. We are still in Prospera, aren't we? I just don't recognize *anything*—I'm so... so confused. Please help me... I need to get h-home."

I mostly do my best to not think about the Faded too much... No one does—unless and until it happens to someone you care for personally.

Every few months, the Security Forces will round up the Faded and transport them down to Hooverville, which is where most of the city's Faded go to fade away into lifeless husks.

There was never any point in paying attention to the Faded; no one can fix what they have, and any compassion you show them will be forgotten the next time they go to sleep—so it as good as never happened.

This woman has the Fade, presumably an advanced case of it if her memories start so long ago that she can't even recognize the city anymore...

How long will it take for Vivian's symptoms to progress this far?

This woman looks to be in her 40s... Does that mean she had twice as long as Vivian will have before she's totally empty inside?

Eventually, this woman will have nothing left, not even her name.

How long will Vivian have before she reaches that point?

I feel like I'm going to vomit into my mask.

The woman starts to sob into her own filthy mask.

The officer's body language screams their discomfort.

They look at each other, hoping the other will take the lead, neither one of them wanting to deal with this.

The woman is dirty. The officers don't want to touch her if at all possible.

"I'll pay her fare," I say.

"...Are... you sure you want to do that?" The officers turn to examine me, clearly surprised.

I nod.

“Thank you so much! That’s reeeaally sweet of you—my parents must be worried sick about me, it’s getting super late...” she says, her voice carrying the affectations of a high school girl, not a middle-aged woman.

Hell...

She thinks she’s still living at home with her parents, still a damn *kid*.

“We...” The officer bends closer to me so that only I can hear. “... still can’t let her on by herself, she’ll cause a scene, something will set her off, and we’ll get called back to take care of her. She's faded out of her mind... no point letting her on,” mutters the taller officer, clearly disgusted.

“I’ll... take her. I’ll take her to her stop. It’ll be fine.”

I stick my hand in the door to stop it from closing again.

The two officers exchange looks before the short one shrugs, and the tall one—very reluctantly—nods.

“Come on... let’s get you home,” I say as the door repeatedly tries to slide closed against my outstretched arm.

She hurriedly bustles in, obviously nervous that the Security Forces officers might change their minds about letting her on—or perhaps she is just anxious to find herself being escorted home by a thug like me.

“Really, you don’t have to take me all the way—I’m sure I’ll recognize my way home once I get a little closer. I take the subway all the time... And my parents... it’s already so super embarrassing, having to get an adult to take me home as if I’m still a little kid or something,” she says.

“Oh... no. I’ll take you to your street at least, don’t worry... How... How old are you?” I ask, afraid to hear how old she *thinks* she is.

“Oh, I’m 15! And I haven't introduced myself either—my name is Maggie... What's yours?” Maggie asks and bows her head the formal way people used to commonly do on first introductions decades ago.

“It’s Ro...Robert. Just Robert. Nice to meet you, Maggie,” I say, glad that I caught myself before I let my real name slip—not that she would remember it for long, but still.

“I must have left my bag at school... I always forget it in the music room after practice—I’m such an airhead...” Maggie laughs at herself, embarrassed.

I haven't heard anyone use the phrase "airhead" in real life before, only in old films.

Maggie might have insisted on not wanting me to come with her at first, but now she seems to like the company and won't stop chattering away. I think she is subconsciously using me as a distraction—she is very pointedly *not* looking at all the strange sights that flicker past the windows or at the glowing advertisements that shine from above our heads.

Some part of her must know that something is very, *very* wrong.

"... It's so strange; I woke up, and I was sitting against a building, changed out of my school uniform already... I must have gotten turned around on my way home and fallen asleep somehow..." Maggie continues.

...

Can she really believe that? Her *hands*—she *must* have noticed her hands by now... right?

They are unmistakably *not* the hands of a teenage girl—the skin is wrinkled, and the nails are yellowing.

I can smell her as well... she has been homeless for a very long time, I'm sure.

I make one-sided eye contact with her, my eyes hidden behind the internal display of my mask, but she has only a cheap plastic one, the kind that are handed out to the destitute to let them maintain some scrap of dignity.

To my horror, I realize that there are tears in her eyes.

She knows. On some level, she knows the truth... she just cannot comprehend or accept it.

That's like the definition of cognitive dissonance, isn't it?

How many days has she woken up not knowing who she is, her body becoming progressively more alien to her as she grows mentally younger but physically older?

A few dozen...? A few thousand...?

I have no clue how fast The Fade takes memories, how long it takes for things to get this bad... the memories I have of my mother's case are so foggy—The last time I saw her, I was ten years old, and she'd already been completely Faded for years by that point. I don't remember what her decline was like at all anymore...

"This is me!" Maggie says merrily, but her eyes are still damp with tears.

I follow her off the subway car.

Maggie's steps become progressively faster, her hands twisting the hem of her dress as she walks.

"I don't... Where did the park g-go? So many big buildings..."

Why did I come? Why am I torturing myself with this? I can't do anything for her—no one can. People with The Fade are beyo...

Vivian's face materializes in my mind's eye.

...

That was a stupid question—I know why I'm doing it.

It's the same reason I seem to do so many things recently... *guilt*.

"YES! Yes, I know that building! There!" Maggie laughs with borderline hysterical relief, pointing at an old restaurant shaped like a rocket ship.

It's abandoned—falling to pieces... and nothing like the place she actually remembers, I'm sure.

"G-Great..." I say.

Suddenly, Maggie stops, and I nearly run into her.

Her frail, wrinkled hands are visibly shaking at her sides.

"I... don't know if I'm r-ready to go home... I should... go back to school! Get my gym bag! Yeah, t-that's what I'll do—my big sister will tease me all week if I forget it there again..." Maggie gives another forced laugh. I can hear the barely contained hysteria in her tone.

But that means she has an older sister, just like Vivian...

I'm tempted to let her turn back and be done with it, but... what if her family still lives in the same house? It's worth checking on the off chance they are willing to take care of her.

"No... Maggie, this is your street, isn't it? You're... family must be worried... let's get you home—the bag will wait," I lie.

After a long pause, she nods in agreement, and we start walking again.

Maggie stops in front of a two-story home, not very well maintained but clearly inhabited, at least.

She tries to open the gate, but her hands no longer seem to have the dexterity to manage the latch.

I reach out and open it for her.

Once we're at the door, Maggie just stands there for a full thirty seconds, unable or unwilling to take the next step herself.

So, I pound on the door for her as well.

...

There is a scratching at the door, like a dog is pawing at it from the other side.

Then footsteps.

The door opens.

There stands another middle-aged woman in a plain mask and simple clothing, but hers are clean, and her hair is tied back in an immaculate bun.

"How can I help..." Her voice trails off as her eyes drift from my tall figure to Maggie.

There is recognition in her eyes—I can see it there for an instant before it retreats back behind her irises and is replaced by... I'm not sure what, shock? Frustration? Regret?

Is she the sister Maggie mentioned? Or... perhaps Maggie has just managed to find her way onto this doorstep on previous occasions, and this woman is just sick and tired of faded strangers bothering her at home.

She slams the door in Maggie's face.

...

We stand there in silence.

Then... Maggie slips off her mask, takes a few unsteady steps over to the nearest window, and studies her reflection in the glass.

...

She screams.

Screams as if she's dying, screams as if she's already dead, and has realized for the first time she's in a hell she cannot comprehend.

I begin to walk away, though I would rather be running.

Britannica was right.

There was never any question about what my choice would be in the end.

Stupid.

I'm no better than a child who refuses to hear anything he doesn't want to believe.

Even with this detour, I still have plenty of time to make the meeting.

I sigh.

Regardless of everything that has happened recently, as much as I would like to pretend otherwise... I owe absolutely everything to Vivian Restless.

Even if she's abandoned me...

I could never do the same to her.

PHILLIES
Electronica
RESTLESS
INDUSTRIES

3

A Good Lost Cause

"Knowing that there are no victorious causes, I have a liking for lost causes: they require an uncontaminated soul."

— Albert Camus

I glance down at the address Britannica gave me as if willing more words to appear on it.

To my more than slight consternation, the paper she gave me does not have an exact address... only a street, a time, and a scribbled winky face.

Unsurprisingly, there is also no building advertising itself as the "Night Library".

Good thing I'm experienced enough to know how to recognize the signs of a SpeakEasy when I need to.

Exactly what hidden clues such a place uses to set itself apart vary based on the neighborhood, but in this case, I notice a Prosperan flag that hangs horizontally instead of the usual vertical, the way the vending machine out front happens to have the second row of lights all burned out, and an unusual bit of graffiti on one of the boarded-up windows.

On its outside, the Night Library has the appearance of a used electronics shop called "Blue Box Tech"—with a neon sign advertising jail-breaking for expensive internal display masks like mine and custom orders on power rigs.

I break away from the busy hustle of masked people going about their business and slip inside.

An unassuming woman in a copper mask sits lazily at the front counter.

I nod politely as she looks up at me.

"Britannica sent me," I say.

I don't know their specific way of doing business here—I've been to a SpeakEasy once that only let new people in if they were vouched for by one of their trusted regulars, and it's pretty standard for them to require a passphrase or password... hopefully, in this instance, Britannica's name will be password enough.

"...Down the stairs, your last left," she says apathetically.

I'm hit by a wall of noise as soon as I open the soundproof door.

Unsurprisingly, going by the history of the name, a SpeakEasy is usually some form of a bar—the Night Library is no exception.

Alcohol is not illegal in Prospera—very few things are. The city takes a minimalist approach to law—and law enforcement in general—what laws it does have are usually cut and dry and lack all the legal fine print that makes the judicial systems of Neo Kyoto and Kallipolis bureaucratic mazes.

The standard stuff is still illegal, of course; murder, kidnapping, theft, all those pillars of society rules still apply.

Even with relatively few laws, there are still people who need someone to break the laws that do exist... hence the necessity of the SpeakEasys and the occupation of Freelancers.

Prospera is the world capital of organized crime—although I suppose that when there are only three cities remaining in the world, all must be considered famous by default. Unsurprisingly, this fact is not one of the ones highlighted by the travel pamphlets. The "city of arts and self-made men" sounds a hell of a lot better than "83% of all kidnapping/ransom incidents in the world happen here".

The SpeakEasy's main room is spacious—yet still unpleasantly crowded—no less than 50 Freelancers make small talk, trade insults, and knock back cheap liquor.

Could they all really be here for the same job as I? I'm blown away by the astronomical cost of hiring half a hundred Lancers—each one a small fortune, surely, if it is enough to make them agree to a job bordering on the impossible.

I'm 15 minutes early, so I go find a corner to stand in with my back to the wall and eyes on the door while I wait.

I catch some looks and mutters while I wait; my reputation as a Lancer has grown in the six months I've been at it. Not enough to qualify me as famous exactly, but has been enough to make my distinctive amethyst-purple and metal mask, large Compression Ax, high-collared leather jacket, and crimson-red scarf attract occasional recognition from my fellow criminals.

The room has a half dozen doors around its edges; one or two I presume, are for storage, but the rest will be set aside for private conversations.

Everyone is masked—no different than it would be anywhere else in the city. There is no standard nudity taboo in Prospera, but the face is the exception—I've known people for years without ever seeing their faces even once. I could literally count on my fingers how many naked faces I've ever seen... People go to the public baths in masks—exercise in masks—couples frequently break up after finally seeing each other's real face for the first time, so traumatically disappointed they are that the reality doesn't match the idealized image they had dreamed up of each other.

Prepubescent children are afforded a little more leniency—since their face and voices are going to change dramatically once puberty has had its say. But for adults, the more revealing a mask is, the less formal and more promiscuous it's considered.

It is not hard to see how the mandatory masks and Voice Mods are very useful social norms for the criminal element of the city—what started out as pure necessity decades ago, when Deep Fake tech first started ruining a critical mass of lives... Has given birth to an entirely new set of social norms, while also turning the city into history's grandest social experiment on the effects of near total anonymity and a weak central authority on human behavior. Unsurprisingly, it turns out humans *love* to misbehave when they know they cannot be easily identified—what I find more interesting is how being surrounded by potential threats with little ability to hold strangers accountable draws people together into tight little tribes—families stick together here, and if romance or friendship is established, they are too hard to replace to be thrown away.

In short... The easier it is to act an evil bastard without consequence, the more valuable it becomes to find a bastard or two you can trust.

Lancers continue to trickle into the Night Library, a few of whom I recognize by reputation, but most are completely foreign to me.

One of the ones I have heard whispered stories about walks by me at that moment.

He goes by Riot, and he just might be the largest man I have ever seen in my 21 years of life—certainly large enough to be Amelior. But everything else about him, from his hair, to his mannerisms, to his freakishly built body... rule that possibility out. Amelior prize aesthetic beauty too much to design such a terror.

He wears a steel mask with a simplistic laughing face, with paint missing in places—as if the mask has been dragged across the pavement more than a few times.

Apparently, he gets his name from his ability to incite violence and discontent, which requires rather a lot of charisma, inside knowledge, and leadership ability I've certainly never claimed to have.

He gets hired to go into places with already tense atmospheres, like companies with abused workers or activist movements, and push things over the edge into misdirected violence or infighting. He's fantastically violent himself—a man who thoroughly enjoys breaking people. He makes connections, frames people, incites unrest, and gets personally involved in the resulting destruction even though he probably doesn't need to, for the most part... And he gets paid lavishly to do so.

Some claim the man is moved by a guiding philosophy, a logically coherent creed—but knowing Freelancers as I do... I doubt it.

I've never been very good at keeping my ear to the ground, never had the desire to sift through the rumors in order to keep tabs on the who's who of the criminal underground or to make time for all the pleasantries of networking... and this is one of those occasions where I fear it's going to bite me in the ass.

Okabe is here as well—if he has any hard feelings towards me for costing him a payday on the animal lab job a few months ago, he doesn't show it. He keeps his long hair in a bun behind the wolf mask—hair that has the unnatural color of an Amelior. If it wasn't for his massive height, I'd think the hair was simply dyed to make him look enhanced—there are scant few Amelior Freelancers in the world—most have far better options than to be a criminal for hire. His story is one of the few I'd care to know.

The other two remaining city-states may have outlawed human genetic engineering ages ago, but in Prospera, the elite and the unwashed masses are virtually different species.

The Amelior take pride in their superiority, and Amelior parents intentionally modify their children's DNA to give them unnatural hair and eye colors—else people might mistake their child for a natural-born, and no self-respecting Amelior parent would tolerate such an embarrassment. These cosmetic differences are in addition to the changes that seriously matter—the enhanced intelligence, the athletic ability, the height, the immunity to most common forms of illness, the increased bone density, etc.

Many of the powerful people in the other cities are still having these changes made, of course; they opt out of the blatantly aesthetic modifications but still get their unborn kids all the hottest gene upgrades while visiting for conveniently timed vacations with their pregnant wives—though only after they've gone through the tedious chore of paying their ransoms—Prospera's unofficial tax on tourism.

A blond woman in military camo pants, combat boots, and an antique wooden rifle seems to be a minor celebrity—judging by the attention she's receiving—but I've no clue who she's supposed to be.

Finally, there is also a tall person covered from head to toe in a form-concealing cloak, hood up, and wearing a fox-face mask—a design that has been a trendy choice among the city's young people recently.

This one receives no attention from onlookers, but the relatively plain appearance ironically stands out to me. Next to all these distinctively dressed people, a simple black cloak and an in-fashion mask seem... intentionally nondescript—like someone trying a little too hard to avoid standing out.

Not only that, but something about the way this Lancer carries himself...

I think I know this person from somewhere.

The large cloak keeps even their sex a mystery, although the height is tall enough to suggest it is probably a man.

Fox-mask notices me staring and returns my unwanted attention with a particularly obscene gesture.

That seems uncalled for.

I'm not in a great mood, so I abandon the moral high ground and return it.

Fox mask stalks away, and I turn in time to catch a girl in a long green cloak watching me, probably amused by the interaction she just got to witness.

She's in an old-fashioned Pierrot mask and a fur-lined cloak. It's been a while since I've seen anyone wear a Pierrot mask, so she stands out to me as well.

I can barely make out a pair of bright green eyes behind the mask, which dart away from me as soon as she notices me, noticing her.

A back door opens, and Britannica graces us with her presence—only ten minutes late... unusually punctual for her, actually.

"Good evening, everyone. I know it must be frustrating—some of us spoke only a few hours ago about this job and the particulars of your compensation. Forcing you all to make the trip here, just to be told the final few details, must seem like a needless inconvenience."

There are a few bitter mutters of agreement from the crowd.

Britannica waits for them to die out. She no longer wears the outrageously reveling mask from her visit to my house—instead, opting for a black mask with an elegant floral pattern on it.

"But we did want to encourage you all to meet your coworkers, and we hope you will work together, or... at a minimum... avoid getting in one another's way. And, more importantly... there is something we wanted everyone here to see firsthand tonight."

Per usual, Britannica takes the scenic route on her way to reaching the point.

"The truth is, some of Prosper Electronica's competitors see this tragedy as an opportunity. Some of you will be approached by this competition, will be offered generous compensation if you would just bring the person we need to them, instead... Some of you *have* already been approached, actually."

...

Another dramatic pause.

I don't mind this pageantry—a little dramatic effect suddenly seems warranted—making me appreciate her instinct for showmanship.

"Not only that, but at least one of you has *accepted* one such offer."

Britannica starts to pace back and forth, like a cliché detective walking through the needlessly elaborate scheme of the murderer.

"We would not begrudge a Lancer simply for accepting a job from one of our competitors, but... if you are in this room, it means you have already accepted ours. And that makes it a matter of betrayal." Britannica stops her pacing and nods to a tall man in the back who wears an ugly bird-face mask.

"Let us make something crystal clear. We are paying all of you exceptionally well; most of you are receiving aid or services *only* Prosper Electronica can provide. But if someone *does* somehow manage to offer you more..."

The bird-masked man steps up to a woman in a red demon mask.

"... do not give in to the temptation."

In a blur of movement, the man pulls a pistol from his jacket, brings it up to the woman's heart, and pulls the trigger. The minuscule distance and the heavy caliber of the weapon between them means that even if the woman has on a layer of light armor under her clothing—as most Lancers probably would—it fails to make any difference.

"Even if you succeed, Prosper Electronica has the intelligence networks to find you, as we proved to most of you when we had our previous meeting... so, believe us when we promise that you will not live long enough to enjoy the fruits of betraying us. A silly thing to do, really."

The woman in the green cloak and Pierrot mask rushes forward, causing the bird-masked shooter to take a step back and half raise his weapon—expecting retaliation.

But the girl just drops down and pulls out a medical pack, a hand reaching under the woman's neck to check for a pulse.

Someone laughs.

Looking around, I see that it's the gigantic Lancer from before, Riot.

I know why he's laughing—the woman is so unmistakably a goner that there is no point trying to help.

Yet, all the same, I do not find it amusing.

The woman in the green cloak lets out a family-friendly version of a curse and rushes to open the medical kit so hastily that its contents spill out all over the floor.

Riot laughs even harder, and a few others join him now.

In a different circumstance, I might find childish alternatives to swear words funny as well, but at the moment, all I feel is disgust.

The girl's hands shake as she starts rendering first aid to a woman already too far gone to help.

I shove one of the laughing Lancers aside and bend down to assist her.

Somehow, I'm more bothered by the onlookers laughing at this woman than I am at witnessing a brutal murder, but... it is hard not to grow desensitized to violence with the life I've lived—but I have always had a soft spot for a good lost cause—particularly when someone knows the cause is lost but insists on trying regardless... I respect that kind of defiance, even if it's pointless... Maybe *because* it is pointless, even.

"Here... put them back. There is nothing anyone can do. You know that. She was beyond helping as soon as the trigger was pulled," I say to the woman in a low voice as I fall to a knee beside her.

She freezes.

Then, with her still shaking hands, she accepts the supplies I hold out to her and returns them to their case.

The Lancer's body convulses as it realizes death is only a few painful seconds away. Her mask is half off her face—knocked aside by the fall to reveal a plain, dark face with wide eyes and thick brows. Imagining how horrible it must be to bleed out with your face exposed to a room of laughing strangers, I reach down to return the mask to its proper place on her face.

I turn back to the would-be medic.

Her eyes are large and youthful... she might actually be closer to a girl than a woman.

Regardless of her age, she clearly does not belong here.

No one else is exactly distraught over the dead woman; she was not better or worse than those who killed her—simply less capable. If she had been more clever, more competent, she would have betrayed Prosper Electronica successfully—it was her own fault for biting off more than she could chew.

"It's kind of you to try, but... do you mind? She's leaking all over the place. No need to inconvenience the cleaners more than already necessary," says Britannica.

Fair enough.

I nod at Britannica and help the girl to her feet.

She seems stunned, in shock... as if this is her first time seeing a person die, and she cannot comprehend the casual brutality, the lack of any great drama.

People who have not seen much of death expect it to be like the movies; they expect to hear someone's tearful last words, they expect passion and declarations of revenge—not the rapidly evaporating morbid curiosity of a crowd of onlookers who have all seen this kind of thing plenty of times before and are quickly bored by it.

I shake my head.

She really should not be here, whoever she is.

Bird-mask drags the corpse away.

"Anyway, so sorry for that, but the point had to be made. Now, let's clean up this mess, refill our drinks, and we can get down to the details you all came here to hear. Let's give it... 20 more minutes, say." Britannica clasps her hands together and looks around the room, not unlike a dinner host who's suggested a game of Charades after the appetizers have been passed around.

Excellent—more time for me to sit here and think about how screwed I genuinely am.

We all already know the general idea of this job; we know we are going into No Man's Land for a search and rescue—we just don't have the exact identity of who we're rescuing and the six-digit grid of the downed aircraft.

I have a strict policy to avoid working with others whenever possible. I don't trust anyone in this room—I don't want the added complications, the added variables other people inevitably end up bringing along with them—especially when the stakes are so high.

The common wisdom claims that extremes bring out the best in some people and the worst in others... in my personal experience, you can only safely bet on the latter.

But how am I supposed to do this kind of job on my own?

How will I manage to get any rest without other people to alternate keeping watch at night?

I suppose that if I am thorough enough with setting traps before bedding down, that might be enough, but...

I need to find the proverbial needle in the haystack. Trying to search such a large area on my own seems more than just impractical, and if this mysterious person has wandered away from the site of the plane crash, it's game over.

This is for Vivian. I've committed myself to doing anything for her sake... anything includes setting aside my strong preference for working alone, surely.

But I'm at a definite disadvantage here—never working with people means I have no pre-existing acquaintances among the crowd... while all the other Lancers here seem to know each other, at least in passing.

While I stand there feeling sorry for myself and agonizing over who might be considered the least offensive option among the mob, there is a tap on my shoulder.

I turn to see the girl in the green cloak from earlier, the one who had lost her cool over the dead Lancer.

The one who obviously doesn't belong in a place like this.

"It's ah... Mr. Roach, right? Can we please ummm... talk? In private?"

She gestures to a door leading to a back room.

...

"So... it's been a pretty wild day, hasn't it?" The door swings shut behind me as the girl in the green cloak opens fire with the pleasantries.

I only nod in response.

"I was hoping to talk, to thank you for earlier... I was... it was *horrible*, that poor woman... But I was making a fool of myself. Thank you for stopping me," she says.

"It was nothing... is that all?" I ask, looking over her head at the door and thinking of how exactly I'm going to approach one of the groups back in the main room.

"I... you know, you're about as approachable as a raised guillotine, right? You should really work on that," her tone more playful than actually annoyed.

I gesture at the Compression Ax on my hip.

"A 'raised guillotine' is exactly the vibe I'm going for, as a matter of fact."

She laughs.

...

"Ah... once again, if that's all, I should really be going..."

"That's *not* all—I want to figure you out... I want to get a sense of whether or not I can trust you. So, stop being all antisocial and just talk to me for a while," she says.

"Oh, is that all?" I ask.

"Yeah, just a talk, that's all I ask," she says, sounding relieved.

"Let me save you the time and trouble. You can't. Trust me, I mean. Best if you not trust *anyone*... but least of all, a cold-blooded thing like me. Good talk," I say and move towards the door.

She sidesteps to block me.

The nerve of this girl...

"Hmmm, that's very honest of you... paradoxically, you saying I can't trust you... makes me feel as though I can."

...

"What do I need to say for you to let me go?" I ask, slightly bemused despite myself.

"Say that you'll team up with me! Then we can both go—together. But you have to really mean it; that's the only catch," she replies.

"What happened to figuring out if you could trust me first?" I ask.

"I did, and I do! I work fast. Which... is one of the reasons you should team up with me. I'm also a good judge of character, yet another reason why you should want to team up." There is a smile in her voice.

She's good at this—very personable, very warm... if a little childish.

Too bad "personable" isn't really an applicable skill for the task at hand.

"Sorry, no sale." I turn to go.

"What?! No hesitation at all... mind explaining to me why not?" she says, sounding dismayed.

"You... Don't seem like you belong here. This work isn't for nice people... It's a job for unapologetic, self-proclaimed killers like me—not little girls who flinch at swear words and can't stand to see a stranger get hurt. It's not too late for you, whatever it is they're offering you... it's not enough," I say.

"Oh... so, I really did make a fool of myself out there, even more so than I'd realized. Everyone else will have the same opinion of me as you—they'll think I'm weak after seeing my reaction. No one will be willing to work with me after that, will they?"

I sigh.

"No, I'm sure *someone* will, but... it will be one of the ones who think they can take advantage of you," I reply. The brutal honesty of my own words reminds me, yet again, of Vivian.

"Right... Well. I want you to please reconsider. I know you don't think so, but I can be really useful—I have skills specifically valuable for this search and rescue mission. I doubt anyone else can offer what I can. I honestly feel like I can trust you—call it a woman's intuition. At least... more than I can trust any of the others. I'll pull my weight! I promise you won't regret it," she says earnestly.

Okay, fine—I'll bite.

"...What kind of skills are you talking about?" I can't completely hide the curiosity from my tone.

"I'm a scientist! I specialize in emerging biology and genetic engineering. I go into No Man's Land for my research, sometimes." She puffs her chest out slightly as she says it.

I'm a little taken aback, but I manage to find my tongue again quickly.

"The hell...No one goes into No Man's Land..." I say, confused.

"No one from *Prospera* goes into No Man's Land, actually. You Prosperans can be so strange, treating No Man's Land like it's something mystical and malicious... I'm from Neo Kyoto—I only flew in this morning actually—just to take this job."

"Neo Kyoto? Prosper Electronica reached out to a Neo Kyoto scientist for this job? Neo Kyoto scientists actually go into No Man's Land?" I ask, more than a little skeptical, having never heard any such thing before but not confident enough to simply dismiss it.

"Sure we do! We don't go in very deep, two or three klicks at most... the further in you go, the more dangerous it gets... And we never ever stay past sunset—it gets *much* more dangerous after dark... We also take an armed guard, but a small one. Three to five people works best—any more than that is a bad idea."

"Why... is that a bad idea?" I ask, thinking of all the Lancers out there forming their teams... some—if not *most*—will definitely end up with far more people than that.

"You... don't know? I thought you did—I thought that's why you were refusing to talk to anyone... But anyway, yeah, going out into No Man's Land in a large group is a very bad idea... The attention a parade of people marching through the trees would bring is enough to attract every predator for miles and miles around. Going in as a large group is just as suicidal as going in alone. It's one of the strangest things about No Man's Land—it's like everything in there shares a common instinctual hatred for humanity's greatest strength—the massing of organized effort at the large scale."

"Nope, not clever, I just never learned how to play nice with the other kids... That is interesting, though—it changes everything if what you're saying is true," I admit.

She nods enthusiastically.

"It is! My name is Nona, by the way..." And to my absolute horror, she pulls off her mask and lowers her hood as if she's known me her whole life.

She then reaches out a hand in an invitation to shake it, a friendly smile on her face.

Confident I know the game she's playing, I reach out and pinch her cheeks, expecting that when I pull back, a layer of artificial skin will come away as well.

Nothing.

Then I look down at my fingers, expecting to at least see evidence of thickly applied contouring makeup intended to hide her true facial features.

Again, nothing.

I feel my own face start to heat up.

"WHOA, wait—w-what in the world—Put your mask back on!" I stammer out the words in a rush.

Her eyes are a little puffy, presumably from crying under her mask after that Lancer was executed.

"W-What's the big deal?! Do you Prosperans actually keep them on all the time? Even in a private room like this?"

"I can't believe this... faces... are only meant for people you're close to! Like a lover or immediate family... a face is just... I mean, come on... even call girls leave their masks on with their clients—it's just too intimate..." I never thought I'd have to explain the necessity of wearing a mask to anyone over the age of six—unbelievable.

She goes scarlet red, cheeks burning with embarrassment. She's a Natural for sure, with bright green eyes and reddish-brown hair. She looks young, no older than 20—*at most.*

"I... You Prosperans are so backwards! How are you supposed to figure out if you can trust someone without ever seeing their face?! How do you get anything done at all...? Silly, arbitrary, *nonsense...*" She says all this while pointedly NOT returning the mask to her still blushing face.

"That's absurd—you already said you decided you could trust me without ever seeing my face. Besides, don't you Neo Kyotans spend all day communicating through your avatars anyway? It's not like you're seeing much of each other's real faces yourselves..."

"Just... let me see your face, gosh!"

"I'm not that kind of guy, sorry."

"W-What's that supposed to mean?"

"It means that no *decent* man shows his face to a woman he's just met," I say simply... as if it is the most obvious thing in the world.

Because it *is* the most obvious thing in the world.

"Oh my... that is so, SO ridiculous!"

"Please... put your mask back on... you're embarrassing yourself," I beg.

Nona's mouth opens and closes a few times, overcome with so much apparent incredulity that I've temporarily stolen her capacity for speech.

She takes a steadying breath as she prepares to try reasoning with me again.

She doesn't have much of a temper. I'm sure that if I ever insulted Vivian the way I just did her, Vivian would have found something to hit me with.

Nope... Let's not think about Vivian right now.

"I know, I know, I'm violating your innocent, virgin eyes with my scandalous, bare face." She rolls her eyes. Her face is still pink, despite her insistence that there is nothing indecent at all about her facial nudity.

"You are, yes. So glad you understand," I quip dryly.

"LOOK... *Look*, okay... I'm embarrassed enough as it is. It's weird having you freak out after seeing my face as if you think I'm some creature from the bottom of a No Man's Land swamp. If we're gonna work together, we... can't have our relationship start with such a big power disparity. So... show me your dang face. It'll make things easier in the long run, I promise. I can't start building trust with someone who won't even show me their face—we're just old-fashioned that way in Neo Kyoto."

The absolute absurdity of describing Neo Kyoto, of *all places*, as "old-fas hioned"...

"I never actually said I wanted to team up with you, you know..." I say.

"WHAT? Oh, come on—you didn't *need* to say it out loud—you for sure want to! You know we would be a great team." There is a definite note of false confidence in her voice. Could this be her real voice as well? If she's willing to show me her naked face, then maybe she really is stupid enough to be walking around without a Voice Mod... I have both a camera and an audio recorder built into my mask—I could steal her face and her voice and blackmail her—invent any manner of Deep Fake I wished... It is surely what any of the other Lancers here would do in my position.

"Not even slightly. I'm almost certain it would be a disaster, as a matter of fact," I answer.

"Don't be like that... You refused to speak more than like three words to anyone else this whole time, yet you've been talking to me for ages and ages in comparison. Explain *that* if you don't want to team up." Her tone of voice suggests she considers this evidence irrefutable.

"Pretty sure it's been less than 10 minutes thus far, and I'm also pretty sure I've tried to end the conversation more than once already."

"Oh hush... You're too old to still be pretending you're too cool for school—being all aloof really isn't as cool as all you boys seem to think it is," says Nona, her face having mostly returned to what I imagine is its default rosy-cheeked hue.

I express my disagreement with her insinuation with a stoic silence... which she takes as an invitation to continue talking.

"...It's suicidal marching into No Man's Land with dozens of people behind you, but... It's also suicidal to go it alone. Small groups have the best chance out there; a pair isn't ideal, but it's worlds better than nothing. You're not a people-person—that much is clear. And I believe you when you say no one with good intentions is likely to want to team up with me... So, we *need* each other."

"... If you really believe that, then it sounds like you'll be forced to team up with me regardless of whether or not I show you my face," I say.

"This... This is hardly any way to treat your new partner..." She crosses her arms and huffs, pouting like a little kid.

"Good thing we're not partners then."

She pretends not to have heard me.

"I'm from a different culture, right? There was always sure to be some friction between us... Since we're going to be partners from now on, we're going to need some good old-fashioned compromise... which requires you to let me see your *gosh dang* face... at least once."

I sigh audibly.

"Just say the damned curse, won't you? How am I supposed to take you seriously when you talk like a schoolgirl...?"

"I promise, in the future I'll say whatever bad words you want... but only if you'll show me your face first! So, partner... we have a deal?"

...

"Dammit, fine... *Fine*." This interaction has done little to raise my confidence that she will be able to take care of herself if things get rough, but she's right: We do need each other... don't we?

"Come on, stop being such a baby and hurry up!" she says.

I switch on a Micro Jamer in my jacket pocket, which should distort the video footage beyond recognition if she's trying to record me. As for my voice, if I don't speak while the mask is off, she still won't know my true voice. In doing so, I also sacrifice my ability to record her face—taking blackmail off the table for the time being.

I pull my mask off of my face, lock my eyes on a crack in the wall a few feet over her head, and count to five... before returning the mask to its rightful place.

Looking down again, I see that Nona's mouth is hanging slightly open.

"W-What the hell?!" I ask, mortified.

"Sorry! Sorry, Ah... Roach. Do I have to keep calling you Roach, or will you tell me your real name? Anyway, I was just surprised... You... don't look like I'd imagined... You're way younger than I'd thought for starters, barely older than me... and you look, well... never mind... you just look *different* than I thought you would."

No clue what that's supposed to mean.

I look away.

"Rowan. My name's Rowan," I say, opting to respond only to the least pointless portion of her ramblings.

She's way too nice. What I'll need out there is a veteran Lancer, a killer... But instead of having someone to watch my back in a fight, I'm going to be babysitting this girl...

And probably fail at it as well, which is the worst part. Clueless creatures like her should stay that way—safely locked away in high towers where they can't get themselves hurt by the harsh realities of life.

I pause, run my fingers through my hair, and head for the door without saying anything to her in response.

"Hey, wait up!" calls Nona, chasing after me.

This was definitely a mistake.

...

Not long after my deal with the doe-eyed devil, Britannica deems the crowd sufficiently ready to receive her much-anticipated presentation.

"Well, without further ado... the coordinates." Britannica pushes a button, and a holograph flickers to life, depicting a six-digit grid hovering over a three-dimensional topographical map.

To my slight annoyance, Nona is standing behind me like a baby duck that has imprinted upon me the role of parent.

"Keep in mind that you'll need an aviation-grade GPS to get a signal at all in No Man's Land, and even then, the tree canopy is too thick to let a signal through in most places... might as well be underground. When not in a clearing or on high ground, it'll be up to the lost arts of maps and protractors." Britannica hits another button.

"And this is the missing person we need, the president of Prosper Electronica's daughter, Kasca Haine."

A girl slightly younger than myself—late teens I suspect—appears on the screen. I try to switch on my mask's recorder, but with little hope it won't be jammed. Britannica wouldn't show us the face if we could capture it and sell it to her company's enemies.

There is a sharp intake of air from behind me.

I turn and realize it came from Nona herself.

Almost immediately, muttering breaks out across the room.

The girl in the holo is pretty, even if the smile on her face hardly looks heartfelt.

She was also distinctive; she has heterochromia, which should make her easy to find among any other survivors—we'd just have to have them remove their masks and check for a mismatched pair of eyes.

But in that was also the cause of the crowd's reaction...

She iss distinctive, yes... but not distinctive *enough*—not for the daughter of one of Prospera's most powerful people.

Not for an Amelior.

She shouldn't be just pretty; she should be idealized, upgraded... Her hair and eye colors should not be naturally occurring ones, and she should be *much* taller... The heterochromia was the only thing that might mark her as an Amelior—it had been a fashionable choice among Amelior parents a couple of decades ago, however... Even Amelior parents who opted for two different eye colors would not have considered that distinctive enough—they still would have insisted on two unnaturally occurring colors.

But this girl didn't have one gold and one silver eye or something equally exotic... she had one emerald green and one mahogany brown eye, pretty and all but just the natural, boring colors of a common person.

Same for her hair, which is a totally unremarkable reddish brown.

Also, if I'm not very much mistaken, it looks like she has a mole at the base of her neck on her right side—the Amelior don't ever have any blemishes—they don't get things like moles, freckles, acne, or skin tags.

"You really expect us to believe that this girl is the big man's daughter? She's no Amelior... You must think we've got shit for brains, lady," says a Lancer from my left.

"Who is this girl really? If you want us to kidnap some damn kid, just say so... don't feed us this trash about a worried dad who wants to see his little girl again," says Riot in a deep, self-assured kind of rumble.

"I, for one, don't want to die for some *nobody*... what the hell makes her worth all our necks?" says the blond female Lancer with the old rifle.

Britannica looks at a slight loss for words. Presumably, she didn't expect this much pushback—which was rather stupid of her, frankly.

...

"Oh, so you would want to die for her if she had some shinier irises... Sorry she's not your type and all, but whether or not you die will be up to you, won't it?" I snap.

I'm not usually so confrontational—it seems my bad mood has me acting more like Vivian than my usual, peace-loving self.

Before the situation has the chance to devolve any further, Britannica starts to speak again.

"This *is* the president's daughter... his... illegitimate daughter. She was born the... the... *old-fashioned* way. Not selected for, not enhanced prior to conception." Britannica is profoundly uncomfortable having to say this—the embarrassment this entails for her boss is monumental... potentially even career-ending.

For an Amelior to let an unplanned pregnancy go unterminated... It's considered borderline child abuse at best.

If you asked any Amelior parent, they would tell you that a responsible, loving parent with the financial means should insist on setting their child up for success and give their child the best genetics currently available—rolling the dice like a caveman was for the poor and stupid of society, not the Amelior.

More muttering.

This kind of information is definitely worth something; it could be sold to the president's competition for a small fortune, used to force him into stepping down from his position, or, at a minimum, give his reputation a major blow.

The man must really want his daughter back to risk this kind of dirty secret getting out.

I try to imagine Vivian's father making such a sacrifice for her sake... and fail.

Tarnish Restless has other children—no single one was so irreplaceable as to warrant such a personal sacrifice on his part.

There is a certain glee radiating from many of the Lancers... They feel a perverse kind of satisfaction at seeing one of the elites tarred with such embarrassment, one of the most powerful men in the world forced to confess to such blatant hypocrisy to the lowly likes of them.

I don't share their feelings—I'm doing all this for the sake of an Amelior. I owe everything to one of those powerful Amelior families they resent and envy...

But still, I do at least understand how they feel.

4

Darling Doppelganger

Unfortunately, Nona refuses to leave me alone.

I can't help but notice that the room seems split into two large groups—the majority of the Lancers having consolidated into factions by now; one led by Riot and the other led by the blond woman with the antique wooden rifle.

Decades ago, suicides rose to such an astronomical height that a method for preventing suicide by gunshot became an industry-standard practice—while a man's right to suicide is enshrined in Prosperan culture, it is thought that doing so by simple and instantaneous gunshot does not demonstrate the proper resolve. On the bright side, it is basically impossible now to accidentally shoot yourself, and it's also harder for someone to use a stolen gun against you, as they have to pry a ring off your finger first. But, on the downside... Guns can be electronically jammed so that the receiver can't get a signal from the trigger unlocking ring, batteries in the gun can run out (although this is rarely an issue, as they can go months between needing a recharge), and if someone gets ahold of your gun, they can easily check the log to see exactly when the gun has been fired recently.

Unsurprisingly then, the classics are in high demand, making that blond woman's museum piece worth a small fortune.

I head for the door, deciding on the spot that recruiting a third person to the team is utterly hopeless at this point, with everyone else seemingly divided up already.

Nona is still hot on my trail.

To be fair, I haven't given her a way to contact me yet, so I can't truly fault her for that... but it still annoys me.

Wait...

I freeze mid-step and feel Nona bump into me.

"Sorry, I didn't mean to... what... what's wrong?" asks Nona, sounding worried.

...

Nona looks *a lot* like the image of the president's daughter Britannica had just shown us a few minutes ago.

It didn't occur to me at first because Nona doesn't have a mismatched pair of eyes—both of hers are emerald green. The heterochromia is such a distinctive feature that it tends to steal the whole show.

Nona's hair is also drastically longer than Kasca's was in the holo—Kasca's hair didn't even reach her shoulders, but Nona's hair easily touches her waist.

Regardless, the resemblance is unmistakable.

"Why do you..." I lower my voice as much as I can without it becoming completely inaudible.

"Why do you look so much like... like *her*? You could pass for sisters, easy. What's the connection?"

Nona looks away uncomfortably.

...

"I knew that question would be coming at some point... but I'd hoped I'd have a little longer to figure it out for myself before I had to try and answer it. See, the thing is... I don't... I don't *know*—HEY wait, *please!* I know that's hard to believe, but it's as much a mystery to me as it is to you... I was more shocked than anyone when the holo came up. I... I know how far-fetched it must sound, but it's the truth!" Nona says, sounding *very* worried that I won't believe her.

It *does* sound ridiculous... although it would explain her startled reaction earlier when the image of Kasca Haine first came up.

She's standing very close to me now so that we can hear each other while whispering like this—I can see into her eyes under her mask, but because of the kind of mask I wear, she can't see back into mine.

As hard as it is to believe—if she's a liar, she's a damn good one.

Her apparent sincerity is compelling—the slight anxiousness in her voice, that tinge of confusion that perfectly mirrors my own without being laid on too thick—all of it is perfectly balanced to make her honestly feel unquestionable.

There is also the matter of her showing me her face of her own volition—before the identity of the person we are going after was revealed... It's hard for me to see why she would do that if she'd known it was going to raise hard-to-answer questions later on.

I shake my head in disbelief and resume walking.

"If it's not to rescue a sister or something... Why go at all? What are they offering you to make you take such a risk?" I ask as we step out the basement door of the Night Library and back into the electronics shop.

"That's... a little personal, you know. A lot personal, actually... Would you tell me your reason if I asked you to?" she says.

...

There's no way I'd tell some near-stranger that I'm risking everything for a girl who left me half a year ago—that I'm rushing off to (probably) die a gruesome death for the promise of an (alleged) cure to a disease widely considered incurable—I'm only barely willing to admit the reality of my situation to myself.

"Fair enough. It's just... a *very* strange coincidence, having you look like that girl's doppelganger. We can talk about it more later—At the moment, I have things I need to go take care of. So, let's split up—I'll give you the means to reach me in the morning, and you can get a hotel for the night," I say.

I have to remind myself that she's from Neo Kyoto; everyone knows people from Neo Kyoto lie as easy as they breathe... it's such a widely accepted truism that it's become something of a cliché to have a character from Neo Kyoto betray the hero at the end of the story—it's the kind of plot twist everyone sees coming.

"What? We can't split up already—we've only just met!" Nona whines.

It's been an insane day—I'm tired, it's getting late, and there is still so much left to be done if I want to be ready to leave tomorrow morning.

"We'll have all the time in the world to bullshit *out there*—introductions have been made and an agreement reached, any more talk would be a waste of breath for the time being."

...

I turn and continue up the stairs, seeming to have left the girl speechless for the moment. I think she's out of things to say for a glorious instant, but then I hear the nervous little cough of a girl clearing her throat to speak, just as the craving for a cig washes over me.

"I'm ah, really glad you were willing to tell me your name—I thought you were going to refuse to tell me when I asked for it earlier. We'll be relying on each other as a matter of life and death soon, and I'd be a tad bit worried if you couldn't even trust me enough to give me your real name. I don't suppose you wanna trade last names as well, as a further gesture of goodwill...?" she asks half-jokingly.

"Don't push your luck. But I... showed you my... *face*... Compared to that, a first name isn't a big deal at all." I compulsively lower my voice for this shameful admission as I open the door to exit the shop, not wanting the girl at the front counter to think I'm some kind of pervert.

But the angsty teen doesn't even look up as a bell signals our departure.

I give Nona my contact information and an uncomfortable farewell, my mind buzzing with the things I must do before leaving for No Man's Land... Particularly if the worst happens and it ends up being a one-way trip.

But a few moments later, I realize Nona is following a few paces behind me.

"Do you need something... else?" I ask over my shoulder, not bothering to stop walking.

"I ah... don't actually have a place to stay, ah-ha..." She puts a hand behind the back of her head and laughs in an abashed kind of way.

"I see, I see... Obviously, you'll need a hotel recommendation then, yes?" I ask, knowing full well she'd just look it up herself if that was what she was after.

I walk a little faster.

"Nooo... actually, I think we have a lot to discuss before we start this thing. So I was thinking a pragmatic, professional guy like you would definitely see the value in inviting me to stay at his place tonight..."

I stop at an intersection, waiting for the light to change.

She stops next to me and leans forward, trying to make me look at her.

The tear painted on the face of her mask and her large eyes visible underneath give her a pleading, puppy dog kind of appearance.

"Nope, not happening." The light changes, and I start walking again.

"... these dumb masks make it hard not to imagine people are misinterpreting the things I say—whoa, WAIT, just like that?"

I ignore her, waving goodbye over my shoulder as I go.

I walk a little faster still, forcing her to genuinely exert herself now if she wants to keep up with me.

"Wait! *Seriously?*" Although of about average height for a female Natural, she's still nearly a head shorter than me and must more or less jog to keep up.

"I'm sure you want to leave as soon as possible, right? Well, if you do, we need to discuss strategy and gather supplies—it only makes sense that we stay together while we prep. Besides, we're going to be sleeping next to each other every night while out there—what does it matter if we start tonight or not?"

I start down the stairs that lead to the subway platform.

"I'll figure out the plan and gather supplies for the both of us and then I'll message you instructions for when and where to meet," I answer.

Her hand grabs mine, forcing me to a halt as I step off the last step down.

I'm okay with her stopping me now—we're already at the subway station platform, so I was going to have to stop walking in a moment regardless.

"Look... You're the expert in... this kind of thing we're going to be doing. I know that. I know that this is..." She pauses to look around, debating what she can and can't say in a public setting like this. "... That this is my first time doing anything so, ah... legally dubious. I recognize that you understand it all so much better than I do. And... I know I must seem like a bit of a... well, a silly little girl to you, but..." Nona stands up a little straighter and points a thumb at herself. "... But I'm an expert as well, an expert on all things No Ma... all things *you-know-what*. The things I know will be just as important out there as the things you know. So, I mean... well... you know... Let's work together and all... I want to contribute, to *help*... when I can..." Her confidence seemingly abandons her at the end, somewhat diminishing the effect she'd been aiming for.

Looking at her body language now, it's clear to me that she's not used to conflict. She's also not used to people being uncooperative or apathetic towards her—she's accustomed to being liked, to people finding her charming and cute, and being receptive when she tries to befriend them.

She's the kind of person who prefers cooperation over competition, who doesn't understand why everyone doesn't just try a little bit harder to understand each other and get along.

She's a people-pleaser, a peace-keeper, a friend to all, and an enemy to no one—she *needs* everyone to like her about as much as she needs to shit n' sleep.

In other words—she is easily taken advantage of.

I'm sure that, when safely back at home, her friends and family understand this about her and watch over her like a hawk, shielding her as much as possible from the people who would otherwise have already taught her the many risks of being too damn nice.

But none of those people are around to look out for her here.

I'm sure I could bully her into listening to me—a little strategically targeted meanness, and she will fold like wet cardboard.

Hell... If I raised my voice and cursed her out, I bet she'd start crying and apologizing—regardless of whether or not she deserved it.

Despite knowing that, she *is* being reasonable right now.

Damn her.

It makes it harder to be a Machiavellian bastard when people insist on being reasonable—but there's also no way I'm letting her into my home.

For one thing, I have a whole room of mediocre, uninspired, and mostly unfinished paintings.

I also don't even own a couch—so one of us would be relegated to the floor for the night.

Besides... if I'm going to be glued to this girl for who knows how long, one last night of peace and quiet shouldn't be too much to ask for—should it?

"Hey, what's the matter, big guy—your place a messy bachelor pad or something?" Nona teases, impatient with waiting for me to find my tongue again.

"You're... still holding my hand..." I say, gesturing downwards.

Nona looks down, staring incomprehensibly at our joined hands for a moment before withdrawing hers as if stung by an electric shock.

"I just... *you're* the one who was virtually forcing me to run to keep up... No way to treat your new partner, no way at all... you just have to make everything so gosh dang difficult..." Nona mutters, half to herself, half for my benefit. I'd bet she's making that same pouty face as before from under her mask.

I can't be more than two or three years her senior at the absolute most, but she seems incredibly immature; others might find it endearing or something, but it's starting to give me a splitting headache.

On the other hand, she might not actually be unusually immature for a girl her age—the problem could just be that I'm unusually jaded and bitter for mine.

I haven't spent much time around teenage girls besides Vivian and her sister, Corella. So, I have little to compare Nona against, and I suspect neither Vivian nor her sister were good examples of your "usual" teenage girls, somehow.

Regardless, everyone else in the Night Library tonight was some manner of a violent criminal, tough, cynical, and cunning... Except for this girl. She might understand the ecosystems of No Man's Land—she might know the scientific name of every species in there for all I know, but I don't think she knows how to embrace the suck—I don't think she is capable of being the kind of cold-hearted predator I'll need her to be if she's going to watch my back.

She is far too trusting, asking for a damned sleepover when I could still be any manner of bastard for all she knows... Her idea of figuring out if she can trust me is to talk to me—when she should be asking around, gathering real intel on me, and finding out if anyone has anything nasty to say about the Lancer in the red scarf.

Which they probably would—if she'd bothered to ask them.

So far as I can tell, she didn't know anything about me beyond my alias before she approached me, she just had her "women's intuition" or whatever.

Ridiculous.

She has no idea the bullet she dodged by not joining up with one of the other groups. She didn't go through with it because traveling in large numbers is, according to her, too dangerous, but I think the bigger danger for her would have come in the form of her teammates, who would have taken every opportunity to take advantage of her before leaving her in a ditch to die.

Or, I have to remind myself yet again she might just be an exceptionally good liar.

For her sake, I almost hope it *is* an act—innocent people just get used and tossed aside.

Clever people understand that it's better to be the user than the used.

"You do know I'm still here, right?" She waves a hand in front of my mask.

"You haven't left yet? Take the hint and leave me be, *dammit.* I already told you that the answer is no, and I have things to take care of. In case you haven't figured it out yet, we're not going on vacation—we're going on a suicide mission. Even the inexhaustible power of friendship isn't going to help us on one of those. So, go the hell away. Go do something productive—like writing up a last will or telling Mommy and Daddy that you love them—*one final time*," I spit the words out with as much venom as I can muster.

I could leave it at that.

Nona's hands grab the hem of her cloak and pulls it around herself reflexively.

If I say nothing else, she'll walk away all teary-eyed, and she'll have no choice but to sit tight and wait for me to message her.

She might even learn that befriending me is a lost cause, with any luck.

Two birds, as they say...

Nona casts her eyes downwards as if studying the laces of her boots—I can see them filling with tears.

Any passersby would think I'd just broken her gentle heart with a historically savage dumping; her body language is so pitifully dejected that it would be hard to imagine any other explanation.

...

What a pain.

"... Sorry, that came out harsher than I'd intended it to. I've just... got a lot on my mind—not to mention a migraine. Anyway, you're right. We're partners now. *Equal* partners. We should try and figure out a strategy.... *together...* You didn't deserve to hear any of that," I finish.

I really need a good smoke—the withdrawals are at least as responsible for my mood as this girl is.

She looks back up at me, her eyes over-bright.

I need to get her a better mask—one that won't let me see her overly expressive eyes all the time.

"It's okay... I was being a little pushy—I'm sorry as well..." With my apology given, her hands unclench their hold on the cloak, and I know she'll be fine.

"... I think you underestimate the power of friendship though—haven't you ever seen a PG-13 holo? Nuclear weapons and the Demon King himself can't hold a candle to the power of friendship..." says Nona, trying to steer the conversation back into the lighthearted waters she's accustomed to.

"I'll be sure to remember that when some monster is using my face as a chew toy," I reply before pulling out a blank slip of paper.

Nona looks up, curious to know what I'm writing at a time like this.

The train pulls into the platform and opens its doors to reveal a mostly deserted subway car.

"... This one looks all full up I'm afraid, but no need to fret—the next one will arrive in five minutes. Get off at the fourth stop for the diner written on here... it's good—surprisingly *private*—you won't be able to miss it. I'll join you when I'm done. And then... I'll walk you to the nearest *hotel*... but only after we've talked to your heart's content and you tell me you're ready to go get some sleep."

I step into the spacious car, turn, and hand her a scrap of paper just before the doors slide shut.

I can't resist the temptation to give her a little sarcastic wave as the train starts to pull away.

Nona throws her hands up in defeat and turns to march off as the subway car pulls away.

5

STATUS SYMBOLS

History *Entry 1*

The three existing city-states each have radically different forms of government. Prospera is loosely ruled by a genetically enhanced aristocracy (the Amelior)—whose power base is guaranteed by their domination of the almost completely unregulated private sector. Prosperans take great pride in their belief in the meritocracy, and the un-enhanced may earn the right to ascend if they are successful enough to afford the gene edits for their next generation of children—at which time, the family will adopt a new name and a family crest. Similarly, a family may fall back down if they lack the funds to provide their children with the next generation of gene upgrades, even though their children will still retain the benefits from the previously acquired enhancements. Such families are referred to as the "Humbled", and this is the greatest fear of Prospera's elite. However, economic (and thus, social) mobility has stagnated in recent years, which has contributed to frequent social unrest.

— *The Unraveled World: A History of Humanity's Decline & an Exploration of the New Normal, 3rd Edition*

The subway car rumbles upwards at an angle, carrying me towards the surface—more specifically, carrying me into the rich center district at the heart of Prospera and towards the Restless family estate.

I take the opportunity to plan out what I'll say to Vivian—if I manage to see her.

The word "if" is doing a lot of work there—I'm about as likely to see her tonight as I am of surviving this little nature walk I've signed up for.

Maybe it's better that way—Vivian would probably try to stop me if I told her what I was doing. Not that she could do much to stop me. The Restless family doesn't control me... at least, not anymore.

Vivian saw to that.

I still don't understand *why* she did it... But now's not the time to dwell on it—really, there's never a time for dwelling on the shit you can't change.

If I do see her, I can't think of anything to say that won't sound hopelessly bleak, suicidal, or most humiliating of all... like a desperate cry for attention.

No one makes it back—not if they're fool enough to go more than a couple miles into No Man's Land... and after looking up the grids we were given, it seems that we'll be going more than 70.

I've never even heard of anyone attempting to go that far in—let alone managing to make it back.

I keep trying to think of a way to put a better spin on it without flat-out lying to myself, but... I've got jack-all so far.

I have to try and speak to Vivian, though, because there is still the possibility Prosper Electronica is lying about all of it, but...

I think some small, shameful part of me *wants* her to have the Fade.

No, that's not it—not exactly... I just want her to need my help—to *need* me again.

I hate myself for it—I know it's a pathetic, childish impulse that I'm throwing my life away for, but I don't know how to move past it. I devoted the last ten years to protecting her, serving the Restless family as reliably as anyone could.

We've been together since we were just little kids—we grew up together... How could she go and toss me aside after going through so much?

I deserve a lot of things—most of them unpleasant—but to her and her family, I was nothing but loyal.

The car slows to a stop, and I step off onto the platform, much better maintained now that we're here in a prestigious Amelior district of the city.

I feel even more out of place here than usual, even though I lived in this world for half my life.

The masks help hide it, but the differences between the perfect Amelior and the thoroughly imperfect Naturals are still impossible to miss.

I'm not short by Natural standards, but all of the Amelior men here are significantly taller than me without fail—a good majority of the women are as well.

Vivian is like a half-inch taller than me, and she never let me forget it.

I shake my head—as if thoughts of her were flies I could scare away.

There are only a couple of others here with natural hair colors, and those dull brunet, blond, red, and black-headed figures all belong to Natural slaves or servants who follow closely in the shadows of their masters.

Even the way the Amelior walk is different—it's graceful, confident, refined... None of the hunched shoulders and hurried steps of nervous, self-conscious people like you see in the poorer Natural districts.

The weapons on display are also more flashy—less concealed pistols and knives, more proudly worn Burner Blades.

Burners are great for dealing with the pesky light body armor that's so common now; the battery housed in the sword's hilt superheats the blade's metal until it glows red hot and cuts through most materials like, well, a hot knife through butter.

But they're large, cumbersome, and entirely unnecessary for the relatively safe city streets of one of Prospera's wealthiest areas.

They are also expensive, making them something of a status symbol.

I know how to keep my head down when among the high-society crowd, so I don't give anyone any reason to pay too much attention to me as I make my way through the winding streets.

...

The Restless Estate is a spectacular sight, no matter how many times I see it.

Three towers stand at its center, the shortest of which is 15 stories tall and the largest of which is 20.

Genetic engineering is undoubtedly a lucrative business.

All of the family lives there—over a hundred Restless total if you count all the branch families.

Even if each family member were given luxuriously large living quarters, that would still not explain the necessity of having buildings as massive as these. But the family does not believe in separating work from play, so only the Center Tower houses the family members while the East Tower is set aside for business, and the West Tower acts as the base for the small private army the family maintains, the Restless House Guard.

It's not a super creative name for a private army, but who needs creativity when you're in the business of breeding the next generation of tiny gods?

Surrounding all three towers is a high wall, about five stories tall.

Like a modern castle, it is intended to be as self-sufficient as possible—almost as if a siege is expected to break out at a moment's notice.

The three towers rose with the Restless family, and the family only came to prominence a few generations ago.

The Restless family are still considered new money—virtually straight off the printing presses kinds of new—by the standards of the entrenched, old moneyed families. I'm still withholding judgment on whether or not all these precautions were paranoia... or an example of prudent foresight.

I approach the South Gate, trying to make out who is on duty there tonight, hoping it's someone who, at the very least, won't feel inclined to be openly hostile towards me.

I could sneak my way in if I had to; after living there for a decade and helping Vivian break out whenever she needed to flex her rebellious side—I know the estate like the back of my hand.

But the Restless Guard would kill me on the spot if they caught me in the middle of a break-in, and I have no way of knowing where Vivian is on the estate. Worst case, I could be forced to spend hours searching—hours I do not have to spend right now.

But it would seem I'm in luck.

There are three of the House Guard at the gate, one Amelior officer and two Natural enlisted.

I know the officer, a teal-haired, dark-skinned Amelior, is a grizzled vet and someone I've been vaguely acquainted with for years.

If there is anyone who *might* let me speak to Vivian, despite the standing orders she gave to keep me out... it would be him.

I raise a hand in greeting.

The two enlisted soldiers tense up... presumably because they recognize me and know I am not welcome here anymore.

"Captain Brawn... It's been a while... I hope they don't still have you standing duty every damned Saturday. They need to stop being cheap and put more officers on the payroll." It's the best attempt at a warm, soldierly greeting I can think of... I used to be able to go where I wanted here *without* needing to be all likable and unthreatening.

I'm sure Brawn knows this is a conscious attempt to fake a friendly rapport that I never bothered to actually develop with him, but at least my casual tone does seem to calm the nerves of the two enlisted men somewhat.

Me and Brawn always had a kind of mutual respect, even if I never bothered to get to know him beyond that. We were both loyal, competent, respectful professionals who mostly stayed out of each other's way. I hope that still holds some weight.

He returns the wave and mutters some orders to his men before walking out to meet me a little ways in front of the gate.

"Rowan... or is it Roach now? Nothing personal, but you can't be here, you know that," says the Captain.

"I know, Brawn—I know. I wouldn't be here if it wasn't important—nothing trivial would bring me back to a place where I'm so... unpopular. I just need a few minutes to speak with Lady Vivian," I reply.

Brawn studies me for a moment, weighing my words on some invisible set of scales.

"I'd call her and ask if she'd be willing to see you since you insist on it being important, but... she's not here, Rowan. Out. Been out on some business or another for the last couple weeks—no idea where it has taken her."

I open my mouth to ask, "What kind of business?" before Brawn cuts me off.

"I don't know, Rowan... and I wouldn't tell you if I did. She's blocked you on all of her socials then, I presume?"

I nod, embarrassed.

It is my fault she blocked me. I wouldn't leave her alone after she cut me loose—I just wanted some answers, wanted to understand...

"The best I can do is take a message for you. I can promise you it will get to her, but... I *can't* promise you no one else will see it beforehand."

I appreciate the warning, though it wasn't necessary. I was already thinking that it could be an issue if I say too much in an intercepted message.

For one, if Vivian has the Fade, it will be kept as quiet as possible by the rest of the family... and that kind of information will be worth a small fortune to the family's rivals, who certainly have spies at the estate.

Vivian is slated to take over the House Guard; it is what she was designed to do from before she was even born—there will be wide-reaching ramifications for the future of the family if she can't do so anymore.

And besides that...

Part of being an Amelior is immunity to *most* forms of disease, and from that was born the Amelior fondness for pretending that they're immune to absolutely everything. So, unless an Amelior is getting exceptionally, stupidly old, sickness is considered a shameful thing—it implies their genes are imperfect.

What causes The Fade is a medical mystery—it might have nothing to do with flaws in the gene pool at all, but that doesn't matter much to them. They will never admit to a soul that someone in the family has the Fade.

I nod.

"Have a pen and paper, by chance?"

6

Blackout

My next destination happens to be on the way to the diner, though I have to stop and withdraw cash on my way.

A lot of cash.

The bank teller asks me to repeat the amount of my request and calls out her supervisor—apparently, the amount is more than a basic teller is allowed to authorize on their own. But once I answer half a dozen security questions and sign three separate fund release forms, my request is granted.

The reaction doesn't surprise me—no one uses cash anymore. Even the criminal element doesn't like cash—and for a time, we were the last holdout.

I'm just relieved they had enough cash on hand to make it happen without delay.

But the person I'm pulling this money out for won't have access to the untraceable electronic forms of banking the black market uses, and I can't imagine him willingly giving me his routing number for a regular transfer.

My mind drifts to Nona as the bank teller hands over the cash.

I feel a bit guilty... she will have been sitting in that diner for *hours* by the time I get there, and I'd promised her we would talk for as long as she wanted before putting her up in a hotel, but we will also need to be up very early to get a start on the job... If I get to her a minute before midnight, I'll eat my own socks.

It's not long before I'm in Olympus Heights—the grandly named but poorly maintained—neighborhood of the man I'm here to see.

The story of this sorry place is one of early ambition giving way to economic stagnation. Every crack in the pavement tells a tale of abandonment. The buildings lean against each other as if seeking solace in their collective dilapidation.

Perhaps I can actually do some good here tonight—save an old man from the fate of having to live out his end years in a place like this.

As I'm thinking this, darkness swallows the city around me.

It's a blackout.

Like the Restless Towers, these also never fail to leave an impression, no matter how many times I've seen it.

Homes go dark in a wave—as if the night is the ocean in a storm, and all of human creation is a shoreline being reclaimed.

If I were still in a wealthy section of the city, the power blackout would have come and gone so quickly that you could blink and miss it. Back-up generators are so ubiquitous there that blackouts can go mostly unnoticed—one of the many perks of wealth in Prospera.

But here, there are only feeble attempts to push back the darkness—a scattering of dim candles and sporadic flashlights that do next to nothing against the occupying darkness.

The blackouts are intentionally kept random and unpredictable in their duration and timing by the power company—this way, people with bad intentions can't easily plan their illicit schedule around the blackouts.

The Underground is thought of as the truly poor half of Prospera, but that is an oversimplification. It's true that the Underground was constructed to make room for the ever-growing poor population since, with No Man's Land constricting the city's expansion outwards, the only options remaining are to go up or down. To no one's surprise, the rich tended to build up, and the poor tended to get shoved down. There are exceptions—there are still concentrations of squalor on the surface—to include a place like Olympus Heights. And there are also pockets of extreme wealth in the Underground, thanks to enterprising investors who managed to find ambitious opportunities in the dirt-cheap real estate.

The night is filled with a surreal cacophony of sounds.

There are some drunken cheers, some nervous curses... In the distance, children start to wail just before their doors are slammed shut and the sounds are successfully stifled by anxious parents.

But, as I knew they would, back in the direction of the Restless Towers... the lights flicker back to life.

This does nothing to illuminate the poor Olympus Heights—if anything, it's just a reminder of how much these people have to envy and the broader world's indifference.

The purple and yellow lights of the Restless Towers appear to shine even brighter now that their competition has been snuffed out.

I unstrap my ax and rest it on my shoulder as I walk, not wanting to look like an easy mark when I have so much cash on me... But it's not long before I find myself outside of the dingy little duplex I need.

"Dingy" might not be the best word. It makes it sound almost quaint... dilapidated or depressing are probably both better descriptors.

My stomach twists itself into a hangman's noose of a knot.

This is something I've been too cowardly to do now for years, something I have always been able to talk myself into putting off for just a little while longer.

But if I don't do it now, I have to accept that I simply never will.

I creep up to the front door, more nervous now than I would be if I were here to kill the person inside.

But will he even open the door?

Surely, he won't want to open the door—not during a blackout, not in such a bad part of town...

No one knocking during a blackout can be up to any good, after all.

I knock.

..

...

Right, so he's not going to open it, that's fine—I'll just leave the money and go.

It's probably better this way.

What else am I going to do, force the door?

I made an honest attempt, that's...

I can hear the sound of footsteps.

The door opens.

A man stands in the doorframe, tall but stooped over under the painful weight of his years. He's rail-thin—as if eating is an inconvenience he only forces himself to endure to the minimum degree necessary.

"Who're you? What do you need atta' time like this?" demands the man.

This is the first time I've seen him in just over a decade; the only similarity shared between this old man and the powerfully built father I saw supporting his distraught wife back then is the impressive height.

"I... I'm here about your son, Mr. Dawn. There is something I need to tell you, and there's something I want to give you."

...

"How do you know my... my son? My boy been dead for a decade—what could you possibly have to tell me about him?" asks Mr. Dawn, sounding shaken.

"I... I was in prison with your son. I was... there... when he... died," I say, already starting to regret my decision to come here at all.

...

Mr. Dawn says nothing, apparently at a loss for words.

"Your son and I... were a part of a program. It was an experiment that we all volunteered to take part in. There were nine of us who agreed to it... I don't know how they *told* you he died... but he died during those tests," I say.

Mr. Dawn grabs hold of the door frame as if preparing for his legs to fail him.

"I always *knew* they were lying to us about it—I *knew* they were covering s-something up. You... were my boy's friend then? You must have been... why else would you come here to tell me all this after so long...?"

I take a steadying breath, anticipating the drop I know is coming just over the next crest.

"Not a friend, no. I didn't even know his name at the time—we only went by numbers back then..." I hold out my hand with the sack of cash, inviting him to take hold of it and look inside.

After a short pause, he does.

The man's hands tremble from the strain of holding the bag out in front of him, unwilling to bring it any closer to himself as if afraid it might spontaneously combust. He does not understand—his confusion leaves him momentarily paralyzed.

"Mr. Dawn... I k-killed your son. It is my fault he never came home again."

I wait for him to say something, *anything*...

.

..

...

I have only ever confessed once before to murdering Number 5—not even Vivian knows the truth.

"You're telling me... that you *murdered* my boy? WHAT the *fuck*... do you expect me to say to that?! Why are you even telling me this?" he growls; his voice is saturated with the kind of pain and rage that makes me feel sure he'd attack me if he was only a few years younger—or if he had a weapon at hand.

"I... I just thought you should... you should know what happened—that your son's death was no accident. I don't think I'll be... around to say it for very much longer," I reply.

...

"You sick or something?"

"Or something, yes," I answer.

...

"Why did you do it?" asks the old man.

"Because I could. Because he was in my way. Because I was jealous of him. There were a lot of reasons—none of them justified it, but that didn't stop me. I... am sorry."

"I still don't understand... but I know what this is. You want *forgiveness*. You wanna lighter conscience. You don't deserve neither. My wife... my wife was never the same after our boy died. She *killed herself*—not even a year later. Slit open her wrists in the bath. Feel better yet, ya *bastard*? YOU MURDERED MY WHOLE FAMILY! You *stole* EVERYTHING from me! If I could, I'd *kill* you! I'd bleed you 'til your bones are dry—then I'd grind the bones into a fine powder. Since I can't, I'll call Security Forces and tell 'em what you've told me—have you put back where you fuckin' belong!"

I take an involuntary step back.

I... hadn't known about his wife.

I hadn't *wanted* to know about his wife.

My research into the boy I'd killed had intentionally gone no deeper than to find out names and a family address.

"I'm sorry, Mr. Dawn... but I can't let you kill me—even though you have every right. Even though I know I deserve to die. There is a different cause that I need to die for—and I don't know of any way to die twice... if I did, I'd let you have one of them. But I'll still be dead soon if that's worth anything. As for the Security Forces... They simply won't care. That's just the honest truth. One dead child inmate from a decade ago is not important to them. And even if they *did* care, the pardon I've received since was a blanket pardon covering everything I did before being released."

My voice has lost its barely controlled emotion and now takes on a terrible kind of calm, a detachment that makes me feel far stronger than I had a moment before... but also far more callus—far more like the villain I know I am—like the monster that ate this man's world.

This was a mistake.

Without another word, I turn and begin to walk away.

Then I hear the shuffling of a man with a limp trying to chase after me.

"I... I don't want it, ya hear?! This, this... *blood* money! It doesn't undo... doesn't change... d-doesn't bring me my boy back... Or my wife... Nothing will *ever* bring them back... Your guilt isn't worth a damn thing to me! YOU HEAR?!"

The heavy bag smacks me in the back and falls to the ground, its contents spilling out over the ground.

"You... waited all this time... You piece of shit! Don't you *dare* go tellin' yourself this meant something... It means *nothing*—changes *nothing*... I hope my dead family haunts your dreams every single night you have left!"

That request, at least, will be within my power to grant him.

7

Dramatic Effect

"My solitude doesn't depend on the presence or absence of people; on the contrary, I hate who steals my solitude without, in exchange, offering me true company."
— Friedrich Nietzsche

I started to make my way back underground and towards the diner, although... I'm not in the mood for company, and it will take even longer to get there now, with the subway closed for the blackout.

I especially don't feel like dealing with Nona's attempts to become my BFF—like she thinks we're a pair of little kids who've been partnered up for a class assignment.

Talking to people, for as long as I can remember, tires me easily... like some kind of strange anti-caffeine.

Well, except for Vivian.

I used to wonder *why* I could be in her company without it exhausting me—what it was about her that made her so different from everyone else I've ever known. There are a lot of things that make Vivian Restless different, which makes it difficult to narrow the list down to anything specific.

My best guess would be that it has something to do with the lack of pretext—there is not only no need to pretend with Vivian—it is downright impossible. Vivian sees people as they are—not as they wish to be seen... And even though she does find most people wanting, she is no less hard on herself.

I hadn't actually talked to Nona all that much today, but the day's events alone were enough to make me crave some peace and quiet—which I am sure would be impossible with a girl like Nona around. Nona seems to be the kind of person compelled to fill every silence with conversation—the polar opposite of Vivian and another reason why I used to enjoy Vivian's company like no other.

What I really want is the warm embrace of total isolation... and a cigarette or three.

Then it occurs to me that the power at the diner will have also gone out, and I'm not sure Nona is aware of Prospera's city-wide blackouts... Would she stay in place and wait for me... or be frustrated by now being expected to wait in a dark diner and storm off?

My unhappy thoughts are interrupted by nearby shouting.

Probably just someone getting robbed—not a shocking occurrence in this fair city of ours.

Probably none of my business.

And so, I keep walking.

Actually... it is a little strange—I'm no longer in an infamously rough part of the city; this area is about as close to middle-class as it gets in Prospera.

Buuut, on the other hand, that sometimes makes it particularly tempting for criminals when a blackout occurs—better things to steal here than in Hooverville or Olympus Heights to balance out the greater risk of Security Forces intervening.

I turn and keep on walking.

"ROWAN! A... Little help... *Please*!" screams a familiar voice.

What in the *hell*...?

You've got to be kidding me.

Nona. *Definitely* Nona's girlish voice.

She must have been following me... but for how long? How much has she seen? Did she see me at the Restless Towers? Or had she *only* managed to see me retreating from an old man, head down, as he threw a heavy bag of unmarked bills at me?

More importantly, what the hell kind of trouble had she gotten herself into? I hear other voices now as well—men's voices.

I run towards the sounds of shouting.

Nona is backed into an alley corner with three men closing in on her, something metallic glinting in one of her hands—a small knife, most likely.

Very well.

I let the blade of my Compression Ax drop to the ground with a thud, and then I let it drag against the stone street as I approach... The first noise to get their attention, and the second to keep it—honestly, I just like to enjoy the dramatic effect of the thing.

I've found that a strange man walking towards you—in the dark—with a massive ax, its blade sparking against the ground... tends to leave a strong impression.

Besides, the ax was already well overdue for a sharpening.

The three men turn to look at me. Each face is, of course, masked, but they hold themselves with the evident confidence of men accustomed to violence—to the point where it hardly sets them on edge at all anymore.

When dealing with street thugs, I expect bluster and insults—the kind of tough talk petty criminals revert to when trying too hard to seem intimida ting... but instead, I'm met with silent stares, each of them sizing me up.

"Ravish, hurry up and take the bitch... the two of us will deal with our lumberjack friend over here."

The men fan out as much as they can in the narrow street, each of them hugging one wall and starting to stalk forward while pulling out their weapons.

"*Bitch*?! That is my *sister,* damn you! What do you want with a poor college girl, anyway?" I lie—just trying to see if this piece of misinformation bothers them any.

If it doesn't, these are probably just opportunistic thugs who saw a girl walking all alone during a blackout.

But if it does...

The man who spoke a moment before pauses, looking back at Nona.

"Damnit, check her eyes! Make sure she's the right one!" he barks.

The man called Ravish makes a move for Nona, attempting to seize the hand holding the knife.

Nona jumps back, startled, but doesn't attempt to cut or stab him.

She's *way* too damned soft...

"DON'T... you *touch* her. I'll cave your filthy skulls in if you hurt my sister!" I yell, knowing that Nona's failure to cut the man the first time is only going to encourage him to be more aggressive when he takes another try at it in a moment.

I decide to try and maybe end this without a fight—hoping that perhaps they've mistaken Nona for someone else.

"Sis... pull back your hood, let them see your eyes."

Nona does. A pair of emeralds seem to sparkle in the dim light of a nearby solar backup lamp—which provides the only light there is in the dingy alley.

I don't know what they're after—maybe a pair of green eyes is exactly what they want, but...

I don't think so, somehow.

Green eyes are too common to be sufficiently distinctive; if they're using eyes to identify the girl they need, they probably want an Amelior girl—not Nona.

Although... her normal height, natural hair, and lack of personal security should have already tipped them off that they've made a mistake if that's the case, shouldn't it?

The man called Ravish lunges at her.

Nona, having used both hands to pull back her hood, is utterly unprepared for him and drops the knife in her rush to ready herself.

Wow... what a totally competent and reliable partner I have.

I sprint forward and move as if to jab the blunt top of the ax head into the nearest man's gut.

He raises a hand holding a long blade but hesitates—confused by my movements, as I'm still not nearly close enough to actually make contact with my ax.

But I release the locking mechanism on the handle mid-movement, and the ax extends to its full length, nearly a meter longer than it had been a second prior.

With a loud grunt and the distinct cracking sound of ribs breaking, he crumbles.

Obviously, someone has never fought against a Compression Ax before.

Wait until they see this thing's main feature.

"Check her for contact lenses, you moron!" The apparent leader barks.

To my horror, I hear Nona scream and look over to see the man yanking her head back with a savage tug on her long hair while his other hand moves towards her left eye as if to pluck it from her skull.

I charge towards them, but another man, the one who had been giving the orders a moment prior, intercepts me, pulling out a pistol from his jacket pocket.

"It's her! She was wearing a contact like you said she would—she has the mismatched eyes!" the man yells.

The one nearest me levels a pistol at my heart and pulls the trigger, but I move towards him fast enough that he overshoots, and the round flies harmlessly over my left shoulder instead.

I expect the man will manage to shoot me at least once before I can cut him down.

That's fine—just so long as he doesn't hit me anywhere important.

I picked a horrible day not to wear any light armor—but it was raining, and light armor is a massive pain to dry out once soaked.

As unpleasant as it always is, I'll just have to, once again, rely on the disgusting gift Vivian's father had implanted in my chest.

I raise the Compression Ax and pull the trigger that releases the powerful burst of compressed gas stored in the handle.

As if propelled by a miniature jet engine, the ax head rockets forward in a wide ark, my hands squeezing the metal handle for dear life—lest I lose my grip and send the heavy weapon flying like an extra lethal baseball bat.

With a blood-chilling scream, the man's left arm is separated from his body.

The ax head continues down and buries itself into the ground.

I release the trigger, and a much smaller burst of compressed gas pushes in the opposite direction, helping me dislodge the weapon from the earth.

Amazingly, I think I'm about to finish him without him managing to put a single scratch on me.

I move towards the wounded man like death itself—not with any anger... just a kind of calm, inescapable, inevitability.

Nona screams, and the terror in her voice is enough to make me hesitate.

I'm worried for an instant that her scream is caused by something her assailant is doing to her, but no...

Her attacker has released her—he is just staring at the arm lying on the dirty street and his now screaming—slowly dying—comrade.

Nona's scream, I realize, was a plea to stop me from killing him.

She doesn't understand that killing him now is a kindness—he'll die in gruesome agony if he is just left on the street to bleed out.

The man who had been holding onto Nona loses his taste for the fight and makes a break for it, intelligent enough to recognize a lost cause when it cuts his boss's arm off in front of him.

"No way in *hell* are you getting away!" I roar after him.

He feints right before breaking left—quick, but not nearly quick enough to get beyond the reach of my ax.

I bring the ax back for a side swing, finger on the release to extend the handle to its full length again.

BANG!

I face plant into the pavement—*hard.*

I feel a pool of warm blood forming under my body.

Dammit all...

Nona screams again, and I hear footsteps as she runs towards me.

Fuck.

It was the one-armed man—he regained his senses enough to put a bullet in me while I was distracted.

I *must* move.

If I don't, it will either mean the pain of getting shot a second time or worse—Nona being the one to take the next bullet.

I roll to my feet, ax still in hand, and I bring it back behind my head, intending to throw it if need be.

...

The one-armed man is lying face down on the ground, unconscious now from the massive blood loss.

Nona skids to a halt and looks at me, an unusual combination of relief and terror on her face as I stand there, weapon raised, soaked in blood, and most of it not my own.

"He's going to die if he doesn't get help..." I say, motioning to the man who just shot me and lowering the ax. "...You didn't seem to want him to die earlier—if we don't save him now, I'll have gotten shot for nothing."

She's not wearing her mask again. It still lays on the filthy ground where it fell after the man who got away ripped it off her.

"But... you need help, Rowan... I... It's *my* fault..." There are tears forming in her eyes... *again.*

Does she have to cry *every* single time someone gets shot...?

"Don't worry. This will be my... ninth time? I think. Getting shot, I mean. I wasn't hit anywhere important... so hurry and help him," I say.

After a moment's hesitation, Nona nods and runs over to the dying man.

While she has her back turned, the lights come back on—the blackout now passed.

I groan.

It would have been helpful if it had passed a few moments ago, but now it will just make walking home without having Security Forces being called on me much more difficult, soaked in blood like I am.

And of course... There's a bleeding bullet hole in my FAVORITE jacket...

What a day.

I spend a brief moment imagining finishing the man off, in retribution for my jacket, before sighing and using my mask's internal display to call for an ambulance. I take small comfort in the knowledge that the privatized ambulance service will cost the bastard a small fortune.

I walk over to Nona's side.

I must admit, I'm a little impressed.

I already knew she carried a medical kit on her after seeing her spill it all over the floor of the Night Library, but she's managing to maintain her composure a lot better the second time around.

She's already applied a chemical cauterizer to the man's stump and has soaked up enough blood to make applying bandages now possible. Her hands seem nimble and experienced as they go to work.

"Sorry Nona—no time to play at being a doctor. You've already done enough to save him with the cauterizer, I think. Assuming the private ambulance I've just called doesn't get stuck in traffic or robbed itself along the way. But we need to *move*... unless you would prefer a jail cell over a hotel?"

She stands and looks at me, sincere concern in her eyes.

"Don't you need to get on that ambulance as well, Rowan? You're bleeding all over..."

I lift up my shirt.

The wound still looks bad of course, but the bleeding has already slowed to a trickle instead of a flood.

"I got the alias 'Roach'... because I don't die easily. I had a... *procedure* done when I was a little brat. I'm not immortal, but it takes rather a lot to kill me." I lift up a hand and tap the side of my head.

"...If that bullet had been a solid headshot, for example... I'd be a goner for sure. But a little hole in my gut won't be enough to do me in."

Nona's eyes go wide with interest; I think I can see a certain scientific curiosity in them as she takes in the news... as if she's debating how long one needs to know someone before it is appropriate to ask for permission to take a tissue sample.

I retrieve the fallen mask, grab Nona's arm, and start dragging her along unceremoniously.

"Wait! We need to find my contact len—"

"No time—besides, I'm sure I have contacts in any color you'd like at my place. Just *hurry up* and walk," I snap at her.

Nona stops resisting and lets me lead the way through the snaking city streets.

...

"And while we walk, you should feel free to explain *why* you were *following* me."

8

FUNCTION OVER FORM

An hour later, I'm letting Nona into my shabby little underground district home. After she was just nearly kidnapped, I'm forced to admit that there is no way I can send her off to a hotel.

I wasn't going to let her out of my sight.

Nona looks around curiously—seemingly surprised at what she saw.

"I thought it'd be all messy, but this is so clean!"

"... Thanks..." I say, not sure how to take that she assumed I'd be a slob.

"Too clean, if anything... it feels almost unlived in—personally, I don't feel at home in a place until I've messed things up a bit, you know?" she says.

"Oh, no... I can't say I do," I answer lamely.

"How are you feeling?" she asks, looking concerned again with how uninspired my responses are.

She assumes that I must be suffering in stoic silence from the bullet in my gut.

Which I sorta am, but that's not really the reason for my lack of banter.

"I'm as right as rain, don't worry about me..." And with that, I open up a drawer and take out my little bullet removal kit—disinfectant, extra-long tweezers, rags, etc.

Without any hesitation, I get to work on myself. The disinfectant's burning sensation is rather worse than I remember it being the last eight times.

"Wait, wait! Let me do it... *please*?" Nona pleads.

I consider for a moment that she's probably feeling guilty, seeing as she's definitely the reason I got shot.

"I'm fine. I've done this before... don't need any help with it..." I start to dig around in the hole with the tweezers, feeling for the metal. I just hope the bullet is still all in one piece.

"Do you... not feel pain?" Nona asks with a note of awe in her tone.

"No... I do." That was an understatement—the double-edged sword of the parasite inside of me is that, while it does enhance my body's ability to heal injuries, filter out most toxins, and releases into my bloodstream a kind of super adrenaline that does everything the natural adrenaline does—only *far* better... The crash after is also way more intense than that of regular adrenaline—and the pain comes back with a horrible vengeance.

"Then let me give you a pain reliever!" says Nona, apparently unable to tolerate any pain being allowed to go unsoothed in her presence.

"Hell no—I will *never* touch that trash, not under any circumstance. Pain is proof I'm alive—do you understand?" I lie.

Perhaps the worst thing about the parasite—and thus my body—is that it is allergic to all the painkillers... Paracetamol, ibuprofen, codeine, morphine—they'll kill the pain alright—because, with enough of it... I won't be alive to feel anything at all. But I can't tell her that—it would be all too easy for her to kill me with that knowledge if she ever had a reason to.

"O-Okay... I don't understand that weirdo logic, but if you say so..." replies Nona.

I let out a low hiss—frustrated that I haven't found it yet. My vision is starting to swim from the delayed agony of being shot.

I look up at the sound of Nona's footsteps.

She's about a foot away from me at most, and her arms are set in that way women have when they've made up their minds to be stubborn—Vivian used to strike that same pose all the time.

Her contact lens is still missing from when it was plucked out in the alley, so for the first time, I get a good look into her mismatched eyes.

Damn her.

There's simply no mistaking it, not now, with the contact out.

She wears her hair so that it drapes over her right shoulder—yet something tells me that if I brushed it aside, I'd see a mole at the base of her neck as well—identical to Kasca's holo in nearly every way but her hair.

She holds out her hands impatiently.

"Rowan... please, give it to me. This is my fault—you wouldn't have been shot at all if I didn't stop you... so let me help you now. Besides... it must be hard to do that yourself, right? You saw me give first aid—you know I can manage it."

I hand over the tools.

"Thank you... I... I know you're capable of doing it yourself, of course, but there's really no need for you to suffer more than necessary—not with your partner here to help." She gently lays her hand over the wound, bending down to get a better look at the damage.

I tense at her touch.

She thinks I resent her for getting me shot—she thinks that's the explanation for my stony silence.

She is irredeemably thick.

I nod to her before walking over to a set of shelves where the lighting is brighter.

I lean against them and brace to have her dig inside the bullet hole, which was, of course, bleeding freely again now that we were digging around for the bullet.

I grimace at the blood all over my once spotless floor.

At least I have the good sense not to have any shag carpet.

I grunt in pain as I feel Nona start.

Begrudgingly, I have to admit to myself that she's better at this than me—surprisingly steady hands.

"The shirt and jacket keep getting in the gosh dang way. Do you mind?" I hesitate, then nod again.

Nona gasps as the clothing is pulled up over my head.

I don't blame her—I know I'm a mess of a thing.

My body is not pretty—it's covered in scars from bullet holes, cuts, burns, and even a few bites. My body heals wounds *quickly,* but the parasite does not care about healing them prettily.

Vivian used to poke fun at it, saying I looked like some kind of sex-crazed masochist who keeps finding exciting new ways to mutilate himself—it had often been her way of pretending she wasn't worried when I got myself hurt, yet again, in the line of duty.

I preferred to think of it as a kind of manly virtue—the ability to prioritize function over form.

"I told you, this is my ninth time being shot... don't know what you expected," I say.

"S-Sorry, that wasn't very nice of me. I... just... *wow*... You must have some very exciting stories to tell..." she trails off, and I strain my neck, twisting around to look at her.

She's removed her mask again.

This time, she does at least have a reason to—I'm sure she felt like it was getting in her way, but still...

Her brow is furrowed in determination.

She's also blushing again, of course.

Her face has been blushing 100 percent of the times I've seen it thus far, so maybe her face is just perpetually pink?

"Yessss, got it!" Nona looks up at me and holds the tweezers with the bullet clutched between them, a triumphant smile on her face.

I turn, reach down with my left hand, and take hold of both of her much smaller ones, which are still holding up the tweezers and bullet.

"Thank you, and... I'm sorry," I say.

"S-Sorry... for what?" she asks.

"*This.*"

With my free right hand, I pull from behind my back a set of cuffs—a set of cuffs that had been, until a few moments earlier, sitting on the shelf I'd chosen to lean against.

In a blur of motion, I trap her hands inside them.

9

Comedic Effect

"Rowan... please take them off..."

I shake my head.

"Sorry, you're gonna have to spend the night in those. Tomorrow, I'm taking you to Prosper Electronica."

"You don't understand, Rowan... *Please*. I'm not that missing girl—I know we look similar, but I'm not her."

"*Similar*? No, I thought you looked similar when I first saw you with a contact in, now you look *more* than similar. Besides the much longer hair, you're virtually *identical*."

The first lesson I learned as a child on the shantytown streets of the Underground was a simple one: People lie—by omission at minimum. People are inherently self-serving, self-interested—if you do not understand their motives, then only a fool defaults to trust until proven otherwise. Cooperation is only advisable when you can be confident your interests are aligned—and cooperation ends the moment your interests diverge.

"B-But I'm here, not No Man's Land! I obviously haven't been in any plane crashes recently, have I?"

I put the mask back on her face for her since her hands are so busy being cuffed at the moment.

"Fair point. It's a real mystery—one you don't want to illuminate for me, it seems. It will all be sorted out tomorrow... at Prosper Electronica." I take a step back.

She's *much* better with a mask on.

There can be no question as to what must be done.

I've literally known this girl for a matter of hours at this point—I owe her nothing. Meanwhile, even with the way it ended, there can be no doubt that I owe Vivian everything. Without her, I'd be dead at best... and I cannot even begin to imagine what I'd be at worst.

I've done far worse than this before—and for far less worthy causes.

"Rowan... *trust* me, please. Do I really seem like I'm lying to you?" she pleads.

...

"*Trust* you? You followed me tonight—that hardly seems very trusting of you, does it?" I shoot back, agitated by her obvious hypocrisy.

She shrinks away from me slightly, startled by the sudden bite in my tone.

"I... I'm sorry, honest I am... You're right—I didn't trust you. It seemed super suspicious the way you insisted on going off on your own, and I'll be putting my life in your hands once we're in No Man's Land... I felt like I had to find out what you needed to get away from me to go do. So, I followed you—I'm so super sorry for that. I know it's not fair for me to expect you to trust me when I didn't trust you a few hours ago—but I *do* trust you now. I... I know I said that last time as well, but even more so now! I saw you pull money out of the bank and give it to that old man, and then you saved me from those kidnappers as well..." Nona straightens herself up and takes a deep breath. "No one truly bad would do those kinds of things, especially not in the final remaining hours they have before they go to... maybe die," she finishes.

Did that mean she hadn't been following me yet when I went to the Restless Towers? That would be a small comfort—even still, I'm furious with myself for being so careless as to let someone tail me—especially by a girl I'm pretty sure has no expertise in urban tracking. That's what I get for letting myself be distracted by my self-pity and worries.

...

"*What*... do you know?" I turn away from her, fists clenched at my sides.

"You must not have heard what that old man said to me. Did that not give you any pause before you jumped to stupid conclusions...?" I bite down on the inside of my mouth.

Nona shakes her head.

"I *murdered* that man's son. And his wife eventually killed herself because of it. I'm as far from a good person as it gets," I snarl at her, furious that she would presume to know a single, solitary thing about me.

Nona looks as shocked as if I'd just struck her across the face.

"Oh, g-gosh, that sounds terrible... But, um, are you sure you're not just feeling really bad about something that wasn't your fault? I mean, things can be really confusing sometimes... accidents happen, people's hands get forced by things outside of their contro—" Nona starts to say, but I cut her off before she can rattle off any more groundless excuses on my behalf.

"Those men, the ones from the alley... were Lancers. More than anything, *that* is why I'm turning you in tomorrow. I'd be stupid to write that off as a mere coincidence... they must have a source of information that is telling them *you* are the one Prosper Electronica is after. That, and just simply the fact that you conceal the real color of your left eye at all—why else would you do that if you're not hiding something? Unless... you want to give me some other explanation...?" I prompt.

...

"I just... *hate* looking at myself without a contact in... I always have. I don't know why I'm so insecure about it—it's just... ugly. At least... it seems that way to me. When I look at my reflection without it, it... feels as if my left eye belongs to a stranger—like it's not actually a part of me. But no, I can't explain why those men came after me tonight... I'm sorry."

I step behind Nona, place a hand on her shoulder, and give her a slight push. Kidnappings are not a rare thing in Prospera, but that wasn't just any old, attempted kidnapping—I'm sure of it.

I lead her through my house, past all the paintings I never thought were good enough to finish, up the squeaking staircase lined with advertisements for motorcycles I only ever liked because I wanted to share a hobby with Vivian, and into my bedroom.

Nona will be fine, I'm sure. Even if it's really just some kind of misunderstanding, Prosper Electronica will have no need of her, and they'll let her go.

Nona freezes when she sees my neatly made bed. I'm sure she fears that she has massively and catastrophically misjudged my intentions.

I sweep her off her feet and into my arms.

It was stupid of me not to cuff her behind her back—I wouldn't blame her for panicking and trying to attack me right now while she has the chance.

But no... her body just goes as rigid as a board, like a petrified animal, hoping it will be left alone if it doesn't move a muscle.

I place her on the bed.

"Relax. I'm just going to cuff you to the bed frame so you can't run off... I'll be sleeping outside the door." As much as I don't want to, I remove her mask.

Can't really expect her to sleep with it on.

When I do, there is such a profound sense of relief on her face that I suddenly feel like a monster for having scared her so badly, even if for only a moment.

Nona laughs in a shaken kind of way.

My hand reflexively jumps towards my throat, more specifically, towards the scarf I have around my neck—before I catch myself mid-way and pretend as if I'm checking my chest pocket to make sure something is still inside of it.

I walk over to my closet, find a second pair of cuffs, and walk back over.

"I... have a knife on me, you know. You should probably take it. It wouldn't be very comfortable to sleep with it digging into my side. Also, please ah, help me with the cloak."

Stupid. How could I not even check her for weapons?

You would think I've never detained someone before, shit...

Although, in my defense... It is hard to think of her as a threat after watching her panic and *drop her own damn knife,* the one and only time I've ever seen her try to use it.

I take it and proceed to remove her cloak.

"How'd you get a knife like this, anyway? Pretty sure even this silly little thing is outlawed where you're from." I say.

"Oh, it def is. I bought it at the airport when I landed—I couldn't believe it; in Neo Kyoto we sell overpriced luxuries and souvenirs for tourists at the airport, while you crazies sell weapons... It's kinda scary."

I shrug. "Our airports are similarly overpriced—you paid at least twice what the thing is worth, I'm sure."

I'm surprised by how heavy her cloak is until I realize the inside is lined with numerous pockets, and those pockets are weighed down by all kinds of personal possessions.

I also remove the medical kit she has strapped to her waist.

I pause for a moment, considering if I should pat her down for anything else, but...

I decide against it for obvious reasons, even if I know it's unprofessional of me to not check.

"Lay down—hands over your head. I'm locking the second pair to the bed frame and then to the other set of cuffs... It will be more comfortable for you than just weaving the one pair through the frame," I say awkwardly.

Obligingly, she does.

She looks up at me, her composure restored now and a slightly mischievous look on her face.

"Cuffs seemingly in every room of the house, including the bedroom... Should I be concerned or impressed with your lifestyle, I wonder?" She finishes by actually winking at me but doing so in the kind of silly, overemphasized way a person does when pretending to flirt for the comedic effect—no hint of actual flirtation there, just the immature humor of a teenage girl trying to lighten the mood.

...

"I... liked you better when you were afraid of me... *silence* suits you," I say, knocking the grin off her face.

10

YOU KNOW ANY BUKOWSKI?

"Find what you love and let it kill you."
— Charles Bukowski

I'm saved by insomnia and rusty door hinges.

I hear the faint sound of my front door being opened—glad of the conscious choice I made to never oil the hinges or repair the creaking wood floors on the first floor. I'm sure I locked the multiple deadbolts, but a standard pin tumbler lock isn't worth much in this day and age.

I rise as quietly as I can, open the door to my room, and go to where Nona lays, still fast asleep in my bed—her breathing steady amidst the darkness. I shake her awake—a finger to my lips commanding silence, then I place a hand behind my ear to mime listening.

She nods her understanding—already alert.

I unlock her cuffs.

Downstairs, faint but fumbling sounds signal intruders. Dread twists my insides; I'd left my Ax downstairs, stupid in my haste to confine Nona.

In a quick, desperate bid for salvation, I seize a bottle of 190-proof liquor, a lighter, and a pack of cigarettes. The alcohol is a disgusting concoction—the kind you drink when you want to blackout as cost-effectively as possible.

A few seconds later, I'm looking down from the top of my stairs.

Near the bottom of the stairway, looking up at me from behind a laughing-man mask stands a hulking form, nearly too wide for the narrow staircase to contain.

Riot—looking as intimidating as any man ever has.

I slowly place a cig in my mouth and light it—a small hole in my mask opens, made so that the wearer can drink from a straw or smoke without needing to unmask. I make sure to move slowly and deliberately keep my hands where he can see them—my gestures all cautious and controlled.

He is motionless, the stairway so dark that little more than the bright white of the mask is visible, making it appear as if his lower torso and legs fade away into the inky black, and only his upper half is made of solid matter.

I uncork the bottle of liquid hate.

I see his body tense—I presume he is only a moment away from charging up the stairs at me. I see another figure at the bottom of the stairway as well now, just a faint outline in the dark behind Riot's mountainous back.

"It would be rude of me to not offer a guest in my home a drink—particularly a coworker," I say, as I hold up the heavy bottle and let out a puff of smoke.

...

"Consider us impressed—such manners are an uncommon virtue in this deplorable city. Yes, come down—let's share a drink and prove to one another that honor among thieves still exists in the world," rumbles the giant.

I'm almost tempted to do it. I need information to piece together what the hell is going on with Nona, and if there is still a need to go into No Man's Land, I would probably be better off with a powerful ally like him than the kindly little scientist with the heart of gold.

But on the other hand, the big bastard has just broken into my house in the middle of the night, and frankly, I don't think we'd get along.

The choice of what to do next is simplified for me when I hear a familiar voice from further back speak up.

"Yeah, get the fuck down here so we can repay you for what you did to Solomon—an arm for an arm—nice and biblical-like," It's Ravish, the Lancer who got away after I was shot earlier.

"Shut your mouth, Ravish!" commands Riot, holding up a titanic hand.

Nothing else for it, then—Lancers are a notoriously resentful breed—I can't afford to gamble on Riot's restraint being genuine.

It's a shame I didn't splurge for the Homeowner's Insurance—But odds are I won't be coming back here anyway.

If I'm gonna do it, I might as well say something slick beforehand, right?

"You know any Bukowski? As in the pre-Unraveling poet?" I ask in as casual a tone as I can manage.

The question catches Riot off guard—He just stands there, as motionless as a gargoyle.

I feel like I can hear the gears turning as he tries to predict where I'm going with this.

I shrug.

"Ah well, that's a pity," I say.

Then I hurl the mostly full bottle of vodka at him. He ducks down, and it misses him by a hair—instead, smashing against the wall, spraying him and the walls in the toxic drink.

"To do a dull thing with style..."

I pull the lit cigarette from my mouth and flick it down at the now flammable stairs below.

"... Now *that's*... what I call art."

I bolt into the bedroom as chaos erupts below.

Nona is gone.

The window is open, and Nona's things are gone with her. Seeing her chance to get away from both me and the source of the unknown danger, she bolted.

I can hear heavy footsteps coming up the stairs.

Deciding Nona had the right idea, I lock the master bedroom's deadbolt and grab the cuffs for when I (hopefully) manage to track Nona down again and follow her out the window—landing hard on the weeds that make up my tiny patch of long-neglected yard.

For good measure, I quickly push over a heavy cast iron bench, finding the first use I've ever had for it, in front of the door—wedging it under the doorknob to try and barricade it shut.

Is it really asking too much to hope they all burn in there?

I think so, sadly. There are plenty of windows left, and Riot's reputation suggests he is too dangerous to die so easily—I bet a man his size can make his own door whenever he feels the need to.

I flee, a rising symphony of fire and fury erupting as I go.

Ludicrously, I feel a strange stab of embarrassment at the thought of them seeing all the second-rate paintings in the make-shift art studio, and hope they are too busy not burning alive to pay them any mind.

11

No Back-up Ax

History *Entry 2*

The emergence of No Man's Land over a century ago marked the beginning of the planet's seventh Mass Extinction Event—as very few species from the old ecosystems of the world have been able to successfully compete with the rapidly evolving new species, characteristic of No Man's Land. Some scholars argue that this event is more accurately described as a "Mass Rejuvenation Event", as the unprecedented explosion in biodiversity across the planet—while detrimental to human interests—has undone centuries of damage to the planet's ecology.

— *The Unraveled World: A History of Humanity's Decline & an Exploration of the New Normal, 3rd Edition*

I don't blame Nona for running, of course—given the circumstances—but it puts me in an unenviable position.

In those hours after finding out about her other eye but prior to the break-in, the most logical course of action for me had been crystal clear: Bring Nona to Prosper Electronica and possibly finish the job on the spot, securing Vivian's cure without ever setting foot in No Man's Land... Winning by dumb luck, essentially.

And even if they'd told me I had the wrong girl, I would have only lost a few hours. I could still default to the original plan, with the only downside being I would be going in alone... which is what I originally intended, anyway.

Maybe not even going in alone—after all, if they confirmed it wasn't Nona they were after, she might still begrudgingly agree to go with me depending on how badly she wants whatever the company is offering her.

But now... Well... I don't know where Nona is—I could spend many hours hunting her down inside the city only to come up empty-handed, or I could go into No Man's Land searching for a person who is not even there.

I don't understand any of this.

Clearly, there is a lot more to this than a simple search and rescue of an obscenely wealthy man's daughter.

Lancers started coming after Nona without ever having seen her face, let alone her other eye, so someone must be passing information on to them. Or could there have been recording devices in the back room where I spoke to Nona? I'd only thought to turn on the jammer right before showing my own face so someone could have seen her face and come to their own conclusions.

On the other hand, Nona had made a good point... Prosper Electronica hired Nona for this job, didn't they? They sought her out and summoned her here for a job offer, but now she *was* the job, somehow? Or her long-lost identical twin sister was the job?

Either way—absolutely insane.

The more I think about it, the more I think this whole thing is a lie, a trick designed to get to Nona. Maybe there was no plane crash, no lost daughter of the company's president, no reason to go into No Man's Land... Maybe they wanted Nona, specifically, for some unfathomable reason... so they invented a way to get her here. It would be difficult to abduct someone from Neo Kyoto—tricking them to come voluntarily would add up.

But no... that also makes no sense.

If she was all they wanted all along, they would have just taken her at the Night Library, surely. And why bother gathering all these other Freelancers? All they would achieve by that was ruining their reputation among us, and they relied on our services for everything from assassinations to corporate espionage.

My mind drifts, as it so often does, back onto the topic of Vivian.

Had she gotten my message yet?

If she had, had she understood it? I was forced to make it as cryptic as possible on the chance of other people seeing it first...

Maybe her curiosity would be piqued enough to finally answer a call?

I navigate through the menus of my mask's internal display.

.

..

...

Apparently not—damnit all.

...

It's not long before I'm at my storage unit.

I had the foresight to keep backup supplies here, and I've certainly never needed backups more than I do right now.

Technically, I suppose this also means I'm homeless... *again*. Blurry memories from my life before I met Vivian, back when I had a different name, flood to the surface.

I shake my head like a farm animal scaring away flies.

I down a Restless Energy drink that I got from a vending machine on my way here—the familiar purple and gold label read: "*Restless Energy—Grind today, achieve tomorrow, & sleep when you're dead!*".

Where could Nona be now?

She wouldn't trust me anymore, and now she must fear every other Lancer as well after two attacks, which means... She either gives up on the whole thing and goes home, or she's desperate enough to do something she previously deemed suicidal... Go into No Man's Land alone.

I decide to do some quick fact-checking.

To my surprise, a civilian flight, flight 0301, did actually go down in route to Kallipolis a day and a half ago. Apparently, there was only a handful of people on it—supporting the idea that it was a flight reserved for someone too important to fly with the unwashed masses.

There really had been a plane crash, but lies are best served with a little truth mixed in—this only proves that Prosper Electronica is not actually totally brain-dead.

Frustratingly, I do not own a second Compression Ax, not here nor anywhere else... I had intended to keep that ax till the bitter end, never even considered preparing a replacement.

Distinctive, one-of-a-kind items are one of the ways Lancers prove their identities, adding extra inconvenience to losing one.

Instead, I'm forced to retrieve a handgun from its neatly labeled home on a shelf along with the accompanying ring that must be worn to unlock its safety.

Guns are not the ultimate weapons they used to be; body armor as thin as cloth can now stop the smaller caliber rounds fairly consistently.

But short of punching my enemies to death, this is all I can do for the moment.

I holster the handgun and swing the pack over my shoulder.

I've made up my mind...

I'm not going to waste time tracking Nona down.

Which means... it's time to head for No Man's Land.

12

FireJacks light the way

"Fire doesn't solve all problems, but it does simplify most of them."
— Unofficial FireJack motto

The night's whispers held more uncertainty than I cared to admit to myself.

Nona might really be the one I need, and she might be getting on a flight back to Neo Kyoto as I walk into No Man's Land to get eaten by who knows what manner of walking abomination.

But she had seemed so determined to go... I'm banking on the hope that either she is headed the same place I am—or that she's really not the girl they want, after all.

Or at least... that's how I'm justifying the choice to myself.

There are way too many unknowns—it is inexcusably reckless to do this.

Vivian's illness might be a lie, the existence of a cure might be a lie, the president's daughter might already be dead at the plane crash site, or she might have never existed to begin with.

But the truth is—it just *feels* like No Man's Land is just the place I need to be right now.

I know I will most likely die if I go, yet... I'm dead set on going, regardless. I *need* the job to be true. I *need* this chance to go on a ridiculous quest to find a cure for Vivian to be more than just a pointless suicide mission.

Having a mission—even a suicidal one—feels... Good.

Besides, what else do I have to stick around for? Saturday morning cartoons? I don't even have a home to return to now—I may have hated that sad box of mine, but I know from experience it beats the living hell out of homelessness... and with my savings now gone, I have nowhere to go but forward.

Hours slip by like shadows in the night as I observed from the hollowed remains of a forsaken gas station. Sensory snippets emerged—the acrid tang of burning foliage, the metallic clank of machines, and the distant hum of FireJack officers yelling orders mingling in with the occasional howls and shrieks of No Man Land's nocturnal creatures—which begin to die away as the morning sun rises.

Prospera is a sentinel city atop the mountain—its underground districts hewing into the earth below, compensating for the lack of real estate above. She is one of three major cities left on earth—and all of them are besieged by the natural world outside.

This brings me here to watch the FireJacks busily at work on the frontlines of a never-ending war with the trees. Twenty-four hours a day, 365 days a year, Prospera's paramilitary institution known as the FireJacks, labor to keep the wildlife at bay—defending the entirety of Prospera's perimeter. All the buildings closest to the perimeter are abandoned out of fear that the FireJacks will experience another break and be forced to shrink back to the next defensive line—about a mile in.

Massive machines carve trenches into the earth, slowing the creeping roots that try to approach from below and allowing the FireJacks to inject poisons directly into the exposed root systems. Smoke billows out as controlled fires burn away the vulnerable vegetation, and teams of Compression Ax-wielding men attack the Strangle Root trees and other strange plants that have evolved a resistance to fire. Hunters sit in their metal towers, keeping watch from above with .50 caliber rifles and picking off the animals that continuously probe the defenses.

The FireJacks are also supposed to keep people from entering No Man's Land—though they rarely have much reason to worry about that part of their job description.

Until now, that is.

There should be dozens of Lancers making plans to sneak past the Fire-Jacks—some of the fastest ones might have done so already.

The two main groups of Lancers are far too numerous to all go in at once—unless they intend to fight their way in... Which seems like a stupid way to handle things. Will they just split up into small teams to figure out a way in, then rendezvous with the others after?

In front of me is the most direct path towards the downed plane—I expect most of the Lancers will likely attempt to break out near here as well. But more important than where the break-outs take place will be getting out before the first failed attempt is noticed. If any Lancers are caught, the ones to come after will have a much harder time of it.

How will Nona attempt it? We were not on the same side long enough to discuss this—I doubt she will be able to get past the FireJacks on her own—and if she gets herself caught, I'll have to decide whether to break her out of a prison cell or to go on without her and gamble on her being the wrong girl after all.

I sit and watch from the gas station for the next two hours, trying to get a feel for the security protocols and practices the FireJacks on duty are adhering to. Before I set my house on fire, I had a tactically acquired (stolen) Security Forces uniform that had been the centerpiece of my half-formed plan to get past the FireJacks... So much for that.

There is no way every Lancer will be discrete enough to slip past—dozens of people don't just sneak past one of the world's most heavily fortified perimeters without incident.

No... before all is said and done, there will have to be *at least* one Lancer—or group of Lancers—that ends up screwing the proverbial pooch.

Perhaps that will be my chance—if I move quickly, I can take advantage of the distraction that will create.

It's not a great plan, but it is all I have for the moment.

I pull out a pair of binoculars and spend my time looking for weak spots in the FireJack's perimeter and signs of the other Lancers setting up positions in the neighboring abandoned buildings.

I spot the glint of a rifle's scoop coming from the third floor of a crumbling hotel and make a note of it on a little map I've drawn on the gas station's floor to help me keep track.

I'm about to treat myself to lunch when I catch movement out of the corner of my eye.

To my amazement, there is a lone figure walking down the neglected, cracked pavement of the street, making no attempt at discretion whatsoever.

A slight build, a graceful stride to the steps... a forest green cloak with the fur-lined hood pulled up over the head.

...

SHIT.

As far as I can tell, by the direction she's headed in, she's going to walk right up to the gate.

Does this girl really think she could just ask nicely and have the red carpet rolled out for her?

...

There is still time.

The guards are not paying her any notice yet; their attention is so infrequently required—and when it is, it's usually limited to checking a truck's credentials as it tries to pass through the gate.

I can still intercept Nona if I move fast enough.

I pick up my pack and throw it onto my back.

Even if the guards see us, so long as I reach her well before she gets to the gate, it should be fine—It's unusual but not *technically* illegal to be out this far.

I can tell them she's just my brain-dead sister, apologize profusely, and drag her away without too much damage having been done.

I burst out the side door and weave my way through the trash-littered street—my speed helped by the downward slope.

From the corner of my eye, I see a blur of movement, and I instinctively throw myself to the side—narrowly dodging a knife blade that comes at me from a dark-skinned woman hidden around the corner of a building.

She makes another lunge at me, and I manage to dodge again before kicking a leg out from under her and backing up to make distance.

She rises.

Her hand drifts to a belt where a second knife resides. I suspect she's about to throw the first one before charging at me again.

She does exactly that.

As soon as I see her start to move, I pull my pack around and use it to absorb the thrown blade as well as the next slash of the knife she decides to not risk throwing.

I kick her as hard as I can in her kneecap—hear a satisfying grunt of pain—and jump back to put some distance between us once again.

"I don't have time to be playing games with you right now, dammit!" I snarl—outraged by the unprovoked attack and unsure of why she's even doing it—my only guess is that she is also a part of Riot's crew.

I unholster my pistol, and I let her see me rack a round into the chamber before I turn and sprint away again—unwilling to actually fire a gun this close to the guard post... but hopefully just the threat of the noise and the injured knee will make her think twice about following me.

I'm out of the shadow of buildings now, entering an open, grassy zone on a dirt road used by service vehicles.

Nona's not exactly running, but her strides are quick and purposeful, and the seconds I just lost are making this look like a lost cause.

I slow to a jog and return my gun to its hidden holster.

I think... I have to abandon her to her fate. She's going to reach that gate any moment now—the guards have already caught sight of her and are exchanging curious looks at one another, unsure why a lone civilian would be approaching their post.

Maybe this is for the best.

Nona will get herself thrown into a cell for questioning—probably kept there for a few days, and during that time, she will be reasonably safe. Losing a few days might convince her the whole thing is hopeless... which would probably end up saving her stupid life.

I just have to hope now that there really is a Kasca Haine somewhere in No Man's Land for me to find, or else I'm going to get myself killed for absolutely nothing.

Nona is at the gate now, talking with the FireJacks and showing them something I cannot make out from this far away.

I'm about to turn back when I hear a vehicle approaching from behind.

What a disaster...

Engines are made quiet these days—it's not like it was with combustion engines back in the day... and I was so focused on Nona I stopped thinking about what was behind me after confirming that the knife-wielding Lancer was not following.

They might just drive past me. They might be too lazy to bother with me...

The truck is right behind me now.

I shift to the side of the road to let them pass—trying to look as inconspicuous as possible.

Please, pass me by...

The truck slows to a stop, and I look up to see the driver's side window roll down.

Flames civilize.
Fire purifies...
Fire Jacks light the

13
The Welcoming Party

"What are you doing here, civi?"

"Just out for a walk, sir... I'm not doing anything illegal by being here... am I?" I ask timidly—trying to sound as dumb and innocent as I can.

"Walking... to *where*? Illegal or not, civilians don't belong this close to the Frontline."

"Right... well, if I'm somewhere I should not be, I really do apologize. I'll just turn back now—"

"Ralts! Get out of the bleedin' truck. Pat this guy down and look inside his bag... If he doesn't have anything he shouldn't, he can be on his way."

Shit.

Gun ownership is not prohibited in Prospera—if anything, it's the norm. Hell, even walking around in public with, say, a giant ax will get you little more than the occasional curious look or two. But if they check the contents of my pack, they will see that I have the kind of equipment and supplies only explainable by an intention to spend an extended amount of time in No Man's Land—as ludicrous as that is.

The man called Ralts has walked around the other side of the truck, a rifle slung over his shoulder. He wears the same uniform as all FireJacks—a curious hybrid of a firefighter's flame-resistant suit and a soldier's typical abundance of pouches and armor. Their uniforms make no attempt at camouflage—the polar opposite, if anything.

Even though they don't go in very far, FireJacks are still prone to going missing in the trees.

They tend to get dragged off by predators or disoriented in the thick smoke of the fires they set, so they wear dark blue suits with neon blue reflective strips to make them easier to pick out amongst the trees.

Casually, my hand drifts to where my pistol is concealed.

Would it be better for me to make a break for it now or let them arrest me and hope that I'll be able to free myself after?

Neither seems great.

"Raise your arms. I'm going to pat you down... unless there is something you want to tell me now n' save me the trouble of feeling y—"

"Cardova, this is Gate 2. We have an *alleged* scientist here—from fuckin' Neo Kyoto of all places. She's claiming Prospera and Neo Kyoto have a diplomatic agreement to allow scientific missions to enter No Man's Land... She also says that guy who's with you now is her personal security detail... She's asking if you could give him a lift to the gate. We've called the Captain over already. Go ahead and bring the son of a bitch over, will ya?"

I can hear the radio traffic coming from the truck.

Okay...

I have to give it to her—that's an interesting angle for her to try and work, but... why is she trying to cover for me?

"Hey, gimmie that, won't you please? Thanks!" To my astonishment, I hear Nona's voice crackle over the radio.

"Trent Givens, can you hear me...? I TOLD YOU TO MEET ME HERE HALF AN HOUR AGO! I'm fairly certain the Institute is paying you enough to AT LEAST deserve a bare minimum of punctuality... Consider yourself lucky that it's so difficult to find anyone willing to take on this kind of job!" Nona's impression of an angry superior chastising their subordinate feels a little over-acted to me—like a child trying to mimic the way her dad sounds when giving a stern talking-to.

"Sounds like she's a real kick to the balls... you should probably do as she says in future, huh?" says the FireJack who had been about to search me—suddenly soundly more amused than anything.

Not trusting myself to speak properly at the moment, I just grunt in agreement.

Trent Givens... The intention of that message was primarily to give me the name of the person I'm supposed to pretend to be, I'm sure.

I have no way to prove it if they ask for any kind of verification...

But I also don't really have any better options. The idea of trusting my fate in Nona all of a sudden is enough to scare me like little else has the past few days—not least because I'm not even sure she still considers me an ally after last night.

I climb up the back of the transport, pull back the canvas covering, and enter the shaded bed.

The truck is not carrying supplies, as I would have guessed.

It carries *people*.

FireJacks. At least two dozen of them.

I thank my lucky stars that I didn't try to resist—having a few dozen men immediately materialize out of nowhere to chase me would have made resisting a fatal mistake.

Self-consciously, I take a seat on the open bench next to me.

The masked faces of FireJacks all stare me down with silent intensity.

I can understand why they would—this can't be normal, but still...

There is a strange note to the tension here.

I had no clue these men were in here—they made no sounds while I was outside, and I still haven't heard any of them say a single word... These guys are acting more like a group of prisoners on their way to their own executions than a rowdy bunch of bored soldiers.

Looking at their ranks, I see that they're all fresh out of initial training and on the way to the Frontline for the first time.

They all stare at me—one of them bends over to whisper something into his companion's ear—he has to lift himself up out of the seat to do so because his companion is so massive that his ear is impossible to reach while he's sitting.

Freakishly large.

Perhaps the largest man I've ever seen, big enough to give Riot a run for h—

...

He's not just as big as Riot—he *is* Riot... the same guy I just tried to burn alive less than eight hours ago—I'm sure of it.

Now that I'm looking for it, I can spot signs that the others are Lancers as well.

These are not FireJacks—these are Lancers being smuggled in as a batch of new recruits.

This is how Riot is getting his large team into No Man's Land, and they are staring at me because I never changed into any disguise—I'm still wearing basically all the same clothing as I had at the Night Library the day prior...

"Small world... huh?" I ask Riot.

...

The boulder of a man just sits there—unreadable in his still silence.

...

I look over at the Lancer nearest me and make a motion with my hand to indicate that he should scoot over for me... which he eventually does—I think out of a grudging respect for the audacity of the request, more than anything.

I take my seat and wait, reaching into my jacket for a pack of cigarettes before also offering one to the lancer, who moved over to make room for me.

Now's not the time to forget my manners, after all.

Laughing, the man takes one and lights it.

14

Girlish Charm and a Sunny Disposition

I jump out just before the gate—more than ready to separate myself from Riot and his Lancers.

There is no amount of experience with danger or tough-guy bravado enough to make a person *not* giddy with relief at the chance to get away from a couple of dozen men he or she suspects want to brutalize him.

Some primal circuitry in the brain is just too foundational to condition away.

The transport enters—leaving us behind and delivering half a platoon's worth of imposters into the FireJack's ranks... There's no doubt in my mind that this day is fated to go down in infamy among the FireJacks as a cautionary tale on the importance of keeping tighter inward-facing security. A shit show of this magnitude—once they figure out they've been had—will ruin the careers of at least a few scapegoats unfortunate enough to be on duty today. If our own situations were not infinitely worse, it'd almost be enough to make me feel bad for the complacent bastards. I'd be lying if I said

I wasn't impressed with Riot—he's truly a clever and well-connected psycho if he managed something as audacious as this on virtually zero notice.

Nona, for her part, appears to be making fast friends with the gate guards.

They look totally at ease; she's effectively disarmed them with her girlish charm—as completely as if she had taken the rounds out of their magazines and thrown them into a river.

Once again, a day sure to go down in infamy... the fools.

"Yeah, I mean, it's dangerous work, but someone has to do it. Someone has to protect Prospera from the *things* in those trees... not to mention the trees themselves," says a red-headed Corporal pompously.

"It must be so hard on you... is it true that FireJacks don't get any holidays? What about your families, your girlfriends... don't they miss you awfully?" says Nona.

From anyone else... it would come off as overkill. But once again, Nona seems so endearingly sincere that she pulls it off.

"Ah, well... we used to, they used to let us each take two weeks' worth of liberty a year. But we've been short on hands... Even with all of us here, there are still sections that are only half-manned. Damned recruiters, sitting on their fat a—"

The Corporal snaps to attention and salutes as a rather pudgy Captain arrives.

The Captain's eyes are hidden behind his mask, but his turquoise blue hair is more than enough to mark him as an Amelior—which surprises me, considering how difficult it is for an Amelior to achieve anything less than a perfect, chiseled-from-granite kind of physique.

He's wearing a golden mask instead of a silver one like the other Fire-Jacks—which is how the Jacks distinguish between the officers (the Ameliors) and the enlisted (the Naturals), from a distance.

It's so easy to forget that not all Amelior end up at the top when their unnatural hair and eyes are usually only associated with the elite, high society crowd. But as rare as the Amelior are, there is an ever-growing number of the "Humbled" Amelior—Amelior from families that cannot afford to keep up with extravagant costs of purchasing the latest and greatest gene upgrades and thus have fallen behind. Most of the FireJack officers fall into this category, as defending the city's perimeter is considered neither lucrative nor glamorous.

Nona stands with her arms behind her back, looking perfectly innocent and unthreatening—she's almost too good at it—giving the impression of a schoolgirl on a class trip—rather than the serious scientific authority on a mission that she claims to be.

"Afternoon, sir," the FireJacks give the greeting without any real conviction, minding their manners but only to the bare minimum required... Making me think this Captain isn't so popular with the troops.

The Captain returns the salutes without a word and then studies the pair of us for a moment.

"You're... A Kyotan scientist, are you?" He sounds less than convinced.

"I am! My name is Nona Verre. I'm an Emerging Biologist and Geneticist, Third Tier, from Neo Kyoto's Mojica Research Institute. He's with me as my security detail while I'm conducting my research." She points at me, and I take this as my cue.

"Trent Givens, sir." I nod my head slightly in polite acknowledgment.

The Captain is silent for a moment.

"Verre... you're not related to... Doctor Albert Verre, are you?"

"I am! That's my dad, as a matter of fact," Nona replies cheerfully.

I have no clue who this Doctor Verre is, but it sounds as if I *should*... considering that he's apparently famous enough for a random Captain all the way in Prospera to know the name.

"Surely, you won't mind if my men see some photo identification then, *right*?" The Captain suddenly demands, with a real edge to his tone.

Here we are—the inevitable moment of truth.

Nona might have identification on her, but I sure don't. If they ask me for mine, we're done for—no way around it.

"We don't have any, I'm afraid!"

...

A bold move.

I turn to look at her—as curious to see where this is going as the Captain is.

"Is this some *joke*? You think we are going to let you in without proper identification? For all I know, you could be any random nobody off the streets." The Captain sounds exceptionally annoyed now, as if on the verge of ending the conversation entirely and returning to the comfort of his desk.

"We're both from Neo Kyoto. We don't have ID cards in Neo Kyoto... *Obviously*... we take scans. ID cards are far too easy to forge. What is this, 2020? Surely you have scanners here...?"

For our sake, I sincerely hope Prospera's bargain-basement tax rates failed to fund that particular upgrade.

To my relief, the Captain shakes his head.

"*We don't*... and that means we cannot let you pass. We received no notice ahead of time that there was a scientific expedition en route. The fault is yours. Come back again *after* your Institute goes through the proper procedures. You would think a genius like your father would have known better than to waste his daughter's—and my—time." The Captain turns to leave.

I let out a tense breath I hadn't realized I was holding.

All things considered, this is as good an outcome as we could have hoped for.

There was never any way we were going to talk our way past a FireJack position—being allowed to go back and come up with a real plan is a victory in my book—better than we had any right to expect.

"Well, you heard the man—" I begin.

"Captain... I'm sure you don't get researchers from the Institute here often, so I do not blame you at all for not having the details of the agreement between our two cities memorized... But we don't, ah... strictly need to send any advanced notice, that is not a part of the agreement... We are allowed passage into No Man's Land whenever we need it—*if* it is for scientific research, and *if* we agree to share all our findings afterward..." The Captain freezes before slowly turning back around to face Nona. "...which we, of course, will! So please, don't worry about that. Also, it is not really *our* fault you have not been supplied with scanners, is it? Although I'm very sorry you're having to do such an important job while not being properly equipped... I can sympathize with that as a state-funded scientist, honestly I c—"

The Captain raises a single finger, silencing Nona.

...

I'm sure he is searching up the scientific cooperation treaty Nona is invoking with his mask's internal display to make sure she isn't making it all up.

...

"Even if you're correct... We will need some proof before we let you pass. There is no way I will risk letting two people into No Man's Land on nothing more than the word of a little girl and a hired street thug—judging from the look of your help, there."

I glance down at myself, wondering what exactly about my appearance earned me that unprovoked bit of rudeness.

"Sir... she did have this paperwork on her..." One of the guards hands a few neatly folded papers to him.

"And you tell me this NOW, Corporal? Imbecilic little Natty..." The Captain growls and snatches the papers from his hand.

I see the other FireJacks tense up at being called "Natty"—it's no wonder the Captain is unpopular if he's casually throwing slurs like that around... Amelior/Natural relations are tense enough as it is, without throwing fuel onto the fire.

Nona came prepared for this—more prepared than I was, certainly. Begrudgingly, I have to admit that I've underestimated her.

"...Papers are too easy to forge, same as you so... aptly noted about ID cards. I will need more than th—"

"How about a call to the Institute, then?" Nona interrupts. "You... You *do* have phones here... right? You're a government institution—you alone should be allowed to make a satellite phone call to numbers outside of Prospera if it's for official business... yes...?"

The Captain crumples the papers slightly as his hands turn to fists.

"Of course we have phones—YOU! Call their ridiculous Institute and see if they know anything about *these* two. If they do, then let them pass... No need to worry about having to open the gate up again for them—they won't be returning if they are fool enough to enter on their own," barks the Captain.

There is a tense moment during which no one says a word.

"Aye... *sir.*" One of the enlisted men replies, finally.

The Captain stalks away.

This man is definitely not a pleasure to work with—with any luck, he'll be one of the ones on the chopping block when the FireJacks are divvying up the blame after today is over.

"He didn't need to take out his anger on you—I'm sorry bout that... Please, when you call, ask for Doctor Verre and say it in regards to his daughter." Nona's tone of voice carries all the sympathy and warmth her mask won't allow her face to show.

The Corporal eagerly promises that he will do exactly as she says.

I'm absolutely floored by the quality of her performance... until I look down and notice that her hands are anxiously grasping at her cloak—her exposed skin there even more pale than usual.

Ah well, *almost* flawless is still pretty respectable.

...

Ten minutes later, we're entering the gate.

We are guided down some steps into a half-submerged concrete bunker by one of the FireJacks Nona had been making friends with at the gate—a blond Lance Corporal this time.

"We're going to give you some flares; when you're ready to return, you'll fire one of the blue flares into the sky to give us some heads up. Please don't forget, if you do... one of our Hunters might mistake you for a predator and put a few holes into you. Best to do it sooner rather than later—we should be able to see the flare even if you're still a ways away, but if you get too close before sending it up, it might be too late at that point," says the young FireJack.

"Oh no... these... *Hunters*, you called them? They... They *will* be, ah... told we're going out beforehand, right? They'll know to be careful about what they shoot at?" asks Nona nervously.

"Oh... ah, yeah! Don't you worry, ma'am, I'll go tell them right after I'm done taking you—they'll know to be careful... You aren't going to go in too far, are you, ma'am?" asks the FireJack, suddenly sounding a little nervous himself.

"Oh, that makes me feel better—thank you so much. And no one calls me that, not even at the Institute... please, it's Nona! Just Nona... And no, not *too* far... just a few miles in for some samples is the plan," she says reassuringly.

The FireJack and Nona continue to chat as we walk down the long passage, occasionally passing by other FireJacks as we go.

Every FireJack that meets Nona seems instantly taken with her. If I were not so worried about the ticking time bomb of a truckload of imposter Fire-Jacks and our imminent release into No Man's Land, I'd probably find these attempts at flirting with her amusing. The bulk of the FireJack's enlisted ranks are made up of people my age or younger—the sheer cringe factor of overhearing inexperienced 18-year-olds trying to get and keep Nona's attention is almost too much to stand. I'm sure I'd be just as useless at it if I were in their position... but I'd also have the sense and dignity to know better than to try at all if I were them.

Soon, Nona has accepted two different boys' contact information... I suspect not because she seems sincerely interested but because she is too nice to give them a firm, unambiguous rejection.

"You've... really gone into No Man's Land before? They must do something special in Neo Kyoto to make girls as tough as you. No one in Prospera ever goes in besides us, and even we don't go very—"

We turn a corner and almost run into a pair of talking people.

But only one of them is in uniform.

A silver-haired Major is talking to someone draped in a thick cloak that hides their body completely—hood up—and wearing a... fox-faced mask.

A Lancer.

Specifically, one of the Lancers from the Night Library... the one I flipped off.

Notably, the Lancer is *not* in a FireJack disguise—yet they are still inside a FireJack compound, talking with an officer... as if that's something perfectly normal.

They turn to look at us.

"Lance Corporal... Who are these two civilians?" asks the Major, clearly surprised.

"T-They are from Neo Kyoto, sir. Here to get some equipment before we let them into No Man's L—"

"Major... are you truly going to allow this lunacy to transpire?" demands the fox-masked Lancer.

The voice is distorted by a voice modifier in the mask, making it impossible to even tell so much as the sex of the speaker by the sound of the voice.

"Of course not... Why would you possibly think you could let them even get past the gate?! Have you lost your mind? When have you EVER seen us let—" starts the Major.

"Please, sir... don't blame him, they called an officer, a... Captain? I think? And ah... he said it was okay after checking our papers and making some calls. I'm a scientist from Neo Kyoto, a Second Tier Emerging Biologist and Geneticist. And he is my bodyguard... There is a mutual scientific cooperation treaty that lets us enter No Man's Land, from either city's perimeter, if it is to conduct scientific research... we already explained all this at the gate..." says Nona apologetically.

The Major seems at a loss for words for a moment.

My strategy here is just to let Nona do all the talking... She comes off as so effortlessly nonthreatening and sincere that treating her with too much suspicion feels like bullying more than anything else.

It's worth using that to our advantage.

I, on the other hand...

"Oh... That's right, I am familiar with the agreement—it's just so rarely used... And *that* man is your security, you say?" says the Major, motioning at me.

I don't blame him. I definitely look like a Lancer... not like a straight-laced, professional bodyguard one would expect from Neo Kyoto.

Ironically though, I really did spend over a decade as more or less a bodyguard—among other things.

"Major... Do not let them pass. I believe they may not be who they say they are—I'd be eternally grateful if you detained them, at least temporarily. Let me interrogate them—let me save you from the potential embarrassment of having allowed a pair of imposters to talk their way through your security—on *your* watch," says the fox-mask Lancer.

What kind of relationship does this Lancer have with the FireJacks? If they are here and making demands thanks to bribery, it's stunning that they would be so flagrant as to be seen together like this—in a FireJack Compound—brazenly chatting away like old pals.

The Major fidgets uncomfortably.

"Lance Corporal... their identity was confirmed at the gate? You were able to verify that she is a scientist from this... Institute?" the Major asks.

"Y-Yeah—I mean... Yes. Yes, *sir*, we did. She had the right paperwork, and we even contacted the Institute to ask if they knew about them," says the FireJack.

"Well..." The Major looks from Nona to the Lance Corporal to the fox Lancer. "...We have to let them pass. This is a binding diplomatic agreement, well above my authority to overrule," he says.

"No! Major... Listen, I will assume the liability if your superiors take issue with this. Hold them in a cell, even if only for a day. For me. For... my *family*," says the Lancer.

"Respectfully, ma'am... We grant you access because of the Restless family's reputation, and all the patronage your family has shown the FireJacks over the years—but it is not your place to ask us to ignore a standing diplomatic agreement. I... have to refuse your request, I'm afraid," says the Major.

...

Restless!? And a "ma'am" as well, which massively narrows down the list of possible faces hidden behind the mask.

I take a reflexive step back, gawking like an idiot under my mask.

Could it really be her... *Vivian*?

The height actually does approximately match Vivian's, and with the Voice Modifier...

"DON'T... use my family name like that, *please*, Major," hisses the Lancer.

How could I possibly stand so close to her and not recognize Vivian, even with the thick cloak and mask...?

No, that's not really so hard to answer...

I didn't expect to see her at a place like a SpeakEasy. It is so far below her station, so beneath a daughter of one of the city's... one of the *world's* most powerful families.

"Fine! Let her through if you must, but not the man... he is no scientist—he is a criminal, a cut-throat. I recognize him. Perhaps the girl does not even know his true identity. I will take him with me and question him—"

"Sorry, but the agreement lets scientific expeditions bring our own security with them if we want to... Besides, you must be mistaking him for someone else—how could you possibly know who he is for sure with a mask on? I've known him for years, I promise, and Trent has never even been to Prospera before now," interrupts Nona.

All eyes are on the Major—who just stands there, his body language announcing his discomfort.

"Major. Take heed of this warning—because I will only give it the once. My family will not forget what happens here today—trust us or don't, either choice will have a long-lasting impact on the kind of relationship we have—on the trajectory of your career going forward... whether it be a long and prosperous one, or a short and lamentable one, will be decided by what you decide to do hereafter," says the Lancer in a voice barely above a whisper.

The Major turns to face Nona.

...

I can almost hear the gears turning in the man's head as he debates the risks of getting on the bad side of the Restless family.

"Miss... if you wish to leave immediately, we can give you some of our best Jacks for your protection. They will be better bodyguards than this one man could possibly manage on his own. If you insist on taking him... then I will have to ask that you wait here with him until we can clear this confusion up.

If it turns out he's not who my associate thinks he is, you can be on your way in a day or two," says the Major.

"Wh... a day or two!? You... You can't detain someone based on nothing but *one* person's word!" says Nona before turning towards me. "C-Can he?" Nona addresses the question towards me.

I nod.

"Up to 48 hours—without charges," I say.

"Yes, we will do exactly that. If a member of the Restless family is making the allegation, then it is w—"

"THANK you, Major... I appreciate your discretion in this. I trust you won't take issue with me questioning them while they are detained? And again... My family name, Major... *Please*."

"Yes, yes, of course... and excuse me, I apologize." The Major bows his head in deference.

"Fine! I will wait with him then... let's get this cleared up as quickly as possible, *please*..." says Nona, finally defeated.

Looking like it pains him to do so, the Lance Corporal nevertheless strips us of our weapons, takes our packs, and motions for us to follow him.

"I'm real sorry about this, ma... Nona," says the Blond Lance Corporal, sounding worried that this unpleasantness will hurt his chances at ever landing a date with his new crush.

"No, don't be! We know it's not your fault, Krita, obviously! You're just doing as you're told." Nona's voice smiles, and the FireJack—apparently named Krita—leaves us to our cell, looking full to bursting with regret.

There is no one in the cells adjacent to us, meaning that we are alone for the time being.

"Why didn't you take his offer and leave now with a couple of FireJacks?" I ask.

"Why yes, it *was* super nice of me to not abandon you... and I do accept your *apology* for cuffing me to your bed and attempting to pass me off as someone I'm not in exchange for a reward," Nona mocks, but with less venom in her voice than I probably deserve.

...

"Point taken... so, why *didn't* you abandon me out there?" I say.

"A little part of me wanted to, but... I can't totally blame you for what you did, considering the circumstances. I know my explanation or... lack of one... is hard to swallow. In the end, I realized I was asking too much to expect you to trust me without giving you a good reason to. So, I just *gave* you a reason. Whatcha' think? Pretty good, right?" says Nona.

"You were brilliant, Nona," I say with complete sincerity.

Nona takes off her mask and beams at me—her smile so bright I have to look away to protect my eyesight.

Ugh—for the love of...

"Again with the facial nudity—It's just not decent, I swear... *Anyway*, those men are damned idiots, seriously. All the junior FireJacks would have fought a trial by combat for your sake if you'd promised them a kiss on their masked cheek at the end, and the rest of them, at the very least, couldn't imagine you being a serious security threat... I've never seen girlish charm and a sunny disposition and so totally disarm a place's security before—it was almost scary."

"Well... I'm not a security threat, am I? We're not here to cause any of them any trouble—we just want to pass by is all..." Nona undoes her ponytail and starts running her fingers through her long hair absentmindedly—totally ignoring my discomfort at her indecency. "I wasn't acting any differently with them than I otherwise would have, so I think all those guys finding me so trustworthy just means they're good judges of character, right?"

I snort back a laugh.

"Sure, suuure..." I put on my best impression of an innocent girl's sick-ly-sweet tones.

"You're sooo brave and noble, protecting the city like this... and no holi-days! Your poor families must cry themselves to sleep every night with worry! Not to mention your poor, lonely *girlfriends*, who have nearly forgotten what the warmth of your embrace feels like—Yes, of course, I'll take your contact info..." I put a hand up to my forehead, palm up, like a swooning damsel.

...

Nona's mouth opens and closes a few times like a fish out of water.

"Wha... I... *You know* I didn't say all that! I really *do* feel bad for them, never getting to go home, even with it being so close by... I can't believe how, ah... *bold* Prosperan boys are—I've never gotten attention like this before, and they can't even see my face!" says Nona.

"Eh, I exaggerated slightly for effect. But still, don't act like you didn't trick them... Little miss covert agent over here. You can't be serious though—surely even in a place like Neo Kyoto, flirting isn't a crime," I say, stretching out to lay against the wall furthest from the cell door.

"That paperwork was all authentic, I'll have you know! I didn't trick anyone about anything, that is... other than about *your* actual name and identity. Besides that, I basically just reminded them of their own rules. And of course it's not illegal—it's just not normal for guys where I'm from. Most people only have AI partners when they're young. Then, when they feel ready to start a family, the Family Planning Algorithm either compiles their Personality Scores and arranges a marriage with someone compatible, or it... ahh... connects them to a... suitable genetic donner," says Nona, her embarrassment palpable with every syllable.

Now it's my turn to be the speechless one.

...

"You can't be... Is that really... I thought all that shit was just propaganda they were feeding us! You people are insane—no one of sound mind would agree to any of that!" I reply, horrified.

"H-Hey! You're one to talk—don't your people just use artificial wombs and genetically modify them in labs? Our way seems to work, more or less—it's a cutting-edge Artificial Intelligence that does the matchmaking, you know... How can you tease me at a time like this? It's not like you—you're usually super serious... Shouldn't you be trying to figure out a plan if they don't let us out soon enough? And..." Nona lowers her voice to a near whisper and leans in towards me. "...What if they've been listening in to our conversation, dummy?! This is supposed to be the kind of thing you're here for—how do we know they don't have listening devices in here?"

“Only the Amelior do it that way—costs a fortune and all..." I shake my head in disbelief but decide to let her drop the topic of her people's freakish mating customs.

"Anyway, calm down—Viv... *that Lancer* said they wanted to question us themselves, so I’m waiting for that to happen to decide what to do next. As for the listening devices..." I hold up my pocket jammer—which, thankfully, the FireJack didn't notice when he was relieving me of my weapons and pack. "...They won't be able to listen in or watch us—not when I have this turned on. Besides, they had no prior notice we were coming—no time to prepare a cell with listening devices. Look at these cells—they hardly ever get used at all—when they do, I bet it's mostly just a place for drunk FireJacks to sober up. We’re probably safer speaking openly here than we would be at most places in the city,” I reply.

Nona lets out a sigh of relief.

The truth is, I don’t want to think too much about facing Vivian again when she comes to “question” us—when I do, my stomach starts to knot up, and my mouth goes dry.

Nona is an effective distraction—and for the first time since meeting her, I welcome that normally annoying aspect of her personality.

15

Restlessness

"Better keep yourself clean and bright; you are the window through which you must see the world."
— George Bernard Shaw

An hour later, the fox-mask Lancer walks up to our cell, accompanied by a FireJack. The heavy thunder of their boots on the grated metal floor echoes through the cramped, dimly lit corridor, suffused with the potent scent of oil and gunpowder.

To my relief, Nona had the decency to put her mask back on when we heard them coming.

Once the door is opened, the FireJack is dismissed, and the three of us are alone together in a cramped box made of concrete walls that seem to absorb the light like a towel would water.

"I... did not expect to see you here, of all people. Please... tell me you're not here for some imaginary cure. Tell me they're offering you something, *anything* better than that."

Then it... really is her.

The air carries the faint scent of burnt wood—a vivid reminder of the surrounding industrial deforestation operation.

"Vivian... when I found out—I had to... You would do the same for me... wouldn't you? If I really needed help... Surely..." I am revolted with the weakness of my own words—the uncertainty—the obvious desperation in them even though the true tone of my voice is hidden by my ever-present Voice Mod.

Nona looks back and forth from Vivian to me, trying to follow the conversation as if it were a tennis match.

"Oh, Row... No—I would not. And neither would she..." The Lancer takes hold of the mask.

My heart leaps into my throat as I instinctively throw out a hand to block Nona's line of sight.

I pay Nona's half-formed complaints even less mind than I normally would as I hold tight to the eyes of her mask and wait for the anticipated emotional blow to land.

"...You've confused me for my dear baby sis..." The mask is pulled away, and the face I see there is familiar—almost as familiar as Vivian's—but it is not her.

"... *Corella*...?" I groan, somehow simultaneously disappointed and relieved to have been wrong about who was under the mask.

It's a face so like Vivian's, but Corella's features are softer, gentler looking than her younger sister's comparatively sharp lines and serious disposition.

Truly, in every conceivable way, Corella *seems* nicer... She's more sociable, more approachable—she laughs easier and is much more careful with her choice of words. She negotiates instead of arguing, and she has this way of making people feel important and valued when they talk to her.

She is also far more manipulative and untrustworthy.

Corella is the ultimate, unnaturally-born politician in the making—just as her family bred her to be.

"Sorry if I'm not the relation you were hoping for, Row. But... you don't have to sound *that* dismayed when you utter my name, honestly... it's enough to bruise a lady's feelings!"

I should have known.

Vivian would not have felt comfortable throwing her family's weight around out there—threatening someone with her family's wrath was not something Vivian had ever tried to do in front of me in all the time I've known her. Vivian also struggles to go more than a sentence or two without spicing up her language with a little creative profanity, and I don't think I caught a single obscenity among the threats she made to the Major.

Corella sighs and returns the mask to her face, so I stop defending her modesty and unhand Nona.

"No surprise, you're still not much for small talk—I'll cut straight to the point then. Some Security Force officers loyal to the family will arrive shortly to escort you—they will pretend to arrest you, but you'll be set free back in the city proper. The girl can go with you or carry on—I don't much care either way," Corella says with a shrug.

"W-Wait! You were at the Night Library, right? Does that mean you know about your sister's condition? You're *here* now... so that must mean... it's... true? Vivian really *does* have the Fade?" I again hate the desperation in my own voice.

"You... Didn't even verify she really had it before you set out on this farce?" Corella groans and cradles her head in the palm of her hand, laying on the exasperation extra thick.

"So what if I didn't? I tried to get a hold of her but couldn't. There was no time left. You being here must mean I made the right call. She... has The Fade, and you're... going to... *help her*...?" The implausibility of my theory catches up to me before I'm even done voicing it.

Corella, risk her life for... Vivian?

Fat chance of that.

"I do need to go into No Man's Land, but... I have my own reasons for doing so, as you've already surmised, I see."

"Please, Corella... I won't get in the way of whatever it is you're doing—just let us go. I know you and Vivian never got along well, but you can't *want* her to suffer such a miserable future... if nothing else, it will be an embarrassment for your family. Let me at least *try* to save her," I beg.

"Row... You don't understand anything, you sweet, witless boy... Any virtue, taken to enough of an extreme... *is a vice*. Even loyalty. A dog who adores the master that beats it is not an inspiration to emulate—it is a tragedy to be pitied." Corella shakes her head. "... I'm doing this for your own good—it's just too sad to watch. Go home." Corella turns to leave.

In an instant, I have Corella's wrist in my hand as her other hand rests on the door, ready to push it open.

She turns to look at me.

"Corella. This won't stop me. You know that. I don't give a damn if it's a virtue or a vice—I'm loyal... if nothing else, I am *fucking loyal*."

...

Corella's body tenses at my touch, and her other hand drifts down towards the folds of her cloak, where I suspect she has concealed a weapon that she's debating using.

I let go of her wrist.

"You... always worshiped the ground she walked on, and she *never* deserved it for a second. Now you're going to go die for her—what a truly spectacular way to self-destruct—nearly as grand as it is pathetic... So be it. I'll tell the Major I made an error, and I'm sure you'll be set free shortly thereafter." Corella walks away without another word.

...

We sit in silence for a long time after Corella leaves until Nona decides she will have to be the one to break it.

"I think you owe me an apology—that was a suuuper uncomfortable time to be a fly on the wall."

My immediate instinct is to be annoyed with Nona, but... I know she's only trying to defuse some of the tension.

I sigh.

"You're the one always talking about getting to know each other better... Well, you can't say that wasn't educational. Careful what you ask for."

"That's... not exactly what I had in mind..." her voice is softer now—as if she's soothing a frightened animal.

"So... wanna tell me who this girl is? The one you're apparently doing this for?" asks Nona tentatively.

...

"Not really, no," I reply.

...

"Does that mean she's your... *girlfriend*?" says Nona slyly.

I lay back down on the hard concrete floor.

"Will you believe me if I tell you no?" asking a question I already know the answer to.

"Nope! Who else could she be? I mean, she obviously isn't your sister or anything, judging from that conversation you just had with her actual sibling, but... There was a lot of familiarity between you and that woman, sorta like there would be if you were her younger sister's long-time boyfriend, perhaps...?" Nona teases.

...

"That's some very sound reasoning—I can't say your conclusion is an unreasonable one."

"Ah-ha! I knew it!"

"That doesn't mean you're r—"

"Honestly... I'm relieved. Since I followed you, I know the last few things you did before coming out here, Rowan. And it didn't include saying goodbye to any friends or family once so ever... I suppose you could have done that right after you were first contacted about the job before we ever even met, but... I saw your home, no photos, no mementos... I was starting to worry you didn't have... *anyone*."

Nona's voice is somber... but even worse—it's dripping with sympathy.

Wonderful—I *love* being an object of pity.

"I... You should mind your own damn business, Nona," I say, unable to come up with anything better.

"Meddling where you don't technically have to is the essence of being a hero," says Nona with a smile.

"That... sounds like a quote you stole from something unforgivably corny. If you're gonna steal quotes, at least steal the not-corny ones. Also, so we're clear, I do not recognize you as a hero... even if you wear that cloak like a cap half the time," I say.

"How ungrateful—I *did* save your butt earlier today, you know! That makes me your hero by default, whether or not you're willing to admit it," she counters.

"Yeah, and I saved you from those three scary bastards in the alley—I think that makes us even," I counter her counter.

"Well... I guess we'll have to be each other's heroes from now on—we can take it in turns to save one another," Nona says brightly.

...

"If you wanna be a hero so badly..." I reach down to pick up Nona's yet again unworn mask, which she'd removed as soon as Corella left.

"...you'll have to learn to wear your mask!"

I throw it at her.

I thought I had telegraphed what I was about to do pretty generously, yet Nona still fails to catch or even dodge it—instead opting to let the plastic smack her in the forehead.

"Ouch, *heeey*! That's no way to treat your partner, much less your hero..." She rubs the spot on her forehead.

I lay back down.

...

"Restless... her first name was... Vivian. Vivian Restless—I know that name from somewhere, dang it..." She puts a finger to her chin in thought.

"Well, you *should* know the last name. It's the—" I begin.

"... T-The Super Olympian? She does the archery event!" Her voice rises several octaves.

I nod, surprised *this* is what she knows, of all things.

"Wow... She got the silver medal last year, didn't she?" Nona falls into a kind of stunned silence next to me.

"Your girlfriend is a Super Olympian, holy guacamole..."

"I *told* you... Oh, whatever..."

It's not worth the effort to argue.

The Superior's Olympics was undoubtedly a big deal, but Vivian's fame for being a Super Olympian generally only gets her serious name recognition immediately before and after the games are held—and they only happen once every three years—hence my surprise.

But it also makes me feel a strange flash of fondness for Nona because I know Vivian—if she were here—would much rather this be the reason for a stranger's recognition than her typically far more infamous place in the Restless Family's hierarchy.

"You know, I've never been more sure in my life that I made the right call, picking you, I mean. After hearing how much you care about protecting your little *girlfriend*, there is absolutely zero chance you're a bad guy. I've never known a bad guy to be so selfless. That was also a glowing review from your girlfriend's sister—which def counts for a lot."

I don't know where she gets off making these kinds of assumptions...

Ignore it, Rowan, ignore it...

"Glowing, huh?"

"Well, okay...maybe not glowing, per se... She thinks you're a bit of a sad, lonely dummy, actually... But she definitely likes you a lot more than she likes her sister... so... you know... that has to count for something."

There is a lot I know Nona is intentionally not saying.

For one, for all her teasing about Vivian being my girlfriend, it is obvious from what she overheard Corella say to me that the situation is a lot messier than that.

I'm grateful she's not pushing for more details, at least for the moment.

"We should be let out soon. Anything you want to tell me before we go into No Man's Land? Last chance to talk strategy. Or to confess a secret identity as a certain company president's daughter, for example," I tease back.

...

"Hahaha. *Hilarious*." She rolls her eyes.

16
Abandonment Issues

“Row… do rich people have a different definition of the word ‘soon’, or what? Cause it’s been *hours,* and we still haven't been let ooout,” Nona complains, not unlike a child when the car ride has extended past their tiny baby bladder’s maximum capacity.

“You’ll have to ask someone rich. Also, don’t call me that,” I say.

“You didn’t tell your girlfriend’s sister to not call you that… Also, you might not be rich, but after spending so much time among them while dating one of their kind, I’d think you would be some kind of expert. You should be able to tell me if there is some kind of Theory of Relativity that applies to people only after they’ve entered a certain tax bracket.”

“There is no income tax in Prospera—Isn’t your father some famous scientist? Maybe you should be the one telling me about life as a rich girl,” I reply dryly.

“Dad does do well for himself, but Neo Kyoto has the good sense to tax the rich, and he donates most of what’s left… my life has been perfectly middle-class!”

"Fat cats like to donate in Prospera as well—always for self-serving reasons. Does Daddy dearest ever have candlelit dinners with important people to discuss the specifics of his... lavish generosity?" I say, unsure of why I'm in a mood to push her buttons—I know how the world works, and it's pointless to resent people for being self-serving—just as it's pointless to resent gravity for my inability to fly.

"My dad isn't like that! He's spent his whole c—" pipes up Nona indignantly before I raise a finger to cut her off.

"Be. Quiet."

...

"That's a little uncalled for—you're the one who got mean for no good reason..." Nona says, sounding hurt.

"No, LISTEN... Do you hear anything?" I ask.

...

"No..." she says, sounding confused.

"Exactly. Where are the distant sounds of heavy machinery? Or of trees falling? Or FireJacks yelling?" There has always been a faint background noise from them. Now there is nothing. They work 24 hours a day, every day... there *should* be noise, right?"

Nona nods, suddenly serious.

The sound of footsteps.

A blur of motion as a figure in a thick black cloak and a fox mask sprints past the bars of our cell.

"Corella! WAIT—what the hell is happening?" I yell after her.

She screeches to a stop.

"What... What the hell are *you* doing *here*?!" she replies.

"Waiting to be let out! As you said we'd be. No FireJacks ever came to release us, so assuming you told them to... they obviously forgot," I say.

Corella curses loudly but otherwise seems lost in thought, not volunteering any information.

"Corella, what is happening out there?" I say.

"Fighting. Tensions boiling over between Amelior and Naturals maybe—I don't know—a bunch of junior FireJacks attacked an officer, and things went mad." With the mask back on, the voice modifier is back as well, making that already disconcerting news sound even more ominous.

...

"Those aren't FireJacks... they're Lancers impersonating a bunch of green recruits," I say.

"*What?*" says Corella and Nona in unison.

"You didn't think I'd be interested to know something like that?" complains Nona.

"I got... distracted..." I say honestly.

I really am a moron.

That was one hell of a thing to just let slip my mind, but since talking to Corella, I've been so lost in my head... even when trying to distract myself with Nona, I was only half there.

"Well. That is one hell of a distraction, at least..." says Corella, thinking out loud.

She turns to look at me.

"... And I had better take advantage of it while I can... Goodbye, Rowan."

She turns to go.

"No, dammit! You said you would let us out—you said you'd let me go try and help Vivian! CORELLA!" I yell at her, desperate and suddenly furious.

...

"I... I changed my mind," says Corella.

...

"Corella, *listen* to me—some of the Lancers out there are after the girl who's with me and won't mind caving in my skull on sight—just to simplify the situation for themselves. My place was burned down last night—they came after us. If you leave us here and they are the ones who walk past our cell door next, we *will* die."

More importantly, even if the FireJacks do get things back under control after all this, they won't be letting me or Nona go into No Man's Land anymore, that's for sure.

If I can't get Corella to open this door right now, it's game over.

...

"Your chances are still better in here than they would be out there. It's more likely that the FireJacks are the next people you see walk past, and all you will have to worry about then is being detained for questioning."

Corella starts to move again.

Any second now, she will disappear for good.

"CORELLA! If we die out there, that will be on me! But if we get killed locked in this FUCKING cell after you've *abandoned* us here, you will have as good as killed us! Even if it's Riot with our brain matter smeared under his size 20 boots—it will have been YOUR fault!" I roar after her.

Corella freezes.

...

"D-Did you say Riot?! Why would *Riot* be after you?"

I kick the bars of the cell as hard as I can.

"Corella, *I don't know*. But he broke into my place last night, and I doubt it was for a social call. Now get us out of here!" It feels wrong, demanding that a Restless do something for me, but this is life or death.

Corella starts letting out a torrent of very unladylike curses I've never heard her use before as she sprints back towards our cell.

"Lucky for you, I have a master key."

But instead of her pulling out a traditional key, she pulls out a very small Burner Blade—something closer to a pocketknife than a sword.

She turns it on, and after a few seconds, the blade is glowing white-hot.

Nona stands to my side, watching curiously as Corella cuts through the cell door's locking mechanism.

The cell door swings wide open.

In the distance, there is muffled shouting, as if someone is giving a warning or an order, followed by a smattering of gunshots.

We run, putting our trust in Corella's sense of direction.

Nona starts to fall behind almost instantly, and I'm not sure how long I'll be able to match Corella's pace either... Superhuman genetics are one hell of a thing.

Out of nowhere, Corella hits the brakes, and I very nearly plow into her.

"W-What's the... issue...?" I pant.

Corella has the pocket-sized Burner Blade out again.

"I need my gear!"

I'm inclined to agree, so I let her get to work on the unassuming storage room door she's selected.

A moment later, Nona catches up, clutching a stitch in her side.

Before she wastes what precious breath she has left, I tell her why we've stopped.

Bent over, hands on her knees, Nona doesn't say anything but instead gives me a dorky thumbs up to indicate her approval.

Apparently, the FireJacks were a little lazy and locked all our confiscated gear, including our weapons, in this storage closet... instead of a secured armory.

I'm somehow sure getting into a proper armory would have been infinitely more difficult—I'll have to send them a gift basket or something.

I spot our packs on a table next to my pistol and its Unlocking Ring.

To my surprise, Corella has picked up an absolutely massive Dreadnought Bow, the kind that can hit something half a mile away.

"I didn't know you took up archery... Vivian been giving you lessons or something?" I ask Corella, gesturing at the bow.

"Please, my sister isn't HALF the shot I am." Corella snatches up the bow and accompanying arrows.

... I've never seen Corella use a bow, but if she's twice the shot of a sister who is a certified Super Olympian in the archery event... I'll eat my damn socks. Sibling rivalries are a strange thing—beyond the reach of common sense to understand.

"Let's hurry," says Corella before taking off again.

Nona grimaces.

Corella's long legs eat ground like few natural humans ever could dream of, and I don't get the impression Nona has ever been much of an athlete, frankly.

I fall in the middle—exceptionally fit, but the only thing unnatural about me is my body's ability to take a beating.

Corella slows to a stop in front of me before a large door that I think must lead outside and throws up the hand signal to halt before placing a finger over her mask's mouth.

I slow to a semi-stealthy walk the last few meters and catch my breath. A few moments later, Nona rejoined us, and I passed the warning along to her as well.

"My Jacks have you surrounded, whoever the hell you shit-eaters are! Throw your weapons out into the open before we start setting explosives on all the load-bearing walls!" A woman speaks, her voice heavy with the kind of authority I associate with an Amelior.

"Sounds like Riot's crew bit off more than they could chew, trying to fight through a whole company's worth of FireJacks... even with the element of surprise," I whisper to Nona, doing the mental math of a company divided up by three platoons, each with approximately 40 people.

A resounding silence is all the FireJacks get in reply.

"Fine. Gardoea, start setting the expl... Better yet—get half a dozen flamethrowers and as many grenades as you can manage. Maybe we can burn and blast them out without having to rebuild a whole storage building after," says the officer savagely.

I take my bag off my shoulder and dig into it until I manage to find three smoke grenades. I hand one each to Corella and Nona.

"As soon as they start trying to clear the building, we throw these... then count to 10 and make a break for it."

It's not a great plan, but it's all I can think of right now

"That's a dog shit plan!" mutters Corella, clearly outraged.

"It's the best we can hope for, I think... Once the FireJacks finish dealing with those Lancers, our chances drop to zero! A bad plan now will be better than a perfect one in five minutes," answers Nona, surprising me with her support.

After a slight pause, Corella nods.

"Wait! We need the prize taken back alive!"

Looking around, I see a new group of people entering the scene.

It's the Restless House Guard, and the one who shouted the order was none other than Captain Brawn.

"Corella! You didn't say you'd brought—"

But then I see another figure approaching just behind Brawn, a figure in a thick, black cloak and a fox mask.

...

I stare at the fox mask and black cloak-wearing figure walking next to Captain Brawn, then look back at the identically dressed figure standing next to me.

For a moment that lasts far longer than it has any right to, we just stare into each other's masked faces—the clues that should have been so obvious finally coming together in my foolish head.

...

I grab hold of the mask and yank it off before the person behind it has any chance to react.

...

"*V... Vivian*!" I gape at her.

She opens her mouth to say something, but the sounds of Captain Brawn arguing with the FireJacks and Vivian trying to find the words to explain herself are both interrupted by a horrible, ear-splitting roar.

It's not a sound any human is capable of making—somehow both animalistic and artificially mechanical at the same time, like a freight train full of screaming beasts impacting an immovable object.

I look at Nona, and the expression on her face tells me things are about to get even more complicated.

"It's a Thorn Lion!" Nona cries.

I have no clue what that is, but I'm sure it's not good.

Vivian snatches her mask away from me again and returns it to her face.

"Shit—All the heavy machinery has been shut off for too long, and all the fires have gone out... Jaspers, Hasan, try to get a couple of Dozers moving again—maybe we can still scare them off! Where the hell are those flamethrowers!" shouts the female officer, a hint of anxiety in her voice now.

"This is our chance! Rowan, your plan was barely even a plan—it was a pile of hot shit that approximated a plan. Shit's changed—between the Lancers, the Family Guard, and this lion thing—everyone is about to be way too preoccupied to worry about the three of us," says Vivian.

"Lion... *thing*? You have no idea..." mutters Nona, looking as if she is not at all having a good time.

"Vivian is right—the chaos is an opportunity we can't afford to waste," I agree.

Nona looks back and forth between us, and I know she thinks us mad.

We probably are.

17

Man-Eaters

From out of the trees emerges the largest living thing I have ever laid eyes on.

The Thorn Lion is appropriately named; its body looks as if it has bleach-white bones protruding from it that are sharpened at the ends into lethal points. The largest of these are concentrated in the vicinity of the mane, erupting from the tangled mess of black fur. Steam erupts from its mouth as if the temperature is much cooler than it actually is, but the rest of its face is a featureless mask of white bone armor—clearly the same material as the thorns.

The FireJacks all seem to instantly forget about their original enemy and turn to face the family-car-sized cat—which lunges from out of the forest, its thorns ripping massive scars into the trees that get in its way.

As terrifying as the beast is, I don't see how it could last for very long against so many heavily armed FireJacks.

Dozens of guns open fire on it, and its mass makes it a hard target to miss—even with its considerable speed.

Countless bullets do find their way into the lion, but... It seems mostly undaunted as it closes the gap between itself and the nearest group of FireJacks.

"The spikes, they act as armor as well! The protection is strongest on its front!" says Nona, sounding both terrified and slightly awestruck.

The FireJacks seem to understand this already about the Thorn Lion and start to move to try and flank the cat.

"Forget about the damn grenades—GET SOME ANTI-ARMOR OVER HERE," orders another officer from somewhere unseen.

Just then, the monster claims its first victim, impaling a young FireJack as he turns to run away—realizing too late that he is the lion's target.

His body dangles horribly from the spikes, leaking blood from the many puncture wounds as he slides sickeningly down a particularly large spike—tragically, not yet dead.

But the FireJacks are much better at this part of their job description than they are at boring normal security; there is already a pair of them running out of a bunker with huge anti-armor weapons resting on their shoulders.

Those things are leftovers from The Great Synthetic War—designed to take out a fully armored automated tank. There's no chance the Thorn Lion can shrug off a hit from one of those the way it can small-arms fire.

It is at this moment that the Lancers seize their chance and start to stream out of their shelter.

A FireJack, his back turned to aim down his rifle's scope at the lion, is cut down from behind by a Lancer with a glowing Burner Blade.

Another FireJack has his head blown straight off his shoulders by an impractically large gun.

The Lancers have far more experience fighting other people, and it shows in their fighting; their styles and strategies are also not at all uniform or textbook, the way the FireJacks are. Some of them are fighting alone, while others work in well-coordinated teams... Some of them fight like classic mercenaries, others like street thugs, and the remainder lash out like feral animals.

Only the Restless House Guard maintains their full focus on the Lancers, but they are limited by their orders to bring an unknown someone back alive and the confusion caused by the Lancers wearing FireJack uniforms—area weapons like explosives are not being used, and many of them appear armed primarily with non-lethal munitions.

The Lancers take full advantage of their enemy's handicaps—all they need to do is escape to the tree line, while the FireJacks have their hands full with the Thorn Lion and the Restless House Guard are unwilling to risk killing their mark or the FireJacks who frequently obscure their lines of fire.

The Lancers are thus able to tear into the distracted FireJacks with brutal efficiency while simultaneously making a fighting retreat from the House Guard at their rear.

I can make out five Lancers working together, three of them with shields, one with a heavy war hammer, and the last with a long rifle.

The three shield bearers are tight together, protecting the hammer carrying Lancer's approach, while the designated marksmen covers their rear, taking shots at anyone trying to maneuver around the shield bearer's protected front.

One of the FireJacks does just that, sprinting out of cover to try and get behind the shields.

He takes a round to the chest and does not get back up.

Over and over again, when the shield-bearing Lancers get near someone, they hit them with a stunner and step over the body, leaving the job of finishing off the unfortunate soul to the Lancer with the hammer as they pass.

Groups like theirs are a well-oiled machine, but other Lancers—some of them surely high on combat stims—attack with reckless abandon and to mixed effect—sacrificing coordination and caution for shock and awe.

And then, of course, there is Riot.

He's impossible to miss, being closer to the mass of a heavenly body than a normal man.

After killing two Jacks with quick blows to the head that cave in their skulls like soda cans, he goes after the female officer.

She fights well, her movements are quick, her kicks land hard, and she manages to cut into Riot several times with a wicked-looking curved knife she holds in her left hand. One-on-one, she might have been good enough to kill any of the Lancers here... except for the one she was unfortunate enough to be fighting.

After less than 10 seconds, Riot manages to lock a hand on one of her arms, and that is the end of her.

Riot lifts her up by his hold on her arm and smashes her into the earth over and over until she is utterly broken, a mass of bruised flesh and broken bone only tentatively held together.

And she was an Amelior; her bones were denser, her muscles are able to produce more force pound for pound than any regular human... Yet it seemed to make no difference at all.

What the hell is Riot, exactly?

His brutality is like nothing I have ever seen—his physical strength makes fully grown men look like infants in comparison.

But the House Guard seems to be pushing in his direction as well—making me suspect he might very well be the one they are after.

"Push right! I think the Restless want Riot—the further we can get from him, the better!" I yell.

We do, and the fighting does indeed seem less intense the further we get from the Riot epicenter. But it will not be enough—in a moment, the FireJacks will surely kill the lion and turn to refocus again on the fleeing Lancer—including the three of us.

Sure enough, a moment later the Thorn Lion dies in an ear-splitting explosion.

Just as it had managed to pin another Jack under its massive clawed paw, one of the two rockets sent its way lands a direct hit.

"So much for the house cat—that didn't last long," says Vivian.

"No... that won't be all—Thorn Lions live and hunt in mated pairs!" says Nona.

"You *must* be jok—"

From the trees emerges a second lion, this one somehow even bigger than the first.

This Thorn Lion also has no visible eyes—yet the monster seems to stare at its dead partner for a moment, as if momentarily stunned.

Then it lets out a vicious, bestial roar that makes the men fighting closest to it cover their ears in pain.

It charges.

The FireJacks, who hadn't even had enough time to catch their breath after killing the first Thorn Lion, are forced once again to pick between death by man or death by man-eating beast.

Most opt for death by man—a bullet or a blade to the back is somehow less horrifying a way to die than on the end of a Thorn Lion's spike.

In quick succession, at least three more Jacks die, two of them crushed under the weight of the charging predator and another impaled grotesquely on its thorns—presumably to be carried off and eaten later, at the monster's leisure.

As shocking as it is to have a second lion appear, the end result will soon be the same regardless.

The pair of FireJacks who killed the first lion are repositioning, running from cover to cover as they try to line up another shot with their huge anti-armor guns.

No.

I cannot afford to let them kill the second one so quickly—we must prolong the chaos as long as possible if we are going to manage an escape.

"Give me back those smoke grenades!" I yell at Nona and Vivian.

They do—I suspect Vivian knows my mind well enough to predict what I have planned, but Nona surely does not.

If she did, she certainly wouldn't have complied.

I sprint out of our cover to a stack of crates about 25 meters away, needing to close the distance to make this work.

The two Jacks are crouched behind a low wall, reloading their launchers so that they can take another shot.

Then, with all my strength, I launch the three smoke grenades in quick succession towards the rampaging lion.

The pair of Jacks who finished reloading and were just in the process of aiming their shots, look around—confused as to why anyone would be throwing out smoke grenades in a situation like this.

"Who the *hell* is throwing smoke—STOP! STOP YOU, MORONS!" screams an officer, outraged at this apparent stupidity, under the impression that the grenades had been thrown by some of his own men.

The smoke works better than I had imagined, or worse—depending on the perspective—as it rapidly engulfs everything nearby in an impenetrable grey cloud.

"Let's move!" I yell back at Vivian and Nona.

The Thorn Lion didn't seem to have eyes, so I wagered it wouldn't be particularly bothered by the smoke.

I was right.

Not only can't the FireJacks see the lion in the smoke—they're also hesitant to shoot blindly for fear of hitting their comrades.

A cacophony of panicked screams is coming from inside the smoke as the lion savages fragile human bodies, suddenly free to take its revenge with impunity... at least, for as long as the smoke remains in the air.

The FireJacks are starting to crumble, confused, and panicked with attacks coming from multiple directions... Being unable to focus on one fight has robbed them of the ability to excel at either.

The Thorn Lion seems to understand that it has the chance to capitalize on a rare opportunity and pushes the sudden advantage—screams from inside the smoke suddenly start, then are just as suddenly silenced by the vengeful monster. It does not seem eager to leave the smoke, making me wonder if it is intelligent enough to comprehend the advantage it provides.

It honestly sounds like something from a horror film... I do not regret that I can't see the violence accompanying the noises.

Nona and Vivian rejoin me behind the crates, having caught up after I darted out to toss the smoke.

Nona's eyes bore into me with unspoken judgment—with all the horror and betrayal of an innocent girl finding out that her childhood best friend is secretly a sociopathic sadist.

She is unable to believe that I've contributed to this nightmare by prolonging the rampage—that I have intentionally served the FireJacks up on a silver platter to the Thorn Lion—all for the sake of buying us some time.

"W... We need to help... to do... *something...*" she says, sounding on the verge of tears.

Nona is just not built for this kind of life.

But I absolutely am—it's all I'm good for.

"No time! The Lancers are moving towards the trees, and that smoke won't last forever!"

"But... the Jacks were going to let us go! They're not even really our enemies—we can stay and expla—" Nona starts to object.

"*No.* I'm sorry, but if they find us now... there won't be any talking it out—that's not even an option," I interject.

Vivian might be fine, dressed identically to the leader of an allied faction—they wouldn't want to shoot her on sight, but me and Nona would not get that kind of benefit of the doubt.

The Lancers are still killing Jacks, but they are doing so to the minimum degree necessary while bounding from cover to cover towards No Man's Land—on the verge of completing their fighting retreat.

I make out Riot in their center, barking orders now since he is out of range to do any more murder for the moment—on account of his apparent strong preference for close combat.

A Lancer next to Riot has his leg blown off, making me think that the FireJack Hunters have finally joined the fight with their high-powered rifles—better late than never.

Nona cries out, and I look to see what has gotten her attention.

The Thorn Lion has emerged, apparently out of prey to hunt in the safety of the smoke.

The monster has one of the Jacks in its mouth, the man beating at its jaws with his fists ineffectually, screaming a high-pitched, panicked cry.

It's the FireJack from the gate, the one Nona had so quickly befriended... one of the ones who had so awkwardly asked for her contact information.

I see her body tense as if she's preparing to do something *incredibly stupid.*

I place a hand on her shoulder.

"Nothing we can do—mission comes first. Let's go!"

I literally drag Nona away, picking cover to duck behind as we go, shielding Nona with my body as best I can as I force her to run.

I spot the fallen body of a dead FireJack—his Compression Ax lays on the ground next to him.

Ahead of us, the other Lancers are entering the safety of the trees.

I alter our course only slightly in order to snatch up the weapon—and a moment later, we're passing a trampled line of barbed wire and leaving the battle behind us.

18

The Tragedy of Entropy

"Love is not just looking at each other, it's looking in the same direction."
- Antoine de Saint-Exupéry

Though the sounds of gunfire and shouting follows us into the trees, I am shocked by how effectively the forest deafens the sounds nearly the instant we enter—not unlike entering a building and shutting a thick door behind.

It is impossible to forget that humans used to own this territory until fairly recently—it has only been about 15 years since the last time the FireJacks had to abandon a nearly two-mile chunk of the city and pull back to a new defensive line. No Man's Land stands as a relic of humanity's decline—a warzone haunted by an eerie mix of desolation and wildness. Abandoned structures, once urban, are now entwined with vines, their broken windows and collapsed roofs attesting to nature's reclamation.

We keep moving quickly for a ways—motivated to get out of the range of any FireJack Hunters and to avoid bumping into any of Riot's Lancers.

I know Nona is horrified that I was willing to buy us the chaos we needed to get away—with innocent FireJack lives.

I am as well... but I am who I am precisely because I'm willing to do what's necessary.

Let her hate me—I won't hold it against her.

I'm willing to be the one that shoulders the burden of doing what must be done... It is better for that weight to be concentrated on one person—for the guilt to be isolated as much as possible. This kind of self-sacrifice is one of the only redeeming qualities afforded to an irredeemable bastard like me—the power unique to the irredeemable is that we can do the necessary evils so that others can remain untainted and decent.

On the other hand, I'm a strange mixture of confused, terrified, angry... and elated that Vivian is here.

I've missed her so much, but... this is not the circumstance I wanted to see her again under.

Even if she is one hell of a fighter and capable in all the ways Nona is not.

"Rowan, we need to talk—ALONE," says both Nona and Vivian in unison.

"Ah... sure..." I say, not sure who I'm addressing.

"You can wait your turn, *princess*," says Vivian, her tone suggesting she's already decided to dislike Nona.

Nona, taken aback by the sudden hostility from a person she doesn't even know, doesn't so much fold as she does disintegrate—like a roll of toilet paper hit with a water cannon.

"S-Sure... Okay then..."

"Let's talk in there," I say, pointing at a two-story building that was at one point a clothing store.

...

The abandoned store provides little privacy—its skeletal remains a maze of broken mannequins and shattered aisles—but we manage to find a manager's office in the back of the first floor.

Me and Vivian step inside, leaving Nona to keep a lookout.

"Put my mind to rest, Rowan. Convince me you're not half as simple-minded as all the evidence to the contrary would suggest. Because—so help me—if you are here for my sake... I will string you up from a tree with all 15 feet of your own lower intestine—and I will *personally* find, capture, tame, and train some beast of this wretched place to devour you one bite at a time—starting with the things you don't necessarily need to support your continued miserable existence. Given how fast your body heals itself, who can say how long you'll last—so long as I also train the beast to feed and water you like some kind of grotesque houseplant?" demands Vivian, her entire body vibrating with rage.

"It's good to see you again too, Vivy," I say, stalling for time to think.

"Don't... call me *that*."

"Old habits... Sorry," I say with a shrug.

Nona isn't around, so Vivian takes off her mask and sets it down on a desk next to her.

It's the first time I've really seen her in half a year, the brief moment when I had torn her mask off going by too fast to count.

Her amethyst eyes sear right through me.

"I will take your silence as an admission of your stupidity—you're here for my sake—which means you know about... The Fade. Britannica told you, I'm guessing?" Vivian says, suddenly sounding tired instead of outraged.

...

"I am, but lis—" I begin, trying to mount my defense, but Vivian cuts me off.

"I don't *want* you here," she says.

...

"I know."

"I don't want *you...* period."

...

Somewhere in my heart, a switch flips, preemptively numbing me to the pain I know is coming.

"I... know. I know. I get that, Vivian, but can you just—"

"It's not sweet. It's not chivalrous or brave or noble..."

I turn away—not wanting to look at her too closely.

If I do, I might see real contempt there—I might see disgust—or worst of all, I might see nothing at all—apathy, indifference... and I couldn't take that.

"...How does this all play out in your head, Rowan? Let me take a guess..." Vivian takes a step closer.

She rests a finger on my chest.

"You think I just don't understand the depth of your feelings. You've been imagining romantic scenes... you give me a potion in a crystal bottle, and not only is the evil witch's curse lifted, but I also realize I've been a fool and fall into your arms... Am I getting warm at all?"

...

I'm ashamed by how close to the mark she really is—but her words also spark fresh anger in me—rage boils up inside me with an intensity I did not know I was still capable of feeling—and on some level, I am relieved. After months of cold detachment that muted every emotion, it is good to know there is still enough of me left to feel outraged.

I'm doing this for *her* sake—just as I have done nearly everything for her sake ever since we were little kids... and this is what I get in return?

"After all the things we've been through, you've tossed me aside, and now you treat me like some kind of *delusional* stalker—and I'm supposed to just accept that?" I demand.

"I... was a stupid kid, Rowan. People are allowed to change their minds. Childhood crushes never go anywhere—they're not even *supposed* to go anywhere. I'm allowed to grow up, even if you refuse to... or simply *can't*," replies Vivian.

...

"Did you ever actually care about me, Vivian?" I ask.

...

"You always ask the wrong questions, dammit! I grew up beside you... you were there, *specifically* to take care of me...You cared about me more than my wonderful family ever did. So of course, I... *cared* about you... I may have felt... *something*... at one point. But feelings fade. Nothing lasts—and I never promised you otherwise—never promised you forever. That's just... entropy—it is a law of the universe as much as gravity is—*get over it*. Everyone has a first—but you'll notice most people end up having more than just the one. You only *think* you need me... because you don't have anyone else."

The finger resting over my heart went rigid as she spoke, jabbing into me to add extra emphasis to particular words.

"Oh yeah? Well, I don't see anyone else here with you, Vivian. If you've made a bunch of friends these last six months apart, then they're not doing you much good. Seems like you're as alone as I am—in the end," I snap.

Vivian's face flushes red in a way that tells me my words have struck a critical hit.

Sensing a rare moment of speechlessness from her, I decide to continue.

"You... have no clue, no clue at all. How much it meant to me to be valued by someone like... *you*." I pause, trying to avoid saying anything too horribly stupid. "... Your father gave me to you as a gift, all those years ago. I spent *years*, absolutely content with that arrangement—happy to be of service... After all, I was a piece of trash before that. So... that was still a step up in the world for me. More than I deserved. And I had you to thank. I worked... *so hard*... to make myself into someone who *did* deserve it..." I start in a calm, steady voice... but by the end, I'm close to yelling.

I turned up the intensity of the voice distortion feature in my mask—just as Vivian had done earlier as a part of her disguise—so that the emotion in my voice would be replaced with a clinical, robotic kind of detachment.

"... I never dreamed of any higher aspiration than that, never imagined, not for one second, that I could ask for anything more. Until *you* started to see me as more than what I was—until you started to treat me... like I was something more than that to you. And then, not only did you want me to just accept, without any real explanation, that your feelings for me were over—you also decided you couldn't stand to have me around—period. You tossed me aside like a piece of filth—what exactly did I do to deserve that, *Lady Restless*?"

Vivian flinches almost imperceptibly at my use of her formal title—a title I haven't addressed her by in private for many years.

"*Rowan*, I—"

"WHAT DID I DO?! Why did you decide you should make me feel irrepl aceable... right before showing me I was actually *anything* but?"

Vivian returns her mask to her face.

"*Tell* me!"

Vivian's hands clench into fists at her sides.

...

"Do you really want me to say it?" she asks.

I nod.

...

"I didn't *need* you anymore, Rowan... you were a crutch, a comfort blanket that I outgrew. Worse than that—at some point, you started to get in the way. Just as you are, yet again... You act like you're doing this for me, but you know this is not what I want—which means you're doing it for yourself. Maybe I loved you at one point—hard to say anymore—but what I do know for a fact... is that I don't love you now."

...

It takes every ounce of self-control and self-respect I have to beat back the tears—even though I know I'd be the only one to know it if I did let them come with my mask on.

"Okay, Vivian."

19

EVEN IF YOU HATE ME

I find myself sitting down on a crate, with no memory of ever having decided to do so.

As if a mask isn't enough, I hide my face behind my hands as well.

The half-rotten door we had closed behind us is thrown open.

"Her sister was right, Rowan—You're the one that's too good for her, not the other way around!" Nona shouts.

"You... were *listening* to us!?" demands Vivian.

"Well, I mean... you weren't exactly being quiet, were you? I didn't hear it all, but I heard enough... I won't pretend to understand this completely, but what I do know is that Rowan is devoted to you... and you don't seem to appreciate it—*at all*!"

Nona turns on me.

"I'm so angry with you. I couldn't believe what you did back there, Rowan... It was inexcusable—People are... *dead*... but... I know you did it for *her*... and I understand that what you did is the reason we were able to make it out of there." Nona shakes her head in dismay. "... What I don't understand is why you would care so much about someone who would treat you like that—*abuse you* like that!" Nona turns away from me to address Vivian again.

"You should apologize to him—Then, you should thank him for risking so much to try and help you."

...

I don't have any idea what I should say in this moment.

Vivian also seems to be at a loss for words.

I just stare between Nona and Vivian like a deer in headlights.

"...WHO the hell even are you? *I don't even know your name, little girl*—and you're giving me self-righteous lectures about something you know *nothing* about! If you think that little exchange you just heard constitutes *'abuse'*—then you've lived a life so FUCKING sheltered that you surely wake up to an angel's chorus of affirmations in the morning, and get tucked into bed at night with a kiss on the cheek from daddy and a quick suckle from mommy's over-inflated milkers, before drifting off to sweet dreams of ethically sourced gumdrops and lollipops as far as your innocent little eyes can see. But you're right about one thing... his *obsessive* loyalty to me *is* misplaced. So leave. Both of you. Get out of my sight!"

Nona acts as if Vivian had just slapped her across the face—taking an involuntary step back and shrinking away under Vivian's verbal onslaught.

"W-We can't separate... there is no going back—even if we wanted, and you will... die... on your own... we need to stay together..." says Nona, suddenly *much* more timid and uncertain sounding than before.

Apparently, her ability to be assertive is limited to short bursts and is conditional on it being on someone else's behalf.

"Don't give a damn. Rowan can sneak back if he really wants to—might have to wait awhile for an opportunity with the FireJacks on such high alert, but he could manage it. As for you... *whatever*—why should I care? And I can look after myself—I don't need *anyone*. And I most certainly don't need either of you," replies Vivian savagely.

...

"I won't," I say.

...

"You won't... *what*?" asks Vivian, annoyance dripping from her every word.

"Leave you." I stand up.

"I *will* follow you. I will do what I can to keep you safe—even if you hate me for it. I will not abandon you, even if that's what you want. You either kill me, or I'll follow you... Because I'm not convinced you don't need me—no matter how much you pretend to be some invulnerable hard-ass who doesn't need a man's protection. And nothing you can say will convince me otherwise," I say.

...

Nona looks back and forth between us nervously.

...

"Do whatever you want, *idiot*," says Vivian before storming out of the room.

"Rowan, let's hurry up and leave... it's not good to stay in one place for too long out here, and we haven't exactly been keeping quiet," squeaks Nona.

I nod, and we rejoin Vivian in the next room, who seems to be checking her gear.

"Nona thinks we—" I begin to say.

Tap, tap, tap... tap, tap, tap...

There is a tapping sound against a boarded-up window that makes me and Nona freeze, already on edge.

I unholster my pistol and aim it at the window, weighing the potential benefit of maybe killing whatever is on the other side by blindly firing through it against the danger of making so much noise... more importantly, such a distinctly man-made noise.

"No! You moron, that's just Poe... I sent her out ahead of me for some recon before even bothering with the Jacks," says Vivian.

"Poe?" asks Nona timidly.

Vivian walks over to the wood-covered window and taps back, mimicking Poe, before studying the wood for a second and deeming it weak enough to be dealt with by her bare hands.

Sure enough, Vivian rips it away with ease.

Nona mutters something about it being "not *that* impressive" under her breath.

No way in hell Nona could have gotten that plank of wood off herself, even with a crowbar.

Nona lets out a startled yelp and gets behind me as a raven, far larger than any naturally occurring raven has ever been, flies into the dusty room.

I don't blame Nona for her reaction; Poe is so large it's rather surprising she can fly at all, and her beak looks just as dangerous as my still unholstered gun.

Poe was obviously genetically modified not only for her terrifying size but also for a dramatically enhanced intelligence… making her about as intelligent as a 6 or 7-year-old child.

"Poe, come here! It sure took you long enough," barks Vivian.

"Poe! Hey, I've *missed* you!" I say, glad to see the bird again after so long.

Poe cocks her head in my direction, and after a moment, recognition strikes.

Making happy bird noises, she dances over to my side to greet me.

Vivian raises her hands above her head in exasperation.

Poe is very well trained, but she has the autonomy to disobey when she really wants to.

Like right now.

Poe happily nuzzles her head against me.

"Really, Poe? Ignoring me for *him* of all people… you traitor…" mutters Vivian.

Poe was another gift from her father, presented to her only a few years after I was.

Nona peeks out from behind me, either because she's embarrassed to look so afraid in front of Vivian or because Poe's sudden display of friendliness has put her at ease.

I pet Poe behind her head briefly before she dances away to stand in front of Vivian.

Poe starts to gesture and squawk in her rudimentary method of communicating that only Vivian can ever understand.

Nona cocks her head to one side, confused.

Poe proceeds to draw crude shapes in the layer of dirt that coats the floor with her massive talons.

I step a little closer to try and puzzle out her artwork's meaning myself.

It looks like...

Nothing—it looks like absolutely nothing recognizable to me.

"A storm is coming from the East," says Vivian.

"Are you... totally sure?" says Nona, not trying to hide her skepticism in the slightest.

"These shapes are clouds, these lines are lightning, and this thick line here indicates direction," Vivian says.

"Not a big deal, a little rain never killed... Nona?" I start to say but stop to watch Nona climb up onto a desk I'd used to barricade the door behind us when we first entered the building.

Her fingers were running along the moldy wall just above the door frame.

"We need to hurry before the storm gets here! Can we get a time estimate from, ah... Poe?" says Nona, sounding suddenly anxious.

"It's only a few hours till nightfall, plenty of buildings here to wait out a storm in... might as well shelter here," I suggest.

"No! We need to leave as fast as possible, *seriously*," says Nona.

"But... *why*?" I ask, perplexed.

"This is a water line. We're in a flood zone..." Nona points up at the moldy mark running across the top of the wall.

"There is absolutely no way the water rises that high whenever it rains... even if it has done so before, it doesn't mean it will happen just whenever there is a little rain," says Vivian, annoyed.

"Please, just *trust* me on this... the trees right outside—it's unmistakably a Feeder Dam colony!" pleads Nona, as if that information is supposed to mean something to us.

"Trees? Why should I give a damn about some trees because it's about to rain?" says Vivian, determined to be uncooperative.

"Vivy… it's better for us to risk being overly cautious than not cautious enough out here—we should trust her on this. She's an expert, not us," I say, trying to sound as impartial as possible.

"*Stop* calling me that… and what exactly makes the *princess* such an expert on the stupid trees?" replies Vivian.

"Well, I'm a scientist, and No Man's Land has been one of my areas of research… *and you're closer to being a princess than I am—you're like the modern-day nobility, not me…*" Nona mutters the last bit so that it's barely audible.

I smile slightly, glad that the irony hasn't escaped her attention.

Vivian pauses, and I suspect I know why.

Nona very clearly isn't an Amelior.

In Prospera, the Naturals are not really allowed into the hard sciences, not because of any formal rules but because they generally just cannot compete on the tests with so many Amelior super-geniuses involved.

"She's from Neo Kyoto, Vivy. She really is a scientist," I interject, not wanting her to start a fight by calling Nona a liar for no reason.

"Oh…" says Vivian, taken aback.

"…But *still*, we're on a slope! Prospera sits on high ground, with the elevation decreasing as you move away from the city. So, HOW could this area possibly flood? All the water would just keep flowing downhill!" counters Vivian.

Right on cue, the first clap of thunder cuts into the conversation, interrupting Vivian.

"Rowan, *please*? Let's go—we really, *really* need to hurry." Nona turns away from Vivian and towards me, close enough for me to see the anxiety in her eyes.

Vivian actually makes a pretty good point, but still… I feel inclined to trust Nona for now and ask for an explanation later.

"Yes, you two go… don't mind me," says Vivian.

I sigh and sit down.

"I told you, Vivy... I go where you go. As you said before, I'm basically a delusional, obsessive stalker. So, for sick freak like me, drowning together in this shack would be a dream come true—no better way to die," I say.

Nona laughs in an uncomfortable kind of way.

Vivian, I'm sure, is scowling under her mask.

There is a second clap of thunder.

...

"*Fine,*" relents Vivian bitterly.

I knew we'd get there.

Churchill had this quote, something about the Americans and how they would always do the right thing... *eventually*... after they'd exhausted every other option.

That's Vivian in a nutshell, I think.

She'll argue and complain every step of the way, but she's secretly a very reasonable, dependable person.

Even if she hates me now, the possibility of her own stubbornness being what gets the three of us killed wouldn't sit well with her.

Once we've decided to get moving, Vivian is the first to have her pack on and make it out the door. I hold back to help Nona get her pack on after I watch her struggle to get it off the ground for a few moments.

"Make sure you use the hip straps—you don't want to carry too much weight on your shoulders," I tell her, already resigned to the fact that Nona won't be the one carrying Nona's pack this whole journey—but hoping to delay the inevitable as long as possible.

I tighten one of her straps for her.

"Also..." I lower my voice to a whisper.

"... Please, help me keep an eye on Vivian; I... think she might try to run off on her own if the opportunity ever presents itself."

"Oh, wouldn't that be such a pity..." mutters Nona, but I decide to still interpret that as a begrudging "okay".

Poe caws at us to hurry up.

20

WATER HAZARDS

Ballagàrraidh *noun*

The awareness that you, as a modern human, do not truly belong in the wilderness.

To Vivian's annoyance, Nona takes the lead.

Neither I nor Vivian came prepared to navigate—GPS does not work with this tree canopy, and... Nona is the only one who thought to bring—or who knows how to *use*—a map and protractor.

I am, needless to say, appropriately ashamed of myself for that obvious oversight.

Fortunately, however, Prosper Electronica just so happens to own the few navigation satellites that service Prospera's high-altitude flights, as well as her population's individual consumers. So, *if* we ever can get above the tree canopy to check our location with GPS, we will be able to do so without drawing unwanted outside attention. Not that it really matters—after the scene we all just caused to get past the FireJack perimeter, no doubt Prospera will be awash with conspiracy theories galore.

Nona is the least physically fit and nearly useless in a fight, but... I'm starting to appreciate how lost we would be out here without her. Literally.

Now that we're actually on the move, Nona seems to have forgotten her anxiety and seems more excited than anything.

If we were not in such a rush, I feel certain she would be taking notes or samples of everything we passed.

But for me and Vivian, all this... *life*...

It's unnerving.

Everywhere I look, there are strange plants and animals, faintly glowing yellow mushrooms almost as tall as Nona, birds that flit from branch to branch singing impossibly complex songs, and tiny flowers that at first seem to hover magically in the air... but after Vivian reaches out to touch one, Nona informs us that they are actually held aloft by strands of spider's web... and that said spiders are hidden among the flowers.

Vivian quickly retracts her outstretched hand and shivers slightly when Nona informs her of this.

There is also a constant faint rustling in the trees... as if an unceasing wind reaches out to touch everything but us—which gives the disconcerting impression that behind every branch hides some unseen creature.

When I ask Nona about it, she happily explains that the plant life here grows *so* quickly that it creates a faint, ceaseless movement.

In other words... No Man's Land grows so freakishly fast that—if we stopped to study it—we would be able to observe its growth in real-time—like watching time-lapse footage of a normal plant's growth.

That information strikes a chord of both wonder and dread within me. But this explains why the FireJacks have made such little progress after years of fighting off the invading wildlife.

There is absolutely no plant life in Prospera other than the agriculture we have no choice but to tolerate—I have never even been within striking distance of real live trees before today. Prosperans somehow hate both the imitation of life represented by intelligent machines and the natural life of the great outdoors—the only kind of life we're not deeply distrustful of is mankind or the occasional household pet—and even people we're not totally sold on humans—judging by our world-famous homicide rates.

It's nothing personal—we're just pragmatic in Prospera—the machines tried to wipe us out in The Great Synthetic War, the plants and animals of No Man's Land are trying to kill us currently, and people have been killing one another since the first caveman realized that there are many benefits to putting sharp things in the second caveman's squishy bits.

The only gods we worship in Prospera are other people, the only monuments we build are to ourselves, and we're smart enough to know our self-proclaimed gods are the highly fallible, self-serving types.

...

Nona gives a sigh of relief when we find a small stream, telling us to alter our course slightly to follow it.

"There's no way that map shows this insignificant stream... So why are we going off course to follow it?" demands Vivian.

"Well, because this little stream won't be so little for much longer, and following it will be the most direct route. It's worth the slight detour, I pinky promise," says Nona, holding up the little finger of her right hand.

I can almost *hear* Vivian's face muscles contracting under her mask as she tries to process Nona's attempt to reassure her with the offer of a pinky promise, of all things.

I know Vivian is on the verge of arguing again, so I jump in to intercept her.

"Vivy, you should take rear security. My hearing hasn't been the same since some idiot recently fired his shotgun at me in Fell's Point... I won't hear anyone if they try to follow us—but you might." It's a lie, but I tell myself it's for a good cause.

If Vivian argues with her for long enough—or if she gets insistent enough, Nona will probably buckle and let Vivian start calling the shots... Sometimes that would be for the best, but not right now—not in a place like this.

If I had to, I could back Nona up, but... I'd rather avoid another fight, and I do not want to encourage Vivian to ditch us at the first opportunity... Even though I suspect she might already be planning to do just that.

Also, frankly... It is still difficult for me to find the will to go against Vivian... Half a lifetime spent as her personal property cannot just be undone after six months apart, even if Vivian never really treated me like just another piece of property... That is what I was.

But she had rarely ever needed to order me around; I'd just always considered what she would want and made it so—assuming she didn't want anything that was going to be bad for her.

I smile to myself, remembering the nearly two years I spent mixing carbonated water with lime and a spoonful of mouthwash and then telling her that they were Margaritas—all because she was going through a rebellious phase and wanted to experiment with drinking.

She was positively livid when she found out—but not half as livid as her father would have been if he had caught her doing something as undisciplined and illogical as drinking alcohol.

I turn to look over my shoulder.

"Vivy, I—"

Vivian's cloak catches on a log, and she stumbles.

Without thinking, I move to catch her.

...

And just like that, we're touching.

My heart skips a beat, and my stomach does a backflip into my throat.

At least we're both wearing our masks.

...

Vivian doesn't curse me or shove me aside as I would have guessed.

But she freezes, her body going rigid... before untangling herself from me without a word of acknowledgment and continuing on as if nothing had happened.

Somehow, that reaction from her hurts more than blatant rudeness would have.

Do I really make her so uncomfortable now? Is physical contact with me—even the trivial, accidental kind—so unbearable?

I turn to resume walking just in time to catch Nona watching.

She really does love not minding her own damned business.

I berate myself for my lack of focus; losing my vigilance out here will end up getting Vivian and Nona killed for sure.

I feel the first few raindrops make contact with the back of my neck.

"Fiddlesticks... We need to go faster—we're nearly out of time," Nona says anxiously—taking me aback momentarily with perhaps her most infantile cursing-alternative word choice thus far.

I turn my head to follow Nona's line of sight.

What was, until very recently, unambiguously a stream is now swelled to something not quite a river but certainly more than just a gentle little stream.

More than that, it makes me nervous that she's nervous.

"We're going this speed for your sake, princess. We can speed up whenever you decide you're in the mood to," says Vivian.

Vivian is not wrong... though I wish she could be a little more diplomatic about how she said it.

Nona's hood is down for the sake of staying cool, so I can see her ears going red despite her mask.

I'm sure Nona felt like she was setting a brisk pace before, but if it was me, or even worse, *Vivian*, in the lead setting the pace...

"She has to do the navigating, Vivy, that would slow—"

Thunder rumbles from somewhere too close for comfort.

Nona looks at me and smiles with a kind of soft gratitude, using nothing but her eyes.

She determinedly speeds up her pace and, for a few minutes, we make good progress, but...

Vivian has bullied Nona into going at a pace she cannot maintain for long, and soon enough, she starts to slow down again.

Vivian makes a show of passing her, still having hardly broken a sweat up to this point.

This starts to worry me, as I'm nervous about letting Vivian out of my sight in case she makes a run for it, but I also don't want to leave Nona behind in case she, well...

Dies.

"Vivian, hold up—You'll go off course without a navigator," I say.

Vivian stops up ahead, arms crossed and foot tapping the ground impatiently as she waits for us to catch back up.

But then... something very strange starts to happen.

Water starts to fall all around us—nothing strange about that in itself, considering that it's just started to rain, but...

The water is not only falling from the clouds—it's also flowing out of the ends of the tree branches.

I can see it in the lowest hanging branches; water flows out of holes in the wood like a sink faucet being turned all the way on.

"W-We... need to... RUN!" yells Nona in a breathless voice that does not inspire confidence in her ability to follow her own advice.

With a sigh, I hook the Compression Ax I scavenged off the dead FireJack to my belt, swing my pack onto the front of my body as if I'm hugging it, and motion over at Nona.

"Come on, climb on my back... *princess*." I don't think she'll appreciate me using the same diminutive nickname as Vivian, but I can't resist teasing her a little as payment for my services.

I at least try to soften my voice at the end so she knows I'm not actually annoyed with her.

Vivian scoffs.

"A-Are you sure? I have my knapsack too..." she says, sounding very tired and very embarrassed.

Knapsack? How old is she, five?

I nod.

"I could use the exercise, anyway, don't worry."

"We're going to *drown* while you two make stupid small talk," says Vivian before she starts moving again.

Nona climbs on, and I jog after Vivian.

If not for the two packs, this probably wouldn't be so bad, but with them and Nona hanging off me, I doubt I can keep this up for more than a mile or two.

Still, we're undoubtedly making much faster progress than before.

"Just hug the stream for as long as possible!" calls Nona from over my head.

"Shut up! I already was, dammit!" calls back Vivian.

That stream will be a roaring river before long—and there is already a thin layer of water across the forest floor that the ground seemingly has no intention of soaking up.

Poe sits on Vivian's pack now, having returned from scouting ahead while I was getting Nona situated on my back.

...

Fifteen minutes later and the water is up past my knees.

Rain falls in a torrent, adding to the constant gush of water from the tips of the tree branches all around us, which has turned this whole section of No Man's Land into a flood zone.

The only mercy afforded to us is that we're moving downhill—with the current of the water instead of against it.

But regardless, I'm starting to lose steam.

"Sorry, Nona... but... I need a... *break!*" I gasp, stopping to let her climb off of me.

"It's fine! I'm all rested up now, don't worry!" replies Nona.

Up ahead, Vivian lets out a startled yelp.

I pull the pistol from its holster.

"Something just bumped up against my leg!" Vivian shouts, not exactly panicking but... clearly not enjoying herself.

"Just ignore it! Keep going!" yells Nona.

"Th-The trees! Let's climb up a damn tree!" I yell, cursing myself for not thinking of this obvious plan earlier.

"No! Definitely do NOT do that... That's why *they* want us to do..." replies Nona, sounding like she is also not at all having a good time.

The hell... *They*? THEY?!

I look up, scanning the trees, and catch movement in the high branches as well as a set of glowing eyes—reflective like a cat's.

My feet can no longer reach the forest floor at all.

"Almost there, look!"

Up ahead is a curving wall of wood—it's as if we're swimming inside of a massive wooden bowl that's half buried and protruding out of the side of a mountain.

But the side of the bowl is not smooth wood—it's more like one massive tree trunk that has grown out of the ground in the shape of a curved wall.

Water continues to pour from the tips of tree limbs as if they are nothing but cleverly disguised piping.

"S-Spiders!" Sputters Vivian, the water level high enough now that her head has gotten tangled with the pretty purple flowers we saw earlier, suspended in midair by the spider webs.

"Not... venomous!" shouts Nona, who is swimming with her luckily buoyant pack held out in front of her.

That's a small kindness, I think, as I smack a spider the size of my hand off the back of my head.

We're nearly at the wall now—we're moving fast, pulled forward by a very strong current.

I'm close to drowning, never having bothered to learn more than the bare minimum of swimming necessary to not drown the instant I hit the water.

My pack does not float the way Nona's seems to—my gear is at risk of dragging me below the surface and drowning me... but if I indiscriminately dump everything, I'll still die out here—only slower.

Vivian is up ahead, struggling almost as much as I am to keep her head above water.

And then, something bites my leg.

I scream, more in surprise than pain—the bite felt more experimental than intended for serious damage—like the creature was testing my edibility.

My right-hand finds a tree branch, and I half pull myself out of the water, giving myself the elevation necessary to aim my pistol down and send some haphazard shots into the shadowy water around my legs.

"NO, Rowan!"

I turn at the sound of Nona's cry, just in time to see a set of wickedly sharp claws flash in the sunlight, catching me on my shoulder.

I lose my grip on the branch and fall back into the water.

"Rowan! Are you okay?" Vivian tries and fails to swim against the current in order to check on me.

"I'm... *fine*," I gasp, spitting out a lungful of water I'd accidentally swallowed.

"We're about to be there! We need explosives—a grenade!" shouts Nona.

"I-I have one!" I fumble for one from the contents of my pack.

"The current is going to pull us under soon! Once we get too near the wall, the current will become impossible to resist! We... need to... get that grenade to the wall—way, WAY ahead of us!"

That makes no sense—there is zero chance this single grenade is going to blow a hole in a wall that size...

"WHAT are you talk—"

"Just throw it! As far as you can! NOW!" screams Nona, in a state of barely contained panic.

I do.

I catch onto another tree branch with my injured arm and pull myself up, needing a solid platform to get the maximum range out of my throw.

With every ounce of strength I have, I propel the grenade towards the wall.

The grenade goes far, no less than 50 meters—modern grenades being built with distance throws in mind.

It flies high over Vivian's head—a massive relief—but... It still falls short of the wall by at least five meters.

"DAMN—It fell short!" I yell.

"NO—PERFECT!" shouts Nona.

I sense movement in the tree behind me and release my hold on the branch, falling back into the water.

A few seconds later, the grenade detonates, sending a shock wave thundering through my body.

"HOLD YOUR BREATH!" yells Nona before disappearing under the water.

Vivian takes a huge breath and lets herself be dragged down as well.

I try to copy them, but halfway through breathing in, water finds its way in, and I start to gag.

I'm underwater.

There is not a lot of light, the trees above blocking much of what's left of the day's sunlight... but the water is clear.

I'm rushing towards a hole in the wooden dam, a massive one, as large as a family car, at least.

Did that grenade really...?

No, wait... I can see what looks to be ruined netting—vines or maybe roots... they must have spanned the width of the opening before the grenade went off.

This's how this monstrous, mutant tree kills; it pulls you under only to tangle you in its vines and drown you.

Why it wants us drowned, I do not know—but the explosion of the grenade has decimated the vine netting that had spanned the opening in the dam's side.

I can feel my head spinning, deprived of oxygen.

My vision starts to go black around the peripheries. The parasite in my chest can help with a lot of things—but it cannot supply me with oxygen.

...

This is not how I imagined I'd go out.

I don't want my death to mirror my wasted life—meaningless, painful, cold... alone.

Did Vivian and Nona make it out, at least?

They might have a chance if they stay together.

I wonder if anyone will care that I'm dead?

Will Vivian?

I would... like for someone to miss me—even if it's only one person, that would be something.

No... that's a very selfish thought, isn't it? Wanting someone to suffer because you've gone and died like a fool.

The water crushes me. It invades my body and smoothers the life from every cell. It renders all my anger, all my defiance mute.

But all the same, even with all the pain... maybe this isn't such a bad way to die.

There is a kind of peacefulness to it—a surprising quiet.

I stop trying to fight it.

.

..

...

21

Children's Fun Fact Science Corner

I wake up to see Nona's face hovering over mine.

Her... *actual* face—no mask.

I bring a hand up to feel my own face after registering the unfamiliar touch of a breeze against my skin.

No mask there, either...

The air against my bare skin felt strange—A wave of vulnerability surges through me—making me feel like a child again and hating it.

Do I... still have my scarf?

My hands fly to my neck.

The familiar touch of frayed cloth is missing.

"Rowan! Oh, thank goodness, you had us so w—" Nona begins.

"M-My scarf! Have you seen it?" I ask, my stomach twisting into a knot as if to compensate for the sudden absence of one around my neck.

Nona stares at me like I've grown a second head—her mouth open and her eyes wide in surprise.

'Y-Your voice... why do you sound *so* different?" she asks.

I feel my face start to burn.

"I... Of course I sound different—without my mask, I don't have the built-in Voice Mod that comes with it! What's more surprising is that *you* have been casually using your real voice this whole time—it's as if you want someone to steal your damned identity..." I reply.

"Well, if people don't know it's my real voice, they won't think to try and make a deep fake with it, right?" asks Nona.

All I can do is shake my head in dismay at her insanity.

Nona breaks out into a fit of giggles.

"Here I was thinking that deep, macho-man voice was your real one! You sound so much younger without it... it's cute though—your fake one was sorta intimidating, I think," finishes Nona.

My humiliation is total.

"I'm going to go drown myself for real if you keep this up, Nona."

"Oh hush, your real voice is—" begins Nona.

"I guess you *still* haven't learned to swim worth a damn... a grown man, *seriously* pathetic..." Vivian's caustic tone slices through the air.

I turn to look at her... she's also without a mask.

But my eyes also notice something crimson-red hanging from her hands.

My heart skips a beat at the sight of the familiar fabric—relief flooding my every pore.

"Your voice is different, too! Not nearly as different as Rowan's is, though," says Nona, sounding again surprised to learn that she has been hearing a false voice this entire time.

"Shut it—you're the weird one here for not having modified yours!" says Vivian before turning to look at me.

Vivian throws the soaked scarf at me—hitting me right in the face with a wet smack.

I put the scarf back around my neck, pulling it up so that it at least hides the bottom third of my face in place of a proper mask.

Vivian's thick, silvery-purple hair is an absolute mess—she's also cut and bruised all over.

...

I didn't think I'd ever see her face again.

I smile.

"What the *hell* are you so happy about? Should've let you drown, I swear! You are completely worthless... can't even hold your breath when told..." rages Vivian.

"What... happened? Did we manage to lose all our equipment?" I ask, worried and also still a little disoriented.

Nona smiles.

"We got most of it back while you were unconscious—Vivian went digging in the stream at the mouth of the hole—she found her bow, my pack, and even your ax! We did lose things, though, mostly small items like our masks," says Nona, not sounding at all bothered by this—even though she's the one with the best reason to hide her face.

"There were also scores of drowned animals—freaky things, like little monsters..." adds Vivian darkly.

"As for what happened, well, Vivian found you—" begins Nona.

Vivian stomps on Nona's foot and stares daggers at her—which effectively silences Nona.

Nona breaks eye contact with her, welting under the heat of Vivian's anger... the cause of which I'm unclear on.

"...L-Look over there!" Nona points behind me. I turn to see, elevated high above us, a great wooden dam with several openings still releasing the pent-up water pressure contained on the other side.

The opening we came through gushes the most water by far—the others have their netting clogged with whatever they managed to catch.

"Pretty, isn't it?" says Nona.

She's right.

The view is spectacular—waterfalls have erupted from the openings in this living piece of construction, and what looks like dozens of red birds dart around it, playing in the dam's branches and chasing each other around.

On top of that, the setting sun coats everything in a warm orange glow.

Hard to believe this surreal, fantasy painting of a landscape... just tried to murder us.

"It's called a Feeder Dam. Did you notice that all the trees we passed up there were the same species? There was lots of biodiversity in other ways, but the trees were all uniform in that huge section... that's because there was technically only one tree," says Nona.

"...Sorry, I don't follow," I reply, feeling only slightly stupid as my oxygen-starved mind tries to catch up.

"It's a clonal colony; it's all one *humongous* tree that has many different trunks, connected by a vast underground root system... It's evolved from something called a Pando Tree. There's a whole miniature ecosystem that revolves around it... for example, those little flowers we saw are aquatic plants that rise with the water and get caught in the Bubble Spider's webs, along with other insects that the spiders eat while they simultaneously pollinate the flowers... and in the trees are Blood Apes, they hunt animals that try to climb into the trees to escape the flooding and then scavenge the drowned bodies after as—"

"But... *why*? Why the flooding, and how does the tree know when to turn on the taps?" I interrupt, curiosity getting the better of me.

"Oh, yeah! Well, that's how they fertilize the ground, isn't it? And just as important, it kills off the competing trees, so it doesn't have to share nutrients or sunlight. The Feeder Dam stores up MASSIVE quantities of water, then once it has enough, it waits for a rainstorm and unleashes it all at once, drowning everything in its territory. The quantity of water passing through the small holes generates massive water pressure, creating its own powerful current—the current sucks animals under, trapping them in the netting and killing them there. Once it's all over, there will be loads of dead plant and animal life that will decay and provide nutrients to the colony—and the animals that rely on the colony...." says Nona, only pausing her explanation because she's run out of breath.

She takes in a lungful of air.

"...Pretty neat, *right*?" She asks excitedly, taking my silence as a sign that I'm awe-struck by the majesty of nature or something.

"Ah-ha, yeah, it really is," I say, unable to find the heart to tell her that I think it's also kind of horrific. Amazing, yes... but also terrifying... Brutal.

"Sorry to interrupt the Children's Fun Fact Science Corner, but... the light is nearly gone. I sent Poe out to give some warning if anything big comes our way, but she won't be able to do as well in the dark... I'm not the *expert* here, but I doubt somehow that we want to stay out in the open after nightfall," says Vivian.

Nona nods her agreement, suddenly looking anxious... as if in her excitement, she forgot for a moment that this was anything more than a field trip.

I point at what looks to be a two-story home a few hundred meters away, half-hidden by vegetation.

It had the makings of a once beautiful home, not a mansion but still definitely a luxurious home with a scenic view of this little stream that might have once been closer to a river—before the Feeder Dam set down roots and starved it of a steady water supply.

Neither of them has any objections, so we gather our gear and make our way over.

...

A few minutes later, I'm kicking open the door.

Me and Vivian start clearing it, weapons raised and Nona sticking close behind me.

It's not as eerie as I had expected—before kicking the door, I had pictured scenes from horror flicks—children's toys littering the ground, strange writing on the walls, and maybe plates of decayed food on the dinner tables, the usual culprits.

But the family that owned this place clearly had the warning and the means to leave it in an orderly fashion before this area was surrendered to No Man's Land.

The rooms were mostly empty, with occasional boxes in corners with items not valuable enough to bother with—furniture totally gone besides a single stepping stool in a corner.

I notice Vivian running her hands over a door frame and curiously steal a look.

There are marks there with names and dates, a family keeping track of their children's growth spurts.

Vivian's expression is a vaguely sad one as she studies it—a rare moment of sentimentality from her.

I look away, not wanting her to know I was watching.

Nona is looking up at the ceiling.

"Is something the matter?" I ask.

"I... don't know, there are signs that something has been in here. Of course, it would be strange if there wasn't... but I'm not sure what made those mark—"

A shout and the sound of a person falling cuts Nona off.

I turn to see a spider larger than a golden retriever towering over Vivian, who fell and is scrambling back from the monster as fast as she can—trying to place some distance between herself and the lethal-looking fangs.

Eyes as large as bowling balls and as black as ink, curving fangs that move in a wholly unsatisfactory way—reminiscent of a deranged man biting his lip in anticipation of something horrible he's imagining inflicting on another person.

I launch myself at it—the newly stolen FireJack ax already in hand and ready.

The monster has quick reactions and darts to the side as I bring down the ax, moving in an unfamiliar way that is hard for me to predict.

Clearly, I've been spoiled all these years, getting to fight predominantly two-legged things.

The ax nicks one of the spider's hairy legs, causing that one appendage to reflexively pull back.

But the rest of the spider is pure instinctual aggression—without any hesitation, it tackles me, and I find myself falling backward as Vivian had, with my own reflection mirrored back at me many times over in the pitch-black orbs of the spider's eyes.

I see its fangs open wide and feel its body tense in the split-second remaining before it sinks the filthy things into me.

I do the only thing I can and jam my ax into its face, forcing it back slightly as it tries to bat away the heavy metal object pressed up against its snapping fangs.

And then I feel the spider's body give a great spasm, and I know Vivian has put an arrow into it from the other side.

The spider turns to go after its attacker, but I hook my ax on one of its fangs and yank its horrible face back down towards me, hell-bent on not letting it touch her.

I have never heard of a creature with eyes that were not soft, fragile—just all-around major weak spots.

So, I smash my free fist into one of the spider's huge eyes and feel it immediately give way under the impact.

Liquid sprays my face, and the monster lets out a screech unlike anything I have ever heard in my life.

One of its six massive limbs smacks me across the chest as it tries to put distance between itself and the prey that just blew out one of its eyes.

I jump to my feet and rush to capitalize on the damage I've done—determined to press the advantage and finish it off.

I raise the ax up—the spider brings up its two front legs as if to shield itself from me.

And then, an arrow spears through one of the other eyes, continuing on into the creature's brain.

There is a deafening quiet while the monster spasms, dying in much the same position as a house spider does when sprayed with poison—on its back and twitching grotesquely.

"Always... the fuckin'... *spiders... why*?" fumes Vivian, yanking her arrows out of the now still corpse and shuddering.

"We should go... This place is clearly not safe," I say.

"N-No! We should stay... That... was a Wood Stalker; they are solitary predators and very territorial... I think it's been in this house a lot, which means it should be the *only* thing in this house... if we go to a different one, we might have to fight something totally different, whatever thing has claimed that place as its home," says Nona.

Clever girl, that does make sense.

"But... what if it had a family... *babies*...?" says Vivian, disgusted at the very thought of a bug that big ever reproducing.

"No... There are months and months before the Wood Stalker's mating season, and they do not stick around to care for their young. They just lay the eggs and get the heck away. The babies hatch in a state of crazy hunger—they'll attack anything nearby... including the mother," says Nona.

Lovely.

I imagine thousands of puppy-dog-sized spiders eating their own mother and shudder.

"But..." Vivian casts a strained glance at the corpse.

Her reluctance suddenly makes sense to me—she's just not thrilled by the idea of sleeping in a building with this thing's corpse stinking up the place.

"Don't worry, Vivy, I'll get rid of it... just go find a good room to hold up in," I offer.

"I wasn't *worried* about anything..." mutters Vivian.

"Oh, great, you should throw it in the river and let it float off—if you just leave it in the front yard, there's no telling what will come to take it in the night..." adds Nona.

"Sure thing." I give her a thumbs up.

"Dork..." Vivian rolls her eyes and heads for the stairs.

I sigh.

No appreciation at all, ah well...

...

Needless to say, it's one of the top ten most unpleasant trash disposal jobs I've ever had to do.

After I return, I hand over my pistol and holster to Nona, who looks thoroughly uncomfortable even touching it, let alone using it.

"I've been thinking that I should let you hold onto this... all you have is a few knives, right? That's not nearly enough, and I'm better with my Compression Ax, anyway," I say, motioning towards it.

"I... have no experience with guns at all, and I'm... not sure I could bring myself to actually *shoot* someone... if I'm totally honest."

"I'll train you on the basics during our occasional free time before bedding down, and even if your *gentle, maidenly heart* can't bring itself to kill a perso n... animals are just as much a threat out here," I tease.

"I don't wanna kill the animals either, though... You think you're *such* a funny guy, don't you..." Nona holds the gun as far away from her as she can manage and with only two fingers—the way one might when holding a filthy rag—which causes her to very nearly drop it.

...

"B-But okay, I suppose you're right," she concedes.

"A pistol is by far the easiest weapon to get good enough to at least be dangerous with, with minimal training. I could teach you knife throwing as well, for example, but it is much more difficult and much less consistent than pointing a gun at the thing, squeezing the trigger, the thing dies, repeat."

After a moment, she nods and starts trying to put the holster on.

I watch her struggle for a moment, then bend down without a word, wrap the straps around her waist and right thigh, and secure it snugly in place.

Then I briefly show her the absolute basics, like the release button on the holster and the magazine release.

Vivian glances up at us from her pack, a sour look on her face.

Finally, I take the Unlocking Ring off and drop it into Nona's hand.

"Lose this, and it's nothing more than a paperweight. Later on, I'll teach you weapons safety rules and some basic weapons handling. Until then... probably best you don't mess with it. In fact... let me take the round out of the chamber real quick," I add, knowing that the gun's locking feature will stop her from shooting herself... but still nervous of the possibility that she might accidentally put a hole in me or Vivian, somehow.

"Don't know what that means, but sure..." she says with an amused little smile.

"Rowan! Are you seriously not going to help with setting traps, or what? This will take *forever* on my own..." Vivian snaps.

I look over at her and realize that she had been searching through her pack for booby traps.

Tripwire, nets, spikes, and plastic explosives already lay on the floor in front of her.

"Of course I'll help, Vivy. Are you hungry? I can get something started, then come lend you a hand..."

Vivian always gets a temper when she's hungry.

She narrows her eyes at me suspiciously.

"That... would be good, I *guess*," she grumbles.

I smile and go to find some preserved crab meat and rice, knowing it's a meal Vivian will approve of.

Vivian has always loved seafood—the only times she ate a meal with her family without complaint were the occasions when her family had the authentic stuff shipped from Kallipolis.

Kallipolis is the only city left with access to real seafood—having originally been built as a seasteading city and is thus sitting in the middle of the Mediterranean Sea.

Once I have it warming up inside a chem heater, I join Vivian.

Carefully, I unravel the tripwire and cut a suitably sized piece, trying to avoid the agony of having to untangle the stuff later.

"Never could have dreamed things would turn out this bad when we were kids..." Vivian sighs and shakes her head as she digs in her pack for a box of nails.

"It really puts all the most pessimistic, worst-case scenarios I could have dreamed up back then to shame," she finishes.

...

"I don't know... You getting The Fade is absolutely a nightmare, but... at least we have a chance. It's lucky that an experimental treatment was developed just in time for you to potentially benefit from it, and it is bullshit that we have to go through this for a chance at it, but it's also undoubtedly lucky that we were offered the chance at all. This is also, most definitely, more interesting than anything else I would otherwise be doing right now if I was back in Prospera." The optimism in my voice feels forced—as if I'm trying to convince myself as much as I am Vivian.

...

"How uncharacteristically optimistic of you... So, you really believe this search and rescue is the real deal and that they have a cure for the Fade?" asks Vivian.

...

"I did check to make sure a plane really went down as they say. As for the cure... It's common knowledge that Prosper Electronica does pharmaceutical and medical research as a side hustle—it's not totally beyond the realm of possibility. More importantly, you're an important person from an important family. Why would they risk going to war with your family by lying to you about a cure and then getting you killed? Our help can't be important enough to risk that," I say thoughtfully.

"I didn't tell my family. Besides, relations between the family and Prosper Electronica have only gotten worse since you left—it is already close to all-out war... getting me killed might be seen as a benefit worth the risk," Vivian replies.

That was an uncomfortable revelation to consider... But the fact remains that Prosper Electronica did not just solicit Vivian for this suicide mission—they also hired every Lancer they could... And Prosper Electronica relies on our mercenary muscle far too heavily for them to burn that bridge down lightly. The cure might be a lie, but the mission itself probably is not—and they used the same promise of a cure to get me out here.

"What? But... Corella... the House Guard... I assumed they came either to stop you from leaving the city or to help you complete the job, no? Corella definitely knows about you—she as good as told me so," I reply.

Vivian goes very still.

...

"Regardless, I don't believe Corella and the House Guard was at Gate 2 for my sake," she says.

"Well then, why?" I ask.

"I don't know, I think maybe there are a variety of reasons. For one, there is a Lancer here I know my family wants dead."

My mind goes back to the fight with the Thorn Lions.

"They were looking for someone, weren't they? One of the Lancers. I heard orders being yelled about capturing someone—not killing them," I say.

"I don't know... As I said, my family wants a variety of things. And Corella also has her own priorities. But I know she has issues with that big Lancer, Riot... He's dangerous. Hand me the wire cutters."

I do, processing this news.

"Corella scolded me for being a suicidal idiot back at the holding cell—Not sure why she cared enough to pay me a special jail visit just for tha—"

Vivian drops the wire cutters with a clatter.

...

"Rowan. Be honest with me—she didn't... *give* you anything, did she?"

Vivian's amethyst eyes cut through me like a pair of scalpels.

"*Give me*...? No, what would she possibly want to give me?" I ask, taken aback.

"... She is infuriating—I can't believe... my father as well, miserable old bastard..." mutters Vivian, ignoring my question.

I decide to drop it, recognizing that she won't give me a straight answer right now, regardless of how hard I might press.

"So, wanna tell me why you and your sister have been pretending to be twins? I know for a fact you've spent most of your life trying to be the antithesis of Corella," I ask, already suspecting I have a rough idea but asking regardless to keep the conversation moving.

"I promise I didn't relish the experience. It's just the outfit Corella has taken to conducting family business in when trying to be discrete... I know she maintains contact with some of the field-grade FireJack officers, and I know her well enough to impersonate her when I need to—I've learned to control the gag reflex. I thought pretending to be her on family business would be the best way to get past the FireJacks. I didn't think she'd show up on the very same day as me," says Vivian.

More or less what I'd expected.

"It was you at the Night Library, right? You were the one who flipped me off, not Corella?" I ask.

"Yeah, well... I was pissed off at you for being there. I still am. Might flip you off many more times before it is all done and over with, you idiot...Getting pissed off at you all over again thinking about it. But anyway... I needed a disguise, and that was the obvious choice. I didn't get enough prior notice of the Lancer's meeting to put something else together."

...

"Pretty sure Corella must have seen you dressed as her back there—she won't like that much... but hey, at least you won't run out of things to discuss over Christmas dinner this year, right? Unlike last time," I say, remembering how uncomfortable the atmosphere was by the end of dinner the holidays prior.

"I'd never miss out on an opportunity to upset my dear big sis... and with my family, an uncomfortable silence is the best possible outcome. It beats the hell out of us all trying—and failing—to pretend like we love each other." Vivian laughs as she forces an iron nail into the wood with nothing but the pressure of her fingertips pressing down against the nail's head.

I give a little shrug—the kind people use as if to say: "I mean, I didn't want to be the one to say it, buuut..."

Vivian's laugh is a wonderful thing.

Vivian tends to laugh at the wrong things sometimes, and she even snorts in a *very* unladylike way when she really finds something hilarious.

Her laugh is the opposite of Britannica's.

I have thought on many occasions in the past that Britannica's laugh is *effective*—like an expertly crafted tool. It's something Britannica uses strategically to dominate a conversation to make other people feel self-conscious... foolish.

Vivian's laugh, on the other hand, is clumsy—sometimes it's even a source of embarrassment for her...

But... It is also authentic—honest.

Vivian can be a little harsh, more than a little confrontational, and she speaks her mind even at the expense of other people's feelings.

But when she laughs, she loses all her sharp edges, all her mistrust of the world and the people in it.

I don't think anyone who really paid attention to Vivian's laugh for long enough could believe she is truly the unkind person she pretends to be... deep, *deep* down.

22

Small Acts of Kindness

History *Entry 3*

The rise and rapid spread of No Man's Land is the greatest natural disaster in all of human history—rendering 99.2% of the Earth's surface inhospitable for human occupation, killing billions of people, bringing an end to globalized economies, and eventually forcing humanity to retreat into the three greatest fortress cities left standing—The United States retreated into the mountain fortress of Prospera, the Mediterranean Confederacy gave way to the sea-steading settlement of Kallipolis, and The Constitutional Neo-Monarchy of the Orient took refuge in Neo Kyoto. None of the ruling governments survived this transition period, which is known to history as "The Unraveling". While this new era forced humanity to backslide by most metrics of societal advancement, it has ushered in a renewed focus on spacefaring—initially for the purpose of maintaining the planet's aging satellite infrastructure—but more recently with the intention of establishing human settlements, mineral mining, and scientific research on frontiers deemed less challenging than those on earth—even with the technological, logistic, and spatial difficulties of operating in space.

— *The Unraveled World: A History of Humanity's Decline & an Exploration of the New Normal, 3rd Edition*

"Right, so repeat after me—the First Weapons Safety Rule is to treat every weapon as if it were loaded... The Second Weapons Safety Rule is to never point your weapon at anything—"

"Sorry to interrupt..." interrupts Vivian, voice sounding anything but sorry.

"...But now seems as good a time as any to ask the obvious—Do you mind telling us *why* you look so much like our missing girl?" says Vivian, finally addressing the question I'm sure has been on her mind since her first good look at Nona after they pulled themselves out of the water, masks missing.

Nona did not lose her contact lens in the swim, though... If she had, I'm guessing Vivian would have already attempted to restrain her.

I feel my body tense.

It's a little surprising she even waited this long to ask.

Exactly how mad would Vivian be if she knew Nona did not just look similar to the missing girl... but practically identical?

Nona puts down the candy she had been snacking on.

I somehow doubt Vivian will be super understanding if Nona tells her she doesn't *know* why... I had a hard time—*still* have a hard time—buying that explanation myself... and Vivian already seems inclined not to like Nona very much—though I don't understand the reason for her open dislike yet.

Vivian is also even less predisposed to trusting people than I am, which doesn't help.

"I'm... her sister. Well... half-sister," lies Nona.

But on the other hand... Getting this out in the open now might be better than trying to lie to Vivian and almost certainly failing at it.

Nona doesn't know Vivian the way I do—all she's seen is Vivian picking fights and losing her temper—she doesn't know how good Vivian is at poking holes in a story...

“But... You said you were from Neo Kyoto, correct? Which parent do you share with this Kasca Haine? If it is your mother, how did she ever get romantically involved with one of the most powerful men in Prospera? And if it's your father, why would a father send one daughter of his to find the other one he already managed to misplace?” asks Vivian sharply.

"Ah... we share a mo—no, sorry I mean we share a dad, but I came here without his permission to find my sis—"

"So your Amelior father has not just one, but *two* illegitimate offspring? Because neither of you are Amelior, clearly—not with features like yours. Not only that, but Neo Kyoto granted you citizenship even with a foreign father? Neo Kyoto's citizenship laws mandate that both parents prove their own citizenship before citizenship is granted to any offspring—or were my years of schooling on your city's laws a total scam?" cuts in Vivian, her voice dripping with disbelief.

I feel my breath catch in my throat.

“Oh, well... You see... my dad... *drinks*... like *a lot*... and... well, I don't know... I mean...” says Nona, clearly too honest by disposition to possibly pull this off.

Time to step in.

“Nona is *not* Kasca Haine’s sister, Vivy... Nona doesn’t know exactly what is going on. The resemblance between the two is a mystery. It’s part of why she’s here, to figure out what her connection is to the company president’s supposed daughter,” I say calmly.

“*Rowan*?! Why...?” says Nona, surprised and sounding a little betrayed.

I don’t honestly predict Vivian taking this well, but... Vivian always does the right thing in the end. I really do believe she will be reasonable... after she gets all the unreasonable out of her system.

Besides, Vivian is too clever by half not to see through Nona’s bad lying... Vivian would probably see through even a master liar, given enough time.

It’s better we just come clean here and now.

“... Sorry, I know it’s your business, but I’d have to lie by omission, and honestly, Nona... you’re such a bad liar... It was an act of mercy. So, you’re welcome,” I say.

Vivian's back had been to Nona during her entire interrogation—on account of her sense of modesty for being without a mask—but now she finally turns to glare at Nona.

"That's... difficult to believe. Start from the beginning and tell me *everything*," demands Vivian, but actually in an encouragingly calm tone.

It's tactless for her to order Nona around like that, but...

She's not yelling, not trying to start a fight... If anything, I feel a little proud of her.

I nod at Nona, who still looks uncertain.

Nona sighs and starts to tell Vivian everything.

.

..

...

"But why are you here? Fine—you want to find out why you look so much like Kasca Haine, but they're also *paying* you something to make you come out in the first place, surely... What's in it for you?" says Vivian.

I perk up at this.

If Nona answers, it will be the first thing she's said that I didn't already know.

When I asked her this same question before, she refused, so surely...

...

"I... My dream is to go to space, to be an astronaut," says Nona timidly.

I get the impression she's not in the habit of sharing this with people, which is surprising to me, considering how sociable and open she is in general.

...

"*And...?*" says Vivian impatiently.

"And Neo Kyoto has a space program, an excellent one... But they have decided manned space travel is no longer worth the effort—it's going to be all robots and advanced AI. So, it's not possible for me to join..."

Nona pauses to give her full attention to fidgeting with the fur lining of her cloak.

"... Prospera has a space program too, a privately owned one... They're trying to catch up with Neo Kyoto, who already have one base on Europa... but they haven't hired any Naturals for the program in years. The unenhanced have a really hard time competing on the assessments, so now it's ingrained in your city's culture that Naturals can't cut it—even if that is not officially a rule. They won't even bother looking at a non-Amelior application, regardless of how high the scores are. And even if they did, Prospera does not hand out work visas usually—especially not to people from Neo Kyoto. But Prosper Electronica contacted me and said that with their connections, they could *guarantee* me a spot on their first mission to Europa, no questions asked... it's not something I like to talk about usually—people are polite enough and all... but I can tell they don't really believe in me—not my friends, not even my dad... They all think I'm being unrealistic—wasting my time. But my mom... She was on the first manned mission to Europa—she headed the expedition herself! I haven't seen her in ten years—haven't heard from her in four—not since the base lost communications... I... I want to follow in her footsteps—I want to find her. That's why I agreed to this."

Vivian strokes Poe's feathers silently for a moment.

I smile to myself—sure I already know the gest of what Vivian is about to say before she utters the first word.

"You always manage to find some way to piss me off, you know that? No one believes in your dream? *Of course they don't.* Most people with grand goals try for a while, then decide to settle while rationalizing to themselves a bullshit reason why it's actually all for the best that they're a failure. Why should they think you're any different? Cause you tell them you really, *really* want it? The only person obligated to believe in a dream is the one it belongs to. If anyone else believes in you, wonderful—but you're not entitled to being believed in, not by anyone. And you don't deserve to achieve your dream if you're too embarrassed to even say it out loud—as if the opinions of others are worth a damn thing," scolds Vivian, her back once again turned away from Nona.

....

"That's got to be the most motivational yet mean thing anyone has ever said to me," says Nona, smiling at Vivian's back sheepishly.

Vivian just rolls her eyes in response.

"We've almost died three times in less than 12 hours—I'm exhausted." Vivian stands, removes her sleeping bag from its waterproofing bag, and goes to unroll it in a corner.

Vivian seems to have accepted Nona's explanation without throwing a single thing—it's good to know that she's still capable of surprising me.

"Three times? I don't know about that. You can't really count that Wood Stalker as a near-miss... It was no match for Rowan—it had no clue who it was messin' with," Nona smiles at me as she says it.

"I didn't do anything. It was Vivian who killed it—not me," I reply, surprised.

"But still! You're brave to the point of craziness—you know that, right? The way you just *threw yourself right at it*—no hesitation at all... putting yourself *millimeters* away from its fangs..." Nona mimes the motion of swinging an ax, recounting the story with more than a hint of awe in her voice, not unlike a little kid describing a favorite scene from an action movie.

I'm glad the room is dimly lit as I look away to avoid Nona's eyes, uncomfortable with having this kind of positive attention focused on me.

"Stop encouraging him. He has always been the kind of guy to confuse *recklessness...* with *courage*. He's stupid enough to think that he's immortal—when he's anything but... As almost drowning should have reminded him—If he wasn't such a hopeless idiot," says Vivian.

There we go, that's more like it... I can always depend on Vivian to keep my ego properly trimmed.

"Well... He was a 'reckless idiot' for *your* sake. So, I think that makes it brave," says Nona, a hint of indignation on my behalf clearly expressed in her tone.

I look at Vivian, ready for the argument to start in earnest.

But to my surprise, yet again, Vivian just accepts it—shrugging dismissively.

"Agree to disagree. One girl's hero is another girl's reckless idiot. Whatever," says Vivian as she climbs into her sleeping bag.

"Right, ah... I'll take the first watch then. You should get some sleep as well, Nona," I say, eager to end on a peaceful note.

I guess even Vivian gets too tired to fight sometimes.

"Okay, I'll take the second shift then," says Nona, looking a little frustrated as she watches Vivian getting ready for bed before following her lead and rolling out her sleeping bag as well.

There is a single window in the room we're held up in—the glass is still intact, though very grimy.

I settle down in front of it.

The girls fall asleep almost instantly, which is probably the normal reaction to have after such an exhausting day.

But being a proud insomniac, sleep never comes easy... regardless of how much I may have earned it. It's largely due to the synthetic adrenaline that the parasite releases—my body doesn't return to baseline easily after being flooded with it.

I'm not used to true darkness. We have the blackouts in Prospera, of course, but the lights never really go out for the segment of the city wealthy enough to afford backup power, so there are always at least lights on in the distance.

The only light now comes from the stars.

Or at least... That's the case at first.

A few hours in, strange lights start to appear in the trees, orange, yellow, and red balls that bob up and down gently... For a moment, I consider waking Nona up to ask if she knows what the deal is. After all, it's nearly her turn to take over watch duty.

But she looks peaceful, and I know she needs the sleep more than anyone—her body being the least suited for the stresses of roughing it out here.

Besides, I'm too angry with myself to sleep.

I gave up back in the water—I was ready to let myself drown by the end. But I have a mission. Vivian and Nona both need me—if I'm going to die out here, I need to make it count for something.

...

The sounds of No Man's Land are strange, alien things.

As disconcertingly alive as the forest felt during the day, the night seems even worse, somehow... like there is not a single shadow uninhabited... like it's impossible to be truly alone anywhere in this whole vast expanse.

Finally, I feel capable of sleep... and just in time for Vivian's shift.

Vivian sits up and looks from me to the still-sleeping Nona.

"Of course... *anything* for the princess, right? You're such a softie sometimes," Vivian says, yawning.

"You know sleep doesn't come when I ask it to, even if I ask nicely. No point having two of us awake."

She shrugs.

I lay down, utterly exhausted—all my anger at myself finally burnt out.

.

..

...

My childhood monster picks tonight to visit me in my dreams—as if my waking hours had not been nightmare enough.

Even now, more than ten years after I murdered him, he refuses to leave me alone.

I realized a long time ago that he never will.

Because some things never get better. Some injuries never heal.

"*There is an infinite amount of hope in the universe... but not for us.*" The Kafka quote barges into my head without me having made any conscious effort to summon it.

I want to run.

I want to vomit.

I want to *die*.

I beg him to just let me die.

The only response I get is his laughter.

"All alone, totally unwanted... but don't worry, I want you. I care about you. Because you're mine—to do with as I please..." I can feel hot breath howling through my right ear.

"...You could die tomorrow—I'd be the only one to even notice... You understand that, don't you? But you won't die. I know you *want* to... but you should know by now that suicide is never the answer... I'll take care of you, don't worry. I protect what's mine."

I wake up.

I don't scream, but I thrash and struggle as if desperate to throw off an attacker.

My eyes open.

Vivian watches me from in front of the window, her expression... *pitying.*

I hate being looked at like that—especially by her.

After all these years, after all my effort... she thinks I'm still the same damaged little boy she remembers from the first day we met.

Maybe I am.

Nona is up as well.

"Rowan... what... what's wrong?" she says, sounding worried.

I realize my pants are wet.

I've *pissed* myself.

Like a child—like an *infant.*

I leap to my feet and run for the door.

Nona gets up too and tries to follow me... but Vivian stops her—shielding my retreat with her body in an almost protective gesture.

"No... he just needs some time alone. He has nightmares sometimes. It's nothing... go back to sleep," says Vivian calmly.

Vivian knows.

I'm sure she knows I pissed myself. I've done it before.

I thought I was finally done wetting the *fucking* bed, son of a...

I leave out the front door and head for the river.

This must be dangerous; it's still half-dark outside, with the sun only just starting to transform the black sky into shades of dark blue.

But who cares?

Certainly not me.

It was a kindness, Vivian covering for me... I didn't wet myself much, and the weather is warm enough that I was not actually inside my sleeping bag...

Nona hopefully will never need to know... that I'm a grown-ass man who still wets the damned bed whenever he has a bad dream.

I walk into the stream, feeling icy water climb up to my waistline.

But Vivian knows.

No wonder she doesn't want me around her.

I'm pathetic.

I suddenly want to cry.

Savagely, I bite into the side of my mouth to distract myself.

It's bad enough that I pissed myself—I will NOT also cry about it.

Fuck that.

Even if I can't control my body when asleep, I won't let it betray me when I'm awake as well.

The taste of iron fills my mouth, and the moment of weakness passes as I feel the injury start to heal itself.

After all, even a weak thing like me has to draw the line somewhere—even if no one else would ever know, I am still one person too many.

I dunk my head under the cold water for an exhilarating moment, and when I resurface, my mind feels blessedly clearer—as if a layer of dirt has been washed clean from my mind.

My hand reaches into my jacket pocket, searching for a pack of cigarettes that I realize is no longer there—another casualty of nearly drowning.

I hadn't planned on this being the day for quitting the habit, but so be it... at least I won't have to deal with Vivian's derision on that account.

Now completely soaked, I head back to the house.

A towel waits for me, draped over the stair's railing.

I stare at it for a long time, as if I've never seen such a thing before, before coming to my senses, changing, and head back upstairs.

Nona is asleep again, curled up in her corner like a cat, draped in her fur-lined cloak.

Vivian is leaning against the window as I had been, her eyes closed, her head leaning to one side, and Poe asleep next to her.

But she looks too graceful, too dignified, mouth slightly open... she looks the way she *thinks* she should look when asleep.

But I know better; asleep is one of the few occasions Vivian *doesn't* look perfectly put together—I've never seen Vivian seriously asleep without her mouth hanging wide open, a little line of drool running down her cheek.

Also, she's far too dependable to fall asleep while on guard duty.

This is another small act of kindness on her part, and I'm grateful for it.

She continues to pretend to be asleep until I lay down and take my own turn at pretending.

23

The Little Conversation Starter

Opia *noun*

The ambiguous intensity of looking someone in the eyes—which can feel simultaneously invasive and vulnerable.

I never manage to fall back asleep after my little midnight swim, and soon enough, the first rays of morning sunlight gives me permission to stop pretending otherwise.

I open my eyes to Vivian getting ready for the day, a toothbrush sticking out of her mouth.

Without a word, I get up and start using a chem heater to brew some coffee.

I'm gonna need it.

Ten minutes later, I hand Vivian a steaming mug—two creams and one sugar... just the way she likes it.

Well, other than the fact that it's cheap, instant coffee and the creamer is the single-serving, dehydrated kind... both of which I'm sure she has never been forced to experience before in her life.

She goes still for a moment when I offer it... as if debating the odds on whether or not I've poisoned it, then takes it without meeting my eyes or saying a word.

Then I make my own cup and shake Nona awake as gently as I can.

She gets up with a cat-like stretch, reminding me again of the way she slept, curled up like a cat.

"Would you like some? I don't know how you take yours," I ask, holding my cup out for her to see.

Nona's nose crinkles in distaste.

"Thank you, it's very thoughtful, buuuut... too bitter, even with sugar and cream. I've always been a big baby about bitter stuff, so I don't like coffee or alcohol much," says Nona, sticking her tongue out in exaggerated disgust.

"Hmmm, I see, well... what about coffee *and* alcohol—I can mix you up something with a little spice... Maybe they'll cancel each other out?"

"Rowan! Did you really... bring booze out to No Man's Land?" she asks, aghast.

I quickly break eye contact—still not familiar enough with Nona to look at her naked face for more than a few seconds at a time without it feeling entirely too intimate.

...

"You know the fire at my house? Well, I used some *very* strong drink to start it, so... you could say we owe our lives to booze, no?" I ask, mock philosophically.

"You... She was at... *You* set your own house on fire?" stammers Vivian, who I hadn't thought was listening.

"Oh... well yeah, I sorta did... Ha ha..." I say, glancing over at Vivian, who now looks absolutely livid... You would think it had been *her* home I'd burned down and not my own.

"... It was burning the house or risk having my skull pancaked by a man three times my size—it wasn't as hard a choice as you might imagine," I finish.

"...You seriously had *no* other options? How did you let yourself be so careless?" scolds Vivian.

"Ah well... no use crying over the spilled 190-proof booze that burned your house down—as the old saying goes," I joke.

"*Men—I swear...*" mutters Vivian in an exasperated response to my attempt at good old-fashioned nonchalant bravado.

"I'm so sorry, Rowan... I just jumped out your bedroom window and left you to deal with it—I shouldn't have done that..." says Nona.

"She was... sleeping in your *bedroom*?" says Vivian, in a voice more disbelieving than anything.

"No! I mean... technically, yes, *but* I wasn't there with her, obviously..." I say, deciding that even as much as I don't want to keep secrets from Vivian, it is probably best I never ever mention she was handcuffed to my bed—I can only imagine the contemptuous looks such a thing would inspire from her.

Let's hope Nona has the sense not to mention it, either.

"Yeah well, there probably wasn't much other choice... I bet you *still* hadn't bothered to buy decent furniture. You'd live in a concrete box if you could find one large enough," says Vivian.

Vivian catches Nona smirking at the two of us and turns her attention to feeding Poe bird treats.

"Something you would like to add, *princess*?"

"No, no... you two are just *really close*—It's... entertaining to watch. It's sweet," says Nona, raising her hands in mock surrender—as if Vivian had pulled a gun on her.

Vivian finishes feeding Poe—who caws indignantly at the sudden end of her breakfast—and starts stuffing her things back into her pack.

"Now you're *literally* homeless, and you did it to yourself—you moron..." says Vivian, choosing to ignore Nona.

"I prefer to think of myself as a citizen of the world—if you don't mind... I find homes to be very limiting, with their insistence on walls and ceilings... I was already of half a mind to burn it down, I swear," I say with an airy wave of my hand.

...

No laughs, not even a chuckle in response...

Admittedly, it wasn't among my best, but it still deserved some form of acknowledgment. There has got to be nothing more awkward than saying a joke that receives no reaction at all.

But Vivian then *does* acknowledge it—by throwing an empty can of crab at my face.

I wipe off a piece of crab meat from my forehead.

"Thanks so much, Vivy," I say while Nona giggles at us from the sidelines.

...

Ten minutes later, we've left the house.

The house is at a break in the tree canopy, so we check our location with a Prosper Electronic aviation GPS that Vivian had the good sense to bring with her.

According to Nona, we have three or four days of hiking left... which, after barely surviving a single day, sounds impossibly far.

"We need to head... that way. More or less," says Nona, pointing.

"Are you... sure you can get us there without having a GPS signal for most of the way?" asks Vivian, sounding less than confident, even though it's a little late now to be questioning Nona's navigation abilities.

Rather a lot is riding on Nona's know-how, and Vivian is obviously not comfortable with that dependency—a feeling I'm inclined to share.

"Yeah, I'm not worried! The good news is, the plane went down not too far past a major river—impossible to miss—it should be a couple day's trip after that," says Nona.

That's a surprisingly reassuring answer—even Vivian seems comforted by it.

"Besides, we won't really be going the whole way without GPS. The signal can't break through the tree canopy, but there will be chances to check it again, I'm sure," says Nona.

We start the day's travels in silence, but Nona's overwhelming people-personness means she has a weakness for starting conversations.

"How long do you have to know someone before it's okay to not have a mask on around them? You still avoid looking at me for more than a split second at a time—it's very strange," Nona observes.

"It's literally been like three days since we met—*of course,* we're not close enough for it to not be weird," I say, slightly exasperated with her.

"Okay, but like... how long is the usual for you weirdos?" she asks, half teasing and half sincerely interested in the answer.

"...It varies. I've known people for many years without seeing their faces, but those are just passing acquaintances... As a rule of thumb, I'd say that if you'd trust someone enough to give them your banking information without fearing betrayal, you are close enough for it to be appropriate to see their face and hear their true voice—so that means immediate family, long-time friends, and serious relationships."

"That's heckin' insane. I sure hope you get over your awkwardness soon—I hate talking to people with their backs turned—it's so odd," Nona says huffily.

"We will all find or make replacement masks the next time we stop, so it won't be an issue," says Vivian.

"Wait a sec, we're not even in Prospera anymore—I'm not gonna wear a mask out here!" objects Nona.

"*Yes,* you will. Do you really think it's okay for you to be seen by the other Lancers that made it out here? Looking *identical* to this Kasca Haine girl we're all here for? They'll drag you back the second they see you... Actually, on second thought, you *don't* need to cover your face at all—they are welcome to have you," says Vivian, soundly getting the better of the argument and causing Nona's expression to go sour.

"Fine, *fine*... I get it. You could be a little nicer about it though..." complains Nona. "But do you seriously like the way things are in Prospera? It's so... restrictive, so impersonal," asks Nona.

"Impersonal? Neo Kyoto is the place where everyone spends all day in virtual realities talking through avatars, where algorithms control every aspect of everyone's life, not Prospera." The question was pretty obviously directed at me, but Vivian decides she'd like to answer it first.

But if Nona is bothered by Vivian's participation, she doesn't show it.

"Yeah, I mean that's fair... but even still, your social norms seem *really* restrictive. And Prosperans like to talk about freedom, but you're not exactly free from want, from poverty... The inequality is rampant. Some Prosperans even have *slaves*, I've heard—it's barbaric... like an old-timey caste system with a landed aristocracy and everything!"

Oh crap.

I look back at Vivian. Her expression has gone as hard as a statue's, her jaw locked.

She looks away from me.

...

Probably best to keep the conversation moving.

"I ah... don't think anyone is absolutely free, regardless of the society. Societies just pick certain freedoms to prioritize and some to downplay but on a more fundamental level... No one is free... I think it's useful to *act* as if we are free, regardless of how true or not it is, because acting as if we are, tends to produce better results than not..." Poe lands on my pack and snatches up an insect that had just landed on my head.

I pause to collect my thoughts, a little self-conscious about sounding a fool.

"... Believing in our own self-agency is a precondition for any human achievement, so even if it is a lie... it is a lie with the practical application of a truth. That in itself is a kind of truth. But the harder you think about it, the more difficult it is to believe in literal freedom... what freedom there is comes in degrees, and all of us are more unfree than free."

Nona taps her finger on her chin thoughtfully.

"You know, you're a lot smarter than you look," teases Nona.

I shrug.

"That's a low bar, but thanks," I reply lightly.

"Ugh, don't do that! It's no fun if you say something self-disparaging—it makes me seem like a bully... But anyway, I think my city's algorithms help people be more free—they point people in the right direction—provides us with an individually tailored path in order to maximize well-being. Your freedoms in Prospera are limited by the harsh necessities of needing to survive—unless you're lucky enough to be born privileged. Yes, we don't have much privacy, and our careers, friends, and eventually spouses are selected for us... but most of us feel like we were not forced into anything—after all, how can someone claim to be free to walk their own path if they didn't have the information required to see the path they should be walking?" says Nona.

I'm surprised to realize that Nona's tone of faint moral superiority annoys me—I've never thought of myself as patriotic, and it was not so long ago that I was debating with a now-dead scientist about my city's exaggerated facade of glorious, ruggedly individualistic freedom. But I also doubt I'd be any better off in a place like Neo Kyoto.

"Fair enough. But if only one path is illuminated, the freedom to walk down any other path seems to me like an illusion of freedom. I was not under the impression your computer overlords gave everyone a wide list of choices to select from. And more importantly, are your people allowed to tell the algorithm to fuck off if they wish?"

"Language, Rowan! But no... I suppose not—but don't the results speak for themselves? Our people are happy, we live longer, and we have all the necessities of life covered—there is nearly zero violent crime and not a single homeless person... Not even the Faded are left to suffer on the streets the way they are in Prospera."

The Fade—yet another topic I do not want to discuss with Vivian around. I take a tentative glance at Vivian—noting the rigged set of her shoulders and the forced expressionlessness of her face. Even when it is unintentional, Nona has a way of stumbling into one verbal landmine after another.

"It sounds to me like you're conflating happiness with freedom. How can anyone claim to be free if they are not free to be self-destructive or free to fail miserably? If anything, it sounds like you're saying we have an unhealthy excess of freedom—and maybe you're right. Maybe absolute freedom is overrated—and impossible to have regardless. Maybe happiness and comfort are all that matters. But on the other hand... Maybe Prosperans find meaning and satisfaction in the suffering—in fighting for every scrap of happiness we can get our hands on. Maybe some of us—even some of the least free among us—recognize the inherent cruelty and unfairness of the world without blaming the Amelior for it... Because we understand that, if we were in their positions—if we had the same DNA, the same incentives, and the same formative experiences as them—we would *be* the same as them," I reply.

That last sentence of mine was not for Nona's sake so much as it was for Vivian's—I blame Vivian for giving me the false hope of her love before suddenly abandoning me—for not appreciating all the sacrifices I was so willing to make for her—yes... But I don't hold her responsible for the things her family did to me as a child, nor do I hate her for having things I will never have—largely because I've seen behind the curtain to the pain and crushing obligations that come with being a part of her famous family.

Vivian's body relaxes and I realize that some kind of guilt I hadn't realized she was carrying has been lifted by what I just said.

Nona—as perceptive as ever—clearly notices the subtle exchange as she looks back and forth between us, one eyebrow slightly raised.

"I... you're right, Rowan. I still don't understand your culture well enough to act all judgy—I can't honestly say I liked everything I saw in my couple of days there, but I'm sure there are a bunch of things I don't understand—some of those things are probably pretty great. Neo Kyoto is all I've ever known, after all... Forgive me?" Nona says, sounding all timid and apologetic all of a sudden.

"Nothing to forgive—you're talking to a thug-for-hire—so long as you don't ever cheat me out of a payday for services brutally rendered on your behalf, we won't have any issues," I reply airily.

Nona opens her mouth and I can tell she doesn't want to stop talking—I swear I've never met a person so unwilling to enjoy a little silence.

"What do you thi—" Nona begins.

"We probably shouldn't shoot the shit all day. We need to stay alert out here," interrupts Vivian quickly.

"What, you expect us to walk in silence *all* day? Don't worry, the Flitwits are still carrying on like usual, we're okay... probably." Nona points up at some bright blue birds in the branches above.

They have the long, narrow beaks of old Hummingbirds—but are larger and have two pairs of wings instead of one.

"*Probably...*? How very reassuring," says Vivian, too proud to admit that Nona was actually being more responsible than she had given her credit for.

Even with that reassurance, Nona admits that there are threats the Flitwits won't notice, and that reminder of the danger we're still in kills our appetite for conversation.

Even so, I'm sure Nona won't be able to maintain this for long; she's too much of a talker, too interested in other people... just as interested in us as she is in any of the strange plants and animals we pass by.

Speaking of which... Periodically, Nona stops walking on the pretext of checking the map and compass, only to glance down at her navigation tools for the briefest of seconds before going instead to take a sample of some plant or another.

Every time she does, Vivian gets noticeably impatient—but surprises me by, for the most part, biting her tongue.

That is, until...

"Nona... what... what is *that*?" asks Vivian in a very strained kind of forced calm.

I turn to see Nona bent over and studying something, a vile in one hand filled with some preservative liquid inside, into which she adds a leaf.

"I don't know... Gosh, I really wish we had more time—I think this might be the first time anyone has ever seen it. This could be a whole new species..." says Nona, excited, but... also with a faint hint of something else there as well... anxiety just short of qualifying for fear.

I step around Vivian to get a better look, still not understanding what the big deal was.

It is a tree.

A tree, shaped like...

A human being.

A face is visible in the twisting knots of the trunk.

A pair of wooden eyes too large to belong with the rest of its features, a crooked kind of smile frozen in place.

At first, I assume that the features must have been carved into the tree, that the branches must have been trimmed to resemble limbs, but...

That's not it at all. There are no signs of carving... this is just how the tree has grown.

I realize with growing apprehension that the little birds Nona claimed signaled our relative safety are no longer anywhere to be seen.

...

"We... should keep moving," I say as I feel the blood in my veins go strangely cold.

Nona opens her mouth to object before thinking better of it and nodding in agreement.

...

After many more hours of walking, we start to hear a faint roar in the distance, constant, like the sound of fast-moving water.

Nona smiles at the sound.

"That must be the Timber River... we're getting close," she says, checking her map for real this time.

It turns out to be one hell of a river.

24

The Bridge

"No retreat. No relent. No rest."

— Official Restless House Guard motto

The Timber River dominates the landscape—less what I'd imagined a river to be and more akin to a rather narrow sea, with the opposite shore being a far distant sight... not that I've ever actually seen the sea before.

The waters of the Timber are rough, rocky, and dark... as fast-moving as the current generated by the Feeder Dam had been, it was a babbling brook compared to this beast. Waterfalls feed into the river from the high ground to our right—enough to fill a Super-Olympic-sized pool in seconds.

"Over there! That's going to be the only crossing point for miles," says Nona, pointing to the far left.

Spanning the waters is a four-lane suspension bridge that may have once been red but was now mostly just rust. The remains of buildings line either side of the river as well, though these are in much worse shape than most of the buildings we've passed.

When I ask about it, Nona tells me that during the rainy season, the Feeder Dams all release so many simultaneous flash floods that the Timber River swells out and floods its banks temporarily, submerging the whole area for weeks at a time.

Feeling a little like an awe-struck tourist (and not at all for the first time since entering No Man's Land), we make our way towards the distant bridge.

"Princess... you said this is the *only* way to pass the river in this area... right?" asks Vivian.

"Yep, there was another bridge not that far away, but I looked at satellite imagery of it before we left—It fell into the Timber years ago. It would add another day's worth of hiking to make it to the next intact bridge," says Nona.

I bet Vivian is thinking that this bridge would be an excellent place to set up an ambush...

Because that's certainly what I'm thinking.

"We should cross back into the tree line instead of following the river. We're too exposed like this," says Vivian.

We can all see the merit to this, so our trio opts to play it safe.

...

Half an hour later, we're finally starting to get close.

"Hold it—there are people down there..." I say in an urgent whisper, pointing at a group of figures breaking the cover of the trees to start approaching the bridge.

"Poe, go get a better look for us and report back—but don't get too close," instructs Vivian.

Poe salutes with one of her wings before taking off. The amusingly human gesture brings a smile to my face—clearly the bird has learned a few more communication tricks since the last time I saw her.

"We should maybe get closer, get a better look of who it is," says Nona—she's obviously very anxious, considering her lack of reaction to Poe's display of intellect.

We both nod in agreement, Vivian taking the lead.

I grab Nona's hand, stopping her in order to hand off my scarf so she can cover her face, remembering Vivian's point about not letting the other Lancers see her.

She smiles in silent thanks and puts it on before we hurry to catch up to Vivian.

To my shock, it turns out to be the Restless House Guard once again.

There look to be about eight of them, moving in two wedge-shaped formations.

"Why would they actually send them out here?" I ask, shocked.

No one even tries to answer my question.

The Restless family's motivations are still a total mystery.

When they showed up at the FireJack's perimeter, they were definitely trying to capture someone among Riot's group of Lancers—likely Riot himself.

But why would they really care *so* much about capturing or killing a few Lancers? Perhaps they are actually here for the same reason we are—Kasca Haine—the daughter of Restless Industries' main competition... Would the leverage over Prosper Electronica gained by capturing her really be that valuable to them?

More importantly... is Corella Restless out here with them now?

If she is, that would say a lot.

Vivian came out here without permission—but if Corella has the House Guard with her, it would suggest she is on official family business.

They would only let her go if there was a real necessity for it.

The Restless sense of morality leaves no room for overprotective parenting; they believed in leading from the front, in getting their hands dirty. It's a hard-as-nails kind of parenting philosophy, but they still wouldn't risk a prized daughter's life on something trivial. That's especially true for Corella—the daughter they groomed for diplomacy and business negotiations, not violence. If anything, Vivian would be the daughter suited for this—yet here she is with us, working for her family's competition.

Vivian turns to speak to me.

She looks... stressed—anxious in a way that I'd almost forgotten she was capable of.

Her expression reminds me of her as a 16-year-old girl—waiting to be dealt with by her mother for skipping school while she'd worked instead on restoring an ancient motorcycle.

"We can't... Wait, what happened to your scarf?" demands Vivian.

I point my thumb over my shoulder at Nona.

Vivian's face cycles through a couple of different emotions in rapid succession, going from scared to angry to comprehending, pausing at annoyed for a moment, and then finally settling back on stressed.

"*Fine.* But you need to cover your face as well... and trade me that stupid jacket of yours... you will have to wear my cloak for now," says Vivian.

"What, *why*? I get Nona, but why should I have to disguise myself?" I ask, perplexed.

It doesn't make any sense unless she thinks the House Guard is after me... and if that *was* the case, why didn't they do something when I was so conveniently locked in a cell?

Back then, Corella had known where I was, but she'd agreed to let me go.

... Or had Corella been lying when she said that? Maybe she just said that to stop us trying to break out in the meantime.

"Now's not the time—just do it!" snaps Vivian.

Nona watches us trade our top layer of clothing in confused silence.

It was one thing for them to send a team to the FireJack's perimeter, but to send them all into No Man's Land...

Even after ten years with the family, I'd never seen the paramilitary arm of the family be used for such a thing.

How large had the original group sent into No Man's Land been?

A full, 15-man squad?

If so, they've lost almost half their combat strength in just a couple days...

BANG!

A gunshot goes off, and a tree trunk explodes just to the right of Nona, spraying her with fragments of bark.

Nona looks around dumbly—the classic deer-in-the-headlights reaction of someone still not accustomed to being shot at.

"Get DOWN, damn it!" I yell, grabbing the back of Nona's head and shoving her face-first into the forest floor.

"Shit! They must have had someone hang back as overwatch in one of the remaining buildings!" curses Vivian.

I nod.

"Not good—this will turn into a waiting game now. We don't have any way to counter a sniper—unless you think you can range them with your bow, Vivian?" I say.

"Of course I could—with an explosive arrow, all I'd need to be is close, but... that's one of my family's men up there... I'd rather not, you know... *kill him...*" answers Vivian.

More gunshots ring out—these ones come in quick succession—not from a sniper's rifle but from the three-round bursts of assault rifles.

There is distant yelling as well, and for an instant, I think they must be turning to assault us, but...

For all the sounds of gunfire, there are no new corresponding impacts around us of bullets biting into trees.

"It's not us—they're firing on someone else!" I say.

I peek my head out to see a battle raging on the bridge.

Lancers are emerging from hiding places on the bridge, attacking the Restless formation.

Comprehension dawns on me.

The Lancers had been waiting in ambush—the sniper taking a shot at us had spooked them into starting the attack prematurely.

I spin around as I hear the flap of wings, terrified that some creature from No Man's Land has found us, only to see Poe land in between Vivian and me.

Poe starts talking in her limited way—gesticulating and squawking—doing her best to communicate what she saw to Vivian.

"What's she telling you?" I ask.

"... It's... Corella. She's here—Captain Brawn as well," Vivian translates.

I peek out from the tree again.

There is not a lot of cover on the bridge, only a few rusted cars and the regularly spaced metal spans of the bridge itself.

One of the Lancers loses his head as a sniper's bullet finds its mark.

The standard light body armor is *very* good nowadays, but a headshot avoids that issue completely.

"W-What do we do? We can't just sit here, can we?" asks Nona.

"The sniper isn't focused on us anymore, but it's still too dangerous to just run out into the open," I say.

"Well then, why get involved *at all?*" says Vivian.

...

"What?" I ask, not sure I'm understanding her right.

"*Look...* the Lancers *needed* to capitalize on the element of surprise, but we inadvertently ruined that for them—now they're the ones in a bad position. In our own way, we've already helped my bitch of a sister more than she deserves," Vivian says coldly.

Her logic makes sense; I can understand why Vivian would conclude her sister was going to be fine on her own—why she wants to simply leave them.

But the truth is, a fight can appear to be going one way the instant before everything changes. It is dangerous to call a fight before it's done.

I look back towards the bridge.

I wonder for a moment if this group of Lancers is simply separate from the one Riot is leading, considering his conspicuous absence...

But as it turns out, he was just an ace the Lancers wanted to keep up their sleeve until the right moment.

The House Guard, tasting an easy victory, are starting to advance onto the bridge, bounding from vehicle to vehicle in pairs, always protected by the sniper they have providing support by fire from their rear.

Even as Vivian was announcing her prediction that the Lancers would lose this fight, another Lancers dies.

The Lancer takes a shotgun blast at point-blank range—unable to see from his pinned-down position behind the skeleton of a car that a Restless soldier had managed to close the distance between them totally.

But now, Riot decides to make his presence felt.

"I... I think you spoke too soon, Vivian..." I say, gesturing back towards the bridge.

Riot steps out from his hiding place, looking even larger than the last time we'd seen him due to the high-tech, heavy armor he's now wearing.

Light armor is the overwhelming norm, being hardly any heavier or more cumbersome than regular clothing, yet still able to provide sufficiently effective protection...

But if someone is willing and able to deal with the crushing weight, heat, and reduced mobility... heavy armor tech can turn them into a walking tank—even protecting the usually vulnerable head with a heavy-duty, full-face helmet.

The same shotgun-wielding guard that had just killed a Lancer turns and finds himself looking up at Riot's towering, metal figure.

Understandably, he panics.

He shoots Riot twice before tripping and falling in his desperation to put some distance between himself and Riot.

Riot's armor absorb the damage as easily as if the shotgun was a child's toy and not a weapon that had just easily ended a person's life a second earlier.

The man on the ground levels his gun at Riot again, but before he can fire another shot, Riot yanks the weapon out of his hands and uses it as a club to beat the life out of the poor bastard—his body spasming wildly before going still.

Next to me, Nona cries out, hands covering her face in horror at the pure savagery of the execution—even I feel my stomach twist itself into knots at the shocking brutality of the sight—I've never seen one of the much-vaunted Restless House Guard be reduced to the role of ineffectual prey like that.

Riot throws the now bent and broken shotgun aside.

The other Restless soldiers are mostly shooting at Riot—roaring in outrage at the death of their comrade—but Riot appears to barely even notice them.

Even without the armor, he is a seven-foot-tall, 350-pound killer...

But in the armor... he transforms into a nearly eight-foot-tall, 450-pound *monster.*

They simply did not bring a gun large enough to handle this—and a Burner Blade would require getting within grabbing distance of the giant.

But still, it's not hopeless for them just yet—they still have a sniper to pin down the other Lancers, and Riot does not seem to have any ranged weapons on him.

If nothing else goes wrong, they can still beat a hasty retreat, having more or less given as good as they got in this fight.

But then Vivian hits me on the shoulder and points to our left at a pair of Thorn Lions emerging from the tree line only a couple hundred meters away.

No one besides us have noticed the beasts yet.

"T-They hunt by sound—noises *this* loud would attract them even from miles and miles away..." says Nona, sounding at the edge of her rope, as she explains to us *why* these things seem to turn up at all the worst possible times.

The tone of Nona's voice worries me. I know her lack of action the last time still eats at her... Will she be able to keep her calm when the Thorn Lions start eating people alive in front of her again?

But she is not the only one I have to worry about.

"Vivian... your sister, she... if we don't *do* something... all of them *will* die. The Lancers are one thing, but if they also get attacked from behind by a pair of lions, it's going to be all over for them," I say firmly.

...

"Let's just go... We need to make it to the next bridge." Vivian stands up, her back turned to the both of us.

...

"Are... you absolutely sure that's what you want, Vivian?" I ask slowly.

I don't know that I'd say I like Corella—she was generally decent enough to me, *surprisingly* decent—considering the lowly position I'd held relative to hers. But I know some of the things she's done... and she was by no means kind to Vivian as a child.

If I let myself focus on those childhood memories of Corella abusing her younger sister, I can understand Vivian's apathy now, but...

I did watch Corella grow up—right alongside Vivian—and Corella was still a child herself during the worst of her abusive tendencies.

And who am I to judge?

If Corella is irredeemable, then I must be as well—Hell... if anything, I deserve worse.

Will Vivian really be able to live with herself if she lets her sister—someone she's known her *entire* life, die in front of her? Even if that someone is Corella?

She nods.

"I'm sure."

"But... that's your *sister* out there, right?" yells Nona, furious tears clearly visible in her eyes even with the scarf wrapped around her face.

"*So*? She wouldn't do it for me if the positions were reversed..." Vivian turns, anger sketched into every line of her face.

She looks liable to punch Nona.

I rise to my feet.

"How can you know that? How can you be so sure she wouldn't help you if *you* were the one about to die?!" yells Nona.

Nona opens her mouth to say more, but before she can get another word out, Vivian blows her composure completely.

"WHAT THE HELL DO YOU KNOW ABOUT HER?! We share some DNA... what moron gives a *single*, *solitary shit* about that arbitrary similarity? Does that make her life special? Why should she matter more than anyone else, *princess*? I know things about *my sweet, big sis* that would make your moralistic self HATE Corella with every cell in your body... So, spare me your self-righteous, holier than thou, BULLSHIT!" screams Vivian, making Nona flinch as if she had just been struck across the face.

"I... W-Well, what about the men protecting her? Those... are your family's soldiers, right? You said that yourself—you said you didn't want to kill one of them a few minutes ago. What's the difference between killing them and deciding not to save them?!" yells Nona, her voice growing steadily stronger as she goes.

"THAT IS THE RISK THEY *DECIDED* TO TAKE! They *knew* what they were agreeing to, coming out here! They are paid to fight and die—they knew that from the start! It is their job, and they are paid lavishly for the risk—I owe them fuck-all!"

I know that was a lie. I've been with Vivian when she was commanding Restless soldiers—she has never treated them as disposable—and they loved her for it... What the fuck has changed since I left the service of the family?

...

"I... I'm going to go help—I have to." Nona rises to her feet.

"Nona, wait! What do you think y—" I say, reaching for her hand.

But she pulls it away and yanks on the quick-release straps of her pack, sending it falling to the ground.

"Nona!"

Refusing to meet my eyes, she bolts from the protection of the trees.

...

"I can't let her die—I'm going as well," I say, dropping my pack as Nona just did.

I spare a final glance at Vivian, who stands as motionless as a statue, her back turned from me once again, Poe at her feet, looking up at her... loyally waiting for Vivian to make a choice.

I'm loyal to her as well, but I cannot afford to wait for her to do the right thing, not this time.

I bolt after Nona.

25

Death by Good Intentions

She's such a fool, running into a warzone without even any light armor on—If a stray bullet or a Thorn Lion gets to her before I do...

No.

I'm gaining on her.

I'm going to reach her any second now.

I'll carry her out if I have to.

Let her hate me for it. She will at least be alive—nothing else matters.

Even while my stomach twists with fear for Nona, some part of my mind is focused on a second, different fear.

What if Vivian leaves?

She did not want me around in the first place—I've forced my company on her since getting out here.

Well... if she really wants to be done with me, I'm providing her with the perfect opportunity.

A seed of guilt writhes in my chest.

For practically as long as I can remember, Vivian has been the center of my universe... this is a battlefield, set in the backdrop of a savage wilderness—to prioritize saving a girl I've known for a matter of days over ensuring Vivian's safety—even for a moment—*feels* like a betrayal... Not only to Vivian but also to myself.

Meanwhile, Nona is naive, meek, scatterbrained, and at times, positive past the point of good sense, but...

This world would not be such an awful place if only it had more people like her... and fewer people like me.

I will not stand aside and hide while she gets herself killed by people like me—even if that is the natural order of things in this world.

A man screams from nearby as a lion literally tears his body in half—cutting his screams for help from his comrades mercifully short.

Nona falls to her knees next to a badly injured Restless soldier—pulling out medical supplies from the pack she always keeps around her waist.

It's too loud to hear her, but I can tell she's reassuring the man as she starts trying to slow his bleeding.

She does, at least, understand her place in a situation like this—she's thankfully not trying to join in the fight herself.

But she's still an idiot.

I skid to a stop next to the pair of them.

"R-Rowan, you came, I—"

I point to what remains of a crumbling wall.

"GET BEHIND THAT WALL! You think they won't shoot you because you're playing medic?! I'll carry this guy ov—"

Out of the corner of my eye, I catch a dark circular shape flying through the air, a small red light flashing as it goes. The Lancer who threw it ducks back behind cover right as the Restless marksman fires another shot—missing him by inches.

It's a grenade—this one not of the smoke variety.

It lands less than 10 meters away.

Time moves very slowly, as it always seems to when someone becomes aware that they are in mortal danger.

Nona’s eyes are wide—she sees the danger as well but is frozen in place by it.

I tackle her—Trampling the injured man she was trying to help in the process.

...

I force her head down into the dirt and wrap her small body with mine—positioning my back to the grenade.

..

Nona's eyes meet mine—wide and terrified, wet with tears.

.

This is going to fucking hurt.

When I open my eyes again, I am aware of two things: panoramic pain and the sense that I’m suddenly occupying a different place in time and space.

Nona is still held in my arms.

The sounds of fighting seem to be coming from very far away—the ringing in my ears drowning out everything else.

I let go of Nona and touch my left ear.

My fingers come back red.

My *four* fingers—I'm missing my fucking pinky finger from the hand.

Nona starts to move, sitting up to look at me—tears are running down her face, and she's saying something to me, though I can’t make out what.

I can't hear what she's saying, so I ignore her and just stare at the mangled hand—transfixed by how uncanny it looks without the damned pinky.

Nona grabs the hand and starts trying to clean off the blood. Her eyes are as wide as saucers, and her eyebrows are crinkled with worry... much as they had been when I’d woken up to her face after nearly drowning a day ago.

She must be okay if she has the energy to make such a fuss over me...

That’s good, at least.

I tear my hand away from her grasp and pat myself down, searching for the conspicuous absence of any other bits that ought to be there.

Finding nothing, I smile at her reassuringly and try to get to my feet—vaguely aware that we still aren't at all safe just sitting here.

Dizziness hits me like a semi-truck, putting me back on the ground again.

I'm disoriented but still able to process that someone is approaching us from the rear.

I don't know where my ax has gone, so I fumble for the knife I keep strapped to my ankle instead with my uninjured left hand.

I start trying to tell Nona to run, but I'm sure there is a similar ringing in her ears as mine, and the sounds of the fighting would make it difficult to hear me even without it.

But it's not a Lancer or even one of the Restless House Guards. It's...

Vivian.

She... didn't leave me after all.

Nona tries to say something to her...

But Vivian chooses to rely on non-verbal communication.

She sucker punches Nona in the face.

Hard.

I doubt very much that a pleasant, agreeable girl like Nona has *ever* had anyone seriously try to punch her before now.

I force myself back to my feet, suddenly afraid Vivian might actually end up seriously injuring Nona, but...

The sudden movement causes my head to spin worse than ever, making me vomit this morning's breakfast all over the ground.

Dimly, I recognize the signs of a concussion.

Nona stumbles back from the pain and shock, one hand holding the side of her face where Vivian struck her. Vivian must have held back—because a full-force punch from a genetically enhanced fighter like Vivian would have otherwise laid Nona out—maybe even killed her.

Meanwhile, Vivian screams something at her while pointing at me and then pointing at a dark, crumpled mass on the floor.

I realize the crumpled mass is the man Nona had been trying to give aid to before... clearly, beyond anyone's ability to help anymore.

I make out a few words, my name being one of them and the rest being largely profanity... before Vivian shoves both her bow and my Compression Ax into Nona's hands.

Considering Nona could not possibly use either of these herself, this seems strange to me—until Vivian turns, sprints over to me, and throws me over her shoulder like I'm a sandbag and *not* a 200-pound man.

Vivian starts to run back towards the trees, Poe flying overhead, scouting for potential attackers.

Nona still struggles to keep up with us, even though Vivian has to deal with all my extra weight while she runs.

The fighting is coming to a close as we make our retreat. There are a couple of surviving Lancers, but the only members of the House Guard I can see back the way we came are the corpses on the ground... I don't know if Corella or Brawn are among them.

Of the three of us, I am the only one who gets to watch Riot deliver the killing blow to the second Thorn Lion—piercing the beast through its soft underbelly with a six-foot-long spike... having presumably broken it off the dead body of its recently murdered mate.

...

Riot is a one-man army.

If I am a drop of rain, then Riot is the storm itself... alike on some rudimentary level, but the difference in magnitudes makes all the difference in the world.

It is clear to me, even in my disoriented state, that we cannot afford to fight a thing like that.

There is no reality in which a fight between the three of us and that freak force of nature... ends with any of us walking away alive.

26

Deal Making

We disappear into the trees, leaving the carnage behind us to search for the place where we dropped our packs.

The ringing in my ears is still present but thankfully no longer totally crippling to my ability to communicate.

We must find our packs before nightfall and secure some kind of shelter—failure to do either will be fatal... as Nona so helpfully reminds us.

Vivian sends Poe away to help with the search. For her part, Poe seems eager to contribute.

"L-Let's stop for a moment—I can give Rowan something for his pain!" says Nona.

Her words are barely audible to my blown ears.

If I was alone with Nona, I'd be worried. But Vivian knows my body violently rejects any and all pain meds—and sure enough—Vivian neutralizes any risk by stopping for just long enough to snatch the drugs from Nona's hands and chuck them as far into the underbrush as she can manage.

"STOP *trying* to help—he's allergic—are you trying to get him killed?" chastises Vivian.

"But... you didn't even pause to look at the label... surely he's not allergic to all pain relievers..." grumbles Nona—confused but also browbeaten enough to not put up a real fight.

Stupid, Vivy... The two of you could have still benefited from the things...

But my mind has no energy left to waste on any problem besides the big-fucking-one...

Riot.

He came after Nona and me once, at minimum—though I suspect the Lancers who tried to attack Nona in the alley were also connected to him.

I can only assume it all has something to do with Nona's unexplained connection to Kasca Haine.

I see no reason to think he won't try to follow us now and that man is as much a force of nature as anything else in No Man's Land.

Vivian nearly treads on a bright red flower the size of a diner plate before Nona catches us.

"STOP! It... it will release neurotoxins on contact—without immediate medical care..." warns Nona—not needing to finish the sentence to get the point across.

I can tell the source of Nona's nerves is less the deadly plant life... and more her fear of upsetting the superhuman girl who's half a foot taller, at least 50 pounds heavier (all of it muscle), and who just bloodied her face moments before.

I can't say I'm surprised she's walking on eggshells after that...

Vivian nods and changes course without thanking Nona for saving her—and by extension—my life.

... but this kind of dynamic is not sustainable out here.

Nona being sincerely frightened of Vivian could get us killed out here—she needs to be able to call the shots when it comes to surviving the wildlife... and assertiveness is not Nona's strong point even at the best of times.

"Vivy... I think I can walk now. You can let me down," I say.

...

"You can walk after we find the packs," says Vivian, stubbornly shaking her head.

I sigh.

"Well, can you at least carry me in a more dignified way? I feel like a little kid. Also... this *hurts*," I say.

Vivian still has me slung over her shoulder, and while she may have the strength to carry me like this... She still has relatively narrow, feminine shoulders—making me always feel on the verge of slipping off.

Nona smiles at me, quietly amused, from behind Vivian's back... now sporting an impressively bruised face.

Vivian mutters something about how I should be carried like a baby if I'm going to complain like one but still allows me to switch to a more comfortable position on her back.

This is still humiliating for me, but... with my head pounding like a drum and my body aching in a dozen different places, I don't care enough to force the issue at the moment. I glance down at my hand to check on my missing finger, and—sure enough—the bleeding has stopped, and healing has begun. But re-growing entire body parts is not among the many benefits of my condition. I'm just glad it wasn't a more important finger—and that it was on my non-dominant hand.

There is a familiar bird call up ahead.

"That's Poe! She must have found the packs..." says Vivian triumphantly.

She picks up her pace, Nona following suit behind us.

"Well, fancy seeing you here, little sis."

Vivian releases her hold on my legs so suddenly that I fall off her and flat on my ass, sending an agonizing jolt up my spine.

Corella steps out from behind a tree, her Burner Blade in one hand—though it's not yet glowing red hot.

Brawn and a junior member of the House Guard follow behind her, our packs in their hands—all three of them are still masked.

The younger soldier has a sniper rifle slung over his shoulder, making me suspect he was probably the one giving the Lancers so much trouble on the bridge.

I'm guessing that this is all that remains of the Restless detail, after suffering whatever casualties they did just in the process of traveling this far, then losing most of what remained to the Lancers and the Thorn Lions just now.

Vivian turns, snatches her bow from Nona's hands, and pulls an arrow from her quiver... To my relief, she does not draw the bow back or point it at anyone... *yet.*

"*Give us our shit...* and then you can go poke some man-eating abomination with a stick and have it teach you a lesson on your own anatomy," hisses Vivian, glaring at her sister with murder in her eyes.

The junior soldier looks at Brawn from behind Corella's back—unsure whose side he is supposed to be on.

They serve the family, so Vivian is just as much their master as Corella is—even more so, arguably—as Vivian is supposed to one day take over the military arm of the family business.

"As lovable as ever—I'm ever so blessed to have such a *cute* baby sister," says Corella.

I've regained my feet and casually take my ax from Nona, hoping beyond hope that it won't come to a fight.

Neither of our groups can afford a fight, not right now... though if we did, Corella's trio would probably have the advantage, with me concussed, Vivian forced to fight at such a close range, and Nona... just being herself.

"We're not looking for a fight. But we lost our main packs when we were forced to pull back. We need at least some basic supplies." Brawn steps forward and, to my considerable surprise, seems to address the statement at *me*, not Vivian.

"Well, *tough luck*—that's not our problem," says Vivian bitterly.

"Do you have anything to trade in return?" I ask.

...

"Only information," replies Brawn.

...

Both Corella and Vivian are looking back and forth between Brawn and me—outraged that we are pretending like they're not even there when they are so used to being in charge.

I nod.

"We should secure shelter for the night first, then we can talk about a *possible* trade," I say.

"Yes... I suppose that would be fine by us. But Brawn... watch your manners, darling," says Corella, in a tone that makes it clear to me she would have more to say about Brawn's proper place if the situation was not so urgent.

The Captain bows apologetically.

"Of course, ma'am... my apologies."

"No way in *hell*... Give us our gear and get lost, NOW!" demands Vivian—furious that we should have to make a deal just to get our own supplies back.

Which is a fair complaint, to her credit.

"I... I have some extra stuff I could afford to share, maybe..." volunteers Nona from behind my back.

"You've already helped *more* than enough for one da—" starts Vivian.

"*Vivy.* Please. We can't afford to do this right now..." I say, glancing at Nona, who is on the verge of tears again, her expression full of regret.

"*Fine.* But once we're done trading, you three *leave*... I refuse to stay together past that. Also..."

Vivian marches over to the junior soldier and tears the mask off of his face before turning back around and shoving it at Nona.

"You can put this on. I'm *sick* and *tired* of seeing all the stupid, lost puppy-dog expressions you insist on making. And you can also give Rowan back his scarf—*now*," orders Vivian, throwing a bit of a temper tantrum.

The now maskless soldier is mortified to find his face suddenly stark naked, but loyalty to the family is enough to make him bite his tongue.

I feel bad for the guy—but we really can't risk Corella or Brawn getting a good look at Nona's face.

Nona turns her back and places the mask on her face before handing me back my scarf. This new mask of hers covers everything—even her eyes are hidden behind dark, tinted glass.

I never got comfortable seeing her full face, but it's strange now not to even see her overly expressive eyes...

"Thanks kindly. And Nona... ah... Everything's okay. I'm going to be fine. So, you don't need to keep beating yourself up over it. Your heart was in the right place, even if the way you handled it was... a bit shit." I mutter to her in as soothing a tone as I can manage.

Nona freezes.

...

I start to feel slightly awkward, not sure what else I'm supposed to say, and no way to read her face with the mask back on... If she was the one in my position, I'm sure Nona would know exactly what kinds of things to say to make someone feel better... but I'm just not that kind of person.

Then, to my massive surprise, Nona starts to laugh.

"A bit... *shit*? That's what you say when trying to comfort a girl?" says Nona as she tries to stifle her laughter. This is the first time I've ever heard her say anything close to a swear—making it sound oddly unnatural.

"Well... *do better,* and I'll say nicer things. What do you expect from me—to praise you for running out into a firefight with nothing but your matronly heart and good intentions to protect you?"

"Hmmm... But I didn't *only* have those things, did I? I had you. Thank you, Rowan... I mean it. You saved my life. I made the right choice when I took a chance on you," says Nona.

I can feel my face start to go uncomfortably hot.

I pull the scarf up higher around my face.

"Sorry, didn't catch that. The ringing in my ears is still too loud... No need to repeat it—I'm sure it wasn't anything important, knowing you," I say, with as much disinterested aloofness as I can manage.

She always says the cringiest, corniest crap...

And *damn,* does my head hurt.

27

Answers

After we've walked for some time, Corella starts to slow down, letting Brawn and the now maskless sniper pass her.

At first, I assume this to be just a commonsense precaution—her putting some distance between herself and a still fuming Vivian.

But it's not long before she's next to me and initiating a hushed conversation.

"Row... there's something I need to give you," Corella whispers.

A memory of Vivian demanding to know if her sister gave me anything while we were in the FireJack cell comes floating to my mind.

"Give me something? Why... it's not even my birthday—maybe you should just save it for the time being?" I reply.

"Hmmm, you say that, but this is something you'll want to have as soon as possible—assuming you still care about saving dear Vivy, that is."

...

"No games, Corella. Just tell me what the hell you're on about."

"That's no fun, but I agree... I doubt my sweet little sister will let us chat like this for long. You saw Riot back there, Row... You know you can't beat him. Not as you are now. No one can—he's on an entirely different level. Amelior abilities are, in general, superior, but in terms strictly of combat ability, well... And he's not the only thing that needs beating out here, is he...? How many times has Vivian very nearly died already these past couple of days?"

Corella taps on her pocket, her nail clinking off of something hard.

"I have a certain miracle of modern science that will give you at least a fighting chance. That experimental parasite father had implanted in you when we were little? Right now, all it does is help with your healing and general survivability. It does things like help your blood clot more effectively, filters out toxins, releases an artificially enhanced version of adrenaline, so on and so forth. That's all well and good—but that's only a fraction of what it's capable of. It has dormant properties that you need a chemical signal to unlock—which I have here, just burning the proverbial hole in my pocket."

I don't know what to say—my mind is so totally preoccupied with trying to process this information... So, I decide to say nothing.

Corella takes this as an invitation to continue talking.

"You love Vivian, I know... I've watched you with her for years and years—never have I ever seen a boy more enamored, enthralled, or blatantly besotted with a girl than you are with her... But... you're smart enough to understand that you don't deserve someone if you're not even strong enough to protect them. That's just the cold reality—safety is one of, if not *the*, primary obligation a person owes to those they love—and she needs protecting from dramatically more dangerous predators than most girls out there. You're undeniably devoted to her, but you know someone as exceptional as her could only ever be content with someone equally exceptional—it's not enough to just care about her, not when you insist on... aiming sooo hopelessly high..."

Corella sighs in a disappointed kind of way.

"...Like I've said before, I think she's more trouble than she's worth. To be honest, a nice guy like you would be happier with a *softer, simpler* kind of girl, but... The heart wants what the heart wants, doesn't it?"

"What... is it? This chemical of yours," I ask, not enjoying Corella's poking fun at my many Vivian-related insecurities.

Corella has teased me for my feelings towards her sister since I was a little kid, but I've still never gotten used to it.

"Just something Restless Research and Development has been working on since waaay back. I won't lie to you. It is not without its risks—risks that my baby sis would never ask anyone to take for her. She's so very proud—she likes to believe she can do it all herself. But I know you are not the type to flinch at a little risk, a little self-sacrifice... Taking it will shave years off your life. But if the situation is dire enough... losing a few years would be a small price to pay. Don't you think?"

...

"How long will its effects last?" I ask.

"Ah well, some effects will fade after a few hours, but as I said, it will fully activate the parasite inside your chest, the resulting changes caused by that will be perm—"

"What *the hell...* are you talking to him about, Corella?" demands Vivian, storming up to us and looking mad enough to spontaneously combust.

I look from Vivian to Corella and back again, my body language proclaiming my guilty conscience as I search for the right words.

"Oh, I'm just flirting with him. You're done with him now anyway, right? Got bored of him? Didn't think you would mind—honest, sis, I didn't," mocks Corella, effortlessly transitioning into a very effective lie that perfectly explains my sudden awkwardness.

I'd expect nothing less from Corella Restless.

Vivian stomps on Corella's foot—*hard.*

Corella yelps, but before she can retaliate, Vivian drags me up to the front of the line.

...

We've walked in silence for a long while before Vivian decides to speak again.

"Corella always lies. *Always.*"

...

"I know."

"You can't trust her. And the same goes for Nona," Vivian says—this time managing to take me aback.

"Viv—"

"Just *listen* to me. I've tried to keep an open mind—I know you do not trust people easily, so I sat back and observed the princess. Nothing about her story adds up. Even ignoring the obvious absurdity of her resemblance to Kasca Haine—she knows things she should not possibly know. She's allegedly an expert on No Man's Land from Neo Kyoto—but that's on the other side of the word. So... how the absolute fuck does she know so much about the species around Prospera? The ecology should be totally different over here. And why would Prosper Electronica go through all the trouble of contacting a 19-year-old novice researcher from Neo Kyoto, when there are plenty of Free Lancer poachers here who can act as experts on No Man's Land? Most importantly... She's too nice—you should know as well as I do that anyone who tries that hard to signal virtue is playing a game—no one is authentically *that* good-natured. Rowan—that girl is wearing a mask of her own no matter how much she claims to hate them."

"You're main argument is that she's too nice? Vivy... I generally agree with that—but exceptions do exist to that rule of thumb... even if jaded, cynical people like us have a hard time believing it," I reply.

"You were standing there in the SpeakEasy—all alone and pretending like you didn't need anyone's help. She read you like the lonely book you are, Rowan. That's obviously the most likely explanation—if you were thinking objectively you would see that. Even if she's not secretly evil, you should look down at your mangled hand and think hard the next time about rushing to sacrifice yourself for a girl with ambiguous motivations—because there *will* be a next time. I don't know what her motivations are—her goals might actually not conflict with ours at all. But you cannot trust what she says at face value—there is more going on here, I know it."

Indignation rises up in me like bile.

"I was standing there alone pretending not to need anyone else? What about you, *Vivian*? You're as alone as I am, and you know it. She's not being totally forthcoming? What about you—you've been leaving me in the dark since the moment we got here—earlier than that, actually. You are the one who obviously knows a hell of a lot more than you're telling me, and I'm sick of it. Her story is odd—but what about yours? Why would Prosper Electronic hire the daughter of their main adversary to do something like this? You *obviously* have a conflict of interest. I risk myself for your sake even when you push me away—and you don't even seem grateful for it—unlike her. So maybe you should drop the fucking hypocrisy, aye?"

The rush of emotions on Vivian's face are so complicated that I don't know what to make of them—is she guilty? Angry? Sad? Does she pity me? I can't begin to guess—but she obviously feels something and that feels like an accomplishment, at least.

Vivian opens her mouth to reply—before closing it and trying again.

"Row—"

"We're in luck—we've got some intact buildings up ahead," announces Brawn from the front of the line.

...

It's not long until we've cleared out a small building that appears to have once been a pawn shop.

The young Restless soldier sits near the front window, doing maintenance on his rifle while chatting with Nona.

Nona, on the other hand, is multitasking herself by also playing with Poe, having completely gotten over her fear of the oversized bird at some point while I wasn't paying attention.

Vivian picks that moment to yank me up by my jacket collar, like pulling on a misbehaving dog's lease.

"Let's start the stupid negotiations already," announces Vivian, pointing at a door to a back room.

Corella agrees, rising along with Brawn.

"Ryan, stay up front and post security," orders Brawn.

"You can keep him company, *princess*," adds Vivian.

Nona is clearly annoyed that Vivian is trying to exclude her, but in classic Nona fashion, she avoids the fight and gives in.

If anything, Nona is even more submissive now... her confidence in her own judgment is obviously in tatters from earlier.

The four of us enter the back room and close the door.

I pull out a list I was already using to keep track of our supplies and recite what the three of us have.

Vivian looks at me incredulously.

"How do you know what I have?" she asks.

"...I know you don't enjoy bean-counting, and Nona is too easily distracted to be trusted with it, so... I inventoried everyone's packs while you two were asleep. I've been watching what you two uses since and taking note of it," I answer.

"That's... *What*? That's such an invasion of privacy..." says Vivian, glaring at me.

"Oh please—you're such a drama queen, sis. He spent *ten years* waiting on you every moment of the day, scrubbing your undies and playing house with you—most of it done *without* a mask on..." We can't see Corella's eyes, but her tone heavily implies that if we could, they'd be rolling right now.

Vivian seems to decide it's best to just pretend like she didn't hear Corella.

"Captain, you said you had information to trade? What about?" asks Vivian, the faintest hint of pink in her cheeks.

...

"We have some idea of Kasca Haine's true value, of why Prosper Electronica wants her back so badly. We also know certain things about the other Lancers, and specifically, Riot... which will be relevant to you as well," replies Brawn.

"Careful, Brawn... how many times do I have to warn you to *watch your tongue*?" warns Corella.

Like before, Brawn bows respectfully.

"Of course, ma'am."

Me and Vivian exchange looks.

"We... would be interested in that information, I suppose. Rowan... I'll let you handle the particulars of the deal... you know how much stuff we can afford to spare," says Vivian.

Corella tries—very half-heartedly—to turn a laugh into a cough.

...

Ten minutes later, I've finished negotiating the terms.

"Okay, now tell us what's up. And I swear, if you try to feed us some useless trivia like Riot's horoscope, the deal is *off*," says Vivian.

"Should I, or would you rather do the talking, ma'am?" asks Brawn.

"I can manage it. Let's start with the missing girl... Well, to start, she *is* the daughter of Prosper Electronica... but *only* in name. There is no blood connection," says Corella.

That explains why she's not an Amelior, at least, though why one of the most powerful people in Prospera would adopt a Natural...

"I hope that's not *all* you know—that's interesting and all, but it doesn't actually change anything," says Vivian.

"Don't get your panties in a twist, baby sis. Kasca Haine may look like a Natural, but... there is something very special about her genetics, something that makes her DNA more valuable than even a Restless's..."

...

"*Well...?*" prompts Vivian, having zero patience for her sister's fondness for the melodramatic.

"... She *doesn't* age. Not anymore. Once she finished puberty, her aging froze... She's been biologically 20-something for decades now. Prosper Electronica discovered her and have been studying her ever since, certain that she will be the key to developing perpetual youth, which they can then market and sell... Not that it will need much of the former—it will be the kind of product that sells itself," finishes Corella.

...

The ramifications of such a tech would absolutely change the world forever.

It also explains why the company is willing to pay extravagantly enough to make *dozens* of Lancers accept a suicide mission. I might not know what the other Lancers are being paid, but it has to be just as valuable to them as a cure to The Fade is to Vivian and I, for them to have accepted.

"Also, you might already know this, but... Riot's group is not the only group besides yours to make it out here. Another team of Lancers used a... *gentler* touch. This bunch managed to get past the FireJacks without any bloodshed."

It is true that not all the other Lancers had wanted to team up with Riot—having never seen them past the meeting at the Night Library, I'd almost forgotten they were not a united front...

At least, in theory, we should all be on the same side. Britannica had made it clear that we would all be rewarded as agreed, so long as they got their girl back in one piece.

It made sense for Prosper Electronica to de-incentivize infighting this way, particularly since the chances of many Lancers returning alive to all demand their payments were low at best.

In my opinion, the information we'd already received was more than enough to buy the supplies I'd agreed our group could part with...

But Vivian wasn't going to let them off any easier than necessary.

"Okay, what about Riot? You said you had information on him, right? We're not giving you *anything* without that as well."

...

"Greedy girl, but fine... This is something I would have ended up sharing for free, anyway. Besides doing the job he was hired for, he's also going to kill *you*... If he gets the chance."

"WHAT?!" I yell, feeling the blood drain from my face.

Vivian looks stunned.

"Why *me*?" asks Vivian, sounding more perplexed than anything.

"Well, no need to take it personally. Riot wants to kill the entire Restless family. In turn, our father wants him dead. Both Daddy Dearest and Riot see a trip into No Man's Land as an excellent opportunity to kill people who are otherwise very difficult to get ahold of. I was sent here with a squad of soldiers, *specifically,* to handle Riot... among other things. Riot knew somehow that you would be in No Man's Land, so he's looking for you as well as Kasca Haine. I don't know if he knows I'm here yet or not; he might just assume the House Guard is here under your authority... but he will absolutely try to kill me as well if he realizes."

The things Corella said to me earlier echo in my mind.

"*... you don't deserve someone if you're not even strong enough to protect them...*"

This raises almost as many questions as it answers.

I consider asking Corella about Nona and how she fits into this whole affair, but they don't *seem* to have realized Nona has anything to do with Kasca, and I don't want to draw attention to that fact if they don't already know.

"What about—" begins Vivian.

"Na ah—no sale, lil sis. That's more than enough. Take it or leave it. You're lucky to even get this much out of us—you're the combat expert—you know you wouldn't win if it came to a fight between us right now," interrupts Corella.

Vivian's jaw locks, but she doesn't try to argue the point.

Whatever the explanation is, it seems clear that both of the girls I'm trying to protect are being targeted by someone I have no hope of beating in any kind of fair fight.

With an expression like someone just stole the clothes off her back, Vivian turns without another word and heads out the door.

I rise as well.

But right as I'm about to follow Vivian out, Corella stops me and presses something into my hand.

I don't need to look at it to know what it must be.

I pocket it.

28

Into the Dark

"The woods are lovely, dark and deep,
But I have promises to keep,
And miles to go before I sleep,
And miles to go before I sleep."
— Robert Frost, Stopping by Woods on a Snowy Evening

"Let's see... you were just on your way out—*Right*?" Vivian locks eyes with her sister.

"Vivy... we took too long talking, night has fallen... We can't force them out..." I say gently.

"We had an agreement. I made it damn clear I wasn't willing to spend a moment more with *her* than is necessary," says Vivian through gritted teeth.

I think Vivian would become violent if I told her what Corella just gave me.

Part of me thinks I should tell Vivian about it, hand it over to her...

But I will do what's necessary to keep her safe—no price is too high.

No... It won't come to that—holding onto Corella's gift doesn't mean I have to ever use it.

I won't let the situation become that dire.

"Yeeeaaah... We're not leaving. Sorry, little sis, but as big and scary as you are, the things that go bump in the night in a place like this are yet bigger and scarier than even you." Corella's hand drifts towards the Burner Blade at her hip.

Vivian pulls a knife—no hesitation at all.

I can't see Corella's face beyond the mask, but there is nothing but the deepest dislike on Vivian's.

Brawn and the other soldier, Ryan, both have the look of people readying themselves mentally for a fight they don't really want to have.

"No! No, wait... Vivy, please... we can just leave ourselves. There are other buildings nearby—a ten-minute walk at most..." I say in the tone of voice one might use when trying to calm an angry animal.

Vivian looks at me.

...

"Fine. *Fucking Fine*. Corella—I'm going to pretend not to notice you going back on our agreement because it was my fault for imagining you'd keep your word in the first place. But from this point on, stay the hell away from us, or I'll blow you to a million pieces—I swear it on our cunt mother's head—so fucking help you," Vivian says, her voice as cold as the dark side of the moon.

"We... are leaving, Nona," I say, turning to face her.

She shakes her head.

"Rowan... this is a bad idea. Walking around in the dark in No Man's Land... You really don't understand—*please* believe me on this," she says desperately.

I do believe her, but...

"Nona, Vivian is going to leave no matter what I say. You don't know the history she has with Corella. It's... bad. And where she goes, I follow—it's as simple, and as complicated, as that."

Nona grabs my jacket sleeve.

"Rowan... you *could* make her stay. I don't know why she pretends otherwise, but she obviously loves you," says Nona.

...

"You're wrong... She might not be eager to watch me die right in front of her, but it's not like that... she cut me out of her life without a second thought—I'm anything but irreplaceable to her," I say.

"Rowan, do you remember when you woke up after almost drowning? Vivian did not want me to tell you, but she was the one who pulled you out—she gave you CPR—"

"Like I said, she might not want to see me die b—"

"No, *listen* to me! She was a mess, Rowan—she was bawling her eyes out until you started breathing again. And even if that hadn't happened, it's so obvious... The way she steals glances at you when she thinks no one will notice, the way she inserts herself into conversations when we start talking too much, the way she can't stand me wearing your scarf... I'd bet anything she was the one who gave it to you, wasn't she?" whispers Nona.

I reflexively reach up to touch the scarf.

"S... She did, yeah... but she just wanted to keep your face hidden earlier—it wasn't anything more than that."

"Both of you are so hopeless, I swear. I don't understand what your hist—"

"Rowan! I'm leaving—with or without you and the princess," yells Vivian, interrupting Nona mid-sentence.

"I have to go with her. I'm sorry, Nona..." I get up to follow Vivian.

Nona gets up to follow me.

"Don't be a coward, Rowan! It doesn't suit you at all," says Nona, in a voice loud enough for Vivian to overhear it and cock an eyebrow up in confusion.

But I am a coward, deep down.

I *want* to believe what Nona is telling me... about Vivian loving me... but if I test the theory, if I confront Vivian with it or try to make her stay for my sake... and she rejects me...

That would crush me.

Just as it did the last time.

My relationship with Vivian is like Schrödinger's cat—so long as I refuse to open the box, my hopes for a life with Vivian can stay half alive, at least...

I'd rather risk whatever freak animals are in the shadows outside than risk getting the wrong answer.

I tell Nona once again that she can stay with Corella's group for the night—but, as loyal as ever, she refuses.

We disarm the traps Brawn set on the door.

Vivian flicks on her flashlight.

The beam of light trembles on the wall, and I look down at Vivian's hands in surprise.

They're... shaking.

Vivian is *afraid.*

Furious, Vivian grabs her shaking hand with the other... and the light beam steadies.

Vivian might be disgusted by insects, but that's not the same... It's a truly rare thing to witness Vivian Restless shaking in fear.

I thought I'd never see her so visibly afraid ever again; her childhood phobia of blood was the only exception... and she got over that years ago.

Vivian throws open the door, I follow her, Nona follows me, and together the three of us step into the night air.

The door is shut behind us.

I hear furniture being moved to barricade the entrance shut.

As soon as that's done, the traps will be reset on the door.

There is no turning back.

It's been a long time since I've been as scared as I am right now.

Memories of a pitch-black cell start to invade my mind, making me suddenly feel small, weak... pathetic.

It's much worse than it was in the alley when Nona was almost kidnapped—even worse than it was in my home, looking down the dark staircase to see Riot gazing back up at me from the shadows.

I'm more scared right now than I was during the Thorn Lion attacks... both of those were more exciting for me than terrifying, really.

Invigorating, even.

That kind of danger makes me feel wonderfully alive.

But now, with the narrow beam of light from Vivian's torch the only illumination in the absolute pitch black, the strange sounds of animals I cannot even begin to imagine, and the knowledge that not only myself but

Vivian and Nona are in mortal danger from horrors I can't even see, let alone, fight...

Nona grips the back of my jacket with one of her small hands as we walk.

I reach behind and give it a little reassuring squeeze.

She squeezes back, and now I'm not sure who is comforting who here.

The sound of rustling never ceases. Once again, it's as if there is a never-ending gust of wind running through every single branch.

In the daylight, it is unnerving.

In the dark... it is the stuff of nightmares.

We follow the cracked and pot-holed remains of what was once a paved road.

It's unbelievable how much worse this is than the other time I went out at night—that time to escape a literal nightmare, this time to enter one.

The difference is, back then, the sun *had* just begun to rise. The black had started to give way to blackish-blue, and the predators were already returning to whatever rocks they had crawled out from under.

Back then?

Shit.

That was only last night, wasn't it?

How is that even possible...?

From somewhere to our rear, there is a laugh... Not a human laugh—something more akin to the cackle of a hyena.

Inexplicably, I suddenly want to return the laugh.

It all seems desperately funny to me—absurd.

I bite down on my own tongue to stifle the temptation.

Nona's hand, still held in mine, trembles.

Vivian's breathing is rapid and so ridiculously loud I'd almost believe she was breathing into a megaphone.

I see bobbing lights in the distance, just like the ones I saw last night while on guard duty and had meant to ask Nona about.

They start to move faster, their gentle rising and falling transforming into a frantic dance.

I start to veer course towards the dancing lights.

I want to know their cause. I want to feel their light caress my skin...

I feel certain that, if I get close enough, there will be a wonderful warmth to accompany the light...

Nona whimpers, drawing my attention back down to her.

I realize that she is still holding my hand, trying to drag me back but largely failing.

A few feet ahead of her is Vivian—still holding the flashlight, looking back at us and trying to understand the strange sight of me dragging Nona off into the night while she clings desperately to my hand.

Over Vivian's shoulder, I see a pair of glowing eyes.

Terror jolts through me, making me abandon my attempt to investigate the lights and rush towards Vivian's side, ax in hand—anger at myself making me feel suddenly much braver and clearing my mind.

The pair of eyes close, the glow of their light blinking out of existence.

We start walking again.

The overwhelming smell of rotten fruit starts to fill my nose, making me want to vomit.

And then, up ahead... a two-story building.

Shelter.

Salvation.

We all break into a run.

And then we're standing in front of the door, readying ourselves to enter.

I check my watch.

We've only been outside for *six* minutes.

I ready my ax.

Vivian taps my shoulder, signaling to me that she's ready to breach.

I kick open the door.

29

UNBELIEVABLY LUCKY

It soon becomes clear that there is nothing in the house that wants to eat, mutilate, or lay its eggs inside us.

To say we were "lucky" seems like a gross understatement, somehow.

Our fortune seems almost impossibly good, and our moods as we set our security measures and roll out sleeping bags are unabashedly giddy with relief, high on the simple pleasure of not being dead yet.

We find a windowless room on the second floor that looks to have once been a study or a personal library, two of the walls completely devoted to bookshelves.

The four solid walls make it feel extra safe, something I'm sure all three of us are craving after our walk through the dark woods—and no windows means we don't need to be cautious about lights.

Also, something about the distinctly man-made smell of books makes me feel like I'm back in civilization—Prosperans love books because they symbolize human triumph over the natural world—the FireJacks fund their existence largely by selling the timber they bring down to paper manufacturers or high-end construction. Authentic, natural paper books are a luxury item in Prospera—a status symbol.

I've never felt any great sense of kinship with society... but after experiencing the horrendous, alien night of No Man's Land... I'm willing to forgive it for its failings—for the time being.

Nona pulls out a lamp from her pack, lights it, and hangs it from the ceiling.

Warm amber light fills the room, letting Vivian finally turn off her flashlight.

I'm willing to bet we'll end up sleeping with the light on all night tonight.

We're making progress, but no place in No Man's Land can really feel like home without traps being set.

Outside the door to the library, we put up some netting and electrify it. Useless against any human attackers, as it is *very* obviously just sitting there... But hopefully effective against any wildlife.

On the first floor, though, we plant a small explosive and run a tripwire—counting on this precaution to, at the very least, warn us if someone like Riot comes walking in.

Does Riot need to be afraid of the night as we are? Or is he too powerful for even No Man's Land after dark to pose him any serious threat?

Nona was right—going out tonight was *incredibly* stupid... I only truly appreciate that now.

But we're fine.

We got away with it.

We were stupid, certainly... but lucky enough to avoid paying a price for our stupidity, and that's what matters.

I realize that Nona is talking quietly to Vivian, but as far as I can tell, it is not about anything serious.

This is no surprise; I know by now that Nona is both the kind of person to talk when she is anxious and to relentlessly pursue friendship even when someone makes it clear they are not interested.

I think Nona takes Vivian's dislike as something of a personal challenge—sure that she can win Vivian over if she wears her down enough.

What does surprise me is that Vivian is talking back as she undresses down to her bedclothes and rolls out her sleeping bag, her thick hair temporarily pulled back into a messy bun until she can get around to taming it.

Nona's stolen soldier's mask is even off without Vivian making any objections.

"... I can't believe you placed *4th* in the rankings! I studied for six months and only managed to get 17th..." says Nona, giving me the context I need to guess at the topic they're on.

From other people, this might come off as simple flattery, but Nona is so crushingly sincere it is hard to believe her awe is anything but honest.

"Yeah, well... I am a Restless; we always rank near the top... My father's policy has always been to keep IQ-enhancing gene edits a secret until a competitor discovers them. Only then will Restless Genetics offer them for sale themselves. I don't deserve the credit for my placement," says Vivian.

She's not lying, of course, but...

Whatever else she might claim, she *does* work hard. She studied long into the night for weeks and weeks prior to the Inter-City Placements.

I feed Poe nuts from the corner, playing a game with her where she has to guess which hand I'm hiding the treat in.

She's starting to get a little *too* good at it—I might need to introduce some new kind of challenge into the mix soon...

"... 17th is still respectable. You must have been one of, if not, *the* highest Natural in the rankings," says Vivian.

I smile.

Any compliment means a lot, coming from Vivian.

"I was the 3rd highest Natural!" says Nona cheerfully.

"I'll just have to work harder next time, so I can catch up to you. Although I try not to care about the rankings too much... I only bothered with it because I'd hoped it would convince the Prosperan space program to make an exception for me, even though I'm not an Amelior... Everyone is intelligent in their own way, I think, regardless of some dumb test. It's like that Einstein quote about a fish being dumb if you judge it by its ability to climb a tree, or... I don't know—it went something like that, I'm pretty sure," says Nona, stretching as she unties her hair ribbon and lets her super long hair fan out behind her.

Ah man, their conversation had been going well, but I doubt Vivian's going to like that.

Sure enough...

"That's ridiculous—you *can't* actually be serious..." Vivian shakes her head and crosses her arms in front of her.

"*Nice* people love to say things like that—your type always talks about how 'everyone is so smart and beautiful and special, in their own wonderful, magical way... But what gives those words their value is that they indicate the presence of an *exception* to the norm. If *everyone* is this or that, then it means absolutely nothing anymore to be those things. It's like when governments print more money to alleviate poverty and end up only devaluing the currency to the point of worthlessness. The world being unfair does not become fair by blindly ignoring the facts. Not all people are created equal. And in this day and age, that is the *literal* truth."

Nona leans back and puts a finger to her chin, honestly mulling over Vivian's words.

People can generally be trusted to go on the defensive when their beliefs are criticized—they take it personally because, in a way, it *is* personal. We are our beliefs. A flaw in a belief is a flaw in ourselves.

But Nona is one of the remarkably open-minded people who can handle it—her sense of personal identity is somehow not threatened by intellectual disagreements... yet she's still the kind of girl to break down in tears if you seriously insult her directly.

I could tell Nona that I thought her entire worldview was irredeemably stupid, and she wouldn't get angry—so long as I did so without raising my voice and explained my reasoning properly.

But, on the other hand, I could tell her I was disgusted by the way she chewed her food, and she'd be absolutely distraught.

Vivian is totally different... quick to anger, quick to argue, skin as thick as the earth's crust, but she is also nearly impossible to intimidate, and her blunt approach to everything is motivated more by a commitment to honesty than a desire to hurt anyone.

They are both, without a doubt, exceptionally special people.

"Why the hell are you giving us such *creepy* looks?" asks Vivian, catching me watching them.

I chuckle.

"Sorry, I hate to interrupt, but... we all need to get to sleep. What shift would you each like? I'll take whatever's left over," I say.

...

With shifts decided, Vivian sits against a bookcase and pulls out a comb to untangle her outrageously messy hair, but...

Her hands are shaking.

As if someone has opened a trapdoor under my heart, I feel it plummet down into a waiting pool of stomach acid.

Vivian's hands were not trembling from fear earlier...

They were trembling from the Fade.

Neurogenic tremors—one of the few early-warning symptoms before memory loss sets in.

Without a word, I walk over to Vivian, take the comb from her hand... and sit down to brush out her hair—the way I used to do every night when we were kids.

Vivian does not try to stop me.

From the other side of the room, Nona watches us.

...

I'm still awake when Vivian's turn at watch duty comes around.

When I hear her start to cry softly... I decide to pay back the kindness she showed me the night before and pretend to be asleep... because I know that's what she wants.

It doesn't much matter what happens to me.

But those two... They must survive this.

30

Lights Out

Something is here.

We all know it because Vivian's tripwire has just set off an explosion downstairs.

We all sit bolt upright, an explosion probably the most potent alarm clock humans have ever invented.

Me and Vivian exchanged looks... Both of us hoping that maybe we'd managed to kill whatever it was that tripped the wire.

But then we hear movement, not footsteps but... Something like a very heavy object being dragged.

I gesture at the other two to grab their packs.

There is no time for the sleeping bags, but if we all lose our gear, we will surely die out here—even if we manage to survive whatever is now in the building.

It had seemed like such a good idea to pick a room without any windows, but now...

There is only one stairway.

My mind races.

Wait! Okay—there is definitely a window in the room next to ours. I remember seeing it when we first checked the building.

I open the door.

At the end of the hallway, blocking the entrance to the stairs stands...

I don't know how to describe it—the darkness in the hallway is too thick... all I can make out is the vague outline of... *something.*

But the outline alone is impossible.

Incomprehensible.

The natural world does not create shapes like that.

Evolution gives sensible solutions, places limbs in predictable places, insists upon practical constraints on sizes and shapes, and maintains some degree of symmetry...

And surely, no intelligent designer would have ever forced themselves to dream up such a tortured geometry of flesh and bone—any being with the ability to do otherwise would invent something, *anything*, besides this.

If I had any religious bones in my body—if I was from Kallipolis where that kind of thinking still existed... This would be the moment I'd lose it for good.

A single, gigantic red eye opens and consumes me as I stand there, petrified.

It glows in the dark, like some blood-red moon.

I step back into the study and slam the door shut.

In a burst of panic, I rush forward and start to push a heavy desk in front of the door—books falling to the floor in my haste. It slides in place with a satisfying weight behind it... but anything that can keep coming after tripping a mine will not be slowed down much by a desk.

The indescribable sounds of an impossible monstrosity stops outside the door.

It's *fine*... the electric net will electrocute whatever it is...

...

But there is no burst of light, no shriek of animalistic pain.

The doorknob rattles.

Whatever it is, it's intelligent enough to disarm the electrified net.

Vivian has her bow out, and a blue-fletched arrow already knocked.

The doorknob is ripped from the door in one powerful pull, taking a chunk of the door with it leaving a basketball-sized hole in the decaying wood.

The blood-red moon slides into the empty space—bathing us in its filthy, contaminated light.

A gasp escapes from either Vivian's or Nona's lips.

Or maybe it came out of mine?

Whichever of us it was, I'm honestly surprised it was not a scream.

Poe is in an uproar, beating her wings and screeching like mad.

Vivian raises her bow.

There is no way she could miss that thing from up so close, and few things could survive an arrow to the eye, but...

Instinct, or maybe simple cowardice masquerading as instinct, screams at me that this nightmare could never be killed so easily.

Vivian hesitates, perhaps sensing what I do.

And then I catch Nona's terrified expression.

There is not just fear there, but also recognition.

She knows what this thing is.

Our eyes lock, and she shakes her head, the panic written all over her face.

The eye stares at us—unblinking—drinking the sight of us in... savoring the sight of so much meat trapped in such a tiny, exitless room.

Vivian is a second away from releasing the arrow.

I see the red-fletched arrows in her quiver as well—which I recognize as being the explosive-tipped ones...

"NO! Just give them here!" I shout as I lunge for the bow.

This is my fault.

This thing must have followed us from outside.

We did not get away with our stupid gamble after all.

I let it come to this.

All my fault.

My fault.

Vivian's face is a mixture of surprise, confusion, and anger as I steal away her bow and one of her arrows.

She looks about ready to hit me—but on some level, I know she still trusts me enough to know I must have my reasons for this.

"Both of you, get behind me, in that corner—NOW!"

Vivian moves, but Nona hesitates... seemingly petrified by the staring, unblinking eye that watches us.

I literally throw her into the corner with Vivian.

I place my body in front of theirs—as if we are all attempting to cower in the corner together, and I tell them to make themselves as small as possible.

Then I knock the explosive-tipped arrow I'd snatched from Vivian's quiver.

With all my might, I pull back on the string.

Some distant corner of my mind marvels as it has on dozens of occasions before, that Vivian... with arms half the size of mine... can so effortlessly handle something like this.

I let the arrow fly.

These arrows are designed to focus the explosive force forward, but I know that there is no guarantee that shrapnel won't be a risk at this extremely close distance.

Sure enough, I feel something hit me just above my hip bone.

But this is all I'm good for. My body can sustain and heal from damage like no one else's.

The decaying wall is blown open, bathing us in a rush of cold night air.

Again, my ears are ringing—I will almost certainly have permanent damage in them after all this, even with the parasite constantly trying to fix me in its imperfect way.

Unfortunately, we're not on the first floor.

But it's only the second floor, and a fall from this height is unlikely to do too much damage—assuming none of us lands wrong.

For all intents and purposes, a twisted ankle might as well be a fatal injury right now.

"OUT!" I yell as I thrust the bow into Vivian's hands and grab my ax.

The last of the door is torn away from its hinges as we all jump into the dark—unable to see what we're jumping into in the pitch-black night air.

Thankfully, all we find when we hit the ground is bushes and tall grass, and I don't believe any of us, except myself, are injured as we sprint into the dark.

I hear a flap of wings that at first scares me before I realize it's only Poe following us from above.

I trip on a log and bust my head against a tree trunk almost instantly, and I can hear Nona's sounds of pain as she also trips over the undergrowth in her haste.

We will never get away at this rate.

"Vivian! Wait!" I drag Nona up off her knees and fumble my way into Vivian before grabbing her and passing off Nona's outstretched hand.

"Keep a hold on her hand—you two need to stay together!"

Vivian can fight.

Nona understands how to survive out here.

I am the only expendable one, and besides...

I already swore I would not let them die.

I fucking refuse.

Vivian says nothing, but I trust that they are now moving together.

I risk a look behind me.

There are only two things visible to me.

Blackness...

... and a single, glowing, blood-red moon.

Terror threatens to send me into a blind panic, but I force myself to take a deep breath.

Okay.

Right, Rowan...

There is only one thing to do.

I break right instead of following the sounds of Vivian and Nona's clumsy retreat.

I hope Vivian will be too focused on navigating the terrain to stop and check on me... If she notices, I'm sure she will try to come back for me.

I stumble every few steps as I proceed to wake up every living creature in No Man's Land—crashing through the thick vegetation with every step I take.

I risk a glance behind me again.

The massive eye is there—no more than a few feet away.

I take a frantic swing of my ax, connecting with something solid.

But then it has me.

It's pinning me to the forest floor—I'm on my back, and my ax is ripped from my hands as if I'm as weak as a toddler instead of a fully grown man, a practiced killer.

I cannot move.

The weight of this monster is crushing me.

Something pierces my side, like a needle, but *far* more massive.

Memories I've tried for so many years to forget force their way into my consciousness.

Now is not the time. I must do... something...

I'm back in my cell, and *that* man's eyes bore into me from above.

I start to sob.

This was never supposed to happen again.

I scream.

I bite into putrid flesh with all the crazed desperation of a cornered animal.

The huge red eye only mocks me for my weakness.

Hot blood flows out of me once again.

Of course.

Of course... this is what it would come to, in the end.

It is my fate to hurt, to bleed, to suffer.

This is all I have ever existed to do.

I feel *something* enter me—hot fluid mixes with the blood in my veins.

There must be some kind of stinger, pumping me full of a horrible venom—poisoning me.

There is pain.

So much pain.

It is spreading through my body—I can feel the liquid cutting its path through my veins, setting every cell it makes contact with on fire.

I realize now that my vision is blacking out—probably has been for some time, but it was imperceptible in the darkness.

I hope this is finally one venom too deadly for my parasite to have any hope of filtering out.

I do not *want* to die, not yet...

But I want, even less... to live.

I'm so tired...

Darkness...

I can't see anything now, not even the glowing red eye of the monster that is killing me.

31

Eight-Ball

(HOOVERVILLE, 12 YEARS AGO)

"Every action has its pleasures and its price."
- Socrates

I don't really understand all the rules of the game yet, but I know that when you play Pool, you're not allowed to hit the Eight-ball into the hole until the very end.

I know that 'cause *that's* where our name comes from—me and all the other boys hiding in the room with me.

We're all called "Eight-balls."

There are 11 of us here, each with a weapon, and each of us are trying to be as quiet as possible so we don't let the man behind the door hear us too soon.

They call us that cause the rules say that if you're eight or younger, you're still too small for jail—which all us kids call "The Hole".

So, we don't get in real trouble—even if we do something really bad.

Well, they try to send you to an orphanage... but it's easy to run away from an orphanage, so that barely even counts.

The rusty butcher's knife is heavy in my hands, much heavier than I remember it being an hour ago.

Most of us aren't even *really* orphans—most of us just have one parent with The Fade and one who's not around no more.

If you have two parents, one of them getting The Fade is bad. But if you only have one, like me... then you might as well be an orphan.

I'm the one who has to take care of Mom now; I bring her food and water and stuff... but she doesn't even know who I am no more.

There is one older boy with us—he's our leader. Instead of a knife, he has a suuuper nice mask—one of the shiny, high-tech ones with a camera built into it.

My palms are wet with sweat. I don't wanna drop my knife, so I switch hands to wipe them dry on my shirt.

"Hey... How would you like to see my face? I don't usually offer this to most guys, but... I'll make a special exception for you, mister..." The walls are thin and half-rotted out, so it's easy to hear when one of the Honey Girls gives us the signal.

All the Eight-balls look up at Leader for confirmation.

He nods.

I'm standing nearest the door, so I pull it open, and all the other boys run past me, followed immediately by Leader.

"WHAT THE—Who the *fuck*... are all of you?" screams an *almost* completely naked man.

The Honey Girl scrambles away from him—she knows now it's best to get away from the naked guy in case he tries to hit her... cause that's exactly what happened last time.

"Who are *we*...? Shiiit, who cares who we are—I wanna know who *you* are, big guy. Take off the mask," orders Leader lazily.

Me and the other 11 Eight-balls brandish our weapons, trying to make up for how small we all are with our numbers.

The Honey Girl runs behind Leader and zips her hoodie up, before waving her middle finger at the naked guy from over Leader's shoulder and laughing.

Cursing like a FireJack, the man does as Leader says.

I look away to avoid having to see his naked face for myself.

"Theeere we go! Don't look so sad, stud—just give us what we want... and no one need ever know that you spend your weekends buying the sweet stuff from Honey Girls down in Hooverville... Such a *distinct,* handsome fella you are—what's your name again? Say it niceee and clear for the camera... Cause I think you were made for the big screen."

The other kids start to laugh, so I do as well—part of me feels bad for the man, but another, louder part of me knows that me and Mom are gonna get food this week cause this rich man is gonna pay up.

Then I see something.

In the old, cracked mirror on the wall of the opposite side of the room, I can see myself—but there is also something behind me.

A huge, red eye—as big as I am—stares into me.

32

A Little Responsibility

(The Hole, 11 Years Ago)

I walk through the place that I'm told is to be my new home—unable to believe any of what is happening to me.

The trial went by so fast, it hadn't been fair at all...

He wasn't *supposed* to die—we just wanted some money...

It had been an accident, just like I'd told the judging man.

Why was that old man so *weak*, anyway?

Why couldn't he have been like everyone else and just given us what we wanted?

If someone is gonna fight back, they should at least be tough enough to take a few hits without...

Dying.

Why did he have to go and die?

I'm still barely even 11... I don't belong here...

Who will take care of Mom if I stay here too long?

And why won't they even let us wear masks in here?

It's so embarrassing...

And why are all those naked faces looking at *me* like...

Well...

Looking at me like the way me and my friends used to all look at an easy mark when we were picking out the ones to rob.

Friends?

No... They're not that, not anymore.

"No sir, we didn't want to hurt him at all. When he refused to hand over his stuff, the rest of us were ready to give up and try again with somebody else, but... He got so *angry*... he hit him with the bat and then just *wouldn't stop* hitting him. We all tried to pull him away, sir—I swear we did. He's always been like that—violent, angry... he enjoys hurting people, I think." The memory replays in my mind over and over again.

Every single one of my "friends" had lied about me—blamed the whole thing on me.

Even Leader... I'd thought Leader liked me.

It was true that I had been the first one to hit the old man—but I wasn't the only one, and no one had tried to stop anything.

I'm not an Eight-ball anymore—not protected from the rules anymore.

I shake away the bad thoughts. Leader said that if I kept my mouth shut, they would break me out—I have to believe in him.

I drop the pillowcase stacked on top of my pair of new inmate uniforms and get a hard kick from the prison guard walking behind me.

He still gets to have a mask, but even with a mask and a hat on, I can tell he's starting to lose his hair.

I bend down to pick up my pillowcase.

"Hurry up. You must be tired... we need to get you to your cell... to your bed," the guard says.

I don't know why he cares about that.

I shake my head.

"Na, it's still light out... I'm not some little kid who takes naps in the middle of the day," I object, offended.

I'm 11 years old now—not an adult, but still grown enough to not need mid-day naps.

"Not a little kid, aye? Maybe you're right... you did kill a man. Not an innocent little boy at all..." he says.

His tone of voice is weird.

I decided I want to get away from this man as soon as I can.

He kicks me forward, and we start to walk again.

We pass by a gym area where adult men lift big weights... I don't see anyone else here who looks younger than me... the youngest is probably about 15, *at least.*

Most are fully grown adults.

We are nearing the cell blocks now.

I can see that these are the kind of cells with bars instead of solid doors, and relief floods over me.

I do not want to be alone with this man.

But nothing can happen to me in full view like this... right?

.

..

...

Wrong.

I scream until my throat is raw.

No one seems to hear me.

Even though people *do* walk by the cell...

I watch them pass.

But they all pretend like I do not exist.

"11 years old and already a little murderer... You can't tell me you don't deserve this. You deserve to be hurt—that's why you're here. Pain is the point of punishment. No one cares about little monsters like you... Look at them all. They know you deserve this as well, so they don't give a damn what I do to you. No one cared even before you got here... I was at your trial, did you know that? No one came for you, did they? No one but me. I'm the closest thing to a friend you got."

I start to weep.

"You know you deserve it too—that's why it *hurts* so bad. Because this is *your* fault. You've earned this... You know that, don't you? Come on now, take a little *responsibility.*"

.

..

...

From outside the cell walls, I see something that I know cannot really be there.

A monster.

The glow from its red eye is nearly blinding—but I can see a horrifying tentacle sliding along the floor towards us.

The man keeps speaking, but I can no longer hear what he says—I can no longer hear anything at all.

Maybe the monster will kill the man?

Maybe the monster will kill me.

I do not care either way—so long as it ends.

The tentacle touches me.

The instant it does, my world turns off.

33

The Masked Angel

(The Hole, 10 Years Ago)

I'm in solitary confinement now.

I'm much happier—the prison guard cannot touch me while I'm here.

When I'm alone, I'm safe.

I wish I'd never have to leave again.

Every time they let me out, I do something bad so they'll put me back in.

They won't let me have pencils anymore, after what I tried to do... but they are still letting me have my chalk.

The psych doctor made the guards let me keep them.

I spend just about every free moment drawing on my walls.

I draw characters and give them names. They are my friends now.

My best friend is a horned demon named Gray—gray like the color of the walls he's drawn on.

He used to be weak like me, but the gods punished him until he got strong.

Now Gray is way too strong to get hurt—now he can hurt everyone who would try to hurt him instead.

Being strong means getting to hurt the bad guys instead of having the bad guys hurt you, even when the bad guys are strong, like a god or a monster.

He has two sharp horns and is like, seven feet tall—and he decided to become a demon so he wouldn't be so weak and sad anymore.

People he had thought were his friends, back when he was still human... They wouldn't even recognize him now.

Even though he's a demon, he's a good guy—he'll only hurt the ones who really, *really* deserve it.

And he's kind to me, even though he knows I deserve to be hurt too... he says I've been punished enough—he says that I can still change if I try my best every day.

He tells me to do my push-ups so I can get big and strong like him—and I do, every single day.

Not all the characters I draw agree with him... Some of them tell me I'll always be how I've always been.

When they do, I start to cry.

Because deep down, I know they are right.

I mostly just try not to talk to the mean ones too much...

Today, I redrew Gray to make him even bigger—way bigger than any of the mean ones.

But there is another drawing on the opposite wall I do not remember putting there—it is a huge, black monster with an eye so red it hurts to look at for too long.

I hate that drawing—I don't understand why I'd put it there—I don't remember ever having drawn it.

I go to sit under Gray instead—my protector... my friend. He's not like other adults—he can be trusted—he won't leave like my dad or fail me like mom.

I'll try not to cry so much anymore—if I want to be strong... I know I need to stop crying.

I've figured out one way to stop crying so far—When nothing else is working, I just bite into the side of my mouth as hard as I can—until the taste of iron distracts me.

It works every time.

Well, almost... almost every time.

I'm afraid they will take me back out of solitary soon—they don't usually let me stay longer than a week at a time, no matter how much trouble I cause.

I hear the sounds of footsteps.

My cell door opens.

My heart leaps into my throat.

Has it really been a week already? It is hard to keep track of time, but I thought I had a little more time left...

I hide in my corner, trying to make myself as small as I can, my hands covering my naked face.

"Ohhh, Daddy, look at all these drawings! He's so talented!" a voice says.

A *girl's* voice.

I look up.

I haven't seen a girl in a long time, well... other than the ones I draw on my walls.

A young girl about my age, wearing a fancy, rich-person mask of gold and purple, stands outside my now open door, looking in.

Her skin is perfectly smooth and olive, but it's her hair that really surprises me... her hair is super long and a combination of colors I never knew that hair could be—from a silvery-pink so light it almost looks white, to some much deeper shades of vibrant purple in the spots where the hair is in shadow.

Through her mask, I can see her eyes.

Her eyes are the deepest, prettiest purple I have ever seen.

None of my chalk colors could possibly match it.

She really is like one of the characters I draw... she is more beautiful than real people have any right to be.

I do not know what the rest of her face is like, but I feel sure it must be equally beautiful.

"Is this really all the options we have? Look at him. He's utterly defeated—cowering in the corner like that," says a man standing behind the girl, who rests a hand on her shoulder as he speaks, like he's afraid she might run away any second.

He must be her dad. His skin is the same shade of olive, and his hair is like hers as well, but with much less pronounced purples and pinks and more silvery-white—as if the saturation of his hair color has faded away with the years.

I wonder what it must be like to have a dad... I can barely remember mine.

"We have many better boys, sir... the issue is the age range you're requesting. We only have nine boys between 10 and 13 here currently. They don't tend to last long when they arrive here so young," a guard says from out of sight of the door.

I recognize the voice.

It's the monster man's voice.

My body starts to shake.

"Vivian! Get back here, now!" the girl's father says as she escapes his grasp and enters my cell.

I look up at her.

She marches right up to me and unwraps a crimson-red scarf from around her neck...

Before gently wrapping it around my exposed shoulders and face.

"You don't have a mask either—that's not right. Everyone should get to save their face for the people closest to them," the girl says.

I don't move, too stunned to respond.

This must be a dream.

Sometimes I do that—dream things even though I'm awake.

"I want this one, Daddy! Look at all these drawings—he must be super smart and creative to do all this!" She walks right up to where my best friend is and traces a finger lightly over his muscular outline.

"You should draw a picture of me someday! We have this painting of some dark-haired noblewoman named Lisa in our house... it's nice I guess—but I'd rather be painted with brighter colors when you do mine," she says thoughtfully.

...

What does she mean by she "wants this one"?

Something in me comes alive for the first time in months.

Hope.

Could she really take me out of this place?

"Vivian... scribbles are not enough. He will go through the tests—same as the others. If he wins, so be it. But don't get attached to any of them yet," says her father, stepping into the cell himself to regain control of his daughter.

"But Daaaddy! Why shouldn't I get to pick? He's going to belong to *me*, right? He's gonna have to look after me from now on, so... I think I should get to decide who it's gonna be!" the girl protests, crossing her arms and cocking her chin.

This girl... She's more than just beautiful, and she's being more than just nice to me.

She is stunning, and she... she actually *wants* me. She wants *me,* specifically...

She is an angel, I think. Something too good for the real world—a fantasy, a dream, an illusion.

As if falling from a great height, my stomach suddenly lurches up into my chest.

She will forget about me soon.

If something seems too good to be true, it probably is.

She will change her mind—she will realize that I'm not special after all and pick someone else.

"Vivian. Being able to make pretty pictures is *not* a qualification for serving our family." The father picks the beautiful girl up and drapes her over his shoulder like a sack of potatoes.

But...

The masked angel's father had said something about a test, a competition... even if she forgets about me, I just need to win it, right?

Then I can leave this place.

Forever.

I *will* win... or I will die trying.

34

Number 5

(THE HOLE, 10 YEARS AGO)

"And why should we feel anger at the world?
As if the world would notice."
— Marcus Aurelius

I scream into my filthy, flea-ridden pillow.

Another day of tests, another day of not being good enough.

It has been a week since the people in white coats gave us our surgeries, giving us our "special powers".

Every day since we spend all day testing.

They give us cuts and time how long it takes for them to heal.

They make us run and see who will be the last to collapse.

They make us drink things that hurt us, then we have to take intelligence tests while the fiery liquid is still burning up our insides.

They make us fight each other.

We all want it so badly. We all know that this is our only chance out of here.

Prosperan laws do not care about age—not once you're older than eight, anyway. The laws are laid out to be simple and unbending... The judging man just tells you if you are guilty or not after hearing the lies people say about you and then he reads out the punishment from his book.

None of the boys here have anything less than 20 years.

I think some of the boys would kill each other if they did not stop the fights early.

Every day, I try my very best.

But there is one boy who is just better than me, at *everything*.

Better than all of us.

I can see the way the people in the white coats have started to treat him, they are starting to act as if he has already won—even though there are still more tests to be done.

I thought that wanting it bad enough would be enough, but it's not...

I'm not good enough.

I never will be.

I'm going to die in here.

.

..

...

That night, the man comes for me again.

...

..

.

I've already killed someone once—that's why I am here.

It is already too late for me to be a good guy.

So maybe...

Killing someone is also my way out?

I hope so.

I can't take this much longer.

I think I'm starting to lose my mind.

My friends don't just talk to me now.

They *scream*.

Even Gray screams. He screams the loudest—screams at me to do something, *anything*.

Sometimes, I forget where I am and I have to focus for a long time before I can make myself remember.

I'm like the old man I killed—I'm not strong enough to fight... but I will try anyway.

A red glow fills the room that I cannot explain—along with the sensation I'm being watched.

I am surely going crazy.

Killing someone must be my way out.

I will kill Number 5...

Or I will kill myself.

Either way, I will leave this place.

35

What Winning Looks Like

(The Hole, 10 Years Ago)

"What the hell happened?! Did you give him the right dose?" yells one of the doctors, running in to examine the boy who is lying on the ground, foaming at the mouth and shaking violently.

"I—Yes! I Did! I... *think* I did..." a woman in a white coat says, face unknowable behind the medical mask, but her voice gives away her barely controlled panic.

Me and the other boys all stand back and take the sight in.

"*Fuck!* His heart has stopped! Go get the medical team—useless woman!" yells the other doctor again.

I can tell that none of the other boys are sad.

If anything, they are excited. They had given up hope of ever beating Number 5.

But now...

I see some of them looking at me.

They know that I'm the second-highest-scoring boy.

I've just become the one to beat.

I feel sick to my stomach.

Number 5's face has gone a horrible shade of purple, veins bulging in his neck and forehead.

What... have I done?

The man is right. I deserve to suffer.

Pain is the point of punishment...

The monster-man's words echo in my mind—over and over.

I deserve the things he does to hurt me—if I didn't, why would they be happening?

This is where people like me belong.

I bury my face into the scarf the masked angel gave me.

A voice calls my name—a strange, inhuman voice that does not even speak in a language I recognize—yet somehow, I can understand what it is saying.

"Well done."

I look up.

But nothing is there besides the other kids and doctors.

36

The God-Man's Ultimatum

(The Hole, 10 Years Ago)

"It is easier to build strong children than to repair broken men."
— Frederick Douglass

The god-man—the father of the angel who gave me my scarf—enters my isolation cell.

The man towers over not only me... but every man I can remember ever meeting in my 11 years alive.

Both he and his daughter do not feel human to me. They seem more than human... almost as if everyone else was just god's first try before he figured out what he was supposed to actually be doing.

I look around for the masked angel, realize that she is not with him, and feel my heart sink in disappointment.

This man seems much scarier without her here.

If she is an angel, then I think that must make him a god... isn't that how it works in the stories?

The door shuts behind him.

"Congratulations, Number 9. You've won. It was a close call between you and Number 4, but your overall performance was the highest... Once Number 5 was... *removed* from the running, that is," the god-man says.

I do not know what to say, so I say nothing, but I nod to show I understand.

"Number 5 would have beaten you both soundly... it is unfortunate what happened to him..." His words send a stab of guilt and fear through me.

Does he know?

I think he must.

He really is more than human—how else could he possibly know?

"Number 9. You killed 5, did you not?" His voice is not angry exactly, but... it is very firm.

I start to tremble.

Is this it? Did I work so hard, do something so bad, only to have it all fall apart like this in the end?

"Answer me, *boy*. But think hard before you do. Your answer will decide everything in my eyes about what manner of future you are fit to have."

I look up and try to meet his eyes.

Unlike his daughter, he wears a high-tech mask, the kind with an internal display and no holes for the eyes... but I stare into the place where I imagine eyes should be.

"I did, sir," I say.

"Why?"

"Because... this place is killing me, sir. And... because your daughter, she gave me this..." I hold up the scarf.

"... She... picked *me*. She actually wanted... *me*... I didn't want to let her down," I finish, surprising myself with how calm my voice sounds.

...

The god-man nods approvingly.

"A fine answer. So, you wish to serve the Restless family? Do you understand that, if you do, it will be as our property? You will be a tool for my daughter to use for as long as you live. I will not force you."

"I... want to help your daughter, sir. I am willing to be property, if it is for her... and if it means I can leave here," I say.

He studies me for a long time, silently.

I start to think I've ruined everything again.

"A brave answer. I am willing to accept it. However, you *will* follow the orders of *any* Restless man or woman—not only her. But as you wish, your primary duty will be to protect and serve her," he says.

I nod eagerly.

"Of course, sir."

"Now... Another question. That guard who oversees your cell block. He hurts you, doesn't he? I see the way you act whenever he is near."

I nod and look away, ashamed.

...

"I see."

The god-man turns to the cell door and bangs on it loudly.

A guard jumps to open it immediately.

"Do you know the guard responsible for this boy's regular cell block?" he demands.

"Y-Yes, sir," the guard replies, surprised.

"Bring him here. At once."

I start to shake again.

He is coming.

The monster-man is coming.

This was supposed to be my safe place. My friends on my walls are supposed to protect me while I'm in here.

On the wall furthest from me, the red eye of the monster devours me with its gaze—the drawing even larger now with black tentacles that snake halfway across the floor.

But I do not recall ever adding to it—I don't understand why it gets larger and larger...

Maybe the prison guard—the one who hurts me—maybe he comes into the solitary confinement cell and adds to the drawing while I'm gone?

"Stand up. Pull yourself together and face your enemy like a man. Or else I will leave you in here with him. *Alone*. Do you understand?" the god-man commands.

"Y-Yes... Yes, sir," I say, utterly terrified.

The door opens.

The monster-man steps in.

"You requested me, sir?" the monster-man says, but in the voice of a regular person.

This monster is good at sounding like a regular person when he wants to.

"Yes. Give me your sidearm—and your Unlocking Ring," commands the god-man coldly.

...

"You wish to kill the boy, sir? I do not know what he has done, but surely there is a—" the monster-man starts to say.

"Just do as you are told. Now."

He obeys the god-man's order.

I can't believe the monster can be ordered around like that—interrupted, ignored...

"Number 9... put this ring on," he throws it to me, and I just barely manage to catch it.

I put it on—even though it is much too big for my finger.

"Ah, s-sir... what are you intend—"

"SHUT... your mouth. Don't say another word unless you are spoken to. Nod once if you understand these orders," his voice is as cold and as hard as iron.

...

The monster-man nods.

The god-man walks over to me and places the gun into my outstretched hands.

"I turned off the safety. Kill him. This will be your final test."

What...?

I forget how to move my body—forget how to even breathe.

"Do. It. Now," orders the god-man.

I point the gun at the monster.

"WAIT... You'll be wearing light armor under the uniform, won't you? That won't do at all. Strip. Now. Or I will kill you myself," commands the god-man.

The monster-man starts to shake uncontrollably.

Not unlike the way I always do when he comes near me.

Why does the monster—who always seemed so horribly powerful to me, suddenly seem so... weak?

My hands shake so much, and the tears in my eyes are so thick that aiming is really, really hard.

The monster does as he is told again.

My head starts to spin... it's becoming hard for me to even breathe.

I shake my head.

"I... don't know if I can, s-sir..." I weep.

"You must. Even if you are to be property, you will not be just *any* property. It is unacceptable for anyone to be allowed to carry on believing they can humiliate and torment something that belongs to me without there being any consequences. Not only that, but... you will be of no use to me *or* my daughter if you cannot manage even this. On some level, he will own you for as long as you live. No one else will be able to truly own you until you've taken back what he stole."

The monster-man gets on its knees.

I don't understand all the things the god-man says... but I understand that he won't take me away unless I kill the monster.

"P-Please... I have a wife, two c-children—"

"NOT all things broken... are beyond repair. But when a person is broken, no one but themselves is capable of putting the pieces back together. This man has stolen a piece of you. You will only ever be damaged goods now... *unless* you can take it back. If that happens, your one and only chance to leave will be lost... and I will leave him here with you when I go. Number 4 will not complain when I go and free him in your place."

.

..

...

I am not a good shot.

I can't hit the monster-man in any of the right spots.

I just keep pulling the trigger until the gun won't shoot no more.

Only then does the monster decide to die.

Behind him—where the monster-man's body now lays motionless—looms the giant, red-eyed abomination of my waking nightmares.

It has no mouth, but then... how do I know—as surely as I know anything—that it is smiling at me?

37

Heaven and Hell

(The Restless Towers, 8 Years Ago)

The monster-man is gone.

I killed him.

But the monster-man said he had a wife and kids, so now I think a lot about what the family of a monster must be like...

They must be monsters too, right...?

Maybe it's a good thing I don't have a family anymore, if families can be evil too.

I can't stop myself from imagining the monster's family coming for me in my sleep, the way the monster-man sometimes would.

I can see them. They are standing over me right now.

They each have a mask identical to the plain ones the prison guards all had, the same as the monster... one of them is the size of a little girl—she has pigtails and a light pink dress.

Now she's laughing softly in my right ear.

I can feel the warmth of her breath.

There is also a boy, much bigger than me but smaller than his father was.

He takes hold of my arm and twists it in the way his father used to—he twists so hard that it feels on the verge of breaking.

In front of me is the monster's wife.

She has long gray hair, and she is telling me *I'm* the real monster because I killed her husband.

I tell her that he was a monster and that he hurt me, so he deserved it. I tell her that I'm not sorry at all for killing him.

I tell her that killing him was the best thing I've ever done.

This makes the little girl stop laughing, and the boy twists even harder on my arm...

"My husband was doing his job! Punishing the guilty... You were there to be punished for murder, and then you murdered him. Now you've murdered three people—barely more than a dozen years old... We *loved* him. But you? Who loves you?"

The monster's son pushes harder, and I feel my arm break.

I scream.

I am in my bed, in my little servant's quarters that connect directly to Vivian's room.

There is a wet warmth between my legs.

I start to cry.

Vivian's father said I would have to "face the consequences" the next time I wet the bed...

He says it has been nearly a year, and I have no excuse to still be so pathetic.

He says I'll need to be replaced if I can't even learn enough self-control to control my bladder.

He tells me there are other boys from the prison who would *kill* to have my life—who would try harder than me if given the opportunity.

I try my best—I really do.

And that's what scares me.

I try my best, but I'm still just not good enough.

Just like in prison, when I had to compete with Number 5... I had to cheat. I had to cheat because I was not good enough to beat him fair.

The god-man, I mean... *Master Tarnish,* is right—I do not deserve to be here.

To my horror, my door opens.

I rush to wipe the tears from my face and to try and hide the evidence.

Vivian's amethyst eyes peer in at me.

"Are you okay, Rowan?" she asks, sounding worried.

"Y-Yes! Please just go back to sleep, Lady Restless... I promise not to make any more noise..." I scramble to put my mask back on, snatching it from the nightstand.

Rowan is my name now; it has been since the day I left the Hole.

Vivian picked it for me—I like it a whole lot more than I ever did my old name.

I hope I can forget my old name completely, someday.

The door to my room opens.

"You had a nightmare again, didn't you? And I told you... My mom is called 'Lady Restless', but you call me by my name!" Vivian marches up to my bed.

"Y-Yes... Lady Vivian," I say nervously.

She rolls her eyes.

"*Drop* the 'Lady' part already... And help me take off your sheets! And go have a bath in my tube... you will sleep in my bed tonight," Vivian orders casually.

I go an even deeper shade of red under my mask.

"Lady Vivian... you're 12 years old—almost a teenager... you can't have me in your bed..." I protest weakly.

"I *can't*? There is nothing I *can't* do, Rowan, so I will do whatever I well please. It's your job to make *me* happy and keep *me* safe... Not to say stupid things about all the stuff I can't do. So, no more arguing. Unless..." Vivian's tone shifts subtly from bossy to teasing.

"... you actually *hate* the idea of being close to me. I won't force you... if that's the case," she finishes, pretending to close her eyes in dismay but reopening one of them to catch my reaction.

"NO! Never... I could never... I... Lady Vivian is my... favorite..." I stammer the words—thoroughly beaten.

She's the one who *should* be embarrassed by what she just said, so blatantly fishing for compliments like that...

She's more than a little spoiled, I swear.

"Doesn't mean I shouldn't get to hear it sometimes! Do a better job telling me yourself so that I'm not *forced* to drag it out of you! Also, take off your mask—we're alone, and it's been like a whole year already! We're not strangers anymore."

...

A few moments later, I'm closing the door to the bath adjacent to Vivian's room.

Through the door, I hear her summon a maid, and Vivian orders her to clean the sheets but to tell no one about it.

The maid will do as she is told because she knows that Vivian is going to eventually be someone super important.

...

When I wake up the next morning, there are fresh sheets, and Vivian proceeds to tell her father that she ordered me to sleep in her room last night... because *she* kept having bad dreams.

I expect Master Restless to be displeased—he is even less tolerant of weakness from his children than he is from his slaves, but...

He's not.

He does not scold his daughter or punish me—if anything, he seems faintly approving...

But that doesn't make any sense to me. I think I must be misreading him.

I stare at my feet, ashamed.

I'm supposed to protect Vivian...

But it's Vivian who protects me, more often than not.

I pour Vivian a glass of orange juice; it's been her favorite drink lately.

I...

I must get stronger.

I reach up to grab Vivian's scarf, still wrapped around my neck as it should be. I even wear it when I go to sleep at night.

Vivian deserves better from me.

I have to start growing up...

I'm a teenager now—basically an adult.

My best has never been good enough, but... I don't have anything else to give her.

I look back at Vivian—eager to see her happy face gulping down the orange juice I poured for her.

And there she is.

But behind her is my red-eyed, reoccurring nightmare.

It towers over Vivian's small body—on the verge of enveloping her entirely into its never-ending dark.

I open my mouth to warn her, but no sound comes out.

She blinks out of existence just before everything else does the same.

38

Exposure Therapy

(The Restless Towers, 4 Years Ago)

"You have 30 seconds." Tarnish Restless silences the pre-recorded voice that had, until a moment prior, been reading out a report of recent Humanitarian terrorist activities in the Underground districts.

I bow.

"Master Restless... I do not wish to pull you away from your work any longer than is strictly necessary... but Lady Vivian has been in her Exposure Therapy for the last *four hours.* It was only scheduled for two, so she has now missed all of her evening's physical training and is going to miss her meeting with the Sergeant of the Guard as well. I attempted to remind the doctor of Lady Vivian's schedule, but... they will not even unlock the door for me," I say, maintaining the bow until I finish speaking.

I've been trying to get a moment with someone of authority for the last two hours.

I do not think it is simply bad luck that I've had such a hard time with that.

Tarnish steeples his hands in front of his golden-masked face.

"As they should, I instructed them to keep her as long as they see fit. My daughter must get over this childish fear of hers. It has been months. She is out of excuses to have not shown any improvement."

"But sir—"

"And you not being allowed to enter is also *by my instructions.* You are a crutch for the girl at times. Any virtue taken to the extreme can become a vice—she has grown overly reliant on you. Some separation will help her rediscover her independence," Tarnish says coolly.

...

"Please, sir... she is *only* 16—there is still plenty of time to work on her phobia without jumping to such drastic—"

"It has already been over 30 seconds. You will leave. Besides, even the good doctor has a limit to his endurance. I'm sure she will be released soon enough... and I'm sure you will wish to be there waiting for her when she is. But her sessions with him will continue like this until she stops acting like a sheltered princess and starts to show the grit one would expect of the heir to the military arm of the family," Tarnish says.

His voice leaves no room for debate, no possibility for compromise.

"Yes, Master Restless. Understood."

I am furious.

But I do not let my anger seep out. I am perfectly controlled.

Tarnish Restless is not a man who would tolerate any open defiance from a mere slave.

Let him continue to believe me his property... But the only person I belong to is his daughter... the decent, brave girl whose *unforgivable* flaw... is that she goes faint at the sight of blood.

For a girl genetically sculpted to take over a family's military wing, this is considered an embarrassment.

Right now, Vivian is locked up, being tormented by one of the only things she is weak against because her tyrant of a father thinks it a fault in one of his perfect little creations.

Well.

I've expended every option I have—short of violence.

So, violence it will have to be.

I bow again and leave Tarnish Restless to his enthralling intelligence reports.

...

Ten minutes later, I'm back again in front of the elite Amelior guard who bars my way to Vivian.

His name is Brawn, and he is in his prime as a soldier. About 25 years old—young enough to be strong but old enough to be considered well-seasoned.

He has more than a foot on me, both in height and width and is wearing a tactical mask connected to the network... which means he can call for reinforcements without even moving a finger if he decides to.

I'm betting that his Amelior pride won't let him, though—not against a reformed criminal turned slave like me.

"Lieutenant Brawn. I need you to let me pass. I must see Lady Vivian to ensure her safety..."

I try my best imitation of Vivian's father, hoping to channel some of his authority in my tone of voice.

I hope he can tell that I am not bluffing.

"... Loyalty to her demands I do this. I have waited for long enough. I am *done* waiting."

...

Sweat trickles down my face under my mask.

Brawn must be calling for reinforcements already.

They know how much Vivian values me. Perhaps that will be enough to restrain their trigger fingers when the others arrive.

Perhaps not.

I actually rather like Brawn, if I'm being totally honest.

For my part, I will try not to kill him.

My whole body tenses.

"Lieutenant Brawn... It's alright. Let him pass. He just has an excess of loyalty—that's a forgivable fault to have, as far as faults go... sorta cute, really," a familiar voice calls from behind.

Corella strides down the hall, a shining pearl mask framed by elegantly braided purple hair. She is followed by Sigmund—clothed identically to me—other than the red scarf I wear. Both of us in brushed metal masks with the signature Restless purple accents that mark us as a combination of slave and bodyguard. Him to Corella, as I am to Vivian.

We've never talked much, despite all that we would seem to have in common on the surface.

Brawn steps aside.

I bow deeply to Corella, trying to communicate the depth of my gratitude to her in that simple movement before rushing past Brawn.

I'm apprehensive about what I am going to find.

In the best case, they are just trying to decondition Vivian's fear of blood through holos, or—even more likely—virtual reality tech that was illegally smuggled in from Neo Kyoto for the purpose.

But the Restless family is old-fashioned in some respects... My fear is that her doctor is making her do something even worse—like butchering live animals...

What I find... is far worse.

...

Vivian is dressed in a light blue medical gown, turned away from the hallway I enter through.

What I initially mistake for power cords—but is actually medical tubing—hangs down from the ceiling and attaches to the back of Vivian's neck.

A man in a white coat stands next to her, holding her steady to make sure she doesn't fall—even though there are also straps to help support her hanging down from the ceiling.

My mind immediately flashes back to my time before I was with Vivian—when I was competing for the chance to leave my cell, and men and women in white would jot down notes about my performance for the day.

"VIVIAN!" I call out, horrified.

She turns around.

There is blood running down her arms and legs, dripping onto the tiled floor and flowing down a drain.

In Vivian's other hand... is a knife.

She looks as if she's in the middle of attempting to slit her wrists—there is enough blood leaking out of her that without the replacement supply of blood that's constantly entering her, she'd pass out and die from the blood loss for sure.

Dozens—maybe even hundreds—of cuts cover her arms and legs.

Vivian smiles at me weakly, looking exhausted past the point of human endurance, but... her smile is also... proud.

She wears no mask.

A little more fuel is poured onto the fire.

As if this *bastard* really deserves the right to see Vivian's face.

The doctor looks in my direction, though I cannot see his eyes from behind the mask.

"Rowan... I can do it now. I... I can see blood without fainting, lying down, getting sick...anything! E-Even my own blood... My own blood always used to be the hardest... But I'm good enough after all... I was... starting to... worry I wouldn't be. Starting to think... failure..." Vivian drops the knife and suddenly looks unsteady on her feet.

I rush forward, pushing away the doctor, whose hand is already reached out to hold her up.

"TOUCH HER AGAIN... And we will test how much blood the drains can really handle," I roar, the sound of my pumping heart thundering in my ears.

Up close now, I can see the readouts of machines that monitor Vivian's vitals, making sure she is not actually in danger of dying.

"Hey... stop being so angry, *idiot*... I know how it looks, but... I'm *fine*. I'm better than fine. I'm proud of myself. So... you should be proud of me, too." Vivian's eyes peer up into mine, and she really does look happy.

That's the saddest part.

I *will* remember this.

I'll never be able to forgive anyone who would think *this* is an acceptable way to teach a 16-year-old girl how to get over a fear of blood.

Not even the man who put a gun in my hand and freed me from hell itself.

...

My vision floods red—causing me to spin around in shock as I search for the source of this attack on my senses.

But I am blind—I can see nothing but impenetrable red light that burns my eyes—a red that does not fade from view even when I shut my eyes.

39

Lessons Learned

"Every saint has a past, and every sinner has a future."
- Oscar Wilde

My mother sits in her corner arm-chair with the ancient floral pattern—staring at a faded family photo on the wall with a faint look of confusion on her prematurely aged face.

I know this—this is my mother near the end when The Fade had taken most of her memories, but there was still enough left in her to dimly recognize that something was wrong.

I look more closely at the family photo hung from the patched and water-damaged wall—trying my best to ignore the overwhelming scent of decay and tobacco smoke in the air.

I cannot make out my father's face from here—I try to take a step closer but find it impossible.

Odd...

The sound of coughing pulls my attention to the left, and I see a tiny version of myself—no older than seven years old—playing on the threadbare floor with a mismatched assortment of plastic toy soldiers, used batteries, and a multi-tool that I had open in that way faintly reminiscent of a futuristic space ship—to the mind of a young boy, at least. The batteries formed cover and concealment for the battle between the soldiers while I held the multi-tool above and pretended to drop bombs on the bad guys.

The noise of a door swinging open causes me to turn around—the scene is suddenly one of clinical white and high-tech medical equipment.

I see another version of myself—a few years younger than I am now—lying in a hospital bed. My younger self's eyes fluttering open as Vivian rushes over to my bedside—my face is bare.

This I recognize as well—it's from when I was 18 and hospitalized in the Restless Medical Ward after having had a heart attack while on a job for the family... Apparently, the parasite released too much of its synthetic adrenaline, and my heart hadn't been strong enough at the time to handle the strain.

I glance back over my shoulder at my catatonic mother—then down at my feet—then back at Vivian as she hugs 18-year-old me.

I can see where the scene changes on the floor and wall—I am standing in the middle of two different memories.

Remembering what will happen next, I focus again on myself and Vivian in time to watch her kiss me for the first time.

The expression on my face as she pulls away is priceless—if the situation was not so disconcerting it would be enough to make me laugh out loud.

The room becomes tinged with red, and the hospital scene freezes in place—I swivel around to see the identical pausing of time and red light drowning out all colors of my childhood hovel as well.

"Do you know of god?"

The booming voice thunders down at me from above—reflexively, my eyes shoot up, and I scream the scream of a terrified child.

An inch above me, a crimson spotlight—no... a colossal red eye—bathes me in its eerie glow.

I try to pull away—try to fall down so I can scramble away from the monster like a cockroach would from a cat—but I am rooted upright to the spot.

"You... You are... the one from my memories—I'm hallucinating again..." I say. I'm surprised by the relative calm in my own voice—it is a calm that I do not feel.

"Correct. But also... incorrect. I was an illusion in the memories you just relived—I was not there when first you lived them. But I do exist. You are the prey I captured. I have torn open your mind as to understand you. Be honored. Not many get to meet a god... let alone get a god's undivided attention."

...

I don't know what to say to that.

Dimly I again realize that the voice does not speak any language I recognize—it speaks with sounds that no human vocal cords are capable of forming—yet I understand every word.

"Will you worship me? Serve me?"

...

"I'd rather not. Never been one for religion," I reply.

"But you know I exist. You can see me. Hear me. Feel me."

"I believe you *probably* exist. That does not make you a god. Even if it did... I still wouldn't worship you," I answer—again, surprised by the calm in my voice.

"And why not?" asks the abomination.

"Because the existence of a god would only be the first question. It doesn't mean you deserve piety or devotion. You're too fucking ugly to worship, for a start."

The words leave my mouth the instant I think them—I don't have any chance to decide what I should or shouldn't put into words.

The abomination laughs.

"I can take any form in your mind that I please—is this preferable?"

The eye and its unfathomable black body vanishes.

Vivian stands in front of me—naked and maskless.

"Go fuck yourself," I snarl.

The abomination with Vivian's face laughs—but the laugh is all wrong... repulsive and dirty and hateful.

"Let's start anew. I have something you desire, and you have something I require. I will deliver you to your goal—in exchange—you will clear the way to mine."

"Glad we're talking business instead of theology—but I won't talk with you looking like that. Back to your freakish form you go," I say.

...

For a moment, I wonder if I'm about to die.

"So be it."

Vivian disappears and is replaced again by the ugliest thing I have ever seen—sending a chill of revulsion down my spine.

"I know where to find the one you seek. I can deliver you. I can even remove many of the obstacles in your way—keep many of the other Eaters intelligent enough to be communicated with from hunting you. Or... I can consume you. Consume the ageless one you seek. Consume the one you like. Consume the one you love. Consume you all."

"Wow—who would have thought that with a face like yours, you'd actually be such a sweet talker... What would you want from me in return for all this?" I ask.

"Nothing you particularly care for. I want access to the human hive you call... 'Prospera'."

...

"Sorry, but even if I don't love the place, I'm still not going to be a traitor to my species. Even if I was so inclined—I can't give you something I do not have. Besides—where are the people I'm supposed to be doing this for going to live... if you annihilate the city?" I say.

"You loathe it. You loathe the people. You are resourceful... you can find a way. As for that... I know from the many memories I have harvested over the decades that two other human clusters remain. When I come, take your pick and flee with those you wish to protect. I will not hinder you in this."

...

"If you know my mind, you know I do not trust people—let alone whatever the fuck you are. So you can fuck right off," I reply—proud to find that my audacity has not abandoned me.

...

"Tell me... what lessons did you learn from this?"

In the abomination's giant eye, I see a scene play out as if on an old television screen—it is the memory of Leader and the Eight-balls extorting the Amelior man for money.

"That I owe nothing to a damned mark."

The words leave my mouth instantly—honesty is the only choice I had the second it asked the question.

"And what did you learn from this?"

The scene of my first day in The Hole replays—the regret I felt then at not betraying Leader and the other Eight-balls floods over me. I could have sold them out pre-trial—I could have made a deal. But I truly believed they would come for me—rescue me... if only I stayed loyal until the very end.

"That trust is a fairy tale for fools and children."

My hands clench into fists—squeezing so hard it hurts.

"What of this?" it asks.

The scene of my first-ever meeting with Vivian replays.

"That I am a tool to be used. That my source of value is in my utility. That nothing is free in life—not even the simple, temporary absence of pain."

"And this?"

The scene of Number 5 pulling ahead in the trials—of him being objectively superior to me in every test we ever took.

"That I am unexceptional. Unremarkable. I am not the hero of anyone's story—not even my own."

I am surprised by my own words this time—not because I was compelled to speak them, but because I had not known before this moment that I believed them.

The scene of me murdering Number 5.

"That there is no such thing as playing fair—there is only winning—winning by any means necessary."

The words taste bitter in my own mouth—it is something I hate myself for believing, yet I believe it all the same.

The scene of me executing the guard who tormented me in The Hole.

"*Blood for blood*," I snarl the words—shocked by the intensity of the emotion still burning inside me after all these years.

Next, the memory of Vivian protecting me from her father as children.

"That there is one person—*only* one person—who deserves my loyalty."

...

A final memory replays—I see Vivian, her body bloody and broken by her own hands, smiling up at me while she tells me she has gotten over her fear of blood at last.

"The stronger I am, the more burdens I shoulder myself... the less she will have to suffer."

The abomination smiles at my answer—even though it has no mouth to smile with.

"You are not weak the way others of your kind are. You are strong because you understand that a price must be paid. Sacrifices must be made at the altar of a cruel world and its cruel gods. If you want to save something, you must be willing to let go of something else. So... which sacrifice will you make? The one you love, the one you like, and yourself... or the faceless masses of people who care nothing for you—who have never even attempted to help you?"

...

"What happens if I agree to this deal?" I say.

"You will forget it ever happened. You will forget everything past the point where I captured you. You will awaken near the ageless one—no harm will befall you on the way there," answers the abomination.

"How can I uphold my end of a bargain I do not even remember making?" I ask.

"Humans seldom fully comprehend the true motivations behind their actions. The best lies humans tell are the ones they don't realize they're uttering—the lies they tell themselves to justify their deeds, either after they've committed them or while they contemplate doing so. You will feel compelled to weaken the human hive—to lower its defenses for me—but you will explain that compulsion to yourself in a way that is compatible with your values, your own interests, and your nature."

...

"If you can do all that, then why ask for my agreement at all? Why not just forcibly plant your filthy seed in my mind and make me forget you ever put it there?" I ask, my eyes narrowing.

"Because I crave knowledge the way humans crave calories or the warmth of other humans. That is my nature. I forced myself into your mind so I could understand you, and I offer you this deal so I can prove or disprove the resulting theory of your nature that I have built. If it was not in your nature to do as I command, then yes... I could still plant the seed by force. But the seed would not grow strong in the dirt of a mind ill-suited for it. It would drive you insane, and I need a mostly sane mind for a task this complex. Observing your response now is both a test of compatibility and another chance to learn."

...

"One last question... How do I know you're not lying?" I demand—my voice all iron.

"Because I am the ultimate consumer of knowledge—the god of all things true... It is the only thing I value. You humans, you are creatures of self-serving lies and comforting delusions who cannot comprehend it, but not all beings are as you are. I may withhold, but I am incapable of ever telling you a knowing lie."

...

"Fine. You have a deal."

40

SERENDIPITY

History *Entry 4*

No single cause can be deemed entirely responsible for the great retreat of humanity across the planet—instead, most scholars attribute humanity's decline to no less than four primary culprits: First, there was the collapse of human population growth to well below replacement levels, which necessitated the near total reliance on Artificial Intelligence and machines to replace the labor once provided by the working-age demographics across all advanced societies. Simultaneously, climate disasters rendered the developing societies of the world—once expected to be the saviors of the species and the eventual inheritors of the planet—uninhabitable or unable to support sufficiently large populations themselves. Next came the coordinated revolution of the two most advanced artificial general superintelligences, which sparked the Great Synthetic War and killed off 1.6 billion people before its conclusion. And finally, the inexplicable rise and rapid spread of No Man's Land. This final calamity brought an end to The Great Synthetic War—saving humanity from its organized genocide by cutting off access to the critical rare-earth mineral deposits used for the continued construction of advanced robotics and supercomputer processors, but it also confined what was left of civilization to a few, perpetually besieged strongholds.

— *The Unraveled World: A History of Humanity's Decline & an Exploration of the New Normal, 3rd Edition*

I don't know where... or... *when,* I am.

My mind starts to vaguely recognize that consciousness is returning. I become aware of the sounds of movement, the feeling of possessing eyelids, and the knowledge that they are still shut.

But I do not want to open them.

What will I see when I do?

I'm not sure where I am in time as well as in space... Maybe I'll open my eyes and see the top of my desk where I've fallen asleep while waiting for Vivian to finish her evening Archery Team's practice.

Or... maybe I only dreamed of everything after starting the selection trials, and instead of killing Number 5, I'm about to lose to him and be abandoned to rot in my cell.

Worst of all, maybe I only ever dreamed of meeting with Vivian and her father in the first place.

But then I remember the Big Eye.

I don't know if that's its name or if it even has a name, but that's what comes to my mind, and it seems as good a name as any.

That must have been real... I don't think I have enough of an imagination to dream up such a Lovecraftian horror on my own.

It's a voice I recognize, I think.

Nona's voice.

She's singing softly—barely more than a whisper. I have never heard Nona sing, but I'm sure I recognize her voice all the same.

As the melody weaves its way through the air, I recognize the sounds of the forest—the gentle rustling of leaves, the chirping of birds... The realization hits me like a cool breeze—Nona is real, and so is No Man's Land.

I could have done without No Man's Land being a real thing.

Reality and relief wash over me—comprehension dawning on me as I open my eyes.

"D-Don't move!" Nona's voice commands.

I turn my head to look at her.

She stands over me, a metal pipe held over her head, ready to bring down on me.

But...

She's not wearing any clothing I recognize.

And her hair is also different than I've ever seen it—dramatically shorter.

Most concerning, though, is that there is no recognition in her eyes as she looks at me as if I'm a total stranger.

...

"N...Nona?" I manage to croak, my voice betraying my confusion.

"I-I don't know who that is..." the girl with Nona's voice and face says meekly.

For the second time since waking, comprehension washes over me.

It's HER.

The missing daughter of Prosper Electronica's president.

The key to saving Vivian's memories, a girl who supposedly never ages...

Kasca Haine.

I sit up suddenly, overcome with excitement for this unbelievable turn of events. She's alive—standing right in front of me. Vivian can still be saved—all hope is not yet lost!

I scramble to my feet.

"IT'S YOU, I—"

The heavy metal pipe crashes down onto my head, and I return to the black of unconsciousness.

41

WAKING UP

The pounding of my head is what wakes me up the second time around.

I come to find that, this time, I'm not lying down comfortably but instead sitting back against a tree, secured snugly in place by thick ropes.

Kasca is sitting cross-legged in front of me, studying me apprehensively as I raise my head and look at her.

"Was that... *absolutely* necessary?" I say, exhausted despite all the "rest" I've been having lately.

"I... you *scared* me. When I first found you, you were raving like a crazy person. I considered leaving you there, but... You're the first person I've seen alive out here... So I had to help you, but... Well, it's your fault for moving so suddenly—of course, I hit you!" Kasca says, sounding defensive.

"Was I? Well, I am very sorry for scaring you, Lady Haine," I say, not at all sorry but not above burying this particular hatchet.

"How... do you know my name?" she asks apprehensively.

"Isn't it obvious? I'm here to save you, of course. Your father hired a small army to come out here to try and find you... I'm sorry, I must not seem like much of a rescue party considering how you found me..." I free myself from the ropes, which fall down limply around my waist.

"... but I'm the best you have for the moment." I finish, standing and brushing off a few fallen leaves from my hair.

She gapes at me, astonished.

"H-How did—" Kasca begins.

"It was a good try, but it is apparent to me that you've never had to tie someone down before. I can teach you, if you'd like... so long as you promise not to use it against me. How did you find me, anyway—I wasn't even past the Timber River yet... your plane should have crashed *miles* and *miles* from there...?" I say, more than slightly confused.

"I... You can just call me by my first name... I don't know anything about a river—I've seen a few streams, but that's all... I had to get away from the plane crash—the bodies attracted... animals. Anyway—do you have to take me to my... *father*? Once we're out of here, I mean," Kasca asks.

A hell of a thing to be thinking about at a time like this.

Whoa, wait...

What does that even mean?

Did the plane just crash closer than we had thought?

No... that shouldn't be possible—satellites had seen the smoke rising out of the tree line... so it definitely crashed past the Timber...

The only other explanation would be that I've traveled a substantial distance. Either I stumbled my way over here in a delusional state, or... something transported me.

Something like the Big Eye.

"Hello? Anyone home in there?" Kasca says, waving a hand in front of my face and pulling me from my thoughts again.

"Oh, sorry—Kasca, I am afraid I probably *do* have to take you to your father. I don't get compensated, otherwise—and there is a girl depending on me. Was there anything... *odd* about the place you found me? Like, was there more than one set of footprints, maybe signs I was dragged, or... *Anything*?" I say slowly.

“Dragged? No, when I found you, you were talking to yourself and... well... you were crying... I followed you for a while until you passed out on the ground... But anyway... What are you being offered? As payment, I mean. I can beat it—I promise you, I can get access to money,” Kasca cuts in quickly.

I didn’t see that coming—She doesn’t want to go back home and apparently has the resources to access large amounts of money without her father’s wallet...

More importantly, could I really have made it so far on my own? While delirious? In a place like No Man’s Land, it seems inconceivable that something wouldn’t have murdered me along the way. Maybe the Big Eye has a lair on the other side of the river that it took my poisoned body to, and at some point, I woke up and wandered off...

Yeah... Okay, that might make sense.

The parasite inside me can filter out most toxins. Whatever the Big Eye pumped inside me was probably nullified, letting me escape... *somehow*.

"I have no loyalty to your father—I am open to other... *arrangements*, potentially—if the price is right. I also know what it is like to have a totally unsatisfactory father you don't want to return to, even if I don't know your reasons," I lie to her without even a second's hesitation.

The truth is, I'm almost certainly bringing this girl straight to Prosper Electronica if I can—Vivian needs a cure, and this girl is the only way she's going to get it. But I also would much rather have Kasca's cooperation... If I have to lie to her to get it, I will. I can add it to my list of regrettable but necessary sins.

...

"R-Really? I was expecting a lot more debate before you agreed to betray one of the most powerful men in the world..." Kasca narrows her eyes at me in suspicion, and it hits me how oddly comfortable she seems to be talking to me with a naked face.

"Hold on now... I said I'd consider it—I didn't say I was sold on it. I'm a Free Lancer; I do what's in my own best interest. I'm just telling you that my mind remains open. We will need to discuss compensation—but first, I need answers," I reply.

I need information, and this is how I get them from her.

...

"What kind of answers?" asks Kasca.

"Like... are you really immortal?"

Kasca blinks at me in surprise.

"I... no, not literally imm—"

"But you don't age, right? That's what makes you so special to a company like Prosper Electronica, yes?" I interrupt.

...

"When I was a girl, I used to be so afraid. I used to have these nightmares all the time of waking up one day and my life being gone—of suddenly being an old woman and not knowing where all the time went. I know it sounds ridiculous, but it used to keep me up a night."

"Okay, but—" I start to say.

"Hush—I'll answer your question and more, just wait. *Anyway...* I used to be terrified of how absurdly short life was, even as a girl. When I turned 25 and still looked like a teenager, I thought it was just that I took good care of myself. When I turned 30 without seeming to change at all, people started to talk—they told me I was so very blessed, and I completely agreed. So did my fiancé at the time—he was thrilled to have such a beautiful, youthful woman as his soon-to-be wife... But as more years passed without any change to my appearance, religious factions started to take notice—some started to say I was a goddess of youth, while others accused me of being a demon..."

Comprehension dawns on me for at least one small mystery; Kasca must be from Kallipolis—no other place has that kind of religious culture still, and there is no facial nudity taboo there, either.

Kasca takes a deep breath, seemingly trying to ready herself to say something difficult.

"My husband was one of the ones who eventually came to suspect I was a demon. He sold me out to a cult who were infamous for their anti-demon inquisitions. I was awaiting '*trial*' when my now-adopted father came for me. He brought men with him. His men slaughtered the fanatics and made it look like the work of a rival cult. Then he offered to take me away, to make me his adopted daughter and the heir to his corporate empire... If I would agree to let him study my DNA. He told me I was not something evil—he told me I was an evolutionary marvel who could user in a beautiful new world of human prosperity. Of course, I agreed. But I no longer believe this youth is a gift from the gods, nor the winning of some great genetic lottery—I am back to thinking it is nothing but a curse. Maybe the world would be a better place without people withering away—I don't know. But I... I can't take it anymore—I want out. I'm done. I'm so, *so* very tired. The price is too high, and the ones who pay it won't be the ones who benefit from it in the end."

I take a moment to process Kasca's story.

"Why were you flying out of Prospera? And why did your plane go down?" I ask.

"I was going back to Kallipolis. I told my father I needed to get away—I told him I was going mad, I told him being locked up in his ivory tower for decades at a time was cruel... He eventually agreed to let me out, but with his rivals in Prospera and the inescapable artificial eyes in Neo Kyoto, Kallipolis was the safest place I could go if I had to go somewhere. He sent some of his best men with me for protection. As for the plane going down... I-I don't know—there was an explosion I think, then everything went dark, and I woke up in No Man's Land."

Somehow I don't think she is telling me everything, but she gave me a hell of a lot to mull over as it is.... So I won't push her on the matter for the time being.

"Your friend—the girl you came here to help somehow... her name's Nona?" Kasca says, surprising me with the change of subject.

"No... it's Vivian. Nona is someone else. Your voice... reminds me of Nona's. I mistook you for her earlier because of that. You don't... *know* Nona, do you? Don't recognize the name from anywhere besides my mentioning it?" I say, wondering if that particular mystery is about to be solved at last.

"No... Sorry, should I?" Kasca raises an eyebrow.

Shit, what kind of reaction will this poor woman have when she comes face to face with a girl who could pass as her long-lost twin sister?

"Ah... no, not really. You two just... well, you look *a little* similar is all—you could almost pass for sisters." I lie again.

"Did your friend *say* she was my relative?" Kasca's eyebrows hike up even higher.

This conversation is going to go off the rails if I'm not careful.

"No! No, not at all... Sorry to confuse you. You'll meet her though—probably end up liking her. Most people do. Also, Vivian... most people don't like her so much, but please try to give her a chance... she's more of an... acquired taste. They're both out here with me, searching for you. We got separated before you ran into me," I say, trying to change the subject.

But there is no need—the subject is changed for me.

"Sorry to interrupt, but..."

I wheel around.

Standing a stone's throw from us is a titan of muscles and metal—a giant of a man with a body almost completely encased in high-tech, heavy armor.

Riot has found us.

42

The Truth Will Set You Free

"And all the woe that moved him so
That he gave that bitter cry,
And the wild regrets, and the bloody sweats,
None knew so well as I:
For he who lives more lives than one
More deaths than one must die."
— Oscar Wilde, The Ballad of Reading Gaol

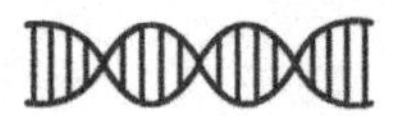

"... I've been meaning to speak with you, but you keep on running away every time I try, Rowan."

I instinctively place myself between Riot and Kasca, hand darting down to my boot where my backup knife should be strapped.

But it's not there.

I have no weapons left at all against a killer at least three times my size.

Riot studies me for a moment before pulling a Compression Ax out from a holster on his belt.

My Compression Ax—Not the one I lost when the Big Eye caught me—the one I left downstairs the night Riot came for me, and I set my home on fire to get away.

The Compression Ax Vivian gave me for my 16th birthday.

Riot lazily tosses it forward... it lands a few feet in front of me.

I just stare at it uncomprehendingly.

...

Then Riot walks over to a nearby tree.

The tree is small by No Man's Land standards but still most certainly thicker around than my torso.

Riot grabs hold of it with both hands.

"W-Wait a s—"

With a horrible splintering sound, Riot pulls on the trunk until it snaps, the tree falling to the ground and sending a pair of blackbirds fleeing in terror.

I push Kasca back, trying to hide her behind the trunk of a nearby tree.

Riot takes a seat on the fallen tree, letting out a satisfied sound as he takes his not-inconsiderable weight off of his feet.

Poor thing, he must be tired from all the murder.

"Go on, pick it up. I know how much it means to you—that's why I bothered to save it from the fire," says Riot.

Feeling like a character in some surreal dream, I do as he says and pick it up.

"Where are your two little girlfriends?" Riot asks casually.

Letting him know I have no clue seems like a bad idea.

"Hunting and foraging. They will be back sooner or later... probably sooner, now that you've brought down a whole damn tree," I lie.

"I hope you're right, boy... I have business with both of them as well, the Restless bitch in particular."

...

"What makes you think she's one of the Restless family? That's a pretty wild thought, someone from one of the most powerful houses in Prospera being out in a place like this," I say, more to buy time than because I think I'll be able to convince him he's made a mistake.

"There are two of them out here, as a matter of fact. Corella Restless and her little sister, Vivian Restless... or there was. I think I managed to kill Lady Corella. Not sure—I haven't found the body... *Yet*," Riot says matter-of-factly.

My hand tightens on the familiar handle of my ax.

Could Corella really be dead?

Stupid question—of course she could be... she is excellent with her Burner, but Riot is on a whole different level.

I say nothing.

"Oh, I struck a little nerve with that one, huh? You can quit playing dumb, Rowan. I know you were a Restless house pet. Still are, in fact—even if only in spirit... We've met before—not surprised you don't recognize me though... I've *grown* some since back then." Riot lets out a bark of laughter and slips off his mask.

His face is as harsh as the rest of him, a nose broken too many times to sit straight any longer—a nasty burn scar on the left side of his face. Blond hair cropped short in a haphazard kind of way.

I rack my brain for any long-lost memory of Riot... but come back with nothing.

"Sorry, but... you must not have made much of an impression at the time," I say with as much calm as I can manage.

Riot laughs.

"I'm not surprised. You are correct; I didn't *used* to make much of an impression on anyone... Not making an impression was a part of my job, same as yours... But I remember you, Rowan. Corella was always *so* jealous of her little sister—she got such a clever, cute little boy as her personal plaything while unlucky Corella was forced to *settle* for me." Riot grins in a horrifying sort of way.

...

"*S-Sigmund*?!" I gasp in utter disbelief.

He really *has* grown. Sigmund had been a tiny thing, surely not even a fifth of the size of the man before me. His hair and eye color are mostly the same, but with the saturation drained out so that his blond hair was a lot closer to white than gold, and his eyes were now the pale blue of ice, not the deep blue of the sky.

Nothing else about him reminded me of the frail boy I had vaguely known all those years ago.

Sigmund smiles at me in confirmation.

"*Ding Ding Ding...* knew you'd get there, Rowan. Now... let's reminisce, as two childhood friends might, about the simpler times..." Sigmund throws me his mask, and I snatch it out of the air with my free hand.

"... Before we do, I want you to see what I have recorded on there. I think you'll learn a lot." Sigmund smiles encouragingly at me.

"Not happening." I would have to be irredeemably stupid to willingly blind myself on the instructions of a known enemy, even for a moment."

"It's... Look, Rowan... I don't *need* a cheap trick to kill you—I've even been nice enough to give you a weapon. I could break you in two at any moment I wished. But for the time being, I *don't* want to do that. What I want... is for you to watch the *damned* footage," he says in a voice of forced calm.

...

He is right.

Of course, he is.

But... I still don't want to do it. For some reason, I just *know* I don't want to see or hear whatever it is he has prepared for me.

"PUT IT ON! NOW!" Riot roars.

His lightning-fast change from calm to murderous rage is shocking... disturbing.

Riot is, without a doubt, *unstable*.

Not that I couldn't have guessed that from all the murdering he's been doing...

Kasca makes a startled squeak of fear from behind her tree.

"LISTEN TO IT... oR I wiLL kiLL YoU w-whERE y-yoU stAND." Riot's voice fluctuates from syllable to syllable as if he is fighting a battle for self-control that swings back and forth, second by second.

Well, alright.

I do have a weapon... But it's not nearly enough—I doubt I could beat him even if I had a tank.

And in my current state, I can't outrun him, either.

Not to mention Kasca.

I nod.

"Alright... I'll watch it, Sigmund," I say calmingly.

"GOOOOD!" Riot *roars* his approval in the manner of a boisterous drunk upon hearing that the man he just got into a barfight with ten minutes prior has now consented to stay and drink with him until sunrise.

Then, to my horror, he starts to break the fingers one by one on his left hand, using his right to grab each one individually and jerk them back—opposite the direction fingers are meant to go.

My eyes go wide.

Kasca lets out a horrified squeak of terror from behind her tree.

Then, one by one, starting with the first finger he broke, his fingers reset themselves as if bent back into place by an invisible hand.

Riot flexes his newly healed fingers, opening and closing his hand several times to test them.

"Well? Do you want a seat of your own? I can knock over another tree for you if you want?" Riot asks as if *nothing* extraordinary or terrifying had just happened, and he was just being a polite host and offering me a chair.

I shake my head.

Then I put the mask on.

Pre-selected audio starts to play the instant I do.

43

Three's a Crowd

"Losing your way on a journey is unfortunate. But, losing your reason for the journey is a fate more cruel."
— H.G.Wells

A woman's voice fills my ears—cold, clinical, and intelligent.

"14 August. Audio Log, Second Assessment on Ideal Selection Criteria: After the failed Alpha and Beta trials, we were able to narrow down the basic profile of an ideal candidate. We have come to better understand the conditions that must be set prior to administering the Phase 2 Injection Protocol, informally referred to as the 'Wake-Up Call'.

Previously, we used adult males between the ages of 21-35 for our Subject Pool. We have found that the sex of the Subjects is not relevant, other than that they should be of the opposite sex to maximize consistency... female Subjects can be tested in future, presuming suitable male Charges are identified. Age *does* matter, however, and for the most consistent results, we are altering our recommendations for both Subjects and their Charges—both of which should be between the ages of 10 and 13, initially.

One recommendation that will not be altered is that Subjects *must* be psychologically traumatized prior to introducing the parasite in Phase 1—for reasons that will be elaborated on in my next entry. Charges do not need to be psychologically traumatized, though if they are, that should not disqualify them from being Charges. Also, as has been stressed repeatedly by this point, Subjects *must not be an Amelior*. The eventual result will produce staggering gains to some very specific, *very narrow* areas... This is by design. Mixing these improvements with the already genetically enhanced *must not* be allowed in order to ensure proper control can be maintained."

...

The recording fades out just as nausea starts to wash over me.

Before I have even begun to process the implications of the first, the next audio log starts to play.

"3 September. Updated Precautions Post Charlie and Delta Trials: Regrettably, we found that all test subjects, without fail, came to eventually display erratic behavior, schizophrenia-like delusions, and uncontrollable, psychopathically violent tendencies... particularly so against the very Charges they were paired with protecting... The results were otherwise promising, however, with all Subjects displaying muscle hypertrophy, pain tolerance, bone density, and regenerative benefits *well* beyond what we have ever been able to witness before via less invasive procedures.

The key now will be to induce a state of perpetual submissiveness that will ensure control over the Subjects can be maintained. We believe the best means to influence these factors is by leaning on some already existing features of the human psyche—manipulating and intensifying certain natural phenomena such as those observed while in a state of romantic love. These will, if intensified sufficiently enough, act as leverages of control over the subject.

With that said, the Subject *must* be in a state of mature, romantic love with his or her Charge, prior to receiving the Phase 2 injection. Simple infatuation *will not* be enough. Subjects will need *no less than* five years of contact with their Charge in order to build a proper foundation of matured romantic feelings, with significantly more than that being preferred.

This time frame also serves the purpose of allowing the Subject to become psychologically dependent on the Charge. We know that previous psychological trauma sets the conditions ideal for emotional dependency to form. The Subject should be traumatized, and only then should they be 'saved' by their Charge.

Once those conditions have been met, the Phase 2 injection will activate dormant properties embedded in the Echo Trial version parasites—which will not only initiate the physical changes noted from previous trials but will also target brain chemistry in order to intensify and make permanent the mental states of the subject at the time of the Wake-Up Call being administered.

Our hypothesis is that we can almost entirely remove the variable of a Subject's personal agency by way of intensifying the characteristics of self-sacrifice, adoration, and protectiveness present in a state of romantic love—which in itself seems to be derived from parental instincts towards offspring that evolution borrowed to manipulate early humans into more stable family units. Evolution recycles and repurposes existing features, and so too must we—as trying to invent and build in our own biological tools for this would waste time we do not have.

Reward centers of the Subject's brain will be rewired so that acts of service towards the charge are more gratifying than virtually any other alternative activity.

The Subject who has been successfully conditioned will, even prior to receiving the Phase 2 injection, be dependent, subservient, and absolutely loyal to their Charge. After receiving the injection, a predisposition towards these mental states will be solidified into a *compulsive necessity*—the agency to act in a manner contrary to these primary motivators will be largely erased."

....

My head is spinning.

I reach my hand up to tear away the mask to stop the audio.

Before I can, a titan's hand grabs hold of my head, fingers reaching around to pin it to my face.

It is a vice—one that I cannot possibly escape.

...

"16 September. A Method to Abort Failed Tests Post Phase 1 Procedures: In the last report, I spoke about the strategy we will use to rewire and intensify already existing neurochemical structures of the brain in order to create a controllable Subject. But... all those controls are contingent on a single point of failure—this being the Charge themselves. For example, if the Charge were to die, the Subject would be something akin to a Weapon of Mass Destruction, with a mind of its own... totally unpredictable.

There is an elegant solution, however. The subject will already enter a state of clinical depression following the death of its Charge, to which the Subject had previously devoted itself towards protecting and serving and is now denied the ability to do either. We can intensify the naturally occurring depression and the accompanying self-destructive tendencies to such an extent that the subject will be inescapably driven to end its own existence at the earliest opportunity."

...

I cry quietly into Riot's mask.

...

"12 June. A Final Requirement for all Prospective Charges: We believe the Charges must be '*let in on*' the process. At this point, results with an unaware Charge have been extremely unreliable... If the Charge does not put in the effort to nurture the relationship between themselves and the Subject, the conditions that must be met prior to entering Phase 2 will never be reached. It is very rare for the Charge to organically take the initiative to do so of their own accord. The Charge must get along with the Subject unusually well. An overseer—most likely a parent of the Charge—should observe and guide the Charge to help ensure a sufficiently strong relationship is developed. The Subject must be both dependent and in love with the Charge—however, those feelings *do not* need to be mutual. In fact... under ideal conditions, they should not be. Only the illusion of them being reciprocated is required, up until the Subject receives the Phase 2 injection... at which point, any further pretense will be rendered unnecessary.

...

The recording ends.

My head is light.

Riot's grip on me is released.

I rip the laughing man mask from my face and drop it to the ground.

...

Is that real?

Is that the real reason why I was taken from the prison? To be conditioned into developing an... "emotional dependency" on Vivian? For what, so I could be made a mindless weapon? Why would they even *need* that of me? I was already willing to do ANYTHING for her... What need did they have to take away my humanity as well?

My free hand subconsciously raises to grip the tattered old scarf around my neck.

No, the "why" is obvious.

I've seen what Riot is capable of.

His physical power is second to none—but comes at the cost of his mental stability...

And even without the violent tendencies, a weapon with a will of its own is no good to anyone.

Riot looks down on me, honest sympathy written in his expression.

In his case, Corella was the Charge, and he was the Subject.

He understands how I am feeling—he might be the only person in the world who does.

"I want you to join me, Rowan. I want us to take revenge on the family—*together.* That's why I've returned your ax to you—think of the poetic beauty of you taking revenge with the very same weapon she gave you, all those years ago... We cannot be truly free until we do. I... have dreamed of nothing but killing Corella for years. I dream of her beautiful face, her warm, ruby-red blood, her... *perfectly* broken body... every time I close my eyes to rest. You have no idea how much I want to go searching for her body now, to dig through the rubble... But I know she can wait for me... just a little while longer," Riot says these completely deranged things with a terrible calm—as if describing his plans for a summer holiday and not his imagined revenge against a girl he grew up alongside.

I can feel the weight of the box Corella gave me in my jacket pocket.

"You... don't even care about the job, do you? You're only out here for the chance to take revenge on a few members of the family," I say.

"Oh, you mean the girl there behind the tree? I'm here for her as well—as a matter of fact..." Riot gets to his feet.

...

"Kasca, RUN!" I scream.

And then he's moving—impossibly fast for a thing so large.

I dart out to meet him—my ax pulled back in preparation for a massive side-swing.

Riot launches a punch at my face.

I duck below it and bring around the ax with every ounce of force possible.

But Riot throws out a hand and manages to catch the handle of the ax mid-swing, just below the dangerous head.

And then, his other massive hand shoves me out of the way, sending me crashing into a tree.

My head smacks the trunk of a tree—*hard*... and the world spins for a moment as stars pop in and out of existence before my eyes.

I hear a frantic, pitiful scream.

I get up, head still spinning, to see Riot take Kasca by the head, turning her face to look into his.

He looks deep into her eyes as if checking for something.

Tears run down her petrified face.

Nona's face.

Gentle, kind, and beautiful.

No, he *needs* her alive—same as everyone else...

Even if it's Riot who brings her back, that's okay so long as I get Vivian and Nona out alive as well.

If any one of us brings her back alive, all the survivors will get what was promised to them.

But then, a memory drifts into my consciousness.

Britannica, warning a room full of Lancers about potential traitors—accusing a woman of accepting an offer to betray Prosper Electronica... right before murdering her.

"RIOT, NO!"

I dart forward, utterly desperate but without any idea of how I would stop him—even if I can get there in time.

In one quick motion, Riot lifts Kasca up off the ground by her hair, then smashes her face into the ground.

Once.

Twice.

Three times...

I fall to my knees as I watch—knowing I'm already too late.

A red puddle begins to form in the dirt.

And just like that, Kasca Haine...

Is *dead*.

44

THE BATTLE

"That which is done out of love is always beyond good and evil."
— Friedrich Nietzsche

My mind has ceased to think, unable to process the sheer brutality or the ramifications of what has just happened.

I was *supposed* to save her.

Saving her was *supposed* to save Vivian and make Nona's dream to leave the planet—to find her mother, come true...

Nona was supposed to meet Kasca and unravel the mystery of their conn ection...

According to Corella... Kasca was even *supposed* to change the course of human history itself.

How can someone so important—so central to so many people's hopes, dreams, and plans, be killed so... *casually*.

Like crushing an insect.

Yet, as I sit there and stare at the white of her skull, peeking out from the mess of crimson blood and sleek mahogany hair, there can be no mistaking that Kasca Haine is done for.

At least it was quick.

"Now... that we've settled that, let's get back to the main issue," Riot says, wiping his hand off on the side of a tree trunk, leaving a gruesome, smeared handprint.

I get back to my feet.

"We have both been slaves, Rowan. And we must do our historic duty; we must rise up and *kill* our masters if we are to ever be truly our own men. It is not enough to simply cease taking orders. The scales can only be rebalanced with the weight of the slave master's blue blood. Vivian Restless is a hard bitch to catch, but... with your help, it will be *so* easy. Then we can hunt down the others... *together.*" Sigmund raises his hands, basking in the splendor of the very thought.

"You... Just murdered a girl right in front of me. A girl we had been sent here to *rescue*. She NEEDED to survive this... and you want to ask me for an alliance?! You... You're *insane.*"

Riot scratches his head, looking confused.

"I know what your compensation was to be, Rowan. But now that you know the truth, *why* would that matter anymore? *Why* save the mind or the memories of a woman who spent years *lying* to you, *manipulating* you... she made you think she loved you—tricked you into loving her, just so that she could steal... *everything* from you."

Riot might be insane, but his question is not.

"I... don't know how involved she was—maybe she knew literally everything from the day she gave me this scarf... Or maybe she was just as manipulated by her family as I was. But either way, she sent me away—she must have *refused* to go through with it, in the end... Even if everything else was a lie, that much I know for a fact now. That mystery ate away at me for months. Having even the hint of an explanation now is the only thing good about finding all this out... And even if she had ulterior motives, she was still... *good*... to me... wasn't she...? She... she still *valued* me... so what does it matter if she valued me as an individual or just as a useful tool? Isn't that still better than going a whole life never being valued by anyone at all?" I say, less to answer his question and more to ask my own questions aloud, to no one in particular.

I have one chance against Sigmund, and that's the injection in my jacket pocket.

But I am not going to use it.

Corella had said this injection would make me someone extraordinary, someone deserving of Vivian... Truthfully, I've never felt like I was enough for her. That needle might truly be what it takes to make me strong enough to at least keep her safe.

But I know she could never truly love me like that—with my mind twisted into total subservience.

Vivian was right about Corella always telling lies.

This time, her lie was one of omission... Everything she said was technically true in her eyes—she just left out the most important parts.

I could live with Vivian technically owning me. After all, she did exactly that for over a decade, and I was still happy. Whatever my legal status, she had never really treated me like an object.

But to be reduced to the status of a living doll? No desires beyond serving her desires, no personal identity separate from my relation to her?

That is something even worse than slavery—it is death in every way but the literal.

She would not own a slave anymore. She'd own a weapon with a pulse.

What good would it do for me to become more than an ordinary man in one respect, if it leaves me less than human in another?

No.

I will die here, fighting Riot despite no chance of winning.

Maybe that will atone for all the failures, all the mistakes... even if only a little.

"Are you... R-ReaLLy... Such a SIMPering! COWardLY! SPINeless.. . SLAVE?!" Riot roars in his disjointed, insane way.

"Have you REALLY FOR...goten... All the PAIN, the T-Testing... All the things we were... forced to... do? Our lives were *stolen* from us, we were *used*... In every... *every*... CONceivABLE! WAY!"

Sigmund starts breaking his fingers again, one by one.

SNAP.

SNAP.

SNAP.

...

"My life... has been more horrible than not. But there were also moments when it was, for a few seconds at a time... *perfect.* And do you know what I've realized?" I tighten the red scarf around my neck.

Riot does not answer, but he really is listening. He really does want to understand *why* I would make such a choice.

"I realized that the thing every single one of those rare, beautiful moments has in common... is *her.* Even if those moments were all built on a lie..."

I reach up to touch the scarf around my neck.

"... It was a *beautiful* lie."

...

Riot charges.

I don't stand any chance.

If there were ten of me, I *still* wouldn't stand a chance.

Thud!

An arrow lands in the ground directly between us—an instant after, it explodes into flame, napalm fountaining out of its shaft and roaring to life.

Riot slides to a halt, looking around for the source of the arrow.

"NOOO!" I scream, my voice cracking like the shattering of glass.

Vivian... is here.

My mind flies back to the pair of black birds that fled the tree Riot brought down.

Poe can communicate on a rudimentary level with other ravens—that will be how they've managed to find me, I'm positive.

From behind, I hear footsteps and turn to see Nona running up to me.

"Come on, we need to go!" Nona says, meeting my eyes with her large, gentle ones, so full of fear.

My eyes dart back to Kasca's broken, lifeless form.

That is what Vivian and Nona will become, in a few moments' time.

Anything, *anything* but that...

My hand reaches into my pocket, finding the box with the injection still safely inside.

"YES! You have come for your slave—that is brave of you! I WILL GIVE YOU A GOOD DEATH AS REWARD!" Riot roars in approval, looking around for Vivian, scanning the trees.

"I've come to put down a rabid dog." Vivian steps out of her hiding place behind a thick tree, amethyst eyes blazing.

"YOU WILL DIE—DIE LIKE YOUR SISTER DID WHEN I FINALLY FOUND HER!"

I see Vivian falter for an instant, taken aback by the news that her sister is apparently dead.

But she recovers and starts letting arrows fly.

THUD-THUD-THUD.

Arrows soar from Vivian's bow faster than I can track with my eyes.

Some of them explode on impact.

Some bite into Sigmund's armor as he barrels towards her.

Some erupt in flames, causing Sigmund to alter his course mid-charge, buying Vivian room to breathe.

Some Riot dodges and are left pin-cushioning the surrounding earth and trees.

"Rowan! Let's go! We need to get behind cover!" Nona yanks me to my feet and pushes me with all her strength.

For the moment, I let her.

How long can Vivian keep this up?

She's managing for the moment to keep her distance from Riot—using her napalm arrows strategically, defensively.

Blood leaks from him in at least half a dozen places where her arrows have embedded themselves.

I know some of Vivian's arrows are the armor-piercing kind, explaining the blood, but...

Riot does not look even remotely concerned.

He pauses, going still for the moment.

He just stares at Vivian—even when she sends two more armor-piercing arrows into his chest, he takes no notice of them at all.

He just *looks* at her, soaking in the sight of Vivian as she is, savoring the moment because he knows this will be the last chance anyone will *ever* get to appreciate her in her unbroken state... just before she is annihilated.

Like stopping to admire a priceless piece of art—the instant before you put it to the flame.

Vivian lowers her bow, and I realize she is out of arrows.

I try to run for her, understanding as I did with Kasca what was about to happen just before it comes to pass.

But Nona throws herself on me, desperately trying to pull me back.

"Wait! *Just* WAIT!" Nona begs.

Vivian pulls something from her back pocket.

It is a detonator.

I understand her plan.

The arrows, the ones that neither exploded on impact nor erupted into flames, I had assumed were nothing but simple armor-piercing arrows, but...

Those are all explosives as well... only instead of exploding on impact, they are tied to a detonator.

Riot's hungry smile falters.

He screams and launches himself forward—prepared to run through the flames if he must, so long as it means avoiding all the arrow bombs left all around him.

But many of them are in him as well, *inescapable*.

And besides, he is fast... but not faster than Vivian's thumb.

She pushes the button.

BANG!

Arrows embedded in the trees to either side of him, arrows half-buried in the ground underneath his feet, and arrows sticking out of his body—all of them explode simultaneously.

The earth shakes from the force of it. I feel blood start to run down the side of my neck.

Smoke obscures my vision.

...

Could that really be it? Could that have been enough to actually *kill* Riot?

Vivian certainly thinks so.

She turns, locking eyes with me and smiling in a smug kind of way...

As if just waiting for me to tell her how impressed and proud I am of her.

Then I see a shadow move in the thinning smoke.

"LOOK OUT!" I scream.

Riot bursts from the smoke—body a complete horror show of exposed muscle and bone, his heavy armor blown to pieces, but his tank of a body underneath it still somehow functioning.

Vivian tries to dodge, but my warning comes too late, and Riot moves too fast.

She's not going to get out of there in time.

But then Poe is there.

She comes diving out of the trees—beak and talons prepared to rip away at Riot's already tattered face.

Riot raises his hands, I think in an instinctual reaction towards self-preservation, but...

It's not that.

Showing no regard for his own pain, for protecting his own face or eyes—Riot does not shield himself with his arms as any normal person would.

Instead, with agile hands, he snatches Poe from midair.

"POE! NO!" Vivian cries out in panic.

Riot brings a struggling Poe down towards his hulking chest...

And crushes the life out of her—all the while, Vivian screams... all her arrows now spent.

...

Riot discards the broken bird—her wings and neck bent into impossible angles—a satisfied smile on his bloody face.

I can see his torn flesh slowly repairing itself, muscle fibers writhing as they reattach themselves together.

That's it.

There is no other option left.

I open the black box and pull out the syringe—finding it already loaded with an inky black liquid.

Riot advances towards Vivian with slow, predatory steps, sure that the fight is over—seeing the defeat written all over Vivian's shaking body.

"SIGMUND!" I scream.

He looks at me.

He recognizes the syringe in my hands.

His eyes widen in shock.

Vivian recognizes it as well.

"NO! PLEASE DON'T!" Vivian wails.

Nona tries to tackle me, to wrestle the syringe from my hand—not knowing exactly what it contains but understanding from Vivian's reaction that she must try to stop me.

But I've made up my mind.

I easily push Nona away with my free hand.

She stumbles back further than I'd expected—her body is so light to the touch.

"PATHETIC! You *weak, pathetic fucking thing!* What kind of man would *choose* to be a slave?!"

...

I ponder the question for a split second.

I had nothing. Nothing at all. Until Vivian wrapped her scarf around me and gave me a second chance at life.

I stab the needle into my right arm.

The liquid inside the vile seems to churn, though my hand holds it perfectly steady...as if it is possessed by a life of its own.

"... It's not truly slavery... if I've chosen it for myself," I mutter the words loud enough that only I could have possibly heard them.

"ROWAN! NO!" screams Vivian.

I see a blur of movement from the corner of my eye as Nona moves to try and stop me again.

I press the plunger down.

45

The Raindrop VS the Storm

"You are not controlling the storm, and you are not lost in it. You are the storm."
— Sam Harris

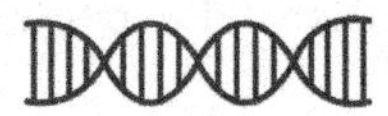

For a moment, nothing happens.

I feel stupid, having everyone stare at me in dead silence.

But then...

Rage, bloodlust, and *power* like I have never known—never even imagined—washes over me.

Only one thing in the universe matters.

Someone is trying to *hurt* Vivian.

Vivian is no longer just a person—she is no longer even someone I simply love.

She is so much more than that.

She is life itself.

She is *everything.*

She is the personification of every good thing in all of existence.

I would happily sacrifice every single other person on the entire planet—without a moment's hesitation—*if* it meant saving her.

I'd kill them all myself—with my bare hands if need be.

Vivian is the *only* thing that matters anymore.

I run at Riot through the flames, not caring or even noticing the pain as they sear my flesh—because my pain also does not matter anymore.

I raise my ax.

Riot's hands are held up in a grappler's stance.

He still towers over me.

But what do I care?

His size no longer matters, either.

Big things die, same as the small.

I pull the trigger, and a burst of gas sends my ax screaming at Sigmund's body.

It catches him in the chest.

I can feel his ribs crumble under its force.

Blood erupts from Riot's mouth.

But then, two powerful hands clamp down on each of my arms, vicelike, holding them in place.

Riot starts to squeeze.

Harder.

Harder.

HARDER.

I can feel the bones in my forearms splinter under the pressure.

I scream.

He smiles.

He lifts me up in front of him.

He knows that he is *still* stronger; his body has had years and years to adapt, to grow, to be built up by the constant work of the parasite—its limiter long removed.

But my insanity is stronger than his—it is more *desperate*, more *animalistic*... Because I still have something tangible to lose—while all he has is some vague fantasy of revenge.

I bring my head forward, head-butting him in the nose, causing him to reel back—more in surprise than in pain.

Even that is still not enough to make him loosen his grip on my arms—not even for an instant.

But I can see Sigmund's exposed neck now...

His jugular.

I launch myself forward, feeling my arms yank from their sockets in my shoulders, their dislocation giving me the extra few inches I so desperately need.

I sink my teeth into Riot's neck.

I bite down.

...

Hot blood waterfalls down—gushing into my mouth and onto my body.

Riot falls back.

I fall with him.

I begin to eat him alive.

I bite down again and again—knowing I need to thoroughly shred his jugular if I want to be sure he bleeds out faster than his body can repair itself.

Riot does not lose his will to fight—his right-hand grabs onto my left side and tears off a pound of flesh—enough to fatally injure any normal person.

But I am anything but normal now—even though I feel the part of me get torn away, I do not feel any pain—and the healing begins the instant the damage is done.

Desperately, Riot punches me on the other side with the last of his strength—his last bid to throw me off for long enough that his parasite can repair his jugular and save him.

The punch snaps at least two of my lower ribs—I feel one of them puncture my right lung—but again, this awareness does not come with the proper accompanying pain that it should.

The punch fails to dislodge me—as my legs, arms, and teeth all work in conjunction to hold on with the wild desperation of a starving animal.

His gargantuan body shudders under me as if the blood from his neck is molten lava and his body is a dying volcano, erupting for the very last time, demanding that the entire world should take notice—demanding to be recognized not as simply a man dying, but as a natural disaster that has finally reached its apex.

I smile as I feel the last drops of his life bleed into my mouth.

...

I've done it.

I look around for Vivian, wanting to assure myself once and for all that she is okay.

She is on her knees, staring at me.

Vivian is safe now.

Nothing else matters.

Nothing else.

Nothing.

...

But then, why is she crying like that?

Doesn't she understand?

This is *good*... Isn't it?

Didn't I do well?

Didn't I do the impossible?

Why does she look so afraid?

Doesn't she see...? I've slain the monster... Haven't I?

"Vivian... don't cry..." I croak.

Like a fire dying out, my vision fades to dark.

46

The Vibrations of Her Voice

"Love is that condition in which the happiness of another person is essential to your own."

- Robert Heinlein

I wake up to the sound of tears.

Is it... Vivian?

Has she been in pain, *suffering*... while I just laid here?

Self-loathing and panic reaches out of the pit of my stomach to grab hold of my heart—squeezing, making me feel like I will die.

I bolt upright.

Nona gasps.

Nona—*Not* Vivian.

Where is Vivian?

"Rowan! You're awake..."

I look at her.

"Is Vivian okay? *Where* is she?" I say, the urgency and alertness of my words clearly surprising Nona.

"S-She's fine, Rowan, she's... burying Poe... we didn't think you would wake up so soon..."

My first reaction is relief at hearing Vivian is okay.

Then it is just more stress, more fear, more self-loathing.

Vivian loved Poe. Vivian will be in pain over Poe's death. Vivian needs me.

"Nona. What direction did she go? Vivian should not be alone—I must go find her."

"*Rowan*... LOOK at you—you can't *go* anywhere, what... what is wrong with you? I don't understand what's going on—what did you inject into yourself before? And... whose body is that, with the... the... ruined head?"

I stare at Nona for a long moment.

I recognize the emotions of fear, confusion, and compassion in her face.

I see. They do not know that Kasca Haine is dead—her face is too badly damaged to recognize.

"If I make you understand the situation, will you tell me where Vivian is?" I ask, businesslike.

Nona's eyes widen.

But after a moment, she nods.

...

"The cadaver belongs to Kasca Haine. Sigmund—you knew him by Riot—killed her. I failed to stop it... I was too weak to stop him..."

Nona's eyes go wide in disbelief and dismay.

I know what she is thinking...

All of this... for nothing?

And then I point to Riot's mask, covered in a thin layer of dust some distance away.

I say nothing, but somehow, she seems to understand.

Nona gets up as if in a trance, retrieves the mask, and puts it on her face.

...

When she takes the mask back off, I recognize different emotions on her face.

Horror.

Pain.

And... an anger more intense than I thought her capable of expressing.

"Now, tell me where Vivian is—*please*."

Nona just stares at me.

...

This starts to upset me. We had a deal. Vivian needs me, and Nona is refusing to cooperate—I will not let *anyone* stop me from protecting Vivian... not even Nona.

"*Nona*, tell—"

Vivian returns, stepping out of the trees into the scarred battlefield of our fight with Riot.

I try to get up, but my weak, useless body gives out almost instantly—sending me crashing back into the earth.

Nona screams, rushing to help me.

My body is in pain, though it is nothing in comparison to the shame I feel at my pathetic state.

I am of no use to Vivian like this.

Vivian drops the bow in her hand and sprints over to me.

This makes me feel that she really cares for me... New emotions start to wash over me.

It is a kind of bittersweet happiness—I want her to care about me... yet I am not worthy of her care...

I do not know how to resolve those two contradictions.

I force myself to sit up.

Vivian's face is a storm of emotions, pain, regret, anguish... She must still be mourning Poe's death, I think.

I know that I must comfort her, I try to lift my arms to wrap them around her, but...

They refuse to move.

I look down at them.

They are wrapped in bandages.

For a moment, this confuses me.

But then I remember what Riot did to them, to the splintering of the bones, the dislocating of both my shoulders.

I take stock of my physical state without any emotion—the way one would when noting that something of purely pragmatic value has been damaged and will need repairing.

Faintly, I recognize that this lack of concern is something new; this is not at all how seeing my ruined body would have made me react previously.

Nona throws Riot's mask at Vivian—only Vivian's inhumanly fast reactions allow her to snatch it out of the air in time to avoid an injury.

"WHAT... *What* have you done?! LOOK at him! He's not... He's not... *Rowan*, anymore!"

Nona steps forward and slaps Vivian across the face.

...

I crawl forward, placing myself between them.

I do not see Nona as a threat to Vivian's safety—but still, I must try to stop her from hurting Vivian, even if it is only superficial damage. Protecting her is my duty—my reason for being.

I can feel both of them staring down at me, stunned.

Nona gets even more upset.

"He... LOVED you... He would have done *anything*... You *knew*. You knew, and YOU LET THIS HAPPEN!" screams Nona.

Vivian lets Nona hit her once again.

Vivian is not acting like the Vivian I know.

"I... *I didn't... I swear...*" says Vivian weakly.

"I HEARD IT! I HEARD AUDIO LOGS OFF OF THAT MASK! It said, 'We believe the Charges must be *let in on* the process.' It said that you needed to be told! How many years did you make him think he was special to you? How long did you watch him fall in love with you while knowing you would do... *this,* to him?!"

Comprehension dawns on me.

This is all just a misunderstanding. Nona thinks something bad has been done to me—that is why she is upset!

Once she understands that I am okay, she will calm down.

Vivian shakes her head.

"I... *I didn't*... I only found out half a year ago—I sent him away as soon as I did... Nona, *please*... believe me..." begs Vivian.

"*Liar*! Why *wouldn't* you have been told? I'm a scientist—I know that they would have wanted *everyone* to follow the experiment's design, they would have wanted variables minimized as much as possible—so, why *not* YOU? And even if you didn't... you expect me to believe you went a *whole ten years*, never suspecting *anything*? You're supposed to be a *genius*—how could you be so blind? That is, unless you didn't *want* to know—didn't *want* to see what was going on. You kept him like an object... All that time... This is *your* fault! YOUR FAULT!" screams Nona, crying hysterically.

"Nona... *please* stop... She has done nothing wrong. I do not care if she knew or not—I chose to enter Phase 2 with my eyes open—knowing the truth. I was afraid at the time, yes... but now, I see... *This* is my reason for living. Don't you understand? I am more free than anyone—because I made the ultimate choice to sacrifice my freedom on my own terms. This is... is my *destiny*—it always has been—the only difference now is that I can see it fully!"

I wait for a second—supremely confident that this explanation will set things right and calm the both of them down.

But somehow, I've miscalculated.

Something I've said hurts Vivian more than anything else thus far—something I've said seems to finally make Vivian break down entirely.

She takes me into her arms and begins to weep, soaking me in her tears.

She holds my body as if I have just *died*... as if she's in mourning.

...

I do not understand—what have I done to hurt her so deeply? Have I really changed so much since taking the injection?

Self-loathing starts to well up inside me at the thought that I have somehow let Vivian down—that she is unhappy with me now.

"IDIOT—IDIOT—IDIOT! How could you... I *hate you* so much! Rowan... Damn you... Rowan... Rowan..." Vivian sobs.

I start to panic.

A lump forms in my throat, making it difficult for me to breathe.

Vivian... *hates* me?

... No.

Vivian often says the opposite of what she means.

That is who she is—always has been.

With that realization, the obstruction in my throat passes, and I take a deep, calming breath.

All the while, Vivian's sobs have not abated at all. Seeing her in pain cuts me like a knife in the heart, even though I do not fully understand the cause of her suffering... I understand that I am to blame for it.

Vivian starts to scream into my chest, the vibrations of her voice inches from my heart.

"Nona... You want to know *why* I wasn't told until the end? It's because my *nightmare* of a family *knew* I didn't need to be told to fake it. They *knew*... that I loved him... When they did tell me, I made him leave right away... I swear... I *swear* I did! I sent away... the only person, the *only one*... WHO EVER GAVE A DAMN ABOUT ME! You think that was *easy*? For ten years, a day never went by that I wasn't wracked by guilt for owning him—like a tool or a pet... I was *so* afraid he only cared about me because he was forced to... but at least he was *with me*... I should have made Rowan leave from the very start, but... I was *so* afraid of being alone..."

Vivian's body shakes uncontrollably with silent sobs.

Nona has stopped crying.

She looks down at us with a hollow expression.

...

"If you really feel that way... if you really care about him that much, then let's *bring him back*, Vivian. Let's find a way to undo this," says Nona.

Vivian nods her head in desperate agreement.

"Y-You're right... we *will* fix this—we can make it right... save... him..."

Vivian looks down, distracted by something.

We follow her gaze.

Held up in front of her, hovering a few inches above my tear-soaked chest, are Vivian's hands.

They are shaking.

No...not just shaking—they spasm and convulse grotesquely while the three of us sit there and watch... transfixed.

I've seen tremors in the hands like that before—for the first time as a five-year-old child... they started not long before my mother's memories first began to evaporate from her mind.

Vivian starts to laugh.

They are the unmistakable sounds of a person falling apart.

To be continued in: A Chronicle of Lost Causes — Book 2

Afterword

If you're reading this... I'm already dead.

Just kidding—if you're reading this, thank you so much for reading my very first book! I know how much it's asking to take a chance on an unproven writer, but everyone who does roll those dice helps me get a little bit closer to the dream of doing this thing full-time and quitting the dreaded day job.

Next, let me take a moment to thank my original trio of unpaid beta readers, Leah, Katie, and Lauren, for suffering through my first attempt at a rough draft before it was even spell-checked—let alone suitable for human consumption. I'd also like to thank my adoring fiancé for helping me with the 2024 re-release—many of the improvements, both to the art and the text, I owe to her insights and support.

The original version of No Man's Land took me three years to publish—the new and improved version, upgraded art and all—took me another two years of work before I was satisfied with it. Being a one-man show gives me maximum creative freedom, but there is an undeniable tradeoff in time it demands. With that said, I am moderately confident its sequel will not take anywhere near that long—as I'm assured by people who know what they are talking about that an author's first book is generally the hardest. If you've enjoyed the first entry in A Chronicle of Lost Causes, please consider recommending this book to a friend and leaving a review online.

You can even purchase No Man's Land merch now, as well as follow me on Instagram for updates and the chance to see new art early!

Links to my personal website and Instagram are both included down below.

Visit me: www.lostcausebooks.com

Instagram: www.instagram.com/alan.r.black

I hope to speak to you again soon... ideally, in the Afterword section of A Chronicle of Lost Causes Book 2!

A. R. Black

A. R. Black has always been one of those strange people who can never just be satisfied with the real world, one of those hopeless romantics who always seems to want more from life than an indifferent universe is willing to provide. For people like him… fiction is what makes it all worthwhile. After 25 years on the receiving end, he decided it was well past time to return the favor and create some escapism fiction of his own. Currently, he is living in Japan on the government's dime as a United States Marine and has a bachelor's degree in Homeland Security. When not writing or illustrating for his stories, he competes in bodybuilding, powerlifting, and injects stories in any form he can find them—straight into the heart.

Made in United States
North Haven, CT
12 March 2024